The Latchkey Murders

THE
LATCHKEY
MURDERS

ALEXEI BAYER

Russian Life
BOOKS

ISBN 978-1-880100-37-0

Library of Congress Control Number: 2015944506

Russian Information Services, Inc.
PO Box 567
Montpelier, VT 05601-0567
www.russianlife.com
orders@russianlife.com
phone 802-223-4955

Cover photograph: Photogio (dreamstime.com).

CAST OF CHARACTERS

Budyonny, Boss (Lt. Col. Ashot Modestovich Martirosyan) - head
   of the Special Crimes Unit, Moscow Criminal Investigations at
   No. 38 Petrovka Street
Baba Dasha - Drozdova's neighbor
Tanya Drozdova - schoolgirl, 11 years
Irina Drozdova - Tanya's mother
Capt. Oleg Gordeyev - head of the murder investigation team
Sasha Grigoriev - medical expert
Nikolai Grushnikov - gym teacher, Drozdova's neighbor
Matvei Nikanorovich Korenev - playwright
Bernard Lazius - psychiatrist, Drozdova's neighbor
Nadezhda - his wife
Marina - Budyonny's secretary
Senior Lieutenant Pavel Matyushkin - police detective, narrator
Natashka - his younger sister
Nastya - pickpocket, friend of Matyushkin
Grigory Oganesov - Chemical engineer
Valeria - his wife
Dima Sadykov - schoolboy
Sergei - Korenev's driver and cleaner
Vova Silin - schoolboy

Tosya (Antontina Ivanovna) - bookkeeper, a friend of Matyushkin
Sevka - her son
Lt. Valera Tumakov - detective
Senior Lieutenant Lenny Urumov - detective, Matyushkin's partner
     and best friend
Zinaida - Korenev's cleaning woman and cook

MOSCOW, 1961

I had yet to announce the death of one human being and the end of an entire world.

Dmitry Glukhovsky, *Twilight*

PROLOGUE

The room is silent. The tulle curtains are drawn to reveal sparkling, recently washed windows. The midday sun, streaming in through the double casement frames, casts a slanted hopscotch pattern onto the rug. Sunbeams play on the chrome-plated music stand and metal locks of a violin case leaning against the wall. The garden outside is buried under a layer of snow almost three feet deep. The sky is luminous, but the winter day is bitterly cold.

Inside, dwarf cacti and an aloe vera plant luxuriate in their orange clay pots on the windowsill. The cracks in the window frames are stuffed with cotton wool that has been glued over with strips of newsprint to staunch drafts. The radiators hum, exuding heat. The room is very hot.

A folding screen divides the room along a diagonal. Its garish pink and orange flowers clash with the oriental rug on the floor. The furniture in the inner half of the room is dark and heavy. There is too much of it. Ranged along the walls, the armoires, sideboards and bookshelves leave too little space for a dining table. A crystal chandelier nearly touches its surface. A Karelian-birch four-poster is squeezed into a corner.

The furniture traps the silence – it is almost palpable, pressing one's eardrums, taut as a piano string. A group of first-graders are playing in the courtyard, laughing and shouting. Their voices resonate in the frozen air caught between the tall apartment buildings, but are muffled by the snowdrifts and the double frames. The silence in the room is complete, undisturbed.

The side of the room that is closer to the window is more airy – there is more light and more space. There is a fold-out sofa bed and a low bookshelf filled with school books. A stuffed bear sits on the middle shelf, dressed in a pair of yellow checkered pants and a white shirt, a scarlet bow tie pinned under its furry chin at a jaunty angle. One of its glass eyes is missing; a black thread dangles from the spot, giving the bear a perpetual conspiratorial wink.

At first glance, the room seems empty. Then you notice a schoolgirl in a chair next to the dining table. She is in her school uniform, in a brown, high-necked dress with a lace collar and a red Young Pioneer's kerchief tied around her neck. She wears a white apron reserved for festive occasions. Her pigtails are tightly braided and tied off with white ribbons. The pigtails stick up in the air – the stuffy overheated air of the room, because she is slumped forward. Her face is pressed awkwardly against the edge of an open textbook. Her arms are stretched out as though she's reaching out for something at the other end of the table. Her violin player's fingers are thin and delicate, with closely clipped pink and white nails. She's eleven, but small for her age and slender.

You might almost believe she is asleep.

ONE

The arthritic elevator in our office building screeched and shuddered to a halt.

It was two o'clock on a wintry afternoon. Lenny and I had had lunch at a basement cafe on the corner of Petrovka Street and the Boulevard Ring, where Lenny was friendly with a waitress. Because of that unfortunate fact, we were compelled to go there for lunch whenever we weren't working on a case.

Lenny was my friend and partner and, in terms of experience at Moscow Criminal Investigations, my senior by a couple of years. I sympathized with his interest in the red-headed waitress, but making me eat their execrable food was going a little too far.

Lenny pushed the elevator door open, took a couple of energetic strides down the hall and stopped. Since I was right behind him, I slammed into him, bouncing back as if I had hit a pillar of salt. Baby face and chubby cheeks notwithstanding, underneath his sheepskin coat Lenny was all muscle.

"What's the matter?" I asked, giving him a shove after I regained my balance.

His head slowly turned from left to right as his eyes followed the movement of two young forensic lab assistants, their high heels tapping an urgent tattoo on the linoleum. Their unbuttoned lab coats flapped and bubbled over their woolen dresses, and as they accelerated down the hall, they looked like two angels ready to take wing and soar to the whitewashed ceiling. Lenny knew them well, yet they ignored him, staring straight ahead, their pretty faces set and focused.

At the far end of the hallway, Valera Tumakov emerged from his office with a thick manila folder under his arm. He had shed his normally pedantic manner and was casting nervous glances right and left. He nodded at us uneasily, stopped and was about to say something, but then seemed to change his mind.

"What the hell—?" Lenny muttered.

Three quarters of an hour before, when we left for lunch, the office had been quiet, even somnolent. Now there was an unmistakable tension gathering along the empty hallways. An ominous silence seemed on the point of exploding.

Tumakov, a sour expression on his face, gave us a dismissive wave and entered another office.

Lenny's head now turned in the opposite direction as he followed Tumakov's partner, Oleg Gordeyev, who was approaching the elevator. Gordeyev wore an overcoat and a fur hat and carried a briefcase under his arm. He brushed past us as if we weren't there.

"What's going on here?" I asked.

"Not now," Gordeyev snapped, his hand on the door handle. "Budyonny will fill you in."

As the doors shut behind him and the elevator cabin began its shaky descent, Marina, Budyonny's secretary, rushed into the hallway and squinted nearsightedly in our direction. She wiped her eyes with one hand and motioned to us with the other.

"Get over here. The Boss wants to see you."

The Boss is Budyonny. He holds the rank of lieutenant colonel and heads the elite Serious Crimes division of Moscow Criminal Investigations, headquartered at Petrovka 38. His real name is Ashot Modestovich Martirosyan, but on account of his magnificent moustache, which rivals the one made famous by the legendary

Red Cavalry Commander Semyon Budyonny, everyone calls him Budyonny. But not to his face, of course.

"Hurry up," Marina pleaded, sobbing.

She had been Budyonny's secretary for more than two months and was getting used to her job: run-of-the-mill crimes no longer upset her the way they once had. But now her face was awash with tears and blackened by streaks of mascara.

Lenny was friends with Marina, too. As a matter of fact, despite having a lovely wife and two delightful small daughters, Lenny was friendly with many different young women. He quickly overtook me, striding down the hallway. By the time I caught up with him, one of his thick arms was wrapped around Marina's shoulders and he was drying her tears with a wrinkled handkerchief he had pulled from his pocket.

"It's shocking, Lenny," she said over and over through her sobs. "How can anyone be such a monster?"

Lenny, his arm still around her shoulders, tried to nudge her gently toward the door to Budyonny's office. Just then the door flew open and Budyonny's massive frame appeared on the threshold.

"Where the hell have you been?" he thundered, his moustaches bristling with rage. "I thought I was perfectly clear. I said urgently."

Budyonny is Armenian and Russian is not his native tongue. But his Russian is good, and under normal circumstances his accent is slight. It gets thicker when he is upset or angry. The guys in his department can gauge his mood by the thickness of his accent and stay out of his way when he is difficult to understand. At the moment, he was almost unintelligible.

Lenny stopped in mid-stride and let go of Marina. For all his bravado, and despite mimicking the Boss's accent behind his back, Lenny was afraid of him. We all were.

But Budyonny suddenly lost interest in him and turned on me, "What the hell are *you* doing here?" he hissed, fixing me with the look of his hooded, bloodshot eyes. "I said I wanted to see Urumov. Is that so difficult to understand, Lieutenant?"

Whenever Budyonny worked himself into a state, trying to explain anything to him was useless and only got him madder.

"Yessir," I replied, clicking my heels and turning around.

"Actually, wait a second," Budyonny called after me. "I need to talk to you, too, Matyushkin."

I stopped and waited a short distance away.

The Boss passed his hand wearily over his face, rubbing his stubble-covered double chin with his short, thick fingers.

"I want you to work with Gordeyev and Tumakov," he said to Lenny. His anger had subsided and he suddenly sounded vulnerable, almost plaintive. "Thing is, some son of a bitch murdered a child, a schoolgirl. Not far from here, in 1st Kolobovsky Lane."

Marina gasped and began to sob again. Lenny, still standing at attention, gave her a helpless look.

I knew 1st Kolobovsky Lane well. It was around the corner from our headquarters and I passed it almost daily on my way to the office. It was a narrow street running more or less parallel to Petrovsky Boulevard and lined with old brick houses.

"Get going, Lieutenant," the Boss said to Lenny and then turned to me once more. "Go and wait in my office."

I squeezed past them. As the soundproof door was closing behind me, I heard Budyonny say to Marina, "Please pull yourself together, girl."

His voice cracked. It was as though he, too, was on the verge of tears.

I waited in the reception area, a windowless room decorated with a couple of anemic house plants and filled with immense, gray filing cabinets that dwarfed Marina's desk, which sat in the corner looking like a piece of doll house furniture. The room smelled of dust and Marina's perfume.

I felt sick to my stomach – because a schoolgirl had been murdered, yes, but also because Budyonny had apparently decided to keep me off the case. Lenny and I were partners and we always worked together.

But not this time. I stood by Marina's desk, drumming my fingers on its gray metal surface.

The Boss came in a few minutes later, alone, clutching Lenny's wrinkled handkerchief in his left hand.

"She'll be back in a minute," he said, motioning to Marina's desk. "I sent her to wash her face."

I followed him into his office. He sighed as he squeezed his large body into a leather armchair. I remained standing by the door.

"It's a nasty case, Matyushkin. Whoever did it, we need to catch him right away. There will be a lot of people watching over our shoulder. Important people, d'you understand?"

I nodded.

"Maybe I should be working on it too," I suggested cautiously. "Since it's a priority case—"

As if he had laid a trap for me, Budyonny angrily snapped, "What you should do is keep your opinions to yourself, Lieutenant. I told you I have a special assignment for you."

I jerked my head up and snapped my heels.

"At ease," he said, relenting. "We're short-staffed. This morning, I got a request from our Leningrad colleagues. They had a robbery at the main branch of the State Savings Bank on Nevsky Prospect. Something went wrong. A clerk died in a shootout and a cop got a bullet through the chest. I was going to send you and Urumov to assist them with the investigation, but now I'll have to turn them down. I just don't have the resources with a thing like this on my hands."

He sighed.

"Urumov will be working on the girl's murder," he went on. "I've got something different for you, Matyushkin."

He sighed again and looked out the window, squinting at the bright winter sunshine. It was a beautiful day. The weather had finally broken after a week of unremitting snowstorms and wind-swept gloom. It was the kind of day – brilliant, frosty and freshly tinged with pink and blue – that makes our long Russian winters bearable.

"I need you to look for a stolen car," Budyonny said at last.

Really? A stolen car?

A girl had been murdered practically on our block and there had been a bank robbery in Leningrad. Yet, all Budyonny wanted me to do was to look for a stolen car?

True, car theft was flourishing in the city, what with the growth in car ownership and the involvement of criminal gangs. There had been talk of a special task force being set up, and Lenny, who had recently acquired a beat-up Moskvich-401 hatchback, was planning to volunteer for it. But our bureaucracy was notorious for its lethargy. Nothing had been done and car theft was still mostly being handled by local precincts.

My dismay must have been written all over my face, because the Boss gave me a stern look.

"I know what you're thinking, Lieutenant. It's not the car I'm concerned about – even though it's a good car – but the owner. His name is Matvei Korenev. I assume you know who he is."

"No, sir. I'm not sure I do, sir."

"Oh, come on. You're an educated man, Matyushkin. Can it really be that you've never heard of Matvei Korenev, the giant of Soviet dramaturgy?"

Shaking his head in disbelief, the Boss informed me that Korenev's plays had been performed by every theater in the Soviet Union, adding that the man was a Hero of Socialist Labor, a recipient of the Stalin Prize, a member of the Supreme Soviet and, most important of all, Party Secretary of the Writers' Union.

"His most famous play is called *The Ardent Heart*. It has even been translated into Armenian, if I'm not mistaken. And now his ZIM limo has been stolen."

I listened to the long list of Korenev's accolades with growing dismay. A theft from a man like Korenev surely wasn't an ordinary crime. And not only because he was a really Big Boss, and every Big Boss expects special attention to be paid to his problems. Worse, all Big Bosses were convinced that a car theft was an extraordinary event in our otherwise crime-free city, and that we at Criminal Investigations needed to drop everything we were doing to dedicate ourselves fully to finding and punishing the culprits.

In other words, Big Bosses believed what they read in the papers, and the papers never reported any crime. Certainly not things like the murder of a schoolgirl or a bank robbery in Leningrad. Big Bosses saw life from the back seat of their ZIM and Volga limousines. Their impressions, gleaned by observing the clean and orderly main streets of the capital while being chauffeured about, were in perfect harmony with the sanitized reports they read in the newspapers.

The only problem was that none of it had anything to do with reality, and when you tried to enlighten them on this point, they preferred to blame the messenger rather than accept the message.

"Your responsibility is to recover Comrade Korenev's car," Budyonny concluded. "And to bring the perpetrators to justice, of course."

"Yes, sir," I said, saluting and turning around.

"Wait a minute."

I stopped and turned to face him.

"When I talked to Korenev earlier today, I told him I'd put two detectives on his case. I meant to send you and Urumov, but now I need Urumov on the murder full-time. Tell the playwright there will be a second detective soon. And, in general, be very careful with him. He's got good connections. We don't want to have any trouble from him. Not at a time like this."

So, my job was also to smooth the man's feathers, I thought bitterly.

"I'm sure we'll get our hands on the murderer quickly," Budyonny said. "Once we do, Urumov will join you on Korenev's case. So, keep him up to date, will you?"

"I'd like to be involved in the murder investigation, too," I said. "In case I work out the car theft in a day or two."

Budyonny nodded and said nothing. I was almost out of his office when he added, "I'm sorry, Lieutenant. You know I would have thrown all my resources on the murder case if I could. But it's not entirely up to me."

Budyonny was a good cop. A case like this made him sick to his stomach, too. But he was a Boss first and foremost, and he had to think like a politician.

Matvei Korenev lived in a large yellow-and-white apartment building not far from Sokol metro station. It was a sprawling behemoth built for the privileged in the first years after the war and was imbued with an over-the-top triumphalism. The entrance was from the courtyard, accessible through a tall arch decorated with a thicket of plaster flags, cannon, airplane propellers and tank turrets, and topped with a colossal statue of a soldier in a steel helmet cuddling a PPSh-41 assault rifle against his chest. A similar arch in the northern wing of the building had a more peaceful theme, with hammers, sickles, saws and other tools of industrial labor. On top stood the soldier's good twin, holding a welder's arc and dressed in a pair of overalls, a face guard pushed back from his forehead.

The door was opened by a middle-aged woman in an English maid's uniform so crisply starched that it encased her body like a suit of medieval armor. Silently nodding in acknowledgment of my request to see her employer, she pointed to a pair of felt slippers and waited while I changed out of my winter boots, looking sternly at the two puddles they created next to the welcome mat.

The playwright's apartment was vast and airy. The windows offered a sweeping view of a park covered in snow, framing the ruins of a church and a skating rink alongside it. On the opposite side of the park, beyond the crumbling brick wall, rose grey cubes of new construction.

The rooms were lined with walnut bookcases that reached all the way to the exceptionally high ceiling. On their glassed-in shelves stood the hardcover collected works of various Russian classics, arranged in strict alphabetical order, interspersed with bronze busts of the writers themselves as well as those of select Communist Party leaders. Display cases contained medals, award certificates and frayed playbills.

The parquet floors of the hallways were slippery and smelled of wood polish.

Still in silence, the maid marched me past an enfilade of chambers that seemed more like rooms in a house museum than a living space, delivering me to a vast dining room. There, she jerked her head in the direction of the dining table and disappeared into the kitchen. Almost immediately came the sound of dishes being dropped into the sink.

Seated at the head of a long table covered with an embroidered tablecloth was a short man with broad shoulders, a round paunch, and a large shaved head. He looked serious and dignified, as though he were sitting for a portrait rather than having his midday meal.

Actually, the room already contained the man's portrait. It was painted in a life-like socialist realist manner and hung behind its subject in a massive gilded frame. The man was shown wearing a simple open-necked shirt with the gold star of the Hero of Socialist Labor pinned discreetly to his chest. He seemed deep in thought, a fountain pen poised in his right hand. A field of ripening wheat undulated outside an open window, stretching as far as the eye could see. A forest rose along the distant horizon, the thin trunks of the birch trees like silver threads woven into the dark green of the foliage. Finely detailed miniature combines, with red flags fluttering over their cabins, were gathering the harvest, moving through the yellow field and raising a column of golden dust. Crop dusters were pinned in the blue enamel sky like frozen insects.

"I'm very glad you came," the man exclaimed, jumping from his chair and giving me a vigorous handshake. "What was your name again?"

Standing up, he was even shorter than I had expected, but remarkably energetic and talkative.

I introduced myself.

"What did you say? Senior Lieutenant Matyushkin? Very nice, very nice. Well, my name's Korenev. Matvei Korenev. I write plays for a living. Take a seat, Lieutenant. I don't stand on ceremony. I have just finished lunch, as you can see. A simple midday meal. Plain peasant food is what keeps you healthy."

"I'm here about your car," I said, finding a crack in the torrent of his words.

In real life, Korenev was dressed in a rough peasant shirt and a pair of ornate Uzbek trousers. He wore Oriental slippers Central Asian style, over bare feet. A pink napkin was tucked into his shirt collar, beneath a glistening, clean-shaven chin.

"I can offer you a glass of cranberry drink. Or a shot of vodka, if you feel a yearning for it in your soul. Or else, a genuine Havana cigar."

I didn't feel a yearning for vodka in my soul or a desire for a genuine Havana cigar. All I wanted to do was to be done there and on my way. But the playwright was limbering up for a long conversation. In the end, I had to sit down and accept a glass of bright-red, viscous cranberry drink that the surly English maid brought out in a ceramic Ukrainian pitcher.

"By the way, Lieutenant," the little man said. "Your boss promised to send me two of his best detectives. I have no reason to doubt that you're one of the best, at least I don't as yet, but as far as I can see you're alone. Unless you can split in two, like an amoeba."

"We had an emergency," I explained patiently, ignoring his sarcasm and keeping in mind Budyonny's instructions. "Most available personnel are working on another investigation."

Korenev's eyes lit up.

"What kind of investigation, detective?" he asked, rubbing his hands. "A murder?"

"I don't know," I said. "It's a developing situation."

"Come on. Tell me at least who got killed."

I shrugged, saying nothing.

"A family quarrel, I suppose?" he went on probing. "A pair of drunks fighting over a bottle?"

"Most likely," I said, shrugging again.

Korenev was disappointed.

"I see," he said peevishly. "All the good detectives are busy investigating a drunken brawl, while the theft of my car is a very low priority. Your boss shouldn't have been making promises he couldn't keep. Now I'm stuck with a greenhorn with no backup, but I suppose I should be grateful for whatever I get."

I gave him a self-deprecating smile that was meant to suggest that I was the best my boss could do, even if I wasn't the best choice for the job.

"Maybe you've changed your mind?" the playwright asked suddenly, switching the subject. "A small shot of vodka, perhaps?"

I shook my head. Korenev picked up a frosted decanter half-filled with a clear liquid that was speckled with the yellow and white shavings of lemon peel, poured himself a shot, clinked his glass against the side of the decanter and threw it back.

"Bottoms up!"

"Ah!" he exhaled with visible delight. "So smooth. An angel's tear, I call it. Pure as driven snow. You're making a mistake, detective."

"Perhaps we should get down to business," I suggested once he sniffed his sleeve, Russian style, to cut the burning in his throat. "Let's get the description of your car."

It was a ZIM-M20 luxury limousine made by the Molotov Automotive Factory. Comrade Molotov had fallen out of favor of late, and the automotive plant had been renamed after someone else, but the limousine was still called a ZIM and was gifted by the government to high officials, party brass, generals and other important people. The fact that Korenev had one meant a lot. He was an even bigger boss than Budyonny had led me to believe.

"The color is black," Korenev said, peeking over my shoulder at my notes. "No need to put that down, detective. ZIMs only come in black. You would know that if you specialize in car thefts."

"How did it get stolen?" I asked.

"How did it get stolen?" Korenev repeated, as though seriously pondering the question. He poured himself another shot of vodka. "Nothing fancy about that, my friend. Over there, across the park, I've got a garage."

He pointed to the window and the snow-covered park outside.

"You can't see it from here because of all the new construction. That's the Composers' Union building over there. They're building an apartment building for their members. My garage is over there, where it's always been. The composers, let the Devil take the lot of them, wanted to steal it from me, claiming it was on their property. Naturally, I couldn't let that happen. I contacted some friends of mine in the government, and the damn composers have since been whistling a very different tune."

The playwright chuckled.

"I don't use the car much," he went on. "I like to stay at home, unless I have a meeting at the Writers' Union. Or the Central Committee summons prominent writers like myself to the headquarters, to give us our marching orders. Of course they instruct us what to write about and what subjects to cover. No literature or theater in the world can exist without close government supervision. Otherwise there will be chaos and decadence."

He gulped down a second shot of vodka, grunted, and continued.

"But if I have no urgent business, I stay at home, at my desk, working. Just as this picture shows."

He pointed to his portrait.

"This is a work by Comrade Alexander Gerasimov, a socialist realist painter of the first order. A genius and president of the Fine Arts Academy. The Tretyakov Gallery is stuffed to the gills with his pictures. By the way, do you happen to know which is the most important body part of a writer? I bet you think it's the writing hand?"

"Let's get back to your car," I suggested, getting exasperated.

"Answer my question, detective. Do you think it's the writing hand?"

I shrugged and looked away. I kept my notebook open on my lap, but I had had nothing to record in it so far.

"Wrong you are, buddy," the playwright exclaimed triumphantly as though I had made an off-the-wall guess rather than refusing to play his stupid game. "That's exactly what I thought, you're no good at detection. It's this that makes you a writer."

He lifted his round posterior from the chair and slapped his rear end, covered in colorful Uzbek trousers.

"I sit on it every morning, seven days a week, including Sundays. I sit and write, write, write. Then I have lunch and take a nap, because writing is not as easy as people who don't write for a living will let you think. And then I go for a long walk. Mine's not a very exciting life, believe me, detective. I've got no reason to take the car out, except in summer, when I go to my country house. And in winter, I keep it garaged until the last of the snow comes off in April."

I wrote it all down. Thirty-five minutes had passed and we were only now getting around to the subject of the missing car. But I could see that rushing the playwright would be worse than useless. He was loquacious and enjoyed hearing himself talk.

"This year was the same story," he went on. "I got my ZIM garaged for the winter and ordinarily I wouldn't have given it another thought until spring. I'm not in the habit of checking on my car all the time, the way some people do who are in love with their motor vehicles. Honestly, I don't understand this obsession. It's just a steel box on wheels, a kind of motorized wheelbarrow, nothing more."

I put down my notebook once again and waited patiently while he explained to me that soon we'll have communism, money will be abolished, and every family will have a private car. Or maybe not. Under communism, nobody will need a car because public transportation will be so convenient and reliable, and free of charge, too, because there will be no money.

"In short, ordinarily my ZIM would have been in hibernation, without anyone disturbing it until well into spring," the playwright said, finally returning to the subject of his car. "Except last night I happened to be looking for my umbrella. Remember the snowstorm we had last night? I own a nice umbrella that is very useful in such weather. It was nowhere to be seen, and I thought I had lost it and nearly gave up looking, until I remembered that the last time I used the ZIM it had also been raining. I figured I must have left it in the car when it was parked for winter. So I sent Zinaida over to the garage to get it."

"Who's Zinaida?" I asked.

"You met her," he said, lowering his voice and casting a fearful eye at the kitchen door. "She cooks and cleans for me. She's what they used to call a domestic. I had to send her to the garage because it was Sergei's day off. Oh, my God, I hadn't realized. Sergei's going to be upset when he finds out. That car's his baby."

"Who's Sergei?" I asked.

"He also works for me. He's my driver, plumber, carpenter, handyman, what have you. He takes care of the car, too. He's a nice young man, honest and reliable – all qualities that are not easy to find these days in young people. I was really lucky to get him, because—"

"So you sent your cleaning woman to the garage," I broke in, trying to keep him on track. "What happened?"

"I don't know what happened at the garage, I wasn't there," the playwright replied testily. He clearly didn't like to be interrupted. "She came back and she was crying: 'There's no car there, Comrade Korenev. It's gone missing.'

"I was sure at first that she'd looked in a wrong garage. So I put on my coat and went to check it myself. Of course she was right. My garage was as empty as a beggar's pantry."

"Could your driver have taken it for a ride?" I asked. "Considering it was his day off?"

The playwright shook his head emphatically.

"Are you sure?"

"One hundred percent."

I shrugged and made a mark in my notebook. Korenev protested, "Sergei would never do such a thing. Never."

"Who has the keys?" I asked.

"I do. I gave my set to Zinaida when I sent her to the garage."

"Is it the only set you've got? Sergei doesn't have his own?"

The playwright hesitated.

"He does," he said at last. "He's supposed to leave them in my desk drawer, but he often forgets. I mean he doesn't want to disturb me when I'm working, and then he forgets. Let me go check."

He jumped off his chair and was gone, returning a few minutes later, relieved and holding a key ring.

"Here they are," he announced. "This one is to the garage."

He demonstrated a long, rusty padlock key.

"Was there any sign of a forced entry," I asked once he sat down again.

"No, they must have picked the lock."

"Or else they had another key. Surely to drive the car—"

"They have their ways of starting cars without a key," Korenev objected. "I don't know how to do it, but Sergei says it can be done. And another thing: there were no tracks in the snow. I mean the only snow in front of the garage was what fell last night. Just a couple of inches. But before that, some son of a bitch had cleared all the snow away. It's the damn Composers' Union, I'm sure. They've been clearing the snow around their construction site. This is what I'd love to do to those composers."

He brought his fists together, one on top of the other, and made a quick twisting motion, as though wringing an imaginary neck. He had large hands with strong, knobby fingers, not at all the kind of hands you'd expect to see on a man who had spent his life sitting on the writer's most important body part, composing plays.

"A little excessive, isn't it?" I said.

"What do you mean?" he asked, a dreamlike expression on his face.

"It's a harsh punishment for clearing the snow in front of your garage."

The playwright shook his head.

"I wouldn't be surprised if they were the ones who stole my car," he said. "They hate my guts because I wouldn't let them have my garage."

"I'd like to take a look at the garage," I said. "But first let me talk to Zinaida."

"What about?" Korenev asked quickly. "I already told you everything she knows."

"I'd like to hear it directly from her."

Korenev smiled uneasily.

"Well, she really didn't see anything. All she did was open the garage door. When she saw the car was gone, she ran straight back here, to let me know."

"Well, I'd like to know then why she didn't look around," I insisted.

"Come on, Lieutenant. She's been very upset by this whole business. She seems to blame herself, even though it is no fault of hers. I don't want her to be bothered."

He still had an ingratiating smile glued to his face, but his eyes were dead serious. He was determined not to let me speak to his cleaning woman, and there was a hint of threat in his voice.

"Very well, then," I said, keeping in mind Budyonny's instructions and deciding not to push the matter further. "At least I hope you don't mind if I took a look at the garage, even though you gave me a full description of what I will find there."

I wasn't sure whether Korenev's smile widened because he appreciated my sarcasm, or because he was happy I had backed down. Then again, it was his car and it was presumably in his interest that it be found.

"Let's go," Korenev said, jumping out of his chair again. "I'll take you there myself. I don't mind skipping my afternoon nap if I get to watch a Petrovka detective at work."

Before we could leave, however, Korenev had to change out of his oriental trousers into a nylon warmup suit with wide piping running down its sides. By the time he had emerged from the depths of his apartment, the word SUOMI emblazoned above five interlinked Olympic rings on his sweater, I was sweating in my winter coat. I observed that Zinaida, who was helping him into his half-length shearling coat, didn't look particularly upset. Just surly.

Korenev spent another few minutes winding a yellow scarf around his neck and pulling on a pair of fur-trimmed gloves. Then, having gotten ready to brave the elements, he showed himself to be a very competent walker. He shifted his short legs quickly, swinging his arms wide as he dashed across the park. His lace-up winter boots, with their thick rubber soles, provided excellent traction on the icy ground.

"Come on, detective, you should keep up," he shouted, turning his beet-red face in my direction, enveloping me in a odoriferous cloud of vodka and garlic. "You'll miss all the clues if you don't pick up your pace."

With me close on his heels, we crossed the park, squeezed through a breach in the wall, and climbed a steep hill along a fenced-in construction site.

"There we are," Korenev announced, stopping in front of a block of six brick garages. "The nearest is mine. The composers already took over the others. But I'm too hard a nut for them to crack with their soft musical teeth. You'll need a set of metal teeth if you think of tackling good old Matvei Korenev, young man."

I caught my breath and looked around. The grey brick garages were squat and solid, somehow resembling the playwright. Their rusty metal doors – once painted green – were secured by thick steel rods and locked shut with heavy padlocks. They looked as impregnable as medieval dungeons.

"Seriously, what if it *is* the composers who stole my car?" the playwright inquired. The idea had become lodged in his brain and he seemed unwilling to let it go. "What if they decided that, if they couldn't have my garage, they'd help themselves to its contents?"

I shrugged, still looking around.

"I'm serious, Lieutenant. If I don't have a car, I would have no need for a garage, right? Food for thought, wouldn't you say?"

The garages abutted the construction fence. The snow lay thickly in the narrow space behind them and formed high, tightly packed mounds against their sides. But the driveway in front had been recently shoveled clean, except for a couple of inches accumulated during the previous day's storm that lay pristine on the ground. By Korenev's garage, the white layer had been churned up by the playwright's rubber soles, plus a set of smaller tracks left by the unfriendly Zinaida. The door of Korenev's garage had recently been opened, too, leaving a black half-moon imprint on the snow. The padlock was back in place.

"What time did your driver leave for his day off?" I asked.

Korenev gave me a sharp look.

"Mid-morning, at around eleven o'clock," he replied reluctantly.

"Did you call the local cops?"

"Should I have? I've got good connections at Moscow Criminal Investigations. I called your boss right away. Frankly, I expected to see a senior investigator assigned to this case. But obviously a car theft gets no more attention at your agency than a wallet with a couple of rubles in it, stolen by a tram pickpocket."

I wondered when he had last been on a tram.

"Who parked the car for winter?" I asked. "Did you do it yourself?"

"Of course not," he replied, still fuming from his tirade. "It was Sergei. I don't drive. I mean I have a driver's license but I hardly ever drive in the city. The traffic here is crazy."

"Do you ever let him use it?"

"What do you mean?"

"I mean does he ever ask to use the car for his own needs? Like to go fishing or to take a girl to the movies?"

The playwright chuckled.

"You don't know Sergei," he said. "He's not the kind of guy who goes fishing. Besides, he'd never take the ZIM out. He'd be afraid it would get damaged or scratched. If it were up to him, he'd just leave it in the garage all the time and keep polishing it and changing the oil. It's his baby."

"So, the car had been here from the time Sergei parked it until it was stolen, whenever that was. Is that right?"

The playwright nodded.

"And you have not been here since?"

"Actually, I never come here at all, except when I need to give hell to the composers. Sergei picks up the car and picks me up in front of my building."

"What about Sergei?" I asked. "Has he been back here since he parked the car?"

"I doubt it. Usually there is a lot of snow in front of the garage. He likes it this way, precisely because by mid-December there is so much snow you can't drive the car out no matter how hard you try. He had no way of knowing the damn composers had cleared the driveway."

Unless he did it himself, I wanted to say.

Korenev must have read my mind.

"I'm telling you Sergei had nothing to do with it," he said. "And the other set of keys is still in the apartment. You saw it yourself."

"I would still like to talk to him," I said. "When is he coming back?"

The playwright hesitated.

"I don't know," he said. "Not today. Tomorrow. But he'll be really, really upset when he learns about the car going missing."

I made a couple of notes in my notebook, marveling at the sensitivity of Korenev's domestic staff. I then walked back and forth in front of the garages, leaving a few more sets of tracks on the virgin snow. There was nothing interesting to see.

"Are there cars in the other garages?" I asked.

Korenev sighed.

"They're all empty now. The composers haven't gotten around to allocating them. I predict a nasty fight when they do. Each one will claim he's a bigger Mussorgsky and demand the right to park his miserable Moskvich under a roof."

At my request, Korenev removed the padlock, a task that required considerable effort on his part. Finally, the rusty key turned in the keyhole, making a loud screeching sound that put my teeth on edge. I examined the padlock for scratches; there were none. The lock was old and solid and felt heavy in the palm of my hand.

It was even colder inside the garage than outdoors. The smell of mold and mouse droppings hung in the air. Lit by a bare bulb swinging from the ceiling, oil cans, gas canisters, old tires, blackened rags, and other junk considered indispensable by all motorists, were stacked against the walls, confirming that Sergei took his duties of caring for the car seriously. The concrete floor was sticky and stained with motor oil.

"What do you think, detective? Have you found what you're looking for?"

"Not yet," I replied.

I bent down and brushed my fingers against the floor. They came up black with dust and grime. I wasn't looking for anything in particular, just surveying the scene.

The playwright's constant prattle would have been annoying under the best of circumstances. But listening to it and doing a job that any local cop could have done better than me at a time when I should have been working on a murder case was unbearable.

I went outside and took a deep breath. The winter day was coming to a close. The sun, dipping behind the concrete apartment blocks in the distance, cast long blue and purple shadows on the snow. I looked behind the garages, where the snow lay mixed with brown leaves and trash blown there by the wind. Then, pulling myself up, I climbed on top of the fence, taking a short step onto the roof.

Seen from that vantage point, the ground around the unfinished carcass of the apartment building was littered with cracked window panes, bathroom fixtures and wooden doors. The rails of a giant crane glittered among the scattered debris. No workers were to be seen anywhere. I wondered whether there had been any the day before, but it was clear even from a cursory look around that the site had not been worked for weeks.

On top of the six garages, the snow lay thick, white and undisturbed.

I jumped down, landing awkwardly in a snow drift and twisting my knee slightly.

"What do you think?" the playwright asked as I straightened out, wincing in pain.

"I think it's pretty straightforward," I said. "It looks like an ordinary theft."

"When do you think it took place?" he asked.

"Before last night's storm," I replied.

"I see," Korenev said vindictively. "I'm sure I didn't need a fancy Criminal Investigations detective to arrive at this conclusion. I could have told you the same thing."

"I've just started to work the case," I said, feeling defensive but not rising to the bait. "I'm sure it will get the priority it deserves once we complete the murder investigation."

"I don't need special treatment. I just want you to do your job."

As I limped back to the metro station, favoring my injured knee and pushing my way through the rush hour crowd flowing in the opposite direction, my mood began to improve. The car theft seemed a cut and dry affair. I felt that once I had a talk with Korenev's driver, the ZIM would be found in no time. I also thought that the playwright had a pretty good idea himself as to what had happened to it. What I couldn't figure out was why he kept insisting on Sergei's innocence and why he had called in Criminal Investigations. But it wasn't any of my concern. What mattered was that I would be rid of him very soon and stop wasting my time, rejoining Lenny and the guys on the murder investigation.

TWO

Lenny Urumov is a walking contradiction.

He is married and, by all indications, happily so. He loves his wife Raisa and their two daughters – one of whom, the younger, he named Raisa. Yet he's forever chasing after skirts, has girlfriends all over the city, and seems constitutionally incapable of meeting a pretty woman without flirting with her. Actually, she doesn't even have to be pretty. As far as women are concerned, Lenny doesn't discriminate.

The Boss partnered me up with Lenny when I first came to Petrovka, less as a learning experience for me than as a punishment for him. Lenny had had a nasty falling out with his old partner, Valera Tumakov, and Budyonny was angry with him.

At first, I didn't think it was going to work out. Lenny's desk was piled high with a mixture of old files and active cases. His case notes were worse than useless: he took them in dog-eared notebooks with tea stains on the cover, and was the first to admit that he couldn't read his own handwriting to save his life. In all circumstances he affected an easy-going indifference and devil-may-care attitude.

But I soon discovered that he had a memory like a steel trap, so he never actually needed to read his case notes. His mind was systematic and logical, categorizing each of the myriad facts he recalled into its proper place. And, while never appearing to be in a rush, he was punctual to the point of obsession.

A few months into my job, I also got a chance to appreciate his dedication to his work. The case involved a recidivist from Sverdlovsk, known by the bizarre nickname Taganka Chef. When we came across him, the Chef was in the process of cooking a very nasty stew. He had gotten his claws into Neal Fyodorovich Bilibin, head bookkeeper at the Central Department Store in the center of Moscow. Bilibin's son had fallen in with a bad crowd and lost a large sum of money at cards. The Chef then bought the son's gambling debts and started turning up the heat on the father. The rules of the criminal community were clear and allowed no exceptions: either you pay your gambling debts or you die. Since the Bilibins couldn't raise the money, the Chef suggested a way out: help him rob the Central Department Store.

That was when the older Bilibin decided to go to the police.

Lenny told him to carry out the Chef's instructions, which were to alert him when the store's safe held a particularly large amount of cash and to leave the back door unlocked. Our plan was to catch the Chef red-handed.

Then it all went wrong.

Neither Lenny nor I were experienced enough to realize that no career criminal would actually put a plan like that into action. Why leave Bilibin behind, since an inside job would be the first thing the cops would think of and the head bookkeeper would be a prime suspect? And of course Bilibin would then finger the Chef.

The robbery was scheduled for the last Friday of the month, which was when the store was set to pay employees their monthly wages. After the bank's morning delivery, the safe would hold over a hundred thousand rubles in cash. On Thursday night we arranged to meet Bilibin in a small park near his house, where he was in the habit of walking his dog, to go over the final details.

We got to the park at the appointed time and waited, shivering in the late October rain and smoking. When, twenty minutes later, there was no sign of Bilibin, Lenny began to sense something was up. We raced to the bookkeeper's apartment, only to be told by his suddenly alarmed wife that a man had come for him two hours before.

"He insisted it was an emergency and they left," she told us.

How could we have been so stupid? The Chef had been planning all along to go into the store the night before, even though there would be less money in the safe. And of course his idea was to abduct Bilibin after the robbery. The missing money would then be blamed on the missing head bookkeeper, whose body, buried under fallen leaves somewhere in the woods between Moscow and Sverdlovsk, would probably never be found.

Lenny figured it out in a flash. The Central Department Store was across the street from the Bolshoi Theater and next to the Maly. Both had evening performances at that hour, and the square in front of them was lively, brightly lit and full of people – including many foreign tourists entering and leaving the posh Metropole Hotel, on the other side of Karl Marx Avenue. The store had closed. The street level display windows were filled with mannequins in elegant clothes and pyramids of radio sets and cameras. The offices on the upper floors were dark.

We found the night guard at the service entrance, slumped in his chair, the front of his uniform soaked in blood. He had been stabbed through the heart, the blade skirting the top of the sixth rib with ghastly surgical precision. The Chef was not kidding around.

Upstairs, the green security light on the ceiling illuminated the small group as it emerged from Accounting. They had emptied the safe and were on their way out, walking single-file toward the back stairs. Two beefy young men led the way, each holding several canvas bags. The Chef brought up the rear and the bookkeeper was sandwiched in-between, being repeatedly nudged by the muzzle of the Chef's thin-barrel handgun.

Neither Lenny nor I was armed.

"Go get help," Lenny whispered silently in my ear.

Lenny snatched a blue salesman's coat, emblazoned with the Central Department Store's emblem, from a coat rack near the back stairs. He slipped into it and stepped out of the shadows.

"Hi, there," he called out cheerfully. "Good evening, Comrade Bilibin. What are you doing at work so late, burning the midnight oil, so to speak? And who are these men with you?"

I lurked in the shadows for a moment, to make sure the Chef wasn't going to plug Lenny on sight. Not that I could have done anything about it if he had.

Taken by surprise, the two thugs froze. The Chef turned around and dropped his right arm to his side, concealing the gun with his body. Lenny didn't seem to notice any of it and continued to blithely advance on the group. In a single moment, he had changed into someone unrecognizable. He suddenly looked soft and slovenly, his shoulders sloping and his stomach, jelly-like, now hung over his belt buckle.

"Who the hell is this?" the Chef asked Bilibin, his voice hard and hoarse.

The bookkeeper hesitated, shifting a terror-filled gaze from Lenny to the Chef.

"It's, um—" he started to reply, then went silent.

"My name is Semyon Moiseyevich Mendelbaum," Lenny answered. "I'm the head of the jewelry department here."

Apparently Mendelbaum was a terribly naive guy, for even then he had no idea what he had stumbled on.

A nasty smile appeared on the gangster's face. His lips spread, flashing a metal tooth.

"Mendelbaum?" he repeated, a note of glee softening his voice. "Jewelry department?"

"I was just locking away some of our more valuable items," Lenny explained as he approached the group.

Then, suddenly, he stopped short. Something must have started to click in his brain, but it was too late.

"Well, you may have to take them out again," the Chef said and struck Lenny in the face.

"What are you doing?" Lenny shrieked as he reeled backwards, upsetting an office chair.

"You'll figure it out in a moment, you idiot," the Chef muttered through clenched teeth and, taking a step toward Lenny, hit him again, this time with the hand in which he held the gun. The blood squirting from Lenny's nose was black in the lurid security light.

"Please don't hit me," Lenny pleaded. "I have a weak heart."

"Go nicely then. Take us to your department."

I don't know whether Lenny knew where the jewelry department was, but he began walking between two rows of counters away from the back door. He was using the sleeve of the salesman's coat to wipe the black droplets dripping from his nose down his chin. The Chef was close on his heels and the two younger thugs, still carrying the loot, were now in the back of the procession. One of them gave Bilibin a vicious kick in the pants to make sure he picked up the pace.

I had seen enough. I turned and, as I tiptoed down the main stairwell in almost complete darkness, I heard Lenny's whining voice, "I have high blood pressure, Comrade. I had a stroke last year. I'm not supposed to get excited."

"Shut up and walk," came the Chef's reply. "I'm not your fucking doctor."

Two uniformed patrolmen were in front of the Maly, leaning on the pedestal of the monument to writer Alexander Ostrovsky, smoking and watching the crowd. It was a cozy posting and the theater-goers and foreign tourists were well-dressed and pretty. The cops weren't at all happy to have to follow me into the darkened store, especially once I requisitioned a gun. Only one of them had his, while the other cop's holster turned out to be stuffed with old newspaper.

I was gone no more than three minutes, but by the time I got back to the third floor – many steps ahead of the useless cops who had gasped like schoolgirls at the sight of the dead security guard downstairs – Lenny had taken the situation in hand. He was standing over the Chef, holding a heavy bronze inkwell. The Chef lay on the floor. Blood – a lot more than had come out of Lenny's nose – was pouring freely from his cracked skull. His German-made P-38 lay next to him. One of his young friends was cowering behind one of the canvas bags of loot. The third thug had escaped, but with the other two in custody he didn't get very far.

When I returned to the office from my extended visit with the playwright, Lenny was waiting for me.

"We got the bastard," he said the moment he saw me, breaking into a triumphant smile. "Caught him right at the scene of the crime."

A glass of very strong tea stood on his desk. Looking smug and pleased with himself, Lenny was fishing oatmeal cookies one by one from a cardboard box, shoving them into his mouth, chewing loudly, and washing them down with sips of tea.

"That's great," I said. "Congratulations. Tell me what happened."

Of course I was happy for them. No detective would object to a crime being solved so quickly – and the perpetrator identified and caught – especially in such a nasty case. But I was also a little disappointed and mad at Korenev, since his stupid car theft – if it was a theft – had kept me from sharing in Lenny's success.

"Get some tea first," Lenny said.

Having broken the big news, Urumov was in no hurry to flesh out the details. He slurped his tea loudly, twisting his lips on the edge the glass to keep from getting scalded. I poured myself a cup and settled down as comfortably as the office furnishings allowed, getting ready to listen.

"What kind of a job did Budyonny have for you?" Lenny asked, offering me an oatmeal cookie with some hesitation, first sticking his nose into the box to see how many he had left.

"Ugh," I replied, making a face. "A stolen car."

Lenny whistled.

"A stolen car?" he repeated in utter disbelief. "With a child murderer on the loose?"

"That's only part of it," I said. "There was a bank robbery in Leningrad yesterday. Firearms involved. One dead, one critical, the gang got away. Budyonny was going to send the two of us up there to help with that investigation, but then there was the murder and, yes, a car theft."

"I heard about the Leningrad robbery," Lenny said. "It all went completely wrong, apparently. First for the robbers, then for the cops, and now for the detectives. The robbers got away and no one can figure out how. But a car theft?"

It wasn't that Lenny was so eager to talk about the Leningrad robbery or my car theft case. Actually, it was the other way around. He wanted to talk about his arrest as much as I wanted to hear about it, and was simply savoring my impatience, waiting for me to give up and start asking questions.

But I was on to him and decided to stir things up.

"That's the thing," I said. "With all of that going on, Budyonny still sent me to investigate a car theft. Of course it wasn't an ordinary car theft, mind you—"

I let the sentence trail off.

"What was so special about it?" Lenny said, pretending to be interested.

"Someone stole a ZIM. From a big wig. The playwright Matvei Korenev. Runs the Writers' Union. Lives high on the hog, too."

Lenny forced himself to look impressed.

"Oh, he's famous," he said. "Did you meet him? What's he like? What happened to his car?"

"You'll probably meet him too," I said. "Because now that you've caught the murderer, Budyonny will want you to give me a hand with Korenev. He specifically asked me to keep you in the loop."

I was ready to continue dragging out my tale, but decided to take pity on Lenny, who was fidgeting in his chair, anxious to talk. Plus, I had had enough of Korenev and his car and was thoroughly bored by the case.

"Well, it's still just a car, even if it is a ZIM," I concluded, pausing meaningfully. "So, tell about the murder."

"Sure," Lenny said, perking up instantly.

Arriving at the crime scene on 1st Kolobovsky Lane in mid-afternoon, Lenny and the guys found the body of Tanya Drozdova, a fifth grader at School No. 128. The victim was in her room in a communal apartment, slumped over the dining table. Her Russian textbook lay open in front of her, along with a notebook in which she had begun to do her homework assignment. At her feet lay her pen and a no-spill inkwell, which had in fact spilled its blue ink all over the carpet and her slippers. The door of the room was unlocked, with the key on the inside. There was no sign of forced entry, and none of any struggle, except for the overturned inkwell. The girl had been strangled. Or rather, her neck was broken.

"He just snapped her neck, like she was a chicken," Lenny said.

Sasha Grigoriev, our forensics expert, said after a preliminary examination that bruises on the girl's throat suggested that she had been strangled by someone standing in front of her. In other words, she had probably been on her feet, facing her murderer, who then placed her body in the chair.

"The inkwell and the pen could have fallen down then," I suggested.

Grigoriev put the time of death at noon, which fit with Tanya's schedule. On a typical day, she would return from school, heat up her lunch in the communal kitchen and eat it in her room. She would then wash the dishes and do her homework. She also practiced her violin.

"At first glance, Grigoriev says there's no sign of—"

Lenny stumbled, his voice catching.

"Of – you know what I mean. Her leg warmers and panties were still on."

Lenny spat angrily.

"But we can't be sure until the autopsy," he added.

Tanya shared a room with her mother. Her father had left them when she was a baby, and he now had another family in Volgograd, a thousand kilometers southeast of Moscow. He saw his daughter during occasional business trips to Moscow, but she never went to see him. He paid child support regularly, but no more than what had been set by the court. Money was always tight. Tanya's mother, Irina, was a proofreader at *Literary Gazette* newspaper and she usually worked late to earn overtime.

Tanya's grandmother used to live with them and pick up Tanya after school. But the grandmother died last March, and this year Tanya had started walking home on her own. On most afternoons, a neighbor, Baba Dasha, was in the apartment. She cleaned the People's Court building on Pokrovka Street, which meant that she worked the night shift. That morning, however, Baba Dasha had some business at the social welfare office that kept her away until late afternoon. So when Tanya arrived home, the apartment was empty.

It was another neighbor, Nikolai Grushnikov, who discovered the body. Coming home a little before one, he was surprised to see Tanya's lunch still on the stove. He decided to knock on her door, even though he didn't know her schedule, as he was a new tenant occupying the room of Tanya's deceased grandmother.

Grushnikov is a gym teacher at a boarding school in the remote suburb of Khamovniki, but had stayed home from work the previous week with an injured foot. In the morning he had gone out to get his sick leave form signed by a doctor at the district clinic.

"I knew there was something wrong with his story right away," Lenny said. "To start with, he was drunk. Like, he was supposed to have gone to see a doctor, but then got pissed somewhere along the way. Or maybe he got drunk after discovering the body, I don't know. He kept shedding drunken tears, describing how he had come upon her. But there was no sign of a forced entry into the apartment, which was suspicious. And Tanya's door was unlocked, too. When I mentioned that to her mother, she was surprised. Tanya had been told to lock her door whenever she was alone and she always did. The murderer had to be someone she trusted."

"Or at least someone she knew," I said. "'A neighbor would fit the bill. Especially a school teacher."

"Just what sort of a schoolteacher this Grushnikov is, Valera Tumakov is going to find out; he's gone to his school. Meanwhile, I'm asking myself, why would he knock on her door? Just because she hadn't had her lunch at one in the afternoon? That's not so strange. Besides, he told us that he didn't know her schedule. I pointed this out to him and he started to get flustered."

"Sounds fishy," I agreed.

"That's exactly what I thought. He told us that the older Drozdova resented him for moving into her mother's room, even though it wasn't his fault. So I put all the facts together and I had a hunch. The dining table where Tanya was found had a polished surface. You could see plenty of prints and smudges. So I point this out to him just as the girls from Forensics start dusting the room for fingerprints and ask him, 'Are we going to find yours here?'

"You should've seen him. He started wriggling and squirming like a fish in a frying pan.

"So I say, 'What if we find your fingerprints here? Are you going to tell me you went around touching the furniture at a crime scene after you found the body?'

"Then he starts to howl: 'Please, comrade detective, I'm going to tell you the truth. This past week, while I was staying at home, I helped Tanya with her math.'

"I take the bull by the horns and ask him straight out, 'Did you kill her, you filthy bastard?'

" 'No, God forbid, I swear, comrade detective.'

"And then came the drunken tears," Lenny said.

"Did he admit it in the end?" I asked.

Lenny turned the cookie box upside down to make sure none had gotten stuck inside. A few crumbs fell out and Lenny brushed them onto the floor with the back of his hand. He got up, walked over to the window and lit a cigarette, even though Budyonny had recently banned smoking in all offices. It was completely dark outside.

"Technically speaking, no," Lenny said. "He thinks he's too clever for us. He keeps bawling and telling us how he liked Tanya, what a nice girl she was. His heart was bleeding for her, because her mother didn't come home until late and the girl was neglected, staying at home all by herself. He started helping her with her math and they got along real well. In other words, he admits coming to see her and lying about it to us, but not to murdering her. He was, he says, so terribly upset when he discovered the body. He didn't know what to say and he was scared, so his first instinct was to lie."

"Why is that?" I asked. "Why hide that he was helping her with math?"

"He says the mother never liked him. He figured she would point the finger at him if she found out he was spending time with Tanya."

Lenny put out his cigarette and began pacing the office. Or rather, since our office was very small and cramped, he took a step and a half from the window to the back wall and a step and a half back toward the window.

"Unfortunately, Valera held me back. I was going to kick the son of a bitch in the balls a couple of times. Then he would have sung like a nightingale."

I shrugged.

"And you can keep your doubts to yourself," he said hoarsely, his brow darkening. I hadn't said a word. But it didn't matter. My doubts must have been clearly visible in my expression. "You didn't see her dead body, Matyushkin, so keep your mouth shut. You were out hobnobbing with the rich and famous and didn't see what I saw."

"It wasn't my choice," I objected.

"Sure," Lenny said. "Do you have any idea what it's like for a father of two little girls to see a dead girl slumped over her homework like that? My girls are about the same age as Tanya. It could easily have been my little Raiska or Zoyka. Makes me want to kill the bastard myself." He paused, his glare darkening. "This case is personal for me, Matyushkin. It can't ever be like that for you or Tumakov. You two should stay out of my way. For your own good."

THREE

Rozhdestvensky Boulevard slouches along the side of a long hill. At the top, by Sretenka Gate, it starts its descent gently, almost tentatively, but gets steeper along the way until it turns into a sheer drop just before reaching Trubnaya Square, where a public toilet is built into the side of the precipice.

The boulevard's central pathway is wide and sanded and framed by two rows of snow-covered benches. Facing the boulevard are stately old buildings now broken into communal apartments, and remnants of mansions once owned by noble Moscow families. Along the inner circumference of the boulevard runs the pockmarked wall of what used to be the Nativity Convent, its surviving buildings adapted to various contemporary uses.

Looking up from Trubnaya, you can't help notice that, under the pavement, just beneath the thin skin of the asphalt, there is still a slice of wild landscape on which the city precariously stands, squatting the way tenants squat in the Nativity Convent's cells. In the original system of coordinates, the last stop of A tram on Trubnaya, where the tram tracks form a loop and runs back uphill, lies on the high left bank of the Neglinka River. The wind-blown expanse of Trubnaya is the river itself, long ago forced underground. But standing on top of it, you can still feel its living current beneath your feet. We have bent the river to our urban will, but its spirit lives on and it gurgles softly below Samoteka Square, along Tsvetnoy Boulevard, and under the extinct Blacksmiths' Bridge. In summer, during heavy July downpours, when rivers are meant to overflow their banks, the Neglinka sometimes bursts out of its sewer and floods the musty cellars of the surrounding buildings.

On the slope of the high riverbank, tram rails gleam like unsheathed cavalry sabers.

In winter, trams take a long rest midway down the slope, testing their brakes. Their electric lights shine invitingly through the bare limbs of the boulevard's poplar trees, making it even more difficult to wait the last cold minutes for the cars to arrive.

Having turned down Lenny's offer to drive me home, I walked briskly to Trubnaya, where I just missed a tram and had to wait twenty minutes for the next one.

I had hoped that the winter air would make my foul mood pass. Back at the office, after Lenny finished telling me about the arrest, and the excitement had worn off, I felt a lump in my throat. Lenny, too, fell silent and, supporting his stubble-covered chin with the palm of his hand, stared morosely out at the dark night beyond our office window.

Arresting the killer wasn't going to bring back his victim.

At first, I was alone at the tram stop, but soon I was joined by an artillery captain in a grey overcoat. He was holding a leather briefcase in one gloved hand and a knitted bag full of potatoes in the other. Later, after a sizeable crowd had gathered, a colonel with the Ministry of Internal Affairs' tags on his uniform arrived, positioning himself a little apart from the rest of us. The captain hastily switched the bag to his left hand and raised his right hand in a salute. The colonel responded by touching the edge of his grey Persian lamb hat and nodding.

Yet he soon shed his self-importance as the cold began to bite. He rubbed his hands together, casting impatient glances up the slope. The artillery captain remained motionless, stoically holding his potatoes and briefcase and staring straight ahead, as though he was on sentry duty before Lenin's Tomb.

I thought about a motorcycle I was in the process of buying. A nice used motorbike was hard to find; one I could afford was next to impossible. Then last summer I ran into a guy selling his war-booty Zundapp. It was a hunk of rusty German steel painted a forbidding shade of gray, but it was a solid machine and it had a sidecar, which made it suitable even for a family. Not that I had a family, as Lenny had been kind enough to remind me earlier, but at least I could afford to buy the bike. Or very nearly so.

The guy selling it was an engineer at the Svoboda Soap and Cosmetics Plant and drove a hard bargain. We haggled all of September and most of October. By the time we were ready to close the deal, the snow had come and the Zundapp had to be placed under a tarp for the winter. The engineer closed our negotiations until spring, but told me that the Zundapp was as good as mine. Zooming up the hill would certainly be preferable to standing on Trubnaya, waiting for the tram, even if riding the motorbike in this kind of weather would be suicidal.

Next to me, two university students were trying to chat up a remarkably unresponsive passenger. They had somehow deduced, from the tip of a nose protruding from a fluffy wool shawl and a pair of green, slanted eyes, that she was a target worthy of their attention.

"What is it that you have in your hand, comrade young lady?"

Comrade young lady had a round object wrapped in newspaper. She was holding it in her outstretched hand, away from her body. She now turned away, patting her package with her hand.

"Seriously, what is it? I'm dying of curiosity."

It is often the case that the shorter, less attractive one in a pair of friends trying to chat up a young woman does all the talking, while his more handsome companion stands next to him, smirking but saying nothing. The taller one had a pair of romantic grey eyes that he held fixed on the young woman's face; they managed to convey tenderness, understanding and superiority all at once. He seemed in no doubt who, if push came to shove, would be her first choice.

Yet for the moment she wasn't interested in either one of them.

"We're intrigued," the shorter boy continued. "If you don't mind me saying so, your package looks quite a bit like a soccer ball. Are you perhaps the famous soccer star Eduard Streltsov in drag?"

His handsome friend extended a hand and started to caress the package with the tips of his thumb and forefinger, as though probing for a nipple under the newsprint. He wore a soft leather glove and the face of a gold wristwatch protruded expensively from beneath the cuff of his tweed overcoat.

"Go to hell," the woman snarled, pushing his hand away.

"Whoa," the handsome one exclaimed, removing his hand quickly and blowing on it as though he had been burned. "Now you've hurt me."

"Get lost."

"Why are you so unfriendly?" the shorter boy asked, regaining the floor. "Your package won't get any smaller if my buddy touches it. What is it, anyway?"

"None of your business."

"Come on, we're opening our hearts to you. Ain't we, Vitalik?"

He turned to his friend, who backed him up with a nod and a smirk.

"I don't give a damn about your hearts," the woman replied.

"You're making a mistake. It's the one organ you absolutely need to fall in love. Don't you want us to fall in love with you? We can either take turns loving you, or love you both at the same time. It's entirely up to you."

"Go to hell."

"Fine," the boy said, finally giving up and taking offense. "The truth is we don't really give a damn about you, either. We're stuck down here waiting for the tram and I thought we might pass the time pleasantly by talking to a nice, intelligent young woman. Obviously, you're neither."

"If you're waiting for the tram, do so quietly and leave other people alone."

The two weren't silent for long. A minute later they were engaged in a heated debate about some fine point of aerodynamics. The short one was once again doing most of the talking, while the handsome Vitalik merely nodded his assent. He seemed a little bored by this new topic and kept casting wistful glances at the unfriendly young woman.

"It's a goddamn disgrace," said a voice next to me.

The man wore a cheap winter hat with its earflaps tied under his unshaven chin. He kept one hand inside his ratty sheepskin coat. A nearly finished Belomor cigarette glowed in the corner of his angrily twisted mouth. He drew on it and gagged, shaking with a fit of visceral coughing that rattled his skinny frame. He sounded like a small, aggressive dog yapping.

"A disgrace, fuck their mother."

He spat the words out, struggling through the coughing.

"Comrade Stalin would never have let it go on like this. He would've stood the public transportation minister against the wall right away, and the lousy municipal bosses against the wall, and the damn lazy tram drivers against the wall, too. He would never have stood for it, Comrade Stalin, them keeping the working man out in the cold like this."

"The tram drivers, too?" the shorter boy echoed him, abruptly breaking off his lecture on aerodynamics. "Really? Have they become too lazy to work?"

He sounded sympathetic, which was probably why the old man missed his sarcasm.

"It's worse than that," he shouted, his voice going half an octave higher. "They're wreckers and saboteurs, the whole bunch of them. Comrade Stalin always defended the working man. That's why the new bosses threw his body out of the Mausoleum."

He stopped short, suddenly catching sight of the Internal Ministry colonel, and concluded sheepishly, his outrage deflated, "I'm a working man myself."

No matter how hard you try to keep the landscape down and pile bricks and mortar on top of it, rivers, hills and ravines will always endure, biding their time under the asphalt. They'll wait for cities to empty out, for buildings to crumble and for roadways to crack, and send forth their grass and saplings through the disintegrating skin of the asphalt. The poplars now lining the boulevard in regimented rows will break ranks and fill all the space with their progeny. Airborne species of other trees will join them and a time will come when the dense woods reclaim the side of the hill. The Neglinka, nameless once more, will wear through the concrete sack in which it is enclosed and flow freely, just as it did for thousands of years before we arrived.

And even now, in its submissive state, you ignore the landscape at your own peril.

Seven years ago, when Stalin died, my aunt Eugenia took my little sister Natashka to see his funeral. She said it was a historic occasion and our grandchildren and their grandchildren would always remember how we buried Great Stalin, the Father of the Nation.

They ended up right there, on the steep downhill of Rozhdestvensky Boulevard. A huge crowd was going down to Trubnaya, where it was supposed to swing left and head toward the Hall of Columns on Karl Marx Avenue. It was March and there was frost in the air. The slope was slippery from all of the snow that no one had bothered to remove, because Comrade Stalin lay dead in the Hall of Columns and all life had stopped.

The crowd was pressing hard. There was a wall of people down on Trubnaya, where the passage to Petrovsky Boulevard had been cordoned off by trucks and Internal Ministry troops. Aunt Eugenia and Natashka were caught on the slope, across from the old Nativity Convent, when those coming down behind them started to press into the ones standing below, and a crush began. Grown-ups and kids, big and small, were all falling down. Those who were behind them, pressed mercilessly forward by the human mass, walked over them, trampling them and churning their bodies into mincemeat with the sharp edges of their heels. The kids were especially vulnerable because they couldn't stay on their feet, and when parents tried to pick them up they were squashed like bugs by the mill of bodies.

When the crush began, Aunt Eugenia picked up Natashka and held her close. Next to her, pressing into her, was a man, a stranger. He saw Aunt Eugenia holding Natashka, wrenched her away, raised her up and set her down on the sea of heads and said, "Run, little girl. May the Lord protect you."

For a few minutes, until she herself fainted, Aunt Eugenia watched Natashka make her way down, hopping from head to head and slipping a bit every now and again as though she were running on wet cobblestones. Even after her own feet buckled, Aunt Eugenia was kept upright and carried by the crowd that flowed down the slope like volcanic lava, bubbling up in screams of pain and curses.

She went down at the very end, just before reaching the drop over the public toilet. The cast-iron banisters had been ripped out and people were falling to their deaths. It was a miracle Aunt Eugenia didn't fall and survived. Her arm was broken in two places and she suffered a concussion, but otherwise she got off relatively lightly.

As to Natashka, she was never found – neither among the living nor the dead.

The way the bodies looked after the crush, it would have been difficult to identify such a tiny child. She wore a reddish fur coat that Mother had made from her own old coat, sewn from fox hides trapped by my grandfather many years before. She also had a green knit hat, another hand-me-down from my mother. Her clothes were distinctive and perhaps could have helped them find her, but the officials weren't going to bother with that. They had more important things to do.

And so those who had been crushed to death on the day of Stalin's funeral – there must have been hundreds of them, if not thousands – simply vanished. They were gone without a trace, as if they had never existed, and my little sister was among them.

I was nineteen at the time, doing my military service, and Natashka was almost eight. She was born a month after the war ended and two months after Father's death notice had arrived in the mail.

It was dark and the temperature had fallen sharply. When I finally elbowed my way out of the tram car at my Kirov Gate stop, my breath came up short and I was shivering in the freezing wind. The square in front of Kirov Metro Station was lit up and the tram stop was filled with people. The conductor rang the bell as a final warning to those who were still trying to storm the back door, and the tram started to roll.

"Holy Mother of God," someone shrieked in my ear.

Suddenly, the square exploded with female voices, with sickening screams and shouts.

"Somebody, help. Stop the tram. Oh, my God, it's gonna cut her in half."

Glancing behind me, I caught sight of the gleaming blue rail, the slowly rolling cast-iron wheel and a pair of winter boots sliding into the narrowing space between the wheel and the cobblestones. At the same time, something black and white and round, eerily resembling a severed human head, hit the underside of the tram with a loud thud. Instead of trying to get out, the woman on the tracks struggled to reach for the round object.

The object eluded her desperate grab, pinballing against the wheel and rolling out, but the macabre sight of it kicking around brought me back to my senses. I dove under the tram and caught the collar of the woman's coat. Straining every muscle in my body, I jerked her up and out.

It all happened in a flash. The tram seemed to linger as though in slow motion, its bell rang once more above my head, and its wheel softly, like knife into butter, fell into the steel groove where the woman's ankles had been a split second before.

I took an involuntary step backwards, propelled by the impetus of my own effort, and felt a sharp pain in my right knee. I had twisted it earlier in the day, jumping off the construction fence next to the playwright's garage, and I feared I had now aggravated the injury. As to the victim, she wriggled free and rushed back onto the tracks.

"What's happened?" an old woman asked next to me.

"A drunk," came a confident reply. "Look at him. He can barely stand up. They have no shame, those drunks, pawing girls in public places. Go home and sleep it off, do you hear?"

The woman I had pulled from under the tram stood on the tracks, intently scanning the ground. I recognized the prickly stranger who had refused to flirt with the handsome Vitalik and his talkative friend. Her shawl had been pushed back, away from her face, and I had to admit that those two had been on to something: she was indeed very pretty.

From my vantage point a few steps away, I could see what she was looking for perfectly well. Her round package had rolled slightly to the side and lay between the newsstand and the ice cream kiosk, hidden in the shadow of the metro station's granite steps.

Limping slightly under the reproachful eyes of the old women at the tram stop, I walked over and picked up the package. It felt heavy, hard as a rock, and extremely cold.

"Is this what you've been looking for?" I asked.

She raised her head.

"Yes, it is. It's mine. Give it back."

For all her prettiness, she was still rude. I had pulled her out from under a tram, preserving at least six inches of her natural height, and had found her precious package. All I had to show for it was a bad knee and a reputation as a lecherous drunk – and now, she was being rude to me into the bargain.

It had been a pretty bad day and I was in a bad mood.

She lunged for her package and I quickly moved it out of her reach.

"Not so fast," I said, my voice mean.

She stared.

"What do you mean, you creep? Give it back to me."

"Watch your manners, young lady," I said. "Didn't your parents teach you the magic word? And don't forget to thank me, too, while you're at it."

"Thank you for what?" she asked indignantly.

"To start with, I just saved your life. And I found your package and have been kind enough to pick it up for you."

She turned away and stood there breathing hard. Yes, she was extremely rude, but her anger was also attractive, and I had to smile.

"By the way, what is it?" I asked, trying to sound less like a cop.

"None of your business."

She really had no idea how to be nice to people.

"Very well," I shrugged. "Then I'm going to figure it out for myself."

I started to pick a hole in the newspaper.

"Hey, what are you doing? It's a frozen chicken. From Hungary. Are you happy? It cost me five rubles. It's a lot of money, five rubles."

"A chicken from Hungary," I said, as though talking to myself. "Fantastic. I'm going to requisition it."

"What?" she exclaimed, giving me an incredulous look. "Are you serious?"

"Of course I am," I replied, choosing to ignore the hatred that twisted her face and that should have given me pause. "How do I know it's your chicken? It was lying over there on the ground. It doesn't say anywhere it's yours."

"Wrong," she exclaimed. "It does say it's mine."

"Where?"

"Let me show you."

She reached for the frozen ball in my hand, but I was ready for her.

"Tell me where," I said, adroitly pulling the chicken back. "I'll look."

"Sure," she shrugged. "Right under the newspaper."

After removing several layers of wrapping, I found a piece of paper pinned to its plastic packaging. It had become soaked and the writing ran in purple streaks, but the word Antonina was still legible.

"It proves nothing," I said. "Antonina may easily be the name of the chicken."

"It's from Hungary," she giggled. "Antonina is a Russian name."

"Fine," I said. "But it only works if your name is Antonina."

"It is," she declared proudly. "Antonina Ivanovna. Tosya for short."

She caught herself, not wanting to get too friendly with me. Nevertheless, she had been thawing little by little, something that could not be said about her chicken. It sat like a lump of ice in the palm of my hand, making it go numb.

"Well," I said. "If our Hungarian friends raised this chicken specially for you—"

"Don't be silly. It's Lenka Skobeleva. She saved it for me from the shipment they got last week. She works at Yeliseyev's Grocery Store. She's a friend from—"

She broke off and added softly: "From school."

And then she really went for it.

The attack took me by surprise and, besides, I had a damaged knee. But, excuses aside, she was strong and tall and good with her fists. She didn't try anything fancy – just struck me in the face and grabbed the chicken. Reeling from the blow, which had been only partly cushioned by her thick mitten, I staggered. Then, overcoming the pain in my knee, I grabbed the chicken back. She turned and doubled over, protecting it with her body like a rugby player. We were now holding onto it together, four-handed, with me enfolding her in my arms.

It was a ridiculous position to be in and, unless one of us was ready to let go, there was no obvious way to end the standoff. She tried to elbow me in the stomach and I had to press hard against her to limit her ability to throw a punch. We were breathing hard, focusing on our silent struggle. Neither of us was gaining the upper hand and neither was willing to give up.

Then suddenly she twisted her head and, our lips meeting over her shoulder, kissed me on the mouth. Or maybe she only twisted her head, and it was I who kissed her, I didn't know how it happened.

Another tram pulled up and the people who had been waiting for it stopped watching our fight and rushed the doors. In their place, a new batch of spectators arrived, who were now watching us kiss.

For a while, we were both still holding onto the damn chicken, but then a kiss proved mightier than a fist and, gradually, I began to loosen my grip on it. My heart was pounding, and it wasn't at all due to the physical effort.

"Get away from me," she whispered as soon as she had full possession of her prize.

She too was out of breath. We broke off and stood facing each other and staring.

She was the first to regain her composure. She turned around, crossed Kirov Street against the light and began to walk away. For a few minutes she and I walked in the same direction on opposite sides of the street. Eventually, however, I had to cross to her side to get to my house. My knee still hurt, I was limping a little, and walked slowly, falling behind her. I was still trembling a little, too. She turned right, into the side street. I followed her.

She turned around, saw me and stopped.

"What do you want?" she asked.

I stopped, keeping a distance of about fifteen paces between us.

"I hurt my knee pulling you from beneath the tram," I said. "I'm trying to get home."

"You're lying," she said.

"This is where I live," I said.

"What's your address?"

I gave her my address.

She mulled it over for a moment.

"So we're neighbors?" I asked.

She didn't reply and began to walk again. But now she walked slowly, letting me catch up. We were almost at the turn to my courtyard. The narrow side street was deserted.

"I'm sorry I punched you in the face," she said. "But it was your fault. You shouldn't have taken my chicken."

"It doesn't matter," I said.

"Does your knee hurt?" she asked.

"It does," I said. "I need to take a rest. You can go ahead."

I stopped and she did too. We stood in silence while I caught my breath.

"I thought you were one of those guys who harass women in the street," she said at last, laughing uneasily.

"I'm sorry," I said. "It's been a pretty rough day at work."

And then, for no reason at all – or maybe because I was tired and disgusted, and had thought of my little sister again, and because she had kissed me and no one had kissed me like that, on an impulse, for a long time, and even though she had not really meant it and had kissed me merely to get her chicken back, it still mattered – for all those reasons taken together I blurted out something I had no intention of saying.

"Something terrible happened today," I said. "Really goddamn terrible."

"What happened?" she asked, suddenly soft and solicitous.

It was such a quick change, I wasn't ready for it.

"Never mind," I said. "I don't want to talk about it. You should go home. I'm better now."

She took a step into the courtyard and then turned around.

"Maybe we should go to the movies some time, since we're neighbors," she said, and added laughing. "Unless you're married. I don't like going out with married men."

FOUR

Tanya Drozdova's apartment was located a short walk from our headquarters, in a squat four-story building with a thick coat of yellow paint over tightly laid brickwork. The façade, facing 1st Kolobovsky Lane, had dentils over first-floor windows and a row of elaborate cornices on the second floor. It occupied almost an entire side of the narrow street. The entrance to the building was through a low archway, as long and dark as a railway tunnel, which smelled of moisture and mildew even in the frozen depths of winter. Tanya's windows gave onto the courtyard and a children's playground planted with a handful of underfed urban saplings.

The courtyard was empty, but as I looked around I spotted the curtains swaying lightly in more than a few windows. Behind them, watchful eyes socketed deep into weathered faces observed my movements. Our newspapers never report crimes, but that doesn't mean that people don't know. Neighbors always know. The official silence only feeds the rumor mill. Whispers radiate from the crime scene and, distorted and embellished with each retelling, spread through the city.

The light bulb on the landing was burned out. The stairwell was lit by daylight filtering from the dusty window between the first and second floor. Several doorbell buttons dotted the side of Tanya's front door. I pressed one at random. The shrillness of the ring behind the door gave me a start as it echoed up and down the dim stairwell.

I waited for a long time after the sound had died down. On one of the upper landings an apartment door squeaked open. There was the patter of stealthy footsteps and a head peeked down over the banister. It drew back quickly when our eyes met and I soon heard the door being shut again.

I waited and then rang another bell. I was about to make use of the keys Urumov had given me when the lock suddenly clicked and the door silently opened.

The entranceway was completely dark. Staring at me from the darkness was a pair of huge, dark eyes.

"You're making too much noise," said a tired voice.

There was a long silence. My eyes slowly became accustomed to the dark and I was able to make out the drawn face and slim figure standing in the doorway.

"Comrade Irina Drozdova?" I asked, sounding much colder and more official than I had intended.

The woman nodded. I introduced myself, showing my Criminal Investigations ID. She didn't so much as glance at it and stepped aside, letting me in. She flipped on the light switch and I found myself in a cluttered, smoke-filled hallway.

Some time ago, Criminal Investigations had circulated a memo instructing us how to talk to victims' families. It was filled with well-meaning clichés about conveying sympathy and reassurances, that violent crime is the thing of the capitalist past, and that the Party and the government are doing their utmost to mop up its regrettable remnants. None was of any use in real life, and only Valera Tumakov had ever tried them in actual situations. In my experience, it was best to say nothing and to get on with one's work. No one needs a cop's sympathy.

"I didn't expect you to be here," I said apologetically.

Lenny had told me that the mother had gone to stay with relatives.

She shrugged. The effort of answering the door seemed to have exhausted her and she sank heavily into an armchair. She lit a cigarette, drew on it greedily, blew out the match and threw it into an overflowing ashtray.

"Have you been staying here?" I asked.

"I have nowhere to go."

She smiled bitterly as she caught me looking at the sealed door of her room.

"Don't worry. I didn't remove any of your seals. Baba Dasha lets me use her room while she works the night shift. She's sleeping now, unless you woke her up with your ringing."

Irina Drozdova was in her early thirties but seemed older. On her drawn, ashen face, her red-rimmed eyes seemed dark and enormous. She raised a small bony hand to her mouth and drew on her cigarette, exhaling the smoke through yellow teeth. At one time she was probably an attractive woman.

"Do you mind if I take a look around?" I asked.

She didn't reply. Taking her silence for assent, I made a cursory inspection of the apartment, looking into the communal kitchen and the bathroom. Everything was pretty much as it would be in a communal apartment in the city, except perhaps a little tidier and cleaner. There was a roll of real toilet paper in the bathroom, not cut-up newspaper. A child's tub hung on the wall, with rubber ducks lined up on a glass shelf. Seeing the ducks, I felt a lump gather in my throat.

"I'd like to go into your room," I said to Irina. "I'm going to take off the seals and replace them when I'm done."

She shrugged and lit another cigarette. In the few minutes I had been walking around the apartment, the pyramid of cigarette ends in her ashtray had grown even higher.

I went into Grushnikov's room first, which had also been sealed by Forensics after they searched it the day before. It had a seedy, slapdash appearance, like a room in a flophouse. An unmade camp bed stood by the wall, with a cheap wool blanket hanging over the edge, revealing grey bed linens and a threadbare pillow. Another wool blanket hung over the window in place of a curtain. A rickety table in the middle of the room contained the remains of a hasty meal: an empty sardine can, its jagged top bent backwards, a mug, a kettle and a small ceramic teapot, its top cracked and crudely glued together. A folded canvas tent, a knapsack and several soiled sleeping bags were stacked in the corner, along with fishing rods and other camping and fishing gear. The room reeked of sweat and stale food.

The only other piece of furniture, a plywood wardrobe, seemed to have been hammered together by Grushnikov himself with neither skill nor care. It contained a suit, a military jacket with its epaulets sliced off, and a Czechoslovakian-made nylon warm-up suit. Sneakers, slippers, sandals, and winter boots were piled at the bottom, tangled with dirty socks, sweatpants, and other athletic clothing.

A set of weights lay on the windowsill. More weights, an expander, and two twenty-kilo dumbbells were scattered on the dusty floor. I lifted one of the dumbbells a couple of times. It required a bit of strength.

"He used to work out with those weights every morning," said a voice behind my back. "Lifting them fifty times and then stretching that rubber thing across his chest. At six in the morning he'd be doing it when I come back from work, the window wide open. Freezing all of us to death with drafts."

I dropped the dumbbell and turned around. An old woman of about fifty stood on the doorstep. She wore a house dress and a pair of discolored slippers.

"Who are you?" I asked.

"I'm a neighbor," she replied readily. "They call me Baba Dasha."

"Did you know that you're not allowed in this room?"

"No need to get all hot and bothered about it, young man. I'm not even *in* this room."

"Let's get out of here," I said, nudging her out into the hallway.

I relocked the door, glued fresh strips of paper over the old ones and applied the Criminal Investigations seal.

"No one is going to get in there," she announced in a conspiratorial whisper. "The Drozdova woman and I are the only ones here most of the time."

Tanya's mother was still in her armchair. She didn't seem to have moved, except to light another cigarette. She stared straight ahead through the cloud of blue smoke swirling around her face.

"Who else lives here?" I asked.

"That's the thing," Baba Dasha said, shaking her head. "The rest of the apartment belongs to Dr. Lazius. It's a strange name. He's a Lithuanian. Or maybe Latvian. He works at a clinic where he treats all kinds of drunks and crazies. If you're a cop, how come you didn't know that?"

"I didn't," I said.

"He's got four rooms. Too many, in my opinion. But of course if we had more people in here, like they do upstairs, it would have been way too crowded. Up there, in No. 44, they've got no room in the kitchen and a line to use the toilet day and night. Especially if somebody has an upset stomach. That's why they keep having fights. Still, it's not fair for the doctor to have all those rooms."

"Does he live there all by himself?" I asked.

"Of course not. He's got two boys, both teenagers. They're good boys, quiet and studious and well-behaved. But they're never at home, none of them. The boys go to a special school where they study numbers. He drives them before going to work. He's so rich, he owns a car. Out early, in late at night. He gave Drozdova some sleeping pills."

"Is he a psychiatrist?" I asked.

"A what? Oh, yes, he is, I suppose. He was married once before and this one is his second wife. The first one died, so to speak."

"What do you mean, so to speak?"

Baba Dasha cast a wary eye up and down the hallway.

"She swallowed some pills she found in the doctor's desk and went to sleep on the tram. The conductor didn't spot her and took the tram to a depot for the night. By the time they found her the next morning she was stiff as a log. Those pills sure are dangerous. No wonder the

Drozdova woman doesn't want to take them. In case she never wakes up, just like the doctor's first wife."

Baba Dasha made a sign of the cross.

"It a sin to do away with yourself," she went on in a whisper. "But the doctor didn't shed many tears for her. He married his new wife right away, almost before they had time to bury the first one. Who can blame him, she's such a looker. The goats in this house all go crazy every time they see her go by, except they don't have a chance with her. The doctor's got everything: four rooms and a Pobeda car, not to mention a well-paid job. Sure, he's old and a widower, and every day he drags her and the kids to ski in the woods or to the opera. But she's happy to put up with it because of all the money he has."

"What does she do?" I asked.

"She's his assistant. She was working for him when his first wife took the pills."

While listening to her, I slowly made my way down the hallway to Tanya Drozdova's room.

"The gym teacher was gaga over her, too," Baba Dasha continued. "Every time they passed each other in the hallway, he'd stare at her like a poor orphan at a chocolate cake in a shop window. He wasn't a bad sort, the teacher, even though he's a murderer. She thought so, too. Except she was too scared of the doctor. She still calls him Dr. Lazius, like she's not his wife."

Baba Dasha appeared to have settled in for a long chat.

"I'm going to go into Tanya's room now," I said. "You'll have to stay outside."

"I don't want to go in there," she replied in a stage whisper. "I'm scared of it."

However, the moment I broke the seals, she poked her nose through the door.

"Too much stuff in here, if you ask me," she commented. "They moved all the furniture in here when her grandma died. She was a hard woman, Grandma Afanasia. She was born here, in this very apartment. They used to have this place to themselves, more rooms for one family than even Dr. Lazius has got. Her father was chief engineer at some factory in the city. After the Revolution they got squeezed and had to make do with these two rooms, sharing their precious apartment with hard-working proletarians like me. And then, when Grandma Afanasia died last March, may she rest in peace, they took their other room away and gave it to the gym teacher."

As she continued talking, I walked behind the Chinese screen dividing the room diagonally into two halves. The half that was closer to the window was Tanya's. It contained a small bookshelf full of schoolbooks; two or three drawings were pinned to the wall. A violin case lay open on the rug, next to a chrome-plated music stand. The sheet music on the stand was a collection of Franz Wolfahrt studies for violin, adapted for intermediate players.

I stopped before the sofa bed and looked at the framed picture of a skinny girl skipping rope. She had been photographed in her own courtyard, in the summer, probably the year before last. The saplings on the playground were in leaf and the windows were wide open. The girl was wearing a short, checkered skirt and white socks. One end of the rope was tied to a pole and the other held by her grandmother. The girl was caught in mid-jump, laughing, her tightly braided pigtails pointing skyward. The grandmother was swinging the rope, her face set in a grim expression.

All of a sudden, I had the impression that someone else had been in the room when I entered and was perhaps still there. The impression was hard to define: a subtle movement of the air, the scattering of dust in the sunbeam by the window, or a fleeting shadow caught in the reflection of the glass over the photograph.

I stood still for a few moments, shifting my eyes from one object in the room to the next, straining my ears to catch any sound except the prattle of the old woman by the door and the pounding of my own heart.

"Go out and shut the door," I told Baba Dasha. There must have been urgency in my voice, because she didn't argue.

I walked around the room, looked beneath the double bed in the corner and behind the heavy armoire. The armoire was locked, with the key still in the door. I turned the key and looked inside, overcome by the strong smell of mothballs.

Nothing. There was nowhere else a person could hide, but the sense that I was not alone had not passed.

Baba Dasha was waiting for me in the hallway.

"Was there anyone else in the room?" I asked her.

She stared at me.

"Did anyone come out of here while I was inside?"

It was a stupid question. I knew there was no way another person could have been in the room or could have left without me hearing their footsteps, no matter how light, on the creaky parquet floor. But I had to ask.

"Of course not," she replied, crossing herself.

"Of course not," I repeated.

I turned to reseal the door and then, almost in spite of myself, quickly opened it and stepped back in.

Nothing.

"That's what I've always said," Baba Dasha whispered as I turned the key in the lock and glued the strips of paper. "It's a strange place. It's full of ghosts. You never know who's listening."

She crossed herself again.

"Small wonder poor little Tanechka was murdered," she added. "It's a cursed place, this apartment, believe me."

She went on whispering about the strange goings on in the apartment. It all sounded like superstitious nonsense and old wives' tales. I stopped listening. Whatever I thought I had seen moving I had probably imagined. But I was quite certain of sensing a very light smell of expensive perfume hanging in the room and that shouldn't have been there at all.

FIVE

This time, the playwright answered the door himself. He was dressed in a pair of dark green velour trousers and a purple hand-knitted vest over a white shirt. His elbows were protected by black cloth pads held in place by rubber bands.

"What's the news, Lieutenant?" he asked eagerly as soon as he saw me.

"Good morning, Matvei Nikanorovich," I said, casting an eye at the two other doors on the landing with their gilded apartment numbers and bronze handles. "I'd like to come in first."

"Oh, yes," he said, raising a finger to his lips. "I understand. The neighbors."

He stepped aside, letting me into the foyer.

"Take off your shoes," he commanded, handing me a pair of felt slippers. "Sergei has just finished buffing the floors."

"You look like you've been writing," I said.

"How did you know?"

I pointed to his elbow pads.

"Not bad, Sherlock," he said, patting me on the back. "Yes, I'm hard at work. The Red Army Theater commissioned a play for the anniversary of the Revolution. It's almost a year away, but that's how it works in the theater. Never too early to start thinking of the next season. But enough about me. Any news?"

"There hasn't been much time to do anything yet," I said. "I'd like to have a talk with your driver."

Korenev stared.

"My driver? Sergei? Why on earth—"

He slapped himself on the forehead.

"Oh, you mean my car."

"Yes, of course. I'd like to ask him a few questions."

"This is not what I'm asking you about." The playwright waved his hand impatiently. "What was that murder your colleagues were working on? The one that made your boss pull his good people off my case?"

I said something about information on ongoing cases being confidential and added, "Where can I find your driver?"

"Don't you start with me, young man," the playwright said sternly. "I've been on the phone with your boss, Lieutenant Colonel Something or Other. Can't think of his name right now, but it's something Armenian. Good people, the Armenians. They stage my plays in Yerevan practically every season. But that's beside the point. He assured me that you will treat me with respect."

"That investigation is still at an early stage," I said.

"Come on," he said, tapping his foot. "I'm a Party Secretary of the Writers' Union. It's a highly sensitive position. I can certainly teach you a thing or two about keeping state secrets. You can tell me anything, share all kinds of confidential information, and you can be sure that your secrets are safe with me."

I tried a different line of defense.

"I don't really know that much myself," I said. "I've been assigned to your case and I'm not part of the murder investigation."

"Then you should've said so right away, instead of giving me all kinds of excuses like 'confidential information' and 'early stages'. At least tell me what you do know. Who got killed?"

"A child," I replied reluctantly. "A schoolgirl."

I didn't want to have any trouble with Budyonny, which would have been inevitable if the playwright decided to complain to him about me.

"A schoolgirl?" Korenev repeated. "Oh, but that's horrible. Who killed her? Hooligans? I hear about all sorts of gangs making trouble in the streets. Something must be done about them."

I said: "They found her body in her room."

Korenev gasped.

"What kind of monster would do such a thing to a child? He must be arrested immediately. I'm sure it must have been a neighbor, a friend of the family, a teacher. I shall call your boss and have a talk with him."

Budyonny was a consummate politician and he knew how to be deferential to figures in authority, such as party functionaries and his superiors in the Internal Affairs hierarchy. He had to be, to rise to his position. But he also had a temper. I feared he might not be able to control himself if he started getting this sort of advice from Matvei Korenev. That was the problem in dealing with Big Bosses: they always thought they knew better and could teach professionals a thing or two.

"A suspect has been arrested," I said curtly.

"Oh, my God. Who did it turn out to he?"

I had to tell him something about Grushnikov – in very general terms, mentioning only that he was a neighbor.

"You see? I told you it had to be a neighbor." said Korenev and then asked quickly: "What makes him a suspect?"

I gave him a brief summary of what Lenny had told me.

The previous night, when I had been swept along by his excitement, Lenny's explanations seemed logical and the evidence against the gym teacher appeared to be overwhelming. But now, recounting it all to Korenev, I realized that our case against the gym teacher was very weak.

"Did he admit anything?" the playwright persisted.

"Not to the murder, not yet. But we're getting there."

"What do you mean?"

Little by little, he was wheedling more information out of me and I didn't know how to fend him off without making him angry. He was as skillful in conducting an interrogation as a Criminal Investigations detective.

"Well, it's a start," said Korenev once I told him that Grushnikov had admitted becoming friends with Tanya. "From now on, I'll expect you to give me regular reports on the course of your investigation. I'm very interested in this case."

I silently cursed Budyonny. I had known from the start that it was going to be a stupid assignment, and now it was taking a nasty political turn. Apparently, Korenev wasn't nearly as concerned about getting his car back as receiving regular updates about our murder investigation. My role would be relaying information to someone who had no business receiving it.

"I feel bad taking you off this investigation," Korenev was saying. "I didn't realize it was such a terrible murder. But thank God it's been pretty much solved without your involvement."

"Yes, it's great," I said. "But I'd still like to get to the bottom of your case. This is why I need to talk to your driver."

"I'm sure he had nothing to do with the theft. And I must warn you, he's very upset about the loss of the car. Far more than I. It was really his baby."

"I'll be gentle," I promised. "But I still need to question him."

"If you insist, Lieutenant. But I can assure you that if he knew anything about it, anything at all, if he suspected anyone—"

I stopped listening and took a step down the long corridor toward the dining room. He stopped in mid-sentence.

"Can you take me to see him," I said.

"Yes, of course," he said quickly. "But you're going the wrong way."

Korenev led me into the other wing of the apartment. His house museum went on forever. Its rooms replicated themselves in an endless enfilade, their sense of not being quite lived-in underscored by the curtainless windows and glassed-in cases containing mounds of memorabilia. It reminded me of the Winter Palace, which I had visited during my military service outside Leningrad.

"Here I have my library, my study and a couple of guest bedrooms," Korenev announced as though he were a museum guide. "And here is a special room for watching television."

A long couch faced a late-model Temp 3 television set standing atop a Karelian birch chest. Next to it was a glass étagère, its shelves crowded with statuettes and porcelain knick-knacks made by the Lomonosov China Works. An electric samovar, its cord plugged into a wall outlet, hissed on a side table. A lamp cast a soft glow beneath an ivory-colored lampshade.

This is where we found Sergei. He was sitting on the couch watching television. He wore a pair of blue overalls and his white undershirt had dark half-moons of perspiration spreading beneath his armpits and around his collar. A brush and a jar of floor wax lay in the corner, emitting a strong odor. In his hands, he cradled a blue and white teacup that looked like it came from a doll house. A dish filled with raspberry preserves rested on his knee.

"Sergei, this is a Criminal Investigations detective. He wants to ask you a few questions about our car," Korenev said as we entered the room. Then, turning to me, he added by way of explanation, apologetically: "He's been waxing the floors. He's taking a break."

Sergei jumped up awkwardly from the couch, oblivious of the dish of preserves. The gluey red substance soiled his overalls and started to drip onto the couch and the colorful rug at his feet.

"Do try to be more careful, Sergei," Korenev blurted, rushing toward him.

"I'll clean it up," Sergei said. "It's no big deal."

As he tried to take a step toward the door, a large dollop fell from his overalls.

"Stand still, you idiot," Korenev shouted. "I'll get a dishrag."

He rushed out, leaving us alone in the room. Sergei stood stock still and seemed to be holding his breath. The preserves slowly rolled down his pant leg.

The TV set was on. Its oval screen flickered black and gray as the test grid, with its series of frequency numbers, went in and out of focus.

It was making a stridulating noise like an oscilloscope in eleventh-grade physics class.

"Watching something interesting?" I asked.

"What?"

"He's been waiting for the afternoon programming to come on," Korenev replied, entering the room with a wet dishrag in hand. He carefully wiped the couch and the rug, shaking his head and complaining under his breath about the upholstery fabric being ruined. He then handed the dishrag to Sergei, who gathered the remaining preserves from his overalls and hobbled out of the room.

"He's been very upset about the loss of the car," the playwright said.

Sergei returned after a very long time, sporting a dark water stain on his overalls. He positioned himself by the doorjamb and announced:

"I don't know anything about the car theft. I was off that day."

"No one is accusing you," Korenev said. "Comrade detective merely wants to ask you a few questions. Is that right?"

"You know the car better than anyone else," I said.

Sergei nodded.

"Were there any dents or scratches on the body? Any kind of damage? Anything that made it stand out?"

"Are you kidding?" Korenev butted in. "He kept it in perfect order. It was as good as new. Any time there was so much as a dark spot on a fender, he wouldn't rest until he'd burnished it away."

Sergei nodded his assent again.

"Now, can you think of anything unusual happening to you recently?"

"Like what?" Korenev asked.

"Like an accident, or an argument with another driver? Strangers hanging around the garage? People asking whether the car was for sale? Anything at all?"

"Everybody knows it's his car," Sergei said, his voice hoarse and sullen. "He's a famous person. No one would ever ask if it's for sale."

He took a deep breath and continued.

"People come up, they want to talk about the engine, like how much horsepower it has and how fast she goes. They say stupid things sometimes. But nothing unusual."

Our conversation went on in this vein for a while and was pretty useless. Yes, he took the car to the garage in October. No, there wasn't much gas in it. Yes, maybe one quarter of a tank, maybe a little less. No, he didn't remember whether he locked the car doors. It made no sense to lock them, because the garage door was padlocked.

Korenev, who had been tense in the beginning, relaxed and started to nod off. Sergei, on the contrary, remained ill at ease and apprehensive. I would have liked to talk to him in private, but I wasn't likely to get a chance – at least not now.

"Anything else?"

Sergei shrugged.

"You know, you asked me about dents and other marks. I can tell this car from any other even if it looked completely different. All I need is to get behind the wheel."

Korenev perked up.

"How can you be so sure, Sergei?" he asked.

"Because cars are like women. Each is different and each one must be unlocked with a different key. And I don't mean the ignition key, I mean a key to her heart. Cars have hearts just like women. There are some that respond to rough treatment. You show weakness and she'll ride you roughshod. Ours has character. A bit frisky she is, but once you show her who's the master, she is yours forever."

"And the master you're talking about is who?" Korenev asked. "You?"

Sergei blushed but didn't back off.

"That's right," he replied and added. "With all due respect."

He turned to me.

"He's a great man and a famous writer, but he's no driver. I mean, he gets behind the wheel, but he doesn't know the car, and the car can sense it. Whenever he takes her for a drive, he gets into trouble. One time he scratches a fender, another he has a flat tire. I'm telling it like it is."

"Well, maybe," Korenev shrugged. "I don't know what it has to do with my ZIM being taken."

"I'm the other way around," Sergei went on, suddenly getting more talkative. We'd finally hit a subject he was interested in. "I feel her when I'm driving her just like I feel a woman when I'm on top of her. I know how to give her just enough gas to make her ride nice and smooth and want to pleasure me. Or else I take her into a couple of hairpin turns to let her show her stuff. Or else put the pedal to the floor so she moans like a widow with a guy who knows his stuff."

A dreamy expression swept over his face. There was a gleam in his eyes and, lizard-like, his pink tongue darted from his mouth, licking his lips.

"Please, Sergei," Korenev said, blushing and frowning. "Comrade detective doesn't have time to listen to your nonsense. As it is, our relatively minor problem is taking him away from other important investigations."

The playwright walked me to the door.

"You shouldn't take him seriously," he said in a whisper. "He is like that sometimes. Strange. You know, he had a difficult childhood, parents dying early, an orphanage. And I told you, he knows nothing about the car theft."

He sighed.

"Are you sure?" I asked.

"What do you mean?" Korenev asked quickly, suddenly alert.

"Don't you think he might know more about what happened to your car than he lets on?"

"I already told you, it's impossible, detective," he said.

"Private drivers often pick up paying passengers when they are not driving their bosses around," I said. "It's a way to make a little money on the side. What if Sergei—"

"Yes, I know, it's an outrage," Korenev interrupted, his indignation completely genuine. "But not Sergei. I can assure you that Sergei would never let a stranger into his car. I mean my car. He even complains when I track dirt into it when my shoes are dirty. Besides, I pay him well."

I shrugged.

"Well," I said, deliberately raising my voice to make sure Sergei could hear me. "I'm not so sure. Right now, the most likely explanation is that your driver took the car out of the garage, perhaps using a spare key or the one he had made, and did a bit of driving on the side."

The playwright grabbed my arm and put a finger to his lips.

"Had you not sent your cleaning woman to retrieve your umbrella and waited instead for him to come home," I concluded without lowering my voice, "I don't believe we would have had a car theft on our hands."

"Boy," Korenev said, once I had changed back into my winter boots and put on my overcoat. "I feel awful bothering Criminal Investigations at a time like this. A little girl murdered and—"

"And the less we talk about it the better," I said, cutting him off as we parted.

I was almost at the entrance to Sokol metro station when Sergei approached me from behind and tugged at my sleeve.

"I want to talk to you," he said, catching his breath. "You know, without him."

He jerked his head in the direction of Korenev's building.

"Did you think of something else?" I asked.

"Yeah," he said reluctantly. "You know—"

He hesitated. We were standing in the middle of a pedestrian walkway and people jostled us as they passed.

"Let's go where we can talk," I suggested.

He shook his head.

"I don't have much time," he said. "I don't want him to notice I'm gone."

He cast an apprehensive glance over his shoulder, as though Korenev was in hot pursuit.

I waited for him to gather his thoughts.

"You asked about people wanting to buy the car," he said at last.

"Yes," I said.

"I didn't want to say anything with him around," he said. "There actually was someone who was interested."

"Really?" I said. "How intriguing. Who was it?"

My interest was too lively to be genuine, but he either didn't notice my sarcasm or chose to ignore it.

"I have no idea," he said. "It was a few months ago. He came up to me at a gas station, while I was filling her up.

" 'A nice ZIM,' he says. 'Very good condition.' "

Sergei was doing a decent imitation of a Caucasian accent. According to him, the man first praised the car effusively and then offered Sergei money. A lot. Ten thousand rubles.

"But he knew it wasn't your car to sell?" I asked.

"Sure," Sergei replied. "What he said was that he had a customer for a hot ZIM. I had nothing to worry about, because he would take the car himself. All I had to do was give him enough time to drive it to the Caucasus before reporting the theft. All he needed was five days."

While listening to him, I noted how articulate and well-spoken he was. Too well-spoken for someone who had grown up in an orphanage.

"That's not all," Sergei continued. "He said he'd pay me a thousand just to let him take her for a spin around the block. He wanted to make sure there was nothing wrong with her. He said he'd pay me even if I didn't go along with the other deal."

"And what did you do?" I asked.

"Well, I figured I'd take him up on it. I wasn't going to let him steal her, of course, but I figured that a thousand rubles was a lot of money and no one would be the wiser if I let him drive her for a few minutes."

"And so, he took the car for a drive and just like that paid you a thousand rubles?" I asked.

"Well," he said. "It ended up being just five hundred, because I insisted on coming along for the ride."

"It's an interesting story," I said, eyeing him derisively. "What do you want me to do about it?"

"Don't you think he must be the one who stole the car?" he asked.

"Really?"

"Who else? He must have figured out where we kept it, waited for winter and stole it. He was full of praise for how it felt to drive her and how well I kept her. It was my fault, of course. I should never have let him take her for a drive."

He broke off, hesitated, and said softly: "I don't want him to know about it."

"Did you go to college, Sergei?" I asked, changing the subject.

He frowned.

"No, not me," he replied. "Why do you ask?"

I shrugged.

"I don't know. I'm just wondering."

"Well, I didn't," he repeated. "Anyway, I told you about that guy from the Caucasus and you can do with it as you wish. I gotta get back now."

"Do you know where I can find this guy?" I asked.

"That's the thing, I know nothing about him. He was just some guy hanging around a filling station on Elektrozavodskaya. I really need to get back."

"I'll be sure to look for him," I said. "In the meantime, I advise you to think of some other way how the car might be returned."

He gave me an innocent look, but he knew perfectly well what I was talking about. I was sure I was on the right track.

"Is that what you think?" he asked.

"Yes. I think that whoever stole the car fears that Comrade Korenev might send him to jail. But I think your boss would be happy just to get his car back. He's not going to ask any awkward questions, and the police could be persuaded to forget about the whole thing."

"Really?" It was his turn to sound derisive.

I, on the other hand, became deadly serious.

"Really," I said. "But only if the car turns up in the next couple of days."

"Well, it's something to think about," Sergei said. "Anyway, it was nice talking with you."

He turned and headed back, walking against the thick flow of pedestrian traffic. He was taller than average and strong, and worked his elbows energetically, forcing the crowd to part as he came through. I watched the back of his quilted work jacket disappear from view. Then I turned and walked slowly toward the metro station.

SIX

Valera Tumakov sat on top of Lenny's desk, having organized into a tall stack various files, folders, and notebooks with yellowed photographs of body parts jutting out of them. He had ignored Lenny's protestations that everything was where it was for a reason and that all the files, folders and notebooks were in perfect order.

Tumakov had once been Lenny's partner and knew him well, but Lenny's peculiar habit of allowing a disorganized workspace still irritated him. Their work styles were a constant source of conflict. They fought like cats and dogs, and in the end Budyonny had to put an end to their partnership. Tumakov was assigned to work with Gordeyev and, since Gordeyev was a captain, it was something of a promotion. But then Lenny got a senior lieutenant's third star on his epaulets, and Tumakov did not. It was Budyonny's way of being even-handed.

Because of the first letters of their last names, the office they shared became known as TU-104 – in honor of the world's first passenger jet, built in the 1950s by the Tupolev engineering firm. The name stuck, even after Tumakov left and I took over his desk, probably because the room's confines faithfully replicated flight conditions on the famous jet. Yet, despite its small size, our office was the favorite place to hold various get-togethers and business meetings. No matter how many additional bodies were crammed into it, it could never feel more crowded than it already was.

Lenny glared at Tumakov. Tumakov was swinging his foot back and forth like a pendulum. Now and again, the rubber sole of his winter boot brushed against the arm of Lenny's chair, making an irritating scraping sound.

Gordeyev, the head of their investigation team, had taken over my chair, having turned it around to face Lenny and Tumakov. He acknowledged my arrival with a nod, but didn't offer to get up.

I climbed on the windowsill and leaned back against the pane. The cold felt nice against my jacket.

The office window was the only thing in our TU-104 that was large, even outsized. When the building was first built, it must have been part of a much larger room: our Petrovka 38 headquarters originally housed a gendarme barracks. But the floor plan had since been reconfigured, so that some offices had no windows, and our tiny one ended up with one that took up the entire wall. It afforded a panoramic view of the Hermitage Gardens across the street, but it was dark outside now and there was nothing to see but a few bluish lights dotting the pathways and glowing through bare tree branches. Rush hour was winding down and red and white taillights flickered in the street below. The window panes reflected the three men in the office as splotches of rumpled white shirts broken by the narrow black lines of their neckties.

They were discussing Grushnikov's interrogation earlier in the day.

"The Boss insists on playing the good cop," Gordeyev said. "Problem is, he can never stay in character for very long."

"At least you have no trouble being the bad cop," Tumakov observed.

Gordeyev ignored Tumakov's remark and continued, "He quickly reverts to his natural self and fixes the suspect with his fearsome black eyes. Then the whole routine goes out the window."

He and Tumakov laughed. Lenny didn't crack a smile, only giving them a gloomy look.

"Go on," he said.

"Once the Boss managed to calm down a little and the suspect stopped quaking in his shoes, we went back to making small talk. You know how the Boss gets during interrogations. He keeps asking about the guy's childhood, his mom and dad, how he got on with his classmates at school, and so on. He thinks it makes him seem friendly. And then we talked about the guy's job at the boarding school and his colleagues and other nonsense."

"His personal life is actually very pertinent to the case," Lenny said. "The Boss wasn't just shooting the breeze."

"Of course not, Urumov. I'll get to his personal life in a moment," Gordeyev responded coldly.

"I'd like you to get to it now," Lenny said under his breath.

"What was that?"

"Nothing. Go on."

Gordeyev shrugged and continued, "You'll be happy to know that Grushnikov wasn't friendly with most of his colleagues. Except maybe Major Kurochkin, the civil defense instructor, although even Grushnikov admits the major could be strange sometimes, on account of having been shell-shocked in the war. And with the vocational trades instructor. They weren't real friends, but liked to share the occasional half-liter after work. On the sly and strictly hush-hush, of course, lest the principal got wind of it."

"She's very strict about drinking," Tumakov broke in. "Alcohol consumption was grounds for immediate dismissal, she said. She's a tough bird."

Gordeyev nodded.

"That's what Grushnikov said, too. The other teachers are all women and he doesn't like any of them. Stuck-up and too brainy, he says. It turns out he doesn't like smart women. Nor does he get along well with Muscovites. They look down on him because he's a provincial and doesn't have appropriate manners. As far as women are concerned, he likes being the boss and is used to women respecting him, not putting him down because he doesn't make use of a handkerchief to blow his nose. What's more, Grushnikov doesn't think the teachers are at all attractive."

"They are not eleven years old, that's why," Lenny commented under his breath.

Gordeyev glanced at the stack of carbon copy sheets in his lap.

"The Boss reverted to being a nice guy and wormed all this out of him about other teachers and women in general. Grushnikov was still a little wary after the Boss's screaming fit, but eventually he relaxed."

"And that was when you came in," Tumakov said, giggling and rubbing his hands.

Valera wasn't a sycophant. It was just the way he was. He made a point of being deferential to Gordeyev and laughing at his jokes, because Gordeyev was a captain and he, Tumakov, was just a lieutenant. Valera always played by the rules, a fact that never failed to infuriate Lenny, who gave his former partner a withering look.

"Not really," Gordeyev said, making a face. It wasn't clear whether it meant that he disliked playing the bad cop – which he did – or listening to smarmy comments from his sidekick. "The Boss felt the suspect needed a bit more stroking. So we talked about the town Grushnikov grew up in, why he never got married, which soccer club he thought was going to win the championship next year, that sort of stuff. The two of them even got into an argument about soccer."

"The Boss roots for Yerevan," Tumakov explained, a fact everyone knew perfectly well.

Lenny looked exasperated by all the beating around the bush.

Gordeyev shared a few more details of the suspect's private life and finally got to the most interesting part. After the preliminaries, Budyonny went over every detail of Grushnikov's leg injury, his weeklong stay at home, and his relationship with Tanya Drozdova, including every conversation he ever had with her and every instance he had helped her with math. Then he shifted to the events of the previous day and made Grushnikov go over everything he had done in the morning and early afternoon, up to the moment he discovered Tanya's body. He checked every detail carefully against the list

Lenny had made after the first interrogation. Then Gordeyev took over, impersonating a Criminal Investigations butcher, and reviewed Grushnikov's relationship with Tanya yet again. Repeating every question Budyonny had just asked, Gordeyev lay into the suspect to ferret out inconsistencies and evasions, trying to throw him off. Then it was back to Budyonny again, and then back to Gordeyev.

"So, did you get anything?" Lenny asked.

Gordeyev shrugged.

"He was flustered, that's for sure, but he's sticking to his original story."

"Damn it," Lenny grumbled.

While listening to Gordeyev, he had been clenching and unclenching his fist.

"But I have a feeling he's going to crack. At times I felt he was on the verge. It's a matter of time, I'm sure."

"Assuming it's him," I said.

They must have forgotten that I was in the room. They turned and looked at me. I couldn't get it out of my head, the doubt I had felt when I repeated Lenny's account to the playwright.

"I'm sure it's him," Gordeyev said.

Tumakov nodded, "Me too."

Lenny just gave me a sidelong look.

Then they forgot about me again. Tumakov shifted to get more comfortable on Lenny's desk and began telling them about his trip to Boarding School 206, Grushnikov's place of employment.

"The principal's name's is Comrade Przhevalskaya. Sixty years old, black skirt, black boots, men's jacket – also black, and cut from stiff wool cloth probably back about 1944, short grey hair, no lipstick, no cosmetics of any kind, nothing. A man's wristwatch on a man's wrist – a stainless Raketa from the Army and Navy Department Store. The one piece of jewelry she wears is the Honored Educator pin on her lapel. Lenin on one wall, Dzerzhinsky on the other.

" 'It's our duty to work with the police,' she says. 'We're an educational institution, we're working to raise responsible, law-abiding citizens.'

"I tell her we're conducting an investigation and she gets a little apprehensive.

" 'Until you tell me what crime you're investigating and who's your suspect, we can't go any further. All my kids are like my own children to me.' "

"It's a boarding school," Gordeyev interrupted. "Most of her kids are difficult. Naturally, she would think it's one of the kids we're interested in."

"Yes, but that's not all," Tumakov said. "Then she tells me she's been working with kids since the 1920s, when the city was chock full of abandoned children and war orphans, and that at every school she ever worked she has had an iron rule: she's got to know everything that goes on. Everything. Her teachers file reports after every class period. She reads each one personally. In other words, she declares that there is no need for me to talk to anyone else at her school. And first I must tell her what crime we're investigating."

"Oh, yes, a rule," Lenny interjected. "Have you ever met a rule you didn't start obeying right away, Valera?"

"It so happens that we have rules, too," Tumakov said, turning to face Lenny. "That's what I told her. Our rules forbid discussing active cases. Then she gave me a long speech about her responsibilities to her kids, and so on."

"I let her go on and when she's done I ask: 'What about your teaching staff?'

"She gives me a look, takes a deep breath and launches into another lecture. How all her teachers are top-notch professionals, very dedicated and personally vetted by her as far as their moral character is concerned. They've got a strong Communist Party cell that she heads, as well as a trade union organization.

"So I say, 'Tell me about your gym teacher.'

" 'Do you mean our current one, Comrade Grushnikov? Because over the years we've had several and not all of them were reliable.' When we finally got to Grushnikov, she got a little cagey and less glowing in her recommendations. Yes, he's dedicated to his work and loves physical culture. He's aware of the importance of athletics in the balanced development of a young person. But he hasn't been working there long, only a couple of years, he's an out-of-towner, so she may not know him as well as some of her other teachers. What exactly am I interested in?

" 'His students? Oh, he loves to spend time with the kids and the kids love him, too. He has no family of his own. He's a loner. Last fall, for example, he took a group of third graders camping in the woods for three days. With tents and sleeping bags.' "

"For three days?" Urumov repeated in disgust. "Third graders?"

Tumakov nodded.

"With tents and sleeping bags," he repeated. "They also have a girl's volleyball team Grushnikov assembled. He coaches them in his spare time. Last year they finished second in a citywide tournament. All thanks to their gym teacher."

"Quite a dedicated guy," Gordeyev said.

"As to his relationship with other teachers, she pretty much confirmed what Grushnikov himself said. Gym is an independent subject, different from the rest of the curriculum. He doesn't seem to have much in common with other teachers. During recess he tends to keep to himself. Not being a Party member, he doesn't attend Party meetings. That's about it. A loner."

"What about his drinking?" Gordeyev asked.

"Oh, that's a whole other story." Tumakov perked up. "She got outraged when I so much as mentioned alcohol. 'Are you kidding? Never at my school. We went through three gym teachers before him, and we had to let them all go because they drank. When I hired Comrade Grushnikov, it was an important condition for his employment. After all, he takes the kids camping.' "

"Camping," Lenny echoed.

"So she thinks that him getting drunk on a camping trip is the greatest danger the kids face," Gordeyev said. "Little does she know."

"She knows people at the City Party Committee," Tumakov continued. "They got him the room that used to be Tanya's grandmother's. Before that, he'd been living in a dorm."

Tumakov shifted again and the entire pile of Lenny's documents, which had been teetering in their precarious pile, hit the floor with a loud thud. Two or three overstuffed files burst their cloth ties, sending their contents flying under the desk and around the room. Lenny threw a murderous look at Tumakov, who shrugged as if to say that Lenny's files had been in a chaotic state to start with, and that shuffling them a bit more made little difference.

"Are you finished with your story?" Lenny asked, his face twisting with rage.

"More or less," Tumakov replied. "As I was leaving, I let it slip that we are investigating a murder.

" 'Is Comrade Grushnikov a suspect?' she asks.

" 'If he were, would you have said anything differently?' I reply.

"She says: 'I don't think so. If Citizen Grushnikov is guilty, he will have to answer for his crime. But until you know for certain that he is, you must be very careful not to cast a shadow upon our school's reputation.' "

Gordeyev chuckled. "So, he's now *Citizen* Grushnikov all of a sudden, and not Comrade Grushnikov? She's already washing her hands of him."

Tumakov giggled.

"She's an old party cadre," Lenny said, not smiling. "That's what they all do. The government declares that the guy you have worked with side by side for the past ten years is an American spy, and you say without skipping a beat: 'How glad I am that our glorious organs of State Security have liquidated this snake. The filthy scum got what he deserves.' "

Nobody said anything.

"Are you done?" Lenny asked, turning to Tumakov and, not waiting for him to reply, declared, "Now listen to what I uncovered while you two were having tea and finger sandwiches with an old party cadre."

"We weren't having any tea," Tumakov protested, throwing up his hands.

Lenny ignored him.

"It turns out that the Russian lit teacher, a nice-looking blonde by the name of Nina Fokina, once caught Grushnikov peeping into the girls' locker room. It was during a long recess and she had gone down to the gym to find one of her fifth-graders. She surprised Grushnikov hanging out by their locker room. He got very flustered when she confronted him. What do you make of that?"

Tumakov and Gordeyev said nothing. They were waiting for him to continue, since he clearly had more to say.

"Then she started asking her students about him. Sure enough, it turned out that he had quite a reputation among players on his volleyball team. Whenever he was showing them how to receive a service or throw a block, he would stand too close and even kind of brush against them with the front of his gym shorts."

"That's disgusting," Gordeyev said.

"I'd like to know how you came by this information?" Tumakov asked, looking straight at Lenny.

"Funny you should ask," Lenny replied, not smiling. "It wasn't very difficult, actually. Unless you take the principal's rules too seriously, that is. I positioned myself next to the gate at the end of classes and waited for an intelligent-looking adult to come by. Soon I saw the blonde Mrs. Fokina and knew I had my source. I followed her to the trolley stop and you can figure out the rest for yourself."

Tumakov gasped.

"You don't have any idea what you have done. You can't imagine what kind of trouble Przhevalskaya will make for you."

"Let her go fuck herself," Urumov cut him off. "The Russian lit teacher, by the way, complained to your friend the principal about Grushnikov. That's the kind of system they've got over there, to rat on each other, as you described. The principal did nothing about it and she didn't mention it to you, either. In order not to cast a shadow on her school's reputation, no doubt."

Tumakov started to say something, but Lenny continued.

"Let me tell you something, Valera. I don't give a damn about her school or its reputation. All I care about is getting this murderous pervert in front of a firing squad. I'll make sure I do, even if I'll have to take down the stupid school or step over the dead body of its principal. You understand?"

Urumov choked on his own anger. Valera was looking at him and shaking his head compassionately, as if he were dealing with a sick person.

It took Lenny a while to calm down. He continued to seethe long after Gordeyev and Tumakov had left, and his mood didn't improve as he crawled around the dusty linoleum, gathering and arranging his files. I helped him as much as I could.

"I was at Tanya Drozdova's apartment this morning," I said. "Did you know that her mother is still there? She says she has nowhere to go."

Lenny lifted his head.

"What do you mean? Her room has been sealed. It's a crime scene."

"She's staying at a neighbor's."

"Oh, I see."

He went back to his files. He was looking for something among the folders.

"It must be here somewhere," he muttered. "Goddamn Tumakov."

"I don't think she should be staying there by herself," I said.

"Yes, I agree," Lenny replied, not listening.

"And one other thing," I persisted. "Do you think there's another way into Grushnikov's room? I mean besides the front door?"

That got Lenny's attention.

"I don't think so," he replied. "Why?"

"I don't know," I said. "I had a strange feeling this morning—"

"Oh, here it is," he exclaimed suddenly.

He had a large photograph in his hand. He got up, walked around his desk and pinned it to the blackboard.

"I should've done it before," he said. "Maybe it would've knocked some sense into Valera."

"Who is it?" I asked, staring at the picture.

"It's Tanya Drozdova. The class picture they took at the start of the school year. What are you staring at?"

That morning, when I saw her picture in her room, I had not noticed it, but now it struck me hard. In the photograph, Tanya looked exactly like my little sister Natashka. I even had a similar picture at home, with Natashka wearing her school uniform and a festive white apron.

"What's wrong, Matyushkin?"

I shrugged.

"Nothing," I said. "Never mind."

SEVEN

The next morning I had a meeting with Nastya.

The morning brought with it a December thaw. Winter comes to Moscow in mid-November, and the snow lays thick and solid until early April, but it is not unusual for the temperature to rise above freezing for a day or two now and again, to give us a brief respite from Old Man Frost, along with wet feet and bouts of the flu.

I woke up at dawn to an urgent tattoo of melting snow against the sheet metal of my balcony, and lay in bed for a long time just listening. I was in no hurry: Nastya, like most people in the world she inhabited, was not an early riser. I had thrown off the heavy covers and stared out the window at the slowly brightening day, the fog enveloping the neighboring roofs and the gray, moisture-laden clouds pressing down on their aerials. I was thinking about my little sister.

How can people disappear so completely, especially in our country, where everyone is always under the watchful eye of the state?

I continued to think about Natashka as I took a shower, got dressed and shoved a rubbery fried egg into my mouth, eating it directly from the frying pan in order not to dirty a dish. Outside, I drew in the unexpected warmth, which smelled deceptively of March and spring, and the first person I saw in the courtyard was Tosya, my pretty acquaintance from two days before. She stood near the Frolov

Lane end of the courtyard, talking to her kid brother, who was maybe seven or eight.

Thoughts of Natashka, who had been stuck in my head all morning, suddenly overwhelmed me. I had to stop and wait for the pain and anger to subside. When they did, I stood a bit longer and observed Tosya and her brother from a distance.

Despite the thaw, Tosya was making the boy put on a hat and tie the earflaps under his chin. He resisted, the way boys his age do, especially when they are being bossed around by an older sister. Only after she stomped her foot in exasperation and made some kind of a threat, wagging her finger in front of his face, did he finally obey – but still with very ill grace.

"Now, the top button," I heard her say.

"I'll be late for school," the boy pleaded and, not waiting for further instructions, slipped her grasp and ran down the street.

"Watch out," she shouted after him. "Thaws are dangerous. You'll catch a cold."

She turned quickly and caught me observing her. I waved, and she frowned back at me. She had reverted to being the unfriendly passenger at the Trubnaya tram stop. But I was glad to see her and to know that she had recognized me.

Nastya was waiting for me on Sretensky Boulevard, near the corner of Kostyansky Lane. She was taking a risk every time she met me, but meeting in the open was smarter than skulking in some back alley behind Sretenka. We were hiding in plain sight, so to speak.

Nastya sat on the backrest of a park bench that was half-buried in tightly packed snow. Melting ice from tree branches overhead dripped all around her; she had to shield the cigarette she was smoking from wayward drops. Her feet, shod in a pair of bright red lace-up boots, rested on the seat. Her long coat was the same color as her boots, its dazzling redness enhanced by its wide, jet-black Persian lamb collar. The coat had enormous shiny, black buttons, and the ensemble was topped off with a silk scarf that was an explosion of colors, dominated by yellow and green. A miniature pill-box hat, also of Persian lamb, sat atop her red hair at a rakish angle, hanging precariously over her left eye.

"Good morning," she said.

The boulevard was empty. No one else wanted to slide around between newly formed puddles on the pathways.

"I'm glad to see you," I said, approaching her.

"You mean it?" she asked, starting to flirt.

"I do. And I also have a question for you."

"I should've guessed," she said, still smiling but clearly disappointed.

Her eyes were instantly watchful. She was prepared not to like my question.

Nastya and I were old friends – if that was what we were. One day, soon after I had been promoted and transferred to Criminal Investigations, I was passing through the Central Market on Tsvetnoy Boulevard. The lingerie shop on the third floor happened to be selling some item that was in high demand and short supply, and whenever something of that sort was on sale at the lingerie shop, women from all over the neighborhood somehow got wind of it and a large crowd invariably gathered, spilling out into the other shops.

I had no idea what was being sold and no need for it in any case. But, passing by, I observed a skinny adolescent with short red hair and freckles skillfully weaving her way in and out of the crowd. Her faded summer dress popped up first in the thick of things, where people were trying to get to the door by working others over with their elbows, then at the fringes of the crowd and finally all the way by the counter, where others had been trying to push themselves to for probably an hour or more.

I positioned myself on the sidelines and began to watch her. My observation post was far enough away not to attract her attention, but not so far away to miss it when she inserted her long, pliable fingers into someone's handbag and pulled out a thick wallet. I was right there, behind her, when she slithered out of the crowd and began to walk to the escalator.

Gripping her shoulder with one hand, I returned the wallet to her still-unsuspecting victim and led the skinny redhead to a door marked "Authorized Personnel Only" on the top floor. Once inside, I showed my Criminal Investigations ID first to the head manager of the Central Market and then to the girl. She made a desperate attempt to get free. When that failed, she went for my face, savaging it with fingernails as sharp as razor blades. The head manager screamed and stood as still as Lot's wife. If it weren't for her second in command coming to my rescue, I would have likely lost an eye. And even with me pushing and the assistant manager pulling at the furious she-devil, it took a vicious kick in the shin to get her off me.

Having exchanged such pleasantries, I took her to an empty office and locked the door behind us, taking out the key and slipping it into my pocket. The summer day was hot and the window was wide open, but I figured that a sheer five-story drop was a sufficient discouragement to anyone thinking of choosing that way out.

That was Nastya.

The Sretenka neighborhood she grew up in was the kind of urban underbelly that city fathers and the top brass in the Internal Ministry like to pretend doesn't exist. It's like a peat fire burning beneath the surface of a green meadow, hidden from the eyes of onlookers. There's a foul odor that fills the air when the wind changes, and occasionally an ember glows menacingly after night falls. Now and again, an unsuspecting outsider wanders into the unfamiliar territory and falls in, getting badly burnt. But it is dismissed as an unfortunate accident, an aberration, nothing more. Nonetheless, when the fire suddenly bursts into the open, with some hair-raising crime, everyone is surprised: Where in the world did that come from? How come nothing has been done about this swamp, this disgusting swarm of criminality? There is a week or two of frantic activity, the police move in and arrest a few local layabouts, but it changes nothing and everything remains as it ever has been. Soon enough, all is forgotten and the fire resumes its smouldering until the next flare-up.

"What are your parents going to say?" I asked Nastya.

She shrugged and replied in a flat voice, "Daddy might punch me in the face. But when he's drunk he usually doesn't need an excuse for that. Mommy couldn't care less. She has other things on her mind."

"I see," I said. "Where do you go to school?"

"I used to be enrolled at the retail trade school. I lasted about six months. I'm not sure if they expelled me or I dropped out."

"How old are you?"

She was sixteen. I wasn't going to arrest her, just recite an abbreviated version of the high-minded warning they teach us at the police academy to pronounce to juvenile delinquents. I was still a well-meaning idiot back then.

"You should turn over a new leaf," I said. "Try to get a job. I'll call your neighborhood officer, he'll keep an eye on you. If you promise me you will give up this life of crime, I will let you go."

She had been sitting with her head bowed and answered my questions in a sullen monotone while staring into the corner. Now she lifted her head and gave me a strange look. She was suddenly very serious and grown-up.

"Let's not kid ourselves, copper. What kind of job am I going to get? And what about my pals who taught me to pick pockets? What do you think they're going to say? Something like, 'Nastya, dear girl, go out and earn an honest ruble, lots of luck in your new life?' Is it what you have in mind?"

"We can deal with your pals, too," I said.

"I'm sure you can," she said. "But don't expect me to help you."

I shook my head. As I said, I was a well-meaning idiot back then, even though my youthful idealism was starting to fray.

"What's your plan for the future?" I asked.

"If you lock me up, my plan is to serve my sentence. If you let me go, I'll be back in the street, picking pockets, until you or some other copper catches me again. Then, I'll go to jail. Then, I'll come out and go back to picking pockets."

I didn't lock her up. I knew that sooner or later someone else would. I let her go.

Then I came to regret it.

The half hour we had spent in the stifling fifth-floor management office of the Central Market was long enough for Nastya to fall in love with me. She did so with all the desperation, determination and clinginess of a neglected adolescent who has finally had someone take her seriously. In her pursuit of me, she proved extremely resourceful. She found out where I lived and kept a watch on the door of my building. Sometimes late at night I would look out and see her standing in the courtyard, her skinny shoulders shivering in the wind. Persuading her to go home was never easy – perhaps because she had no real home to return to.

When spring came, she cut lilacs growing wild in Sretenka courtyards and left huge piles of them on my doorstep, timing it perfectly for me to trip over them as I rushed off to work.

She once gave me a watch for my birthday; I have no idea how she found out when it is.

"Is it hot?" I asked her.

"Are you crazy? Would I give a copper a stolen watch? I paid for it with my own money."

"Which you earned by putting in hours of honest work, I'm sure," I said, hating myself for my dumb cop's humor.

"Everyone makes a living as best they can."

One night – it happened after her first stint inside – she tricked me into going with her to a godforsaken vacant lot in Potapovsky Lane, claiming she had a body to show me. I expected to see a dead body, but it turned out to be a live one instead – hers. She threw off her top and attacked me with kisses.

I thought that after I had fought her off and, picking up her blouse from the rubble-strewn ground and handing it back to her, she would get mad and leave me alone. I was wrong.

"I know why you don't want me," she said when she caught her breath. "It's the tattoos I got inside. But I'm glad you turned me down. My buddies wouldn't approve if they caught me sleeping with a copper."

Her breasts and arms were blue from all the tattoos she had gotten in prison.

Nevertheless, after that night in Potapovsky, I saw far less of her.

"What do you want to ask me, copper?"

Since our first meeting, we had had an unspoken agreement: she didn't rat on her pals and I didn't ask her about anything that could land them in jail. But as long as we stayed on general subjects, she provided me with valuable information about Moscow's criminal underworld – a subject she seemed to know like the back of her hand. Her information was always current, first-hand and accurate.

"I'll get to it in a minute," I said. "Tell me how you've been getting on first."

"As you can see." She showed off her red boots. "How do you like my new look?"

"Devastating," I said admiringly.

"Glad you like it. You may end up falling in love with me, after all."

"So, business has been brisk?"

She nodded. "Highly skilled, hard working professionals are always in demand. And you? When are you going to make colonel?"

"Probably not this year."

"How come? Not catching enough criminals or not enough criminals left to catch?"

"Both."

"That's too bad. You'd look good in one of those hats colonels get to wear. Persian lamb, just like mine, only grey. I can't wait to see my cellmates' faces when I go walking down Gorky Street arm in arm with a police colonel."

She giggled and then turned serious.

"Enough kidding around. I know you're itching to ask me your question."

"Very well then. Who handles cars in the city?"

Nastya gave me a sharp look.

"Depends on what kind of cars."

"Hot ones, naturally."

"There are different kinds of hot cars. Make, model, where it was stolen, how."

"This one's a little tricky," I said. "I'm looking for a ZIM limo."

Nastya guffawed.

"Are you nuts, copper?" she said when she stopped laughing. "ZIM limos don't get stolen. Only government people use them, sitting in the back seat and having uniformed lackeys chauffeur them around."

She laughed some more.

To be honest, something in Sergei's manner the day before had made me apprehensive. There was a kind of defiance in him, as though he wanted to challenge me. I knew he had heard my conversation with Korenev – I made sure he would – and followed me to the metro station in order to tell me that ridiculous story about the Caucasus man at the filling station. I offered him a safe way out, but it didn't look like he was going to take it. And there was always an outside chance that the ZIM had actually been stolen. In either case, the car could have already made its way into the fences' network, which was why I wanted to talk to Nastya.

"But if one were stolen nonetheless—" I said once she had stopped laughing.

"So, there *was* one stolen? Is that what you're telling me?"

"Yes. I want to know whether there is a market for a hot ZIM."

"There is a market for hot everything. But not for a hot ZIM. You might as well drive yourself straight to jail if you go around riding in a hot ZIM."

"Very well then. If you can't fence the car, what about its parts?"

She thought it over.

"Maybe," she said after a while. "With cars like that, even if it wasn't stolen by a professional, getting rid of it would require professional help."

"Exactly," I said. "And there must be someone who controls that business."

"It's the only reason you keep calling me, copper," she observed bitterly. "It serves me right. I shouldn't be hobnobbing with your kind."

I expected her to keep complaining, but she suddenly leaned over and lowered her voice.

"Rubashkin," she said.

"What?"

"Rubashkin," she repeated even more softly. "He's your man."

"Who's Rubashkin?" I asked.

"Be quiet," she hissed. "No upscale car is stolen in Moscow without Rubashkin knowing about it. He controls the market."

"So, there *is* a market for a hot ZIM after all?"

"There is a market for spare parts. You can make more money selling parts, and it's safer, too, even though it takes more time. You might be able to fence a hot ZIM if you take it out to one of the Central Asian republics or to the Caucasus. But I still kind of doubt that Rubashkin would have anything to do with an idiot who goes out and steals a ZIM."

"What do you think of this scheme," I said. "A guy from the Caucasus approaches a driver and offers him money to look the other way while he steals his boss's car. The thieves need five days to drive it where they want to sell it before the driver raises an alarm. Could something like this be done behind Rubashkin's back? Or with the help of Rubashkin's competitors?"

Nastya rolled her eyes theatrically.

"Copper, Rubashkin hasn't got any competitors. All his competitors own small plots of land at Vagankovo Cemetery. The day he gets a competitor he can't handle is the day I'll send you a personalized invitation to his funeral."

"Well," I said. "In that case, if you hear of someone shopping a hot ZIM, be it to Rubashkin or to one of his competitors at Vagankovo Cemetery, maybe you'll give me a shout?"

"Maybe," she said.

She hopped off the bench and started to walk away, ignoring the puddles and stepping right in every one. I kept my eyes on her – a gaudy bright spot against the gray snow – until she reached the Sretenka exit.

She never looked back.

EIGHT

Once Nastya's red coat disappeared around the corner, I too got up to leave. I had no news about the car and therefore no reason to go to see the playwright again. Besides, I had not yet submitted my initial report on the car theft and I knew that the Boss was expecting it.

"Where were you?" Lenny snarled at me the moment I stepped into our office.

I neglected to mention that our TU-104 was usually overheated in winter. Along with a huge window that originally belonged to a much larger room, we had inherited a full-sized radiator that hung beneath the windowsill. It was nice in the dead of winter, but unpleasant in fall or spring. Now, despite the warm spell outside, it was going full force, and its red-hot cast-iron chambers emitted the smell of burnt dust. Oblivious to the heat, Lenny was sitting at his desk in his winter coat and hat.

"I was working on the car theft," I said.

"Who the hell cares about the goddamn car theft?" Lenny snarled, jumping to his feet. Then, when he saw that I was about to remove my coat in the steam bath that was our office, he commanded, "Keep it on. We're leaving."

"Going where?" I asked, but left my coat on.

Lenny was my superior and could give me orders, but I still had the right to know where we were off to.

"We're going to Butyrka, to interrogate Grushnikov," he said, his face twisting with barely controlled rage. "I would've gone already and been done with him, except Budyonny told me to take you along."

"I thought—" I said, but Lenny cut me off.

"Who cares what you thought. You should take a look at this."

He handed me a thin file. It contained the results of Tanya Drozdova's autopsy typed on thin, transparent paper. I picked up the stapled carbon copies and started to read. But Lenny was too impatient to wait for me to finish. Besides, we were both sweating in our coats and had started to walk down the hall toward the elevator.

"She wasn't raped," Lenny said as he led the way. "At least not right before she was killed. But you know what Grigoriev found out?"

Lenny choked up and stopped in mid-stride.

"She's had sex. That scum Grushnikov! She was just eleven, for God's sake."

"Was there anything else?" I asked.

"Don't you think that's enough?" Lenny asked over this shoulder as he resumed walking.

I started to leaf through the folder, but Urumov turned and pulled it out of my hands.

"There is nothing else. All the preliminary findings were more or less confirmed. Grigoriev thinks he might have been wearing gloves as he strangled Tanya. There are no fingerprints on the body, but enough on the surface of the table and all over the room to get him executed."

"Wait," I said. "If Grushnikov wore gloves, why are there fingerprints on the table?"

"I don't know. They might have been old ones, from the day before. He had been helping Tanya with her homework that whole week. Or at least that's what he keeps telling us."

"Why do you need me?" I asked while we were riding down in the elevator.

"I don't," Lenny replied. "But Budyonny thinks I do. He thinks the bastard's ready to confess and you, a nice and priestly type, are best suited to hear his confession. I'm not kidding. You're a new face, somebody he hasn't seen yet, and if you're gentle with the bastard, Budyonny thinks he might take to you."

"And what about the stolen car," I asked. "What did he say about that?"

We were getting out of the elevator now, with Lenny leading the way again. He turned toward me without breaking his stride.

"Get moving," he said. "You're on this case until the guy is convicted."

Lenny got down to business the moment the steel door slammed shut behind the foul-smelling bulk of Sergeant Molotov, the infamous senior guard at Butyrka Prison. He had been working himself up into a lather while I straightened my sheets of paper and pencils on the desk, getting ready to take notes. Once alone with the suspect, Lenny jumped up from his chair and took two quick strides toward him.

"You, scum," he hissed into the man's face. "You dirty pervert. You make me sick."

Grushnikov had a dark, pockmarked face with prominent cheekbones that rose like stone redoubts toward a pair of small, watchful, closely-set eyes. The black irises shifted nervously from one object to the next, as though they had a life of their own. His hair was coarse and brown, with deep widow's peaks on the sides of his sloping forehead.

Lenny pushed closer, crowding in on him and making him take a step backward. Grushnikov's eyes began to dart back and forth even faster.

"Why are you insulting me?" he asked, trying to sound calm and not succeeding very well.

"You know perfectly well why," Lenny replied, taking another step toward him. "Because you are a pervert and scum of the earth. Let's start by you telling me what you were doing peeping into the girls' locker room at your school. Were you jerking off? Come on, out with it. Were you?"

"Who told you that? Have you got any evidence?"

"Evidence? What evidence of you jerking off do you want me to produce?"

"I know who told you," Grushnikov exclaimed. "It's that Fomina woman, and it's not true! She's been spreading lies, and even went to the principal with them. Comrade Przhevalskaya conducted an investigation and saw right away that there was no truth in her accusations. She wouldn't have kept me on the job if it were true."

"You were getting off watching your students," Lenny said, ignoring Grushnikov's explanations and thrusting forward. The gym teacher now had his back against the wall. Lenny was in his face, depriving him of breathable air. The guy tried to pull back and hit the wall hard with the back of his head, groaning.

Grushnikov was a tall and powerful man, solidly built, with big strong thighs and the overdeveloped torso of a body builder. Moon-shaped pectorals stretched the rough fabric of his prison robe, a size too small for him. His arms were massive, hanging off his shoulders like whole hams at a sausage plant. Lenny was nearly a head shorter, paunchy and not in a particularly good shape. But if it came to a fistfight between these two – and not in police custody, where Lenny had an unfair advantage, but out in the open, man to man – I didn't have any doubt who would have the upper hand.

Neither did Grushnikov.

"And what about your volleyball players?" Lenny continued, relentlessly pressing into Grushnikov. "You were pawing them, too, weren't you?"

Grushnikov's face, which after two days of detention had acquired the characteristic earthen tinge all inmates get, grew pale and his lips began to tremble, but he made an effort to regain control of himself.

"Get out of my face," he said, his voice shaky. "I wasn't pawing anyone. This is all nonsense."

The interrogation room was narrow, with a high ceiling, its exposed brickwork painted purple – the color of calf's liver. Five high-voltage electric bulbs hung on long cords, heating up the room. Grushnikov's forehead glistened with perspiration.

The prison was more than a century old, and those who built it knew that a high ceiling could be more oppressive than a low one.

While Lenny was softening up the suspect, I sat quietly behind the desk, not interfering. The lamps cast a bright, dramatic light onto the proceedings. The interrogation room looked almost like a stage, and Lenny and the suspect had a mannered and exaggerated style of acting, as though they were performing in some bad police drama.

I was halfway between being another actor in this sordid production and its audience of one. I had not taken any notes, as there wasn't anything to record yet. We had sketched out a plan for the interrogation beforehand, while driving to Butyrka in Lenny's ramshackle Moskvich, but he was so far off script that I had absolutely no idea where it would end up.

"What about Tanya Drozdova?" Lenny asked.

After his furious early assault, he was suddenly quiet. I, on the contrary, grew tense because I sensed that it was a deceptive calm, a pause before a storm.

"It's another lie," Grushnikov protested. "I never spied on her, I swear. Never."

"Who said anything about spying?" Lenny asked, his voice getting even softer.

Grushnikov, on the other hand, was missing the implications of Lenny's ominous calm. He must have thought that it was a good sign, an indication that his vehement denials were starting to have an effect.

"Of course I wasn't spying on her," Grushnikov exclaimed. "And I wasn't spying on any of the girls at school, either. That's what I've been trying to tell you."

"Who said anything about spying?" Lenny repeated.

"You did."

"You weren't spying on her," Lenny said thoughtfully, looking away. He appeared to be addressing the purple liver-colored walls rather than the suspect. "You were screwing her, you bastard."

The soft buzzing of the extremely bright overhead lights was suddenly audible in the deep silence that fell over the room. The gym teacher stared at Lenny. It was as though he couldn't quite figure out whether Lenny was being serious or making some grotesque, sick joke. After what felt like an eternity, he finally thought he had it figured out – and he got it dead wrong. His pockmarked, tense face dissolved into an incredulous smile.

It was too much for Lenny to bear. He raised his right hand, its index and middle fingers sticking straight out like a double-barrel gun. He had short, stubby, hairy fingers worthy of a descendent of several generations of kosher butchers in the Ukrainian city of Poltava. They were scary fingers, especially when they were being jabbed into your face, aiming for your wide-open eyes. Grushnikov instinctively threw back his head to avoid being blinded and hit the wall again, much harder this time. There was a dull thud. At the same time, Lenny kneed him savagely in the groin. The gym teacher gasped. As he doubled over in pain, Lenny gave him a short hook in the solar plexus.

It all happened in a flash. I couldn't have stopped Lenny even if I had tried. It was a fitting denouement for the cheap police melodrama.

We picked Grushnikov off the floor and sat him on a metal stool. He was barely conscious. Lenny went down to the first-floor bathroom and returned a few minutes later with a beat-up tin can filled with icy water. He poured it unceremoniously over the suspect's head.

Grushnikov perked up, wincing as the water trickled down his back, then wiped his face with a rolled-up sleeve of his prison tunic and turned away.

"Very well then," Lenny said. "Let's start from the beginning. Let's talk about Tanya Drozdova. When did you first rape her? And what made you murder her?"

Grushnikov was silent, looking away.

"I'm sorry, I didn't hear that," Lenny said sarcastically, cupping his hand to his ear. "What? She was going to expose you? That's why you thought you had to kill her? Who was she going to tell? Her mother? A teacher at school? A friend? As you see, we have already figured out the big picture. All we need from you is to fill in a few small details."

Grushnikov continued to ignore him.

"Listen very carefully, scum," Lenny said, leaning close to him and lowering his voice to a hoarse whisper. "You tell us everything that happened and I promise you you'll have it easy from now on. No one will bother you any more, you'll keep your solitary cell through your trial. Eat government rations, walk for an hour in the courtyard every single day, rain or shine, get your death penalty in due course and enjoy life while it lasts. We all have to die someday, one way or another, and your death will be easy and painless. Do you agree?"

Grushnikov didn't answer.

"But if you go on lying to us," Lenny continued, putting a lot more steel in his voice, "I'll make sure we put you in a common cell with hardened criminals, recidivists and the like. Do you have any idea what they do to rapists of little girls, those hardened criminals? You can take it from me, you pervert: by the time they're through with you, you'll be eager to face the firing squad."

Grushnikov waited patiently for Lenny to finish giving no sign that he had heard him.

"I'm not going to talk to this man," he said, turning to me. "I know you're no better. Your job is to be the good cop to his bad one. But I think this guy really enjoys beating up people who can't fight back."

I couldn't help being impressed by Grushnikov's courage.

"Does this mean you're going to sign a confession if I leave?" Lenny asked. "I'm so committed to your conviction that I might be willing to humor you."

Grushnikov said nothing. Lenny's methods had yet again yielded a splendid result, I thought bitterly.

"You win," Lenny said after a long, heavy silence. "I'll leave you two alone. But when I come back, you'd better admit everything. Is that clear?"

Before going out, he turned and gave us both a withering look, as though we were accomplices in a hateful crime.

"What now?" I asked when the door slammed behind him. "Am I going to hear the truth?"

"You are," he said. "But you're not going to like it."

"That's right. It's not a very pretty story."

"No," Grushnikov said, shaking his head and grimacing in pain as he rubbed the top of his stomach. "You're not going to like it because the truth is not what you want to hear. You want me to sign a confession, regardless of whether it's true or not. Your idiot partner wants to beat it out of me. I have nothing to hide. I did love Tanya, I admit that, but I loved her like a daughter. Then you're going to say I raped her. How could I have? She was eleven years old."

"That's exactly what's so disgusting," I said.

"I still can't believe someone would strangle her. She was a special little girl. She was so vulnerable. You know, her own father never even gave her a birthday gift. Kids needs fathers, especially girls."

"So you wanted her to be your daughter? Did she want you to be her father?"

He didn't reply.

"Why is it that Tanya's mother knew nothing about your familial relations?" I asked.

"Tanya's mother hated me," he said.

"Was there a reason why?"

"She didn't need one. I moved into her mother's room, that was enough. I understand her feelings, but what was I supposed to do? I had waited for a room of my own for two years, and the school principal had been dangling it in front of me like a carrot in front of a donkey. It wasn't my fault her mother died. They were going to take their extra room away in any case."

"Have you had relations with other women since you moved to Moscow?" I asked.

Grushnikov, who had started to relax since Lenny's exit, suddenly became tense and nervous once again.

"Why does it matter?" he asked quickly. "Does it have a bearing on this case?"

I shrugged. "I think it does. Did you ever try to date another teacher?"

"Another teacher?" he laughed. "At the boarding school? They're not my type. Besides, even if I liked one of them, where would I have taken her? I've only had a room of my own for a few months. Before that, I'd been living at a dorm, seven guys all bunking together in one room."

"No sex for two years, then?" I asked.

He sighed.

"Every few weeks a bunch of us got together on a Saturday night to go visit the girls at the house painters' vocational school. They were also out-of-towners, like us, Russian country girls and young girls from Central Asia, living in Moscow by themselves. We would buy a few bottles of cheap red wine for the girls and a bottle of vodka for us, plus another one for the dorm manager. For a bottle and a ten-ruble bribe he'd let guys in and look the other way. We'd get drunk quickly, divide into couples depending of which guy liked which girl, turn out the lights and go at it. In silence, of course, because the walls between the dorm rooms were paper-thin. The manager gave us an hour for the whole thing."

He sighed, caught himself and added quickly.

"They were of age, those girls. Twenty to twenty-five. Some were even older."

"Charming," I said.

He fell silent and I thought he was done. A confession didn't seem to be coming. He was either very clever or, actually, innocent. It was time for me to call Lenny back.

"You're the cops and I'm the suspect," Grushnikov said suddenly. "You hold all the cards. I'm sure you'll be able to frame me one way or another. Most likely, I'll be sentenced to be executed, because it's a terrible crime and the killer deserves the penalty of death, regardless of whether Tanya was raped before she was killed or you're lying to me the way you cops often do. Once I'm convicted, you and your sadistic colleague will get a medal and a new star on your epaulets, and everyone will commend you for catching the killer. But the real killer will go free. This is why I'm not going to sign a false confession. This way there will still be a small chance that someday this case will be reopened and properly solved, that Tanya's real killer is brought to justice."

As I listened to him, a thought popped into my head. I kept fighting it and chasing it away, but it was persistent. Or rather, it was a realization that if an innocent man was framed for Tanya's murder it would be another life senselessly thrown away. Like Tanya's. Or like Natashka, my little sister. I must not allow it to happen.

Waiting outside seemed to have gotten Lenny even more exhausted than interrogating Grushnikov. He was a sloppy dresser to start with, but now his clothes were wrinkled as though he had slept in them for a week. Perspiration had stained the armpits of his jacket.

He and Grushnikov came face to face in the narrow prison corridor and Lenny glared at the gym teacher.

"I should have hit him harder," Lenny said to me. "And I'd really love to transfer him to a common cell. Just for one night."

Despite his exhaustion, his rage had not been dampened while he waited.

"You know we have no authority to do that," I said and then added very reluctantly, knowing how Lenny would take it: "Besides, I'm not quite sure he did it."

NINE

Later that day I took the metro to Mayakovsky Square station, exiting up the stairway that empties in front of Tchaikovsky Concert Hall. I made my way past a well-dressed, perfumed crowd and, crossing Gorky Street, used the maze of side streets to get to 1st Kolobovsky. I stood for a few minutes in the courtyard, gathering my thoughts before entering.

"You again," Irina Drozdova said when she opened the door. "Baba Dasha has just left to go to work. I'm the only one here."

She was sitting in the same armchair. The ashtray had been recently emptied, but it was rapidly filling up again with ash and cigarette butts.

"I'm actually here to see you, Irina Borisovna," I said. I had looked up her full name and patronymic in one of Urumov's files.

She gave me a shrug, which was a lot like a shiver.

"Your colleagues have already questioned me. I told them everything I know. I have nothing to add, especially as far as the killer is concerned. In all the time he lived in my mother's room, we didn't exchange more than ten words with one another."

"I wasn't going to question you," I said. "This isn't even my investigation. I just wanted to ask you whether you couldn't go and stay somewhere else for a few days. With a relative or a friend perhaps?"

She gave me a lifeless smile.

"I don't have anywhere to go. I don't mind being here."

"I don't think you should be here on your own," I said.

"I don't mind being here," she repeated mechanically.

"I'm serious, Irina Borisovna. I think it would be best if you went away for a few days."

"Thank you," she smiled again. "I understand your concern. You wouldn't want to see the mother of the victim doing away with herself. It won't look good. Don't worry, I won't kill myself. I promise."

"Please, Irina Borisovna," I protested a little too strongly, because the possibility of her committing suicide was exactly what I had been worried about. But not because it "wouldn't look good."

"I think you should be with other people at a time like this. You shouldn't be alone."

"But I am not alone, Lieutenant. Tanya and my mother are here with me. This apartment used to belong to my mother's family. My mother was born here before the term 'communal apartment' was invented. My mother and I spent the winter of 1941 here. My father was at the front and all the neighbors had been evacuated to the Urals or to Tashkent. We were all by ourselves here. It had been ours once, and it was ours once more, even though the Germans were just outside the city. My daughter was born here, too. This is where we brought her from the hospital and this is where she died. It's home to me and I don't know any other."

She put out her cigarette and shook a fresh one from the pack on her lap. I held a match for her and got out one of my own Laikas. We smoked in silence.

I couldn't quite think of anyone to suggest for Irina to stay with. My Aunt Eugenia would have been perfect, except – well, except for Tanya Drozdova's extraordinary resemblance to my little sister Natashka, which would probably kill her. Natashka's loss was the great tragedy of my Aunt's life, she was racked with guilt for her role in that tragedy and the guilt never left her.

Irina sighed.

"When Mother died and they took away her room, I knew it was the end," she said. "The end of everything. I didn't know it was going to be this painful and come so soon, but come to think of it, there is a kind of logic to it."

"There isn't," I said firmly. "There is no logic to it. Just crime. And the killer will be found and punished, I give you my word."

"But it makes a *lot* of sense," she continued, ignoring me. "My grandparents had a very large family, tight-knit, accomplished, loving. Then, one by one they were all gone. Two of my mother's brothers were killed in the Civil War, one fighting for the Reds and the other for the Whites. Another brother was shot in the street by drunken soldiers – just like that, for no reason. Her older sister and her husband emigrated and we have not had any news of them since, from France or wherever else they ended up. Who knows if they're even alive. Grandfather, who was one of the best industrial engineers in Russia, was arrested and convicted as a wrecker. He spent ten years in the camps and came back a broken man. My father was killed in the war."

"Mine too," I said.

She shook her head and looked at me, as though she only now became aware of my presence.

"I probably shouldn't be telling you this," she said, shaking her head.

"You need somebody to talk to. My father was killed in the war too."

"Lots of people lost fathers," she said wearily. "One way or another, the entire family disappeared until only Tanya and I were left. And now I'm all alone. And all this time this apartment, the place where my mother's large, happy family once lived, has been taken away from us, room by room."

"Actually," I said, "I wanted to ask you something. Is there a door between your room and your mother's?"

Irina gave me strange look.

"Which rooms?" she asked.

I had a feeling she knew exactly what I was talking about but was playing for time.

"Between your room and the one that was occupied by Comrade Grushnikov," I said.

"Why, there used to be one. In the old days, ours used to be the living room and my mother's the dining room. They used to be connected by a door. But it was nailed shut years ago. It's behind the armoire in my room."

"Is there a chance it could have been opened recently?" I asked.

She started to say something, but was interrupted by loud voices and peels of laughter coming from the landing outside the apartment. There was a rustling sound against the wall and something fell heavily, preceded by shouts of warning and more laughter. A key turned in the lock and the door flew open, admitting a cloud of frosty freshness into the airless, smoke-filled hallway. At first it seemed as though a crowd of young, happy people burst in behind it, but in reality there was only a tall, trim and youthful middle-aged man, a young woman and two teenage boys. All were bright, good-looking, tall and cheerful. They had pink cheeks and white teeth and their entire group exuded health and happiness.

They were carrying skis and ski poles on their shoulders. The man was telling them a story and the boys were roaring with laughter. The young woman, coming in behind them, smiled indulgently. I couldn't help noting how beautiful she looked. Prosperous and well-cared for, but also extremely beautiful.

Seeing Drozdova, the man broke off and the boys clammed up. They greeted her softly and politely and a little shamefacedly, hurrying by and averting their eyes.

There was a brief delay at the door leading to their half of the apartment, when the man dropped his keys. While he was picking them up and looking for the right one, the boys shifted impatiently, still looking away. A new burst of laughter reached us as the door swung shut behind them.

The young woman remained standing in the hallway, looking back at Irina. There was a strange expression on her face that made it almost ugly. I had seen this reaction before to people touched by tragedy: it's as though the victims were guilty of their own misfortunes or could infect others.

It was only for a brief moment. The door opened again and the man called out:

"Nadezhda, what on earth are you waiting for? Come, your clothes are all wet. You're going to catch a cold if you don't hurry up and change."

The woman smiled at her husband and became radiantly beautiful once more.

"Dr. Lazius and family," Irina observed. "They go skiing in Ostankino Park after work. They're a close-knit bunch. They love each other and spend all their time together. They always find so much to laugh about. It's as though they were, in a way, a reincarnation of my grandmother's family. All that's left of us is ashes."

"Irina Borisovna," I began.

She was looking at me through a cloud of blue smoke, waiting for me to go on. Maybe Aunt Eugenia could be a solution, after all, I thought. She had so much compassion, lavishing it on her down-and-out neighbors in her dingy, small town thirty kilometers northeast of Moscow.

"No, nothing important," I said, shaking my head. "Perhaps I had better go talk to Dr. Lazius."

"Go ahead," she said. "He's a good man."

The Laziuses had something of a separate apartment behind their door, with two bedrooms located off a narrow corridor. The larger bedroom was the boys', and it had been divided by a partition, giving each a half of a barred window facing the street. The smaller bedroom – which was still pretty large by the city's standards – was a master bedroom and at the end of the hallway there were two more rooms. All were furnished in a comfortable and elegant style but without ostentation or excess of any kind. The place was clean, tidy and rational – very much the way you'd expect this family to live.

I had a chance to stick my nose into each room by turn while Dr. Lazius and I walked toward his study.

"I have already been questioned by two other detectives from Criminal Investigations," Dr. Lazius announced. "Twice, as a matter of fact. They checked my alibi, but I don't mind repeating to you as well, that on the day of the murder I was at my clinic, teaching a class first thing in the morning, then seeing my patients in late morning and early afternoon, and then teaching again in late afternoon. As a rule, I'm rarely if ever out of my clinic during the day. Besides, the clinic is located on the outskirts, almost out of town and a long way away from here, even if by driving I could have gotten here very quickly."

"Yes," I said. "I read your responses in the file."

"Nevertheless, I'm entirely at your disposal," the doctor went on. "I'll be happy to answer any additional questions you might have. Repetition is the mother of learning and it is imperative investigators scrupulously learn all the circumstances surrounding the crime in order to identify the perpetrator. Oh, I see. You wish to talk about Comrade Grushnikov."

Dr. Lazius spoke with a Baltic accent. Or perhaps it was a mannerism of his, an affectation he had developed to express himself by enunciating every syllable with considerable care and clipping his words.

His study was even smaller than our TU-104 office, and filled with bookshelves that rose to the ceiling. His books were in German, French and English, as well as in other languages I couldn't identify. Russian books all dated from the nineteenth and early twentieth century, all solid editions bound in fraying leather, their titles printed on their spines in gilded letters with old-style spelling. The bookshelves also held photographs, mostly ancient and yellowed, group portraits of old men with luxurious facial hair and young men in winged collars and bowler hats. Some were signed in Gothic script. Glancing at one of them, I spotted young Dr. Lazius dressed in a student coat with two rows of brass buttons. His bony face was framed by shoulder-length blond hair and he sported a sparse goatee, also apparently blond.

My host closed the door and offered me a comfortable armchair, positioning himself behind his desk. On the opposite wall, over the doctor's head, hung a small seascape, a becalmed northern sea. A desk lamp shed soothing yellow light around the room.

"You may be wondering why I closed the door," the doctor addressed me after a short pause. "It's on the account of my boys. I do not subscribe to the modern view that young people should be thrust into the world early in life and be exposed to the kind of dirt and nastiness we habitually encounter in our existence. Surely they will come to know all of it in time, but I want them to grow up at their own pace. Of course, in this particular case, they couldn't be kept completely in ignorance, I'm well aware of that."

I nodded.

"Anyway, back to Comrade Grushnikov," he said.

He hunched over, brought the palms of his hands together and placed them under his chin. He kept silent for a long time, staring at the heavy dark-green curtains from under half-closed eyelids. Five minutes passed with us sitting silently across the desk from each other. Finally, I decided to break the silence.

"Did you notice any strange behavior in him? As a psychiatrist you—"

He raised his hand, bidding me to stop. He remained immersed in his thoughts for several more minutes while I bit my tongue and waited.

"You must realize, Lieutenant, that I didn't have much contact with Comrade Grushnikov – and none at all in a professional capacity," he began. He spoke slowly and deliberately, taking time to search for the correct word. "I mean in my capacity as an analyst. Even our encounters in the apartment, in our capacity as neighbors, were mostly cursory and never frequent. Of course, I would run into him in the kitchen now and again and we would exchange a word or two as is customary between neighbors. Civil relations must be maintained as long as people are forced to share their living quarters with strangers."

He fell silent again.

"But no more than that," he resumed after a while. "I'm a busy man. My work takes an inordinate amount of my time, and, as you have seen, I have a family, a wife and two young children. We do try to spend as much time together as our busy schedules permit. We go to the theater, to fine art museums, we attend important cultural events. "

I thought back to the well-dressed, fragrant crowd I had skirted at the entrance to the Tchaikovsky Concert Hall an hour before. I had felt out of place there, but the doctor and his family would fit in perfectly.

"We do a lot of sports," the doctor went on in his slightly stilted Lithuanian way. "My wife is an excellent amateur swimmer and we often go to the pool on Kropotkinskaya Embankment. In winter, we ski. Are you a skier, Lieutenant? You're not? It's a pity. The former Sheremetyevs' Estate at Ostankino is probably the best place in Moscow for cross-country skiing.

"But again, we have digressed, Lieutenant. I'm not certain I could be of much help to you. You see, I should mention that I'm not in the habit of analyzing people I meet outside my practice. I do plenty of that during my work hours. But since you have asked me, I suppose I would be on fairly safe ground if I said that I did observe certain psychological abnormalities in my neighbor. Nothing very concrete, mind you, and I hope you understand that this is not an official diagnosis. Still, there was behavior that revealed certain narcissistic personality traits and some deep-seated neuroses, such as wounded pride, exaggerated *amour propre* combined with a measure of classic male insecurity. All that physical exercise, endless weight-lifting, body-building, working the chest expander. I suppose you know that the desire to become good-looking by losing weight or building musculature is a sure sign of inferiority? It suggests a hope that women will fall in love with you because of your looks, body or physical strength and disregard your other shortcomings, such as small penis or poor performance in bed?"

It was news to me, but I nodded all the same.

"In Comrade Grushnikov's case, this inferiority complex appears to have been exacerbated by lack of normal, regular sexual activity. I do not make it a habit of prying into other people's private lives, but

I have never actually seen a woman visiting his room. Perhaps there was a measure of – how shall I put it – homoerotic deviancy. Come to think of it, I would have liked to interview one of his sexual partners – assuming there has been one. I don't believe Comrade Grushnikov was ever married."

I shrugged. Dr. Lazius was going into far greater psychological detail than I had expected.

"Under propitious circumstances," he continued, "such personalities may develop certain neurasthenic traits. I stress the word 'may' because in human psychology nothing is ever certain. Just as there are no two sets of identical fingerprints, so there are no individuals in the world who share the same psychological makeup. Anyway, in certain circumstances men like Grushnikov may develop the fear of adult, sexually initiated, self-confident women and instead become attracted to inexperienced young girls who would not be in a position to judge, criticize or compare them to other men. While they are scared to assume the traditional dominant male role in a relationship with an adult woman, they could become a mentor or a father figure to a child."

"A father figure?" I repeated, thinking back to what Grushnikov had told me during the interrogation. "Could this lead to a murder?"

Dr. Lazius sighed.

"Again, I wouldn't say *lead*. Such deviant behavior may propitiate a natural tendency toward murder. As I said, in each patient mental illness takes a different form. Some do not see relations with a minor as morally repugnant, but fear being exposed. Such individuals can kill when they are threatened with exposure. But, then again, to become a killer a person must either be a terrible coward or already predisposed to murder. In another case, the patient may realize that what he is doing is wrong but, being a narcissist, be incapable of admitting his guilt. He may blame the victim and this could also lead to murder."

"Why? For leading him astray?"

"Precisely. For leading him astray."

I was thinking it over.

"However, both your hypotheses suggest that the killer, either Grushnikov or some other person, had had sexual relations with Tanya," I said at last.

"Do you mean to say that Tanya was not sexually abused?" he said in surprise. "That's very, very strange."

"I can't really talk about it," I said.

I wasn't going to tell him about the results of the autopsy, but he took my words differently.

"In this case, I'm sorry." The psychiatrist thought it over, trying to fit this new piece of information into his logical construct. Finally, he sighed. "Well, as I said, I've been expounding a theory, so to speak, and a few pure conjectures. Nothing that would stand up in the court of law."

"Speaking of the court of law," I said. "Your professional assessment of Grushnikov's personality may prove useful if he is charged with Tanya Drozdova's murder."

"I'm flattered that you think so, Lieutenant," Dr. Lazius replied coldly. "However, I don't think I can be an expert witness in this case."

"Why not?"

"Ah, well, there are plenty of good reasons why not. First of all, I know Grushnikov personally, I have been his neighbor for a number of months, and, if truth be told, I dislike him. Believe it or not, he has been making passes at my wife and, even though I have not been so ill-mannered as to say anything to him personally, he should be under no illusions that his behavior has gone unnoticed. Mind you, he's not unusual in this regard: my wife is a very attractive woman. Needless to say, he never had the slightest chance with her. Nevertheless, it certainly has not made me see him in a favorable light. I don't know if you're familiar with *The Odyssey*?"

I shook my head.

"It's an Ancient Greek epic written by the poet Homer. I assume you've at least heard the name, Lieutenant. In a very long poem, Homer recounts the travels of the Greek hero Odysseus who, for one reason or another, took ten years to return to his homeland after previously spending a comparable amount of time besieging and pillaging the city of Troy. While he travelled, a number of kings and princes sought the hand of his beautiful wife Penelope. They all assumed that her husband was dead – which was, after such a long absence, highly likely – and, technically speaking, there was no reason for them not to court her. Nevertheless, when Odysseus finally returned, he put all of his wife's suitors to the sword. Do you see my point?"

I nodded.

"Anyway, we keep digressing from Comrade Grushnikov. Perhaps because he is not such an appealing subject. My second reason for not wanting to share my views on his personality with the general public – much less to testify in the court of law – is that I am not at all convinced that my analysis of his personality is correct. As you have just seen, I surmised wrongly that he had had sexual relations with Tanya Drozdova."

I gave him a noncommittal shrug.

"Quite frankly, I'm still surprised. Of course I'm not at all casting aspersion on the professionalism of your forensics staff. Still, if I were you, I'd do a far more thorough search of his room. Men with psychopathic tendencies also tend to be fetishistic. They transfer their desire onto objects. Most often, it is article of clothing, usually of intimate nature. Socks, underwear, toiletries."

"His room has been thoroughly searched," I said.

"Maybe you and your colleagues didn't know what to look for."

He lapsed into another of his long silences.

"But I have not yet told you the most important reason why I'm not going to pass professional judgment on Comrade Grushnikov – or anyone like him, for that matter," he said when he came to life once again. "The problem is that human sexuality and deviant sexual behavior lie well outside my field of competence. Or, to put it bluntly, I don't know much more about it than you do. Appearing on a witness stand as an expert would be unethical. Worse, it would expose me to ridicule. My distinguished colleagues who spent years specializing in this area would laugh at me and my conclusions."

"And what is your area of specialty, Doctor?" I asked.

He nodded mournfully a few times before replying.

"I specialize in other kinds of psychological deviations," he said. "My patients present little danger to society and don't often come into contact with Criminal Investigations. Their disorders cause grievous harm to themselves. My specialty is suicide."

"Oh, yes," I blurted out. "Of course. Your first wife—"

Suddenly alert, Dr. Lazius turned and gave me a sharp look. He had steely gray eyes that seemed to drill a hole through my skull with their unblinking, intense stare.

"Would you care to explain what you mean by this insinuation, Lieutenant?" he asked.

"I meant," I muttered. "Your first wife—"

"I'm sorry, I don't understand what you're trying to say."

His voice grew softer and, suddenly, threatening.

"I thought your first wife committed suicide, sir," I said, cursing myself for bringing up the subject.

An ugly grimace contorted Dr. Lazius' handsome, intelligent face. He turned beet-red with anger and got up from his chair.

"Who on earth has put this kind of nonsense into your head, Lieutenant?" he asked in a hateful whisper.

I wished I could somehow evaporate from his study. Dr. Lazius was now towering over me as I tried to shrink into the upholstery of his overstuffed armchair.

"Who told you this?" he insisted.

"It must have come up in the course of the investigation," I said feebly.

His mouth twisted in disgust.

"You should be ashamed of yourself, Lieutenant. What does dirty gossip have to do with your investigation into the death of a little girl? My wife died of natural causes. The cause of her death was a heart attack. It's all good and well for old wives in the courtyard to gossip about it, but I absolutely refuse – do you hear me, Comrade? – to stand idly by while this idiotic hearsay is being repeated by the police. I would advise you not to take on faith every piece of gossip you hear. I'm not an expert in detection, but I strongly doubt that at Moscow Criminal Investigations it would be considered professional behavior. "

"Are you alright?" came a voice from behind the closed door.

The door opened and Dr. Lazius's second wife appeared on the threshold. She had a concerned look on her exceptionally beautiful face.

"Everything is under control, my love," Dr. Lazius replied, no longer shaking with anger but still glaring at me from across the desk. "Comrade detective and I are having a little chat. And anyway, he's about to leave."

TEN

Two levels below ground in our headquarters building, in the basement, was a place known as The Cellar. In The Cellar there dwells a librarian with the unkindly nickname Baba Yaga, or The Witch. Baba Yaga was a prematurely gray, unmarried woman with deeply lined, chalk-colored cheeks, bleached eyes and a wart. She presided over a special archive set up in the early 1950s by the then director of Criminal Investigations, Colonel Konstantin Grebnev. It contains a wealth of information about various incidents that, while not necessarily criminal, could for one reason or another be of interest to investigators, such as natural or man-made disasters, extreme weather phenomena, traffic accidents, drownings, fires, unexplained or unusual deaths and – of course – suicides.

Suicides were special. They were looked up so often that they were kept in a section of their own.

Despite an appearance that did indeed bring to mind the scariest of fairy tale-inspired childhood nightmares, Baba Yaga was, deep down, a kind-hearted woman, extremely helpful to those who were on good terms with her and who showed her a modicum of respect. Her real name was Zoya Georgiyevna.

It was early morning and I was her only visitor. She promptly got out two thick folders covering the second half of the 1950s. Sneezing from paper dust and squinting at the pale, age-worn lines, I started by scanning the last names and then, finding no Laziuses in any of the reports, separated all files related to women and began leafing through them in order. The first Mrs. Lazius could have been entered under her maiden name, for instance.

If her body had been found at the tram depot, the way Baba Dasha had said it was, the case would have immediately leapt off the page. Yet I kept an open mind, making allowances for the fact that, in retelling, such stories can be altered beyond recognition, and that the discovery of a frost-stiffened body on a tram that had been parked overnight added exactly the kind of macabre touch that old wives love. The doctor's harangue had humbled me, and I was taking extra care to check Baba Dasha's information. Lazius was right: gossip had to be taken with an extra pinch of salt.

On the other hand, where there was smoke there had to be fire.

Baba Yaga soon joined me, taking half of the files, so that we got through the tall stack in half the time. There was no mention of any tram depot, and no case that resembled Baba Dasha's tale in any way.

Baba Yaga arranged the files in their original order and took them away. We then made short work of the next two years, and got the same result – which is to say, found nothing at all. It made no sense to look at more recent dates and there were no earlier ones. After skimming through two other stacks containing reports of people found dead in the street and on public transportation, as well as unidentified bodies, I had to admit that Lazius had been telling the truth, and that the suicide story did not check out. But, then again, it was not surprising: old women spending their days sitting on benches in Moscow courtyards have a lot of time on their hands and nothing better to do than invent wild tales and spread unsubstantiated rumors. It had been entirely my fault to have fallen for one of them.

I had gone to The Cellar so early because Lenny and I were meeting Gordeyev and Tumakov at the office to discuss the progress of our investigation, and to map out the course of action over the next few days. I was finished and up at our office at five minutes to nine. The others had already gathered and were waiting for me. Gordeyev and Tumakov greeted me in their usual manner by exchanging handshakes, whereas Lenny looked away, said nothing, and deliberately withheld his hand. He was tense, like a wound-up spring waiting to uncoil. I had felt it last night, too, when he was driving back to the city from Butyrka. It was as though Grushnikov's interrogation had opened a rift between us and now he was letting me know that we were on opposite sides of the barricades.

Tumakov, who had been sitting in my chair, made an attempt to climb on top of Lenny's desk again, but Lenny rebuffed him savagely. "Go sit somewhere else, will you?"

"So, I guess it didn't go well last night?" Tumakov asked with a smirk.

He was familiar with Lenny's moods and temper tantrums and he always responded to them with a heavy dose of sarcasm, which made Lenny all the more furious.

"Correct," Lenny replied, addressing Tumakov but looking at me. "Actually, it's much worse. The pervert managed to convince Senior Lieutenant Matyushkin of his innocence. For some reason, it wasn't difficult, and Senior Lieutenant Matyushkin here is now Grushnikov's most ardent supporter, even though to the rest of us it appears to be an open and shut case."

Gordeyev and Tumakov stared at me.

"He didn't convince me that he's innocent," I protested, still hoping to turn the whole thing into a joke, "It's you who didn't convince me that he's guilty."

"If he signs a confession, there won't be any further doubt," Gordeyev observed.

"I'm not sure he'll sign a confession," I said. "In fact, I'm sure he won't."

"Oh, yeah?" Lenny exclaimed. "Of course he won't sign anything now, because he's not blind and he can see that he's twisted you around his little finger. But I'm telling you, if I could get him to spend a night in a cell with a couple of career criminals, he'd crawl back to us on his hands and knees, begging us to let him sign whatever we want him to sign."

"You may well be right," I said, shrugging. "But that won't necessarily prove him guilty. Be that as it may, he gave me a pretty convincing reason why he won't sign anything. He said it would be like covering up for Tanya's real killer."

"Agh," Lenny cried out in exasperation. "But he *is* Tanya's real killer. Get it through your thick skull, will you?"

Lenny and I don't always see eye to eye, but he had never before been so hostile when disagreeing with me.

"It's your opinion," I said. "I'm going to reserve judgment until we get more solid evidence."

"Pavel has a point," Gordeyev said thoughtfully. "Yes, it would be nice to have his confession. But all we have on him are fingerprints on Tanya Drozdova's dining table. Nothing else, really."

"We've got the testimony of the Russian lit teacher," Lenny objected.

"It won't be enough to convict him," Gordeyev said.

"There you go. You see what you've done, Matyushkin?"

Lenny glared at me. Now he was suddenly outnumbered, and he was convinced that it was all my fault.

"There may be more evidence in his room," I said. There was no point of antagonizing my partner any further, now that I had made my point. "I went to see Grushnikov's neighbor, Dr. Lazius, last night. He's a psychiatrist and a luminary in his profession. He suggested that if Grushnikov had sexual relations with the victim, he might have kept some of her things in his room. I guess he meant her panties or something along those lines. Perverts who go after little girls are also typically fetishists, according to Dr. Lazius."

"We searched his room pretty thoroughly," Tumakov said. "The scene of crime unit went over everything with a fine tooth comb."

"They may not have known what to look for," I said, echoing Dr. Lazius.

"How come the doctor knew that Grushnikov had had sex with Tanya?" Lenny asked, his voice truculent. "Grigoriev's report was finished only yesterday morning. Was it you who told him?"

That was an outrageous suggestion, one he wouldn't have made if he had been his normal self. He knew I would never have disclosed that kind of information to an outsider. Something about this case was making him crazy.

"Of course I told him nothing of the kind," I said. "That's the thing. He got the idea on his own, which is not that hard, you know. If an eleven year-old is strangled by a man, it begs the question whether she was raped. Anyway, Lazius is more in your corner. He believes that Grushnikov has serious emotional problems and that his problems are sexual in nature. I even suggested that he might be called as an expert witness for the prosecution if Grushnikov is put on trial."

"It's not a bad idea," Gordeyev said.

Our office door opened without warning and Lenny shouted over his shoulder. "Get out. We're in a meeting."

Having received no reply, he repeated savagely into the sudden silence, "I said, get the fuck out of here!"

Only then did he turn around – and instantly leap to his feet while at the same time trying to salute and knocking a stack of folders from his desk to the floor. Loose sheets of paper went flying in every direction.

Budyonny considerable bulk was lodged in our doorway.

"I'm sorry, Comrade Lieutenant Colonel. I didn't know it was you."

"At ease," Budyonny said, steering himself through the door as though he was an aircraft carrier sailing into a small harbor. "Carry on. I just want to listen in."

He was half in, half out. Our tiny TU-104 simply couldn't accommodate him. There was a brief shuffle as Lenny let Tumakov sit on top of his desk – now that the damage had already been done a second time – and climbed onto the windowsill. Ordinarily, the Boss never graced his staff's offices with his presence, so this was clearly a special occasion.

"Please sit down, sir," Lenny said, offering him his chair.

"I'll stand. Ignore me, comrades. Go on with whatever you've been discussing."

"Where were we?" said Lenny. Budyonny's presence unnerved him. "Oh, yes. You were saying something about Dr. Lazius, Lieutenant Matyushkin."

"Yes," I said, "Dr. Lazius thinks we ought to take a very close look at Grushnikov's room, because we might find something that would connect him to Tanya. Also, doesn't he have some kind of an office or a desk at the boarding school?"

"Yes," Tumakov replied readily. "Only we may not get the principal's consent to search it."

"I don't think we should ask," Lenny said.

"How can you say that?" Tumakov was instantly incensed. "She's a Party veteran. She can cause us a lot of grief if she chooses to. As it is—"

Another fight was brewing now, between Lenny and his former partner. Budyonny, eyeing one and the other in turn, frowned. Gordeyev felt it was time for him to step in.

"Dr. Lazius knows what he's talking about," he said, turning to the Boss. "Matyushkin has suggested to him that we might want to use him as an expert witness, to testify at Grushnikov trial. He's a world-renowned psychiatrist and he had an opportunity to observe Grushnikov for a few months at a close range."

Budyonny's reaction took us all by surprise.

"No need to tell me who he is, Captain," he roared at Gordeyev, then turned to me. "Who the hell authorized you to talk to Lazius, Lieutenant, much less offer him to be an expert witness at the putative future trial of a suspect?"

I attempted to say something but the Boss thundered right over my objections.

"Dr. Lazius is no expert witness for you. He's a victim's neighbor, which makes him a suspect."

"He has an alibi," Gordeyev said. "And so does his wife. We've checked them both. They're clean."

"Don't interrupt me, Captain." Budyonny was full of rage now. "I've asked you to give these guys a hand, Lieutenant, no more than that. Your main job is to investigate the theft of Comrade Korenev's car. I just got off the phone with him. He said you have not been to see him in three days. I want you to get back on his case right away. And I'm still waiting for you to submit the report of your preliminary findings."

"Yes, sir," I said. "I'm sorry, sir."

"And when you get to him, Lieutenant, make sure he knows that, as soon as we successfully complete this investigation, I'll put two more operatives on his case. Three more. Understood?"

"Yes, sir."

"Go right away, Lieutenant. I don't want you to be sitting here wasting your time."

I gathered my coat. Budyonny moved aside to let me through and then followed me out. For a few seconds we walked side by side down the corridor, in silence.

"Just humor him as much as you can, Matyushkin," the Boss said as we got to the elevator, his tone much gentler now. "Within reason, of course. Use your discretion. As to the psychiatrist, I think he's full of shit. They all are, starting with what's his name? The German?"

ELEVEN

Korenev greeted me with studied reserve.

"I had a talk with your boss," he told me even before I had time to change into his felt slippers. "He said you're now going to cooperate and pay some attention to my requests."

He stood in the doorway with a starched napkin in his hand while I struggled with the wet laces of my boots. I had once again caught him at mealtime. It was pretty much the same as on my first visit: we proceeded to the dining room where he quickly shoehorned his butt into an armchair at the head of the table and assumed a solemn pose, as if sitting for the painter Gerasimov. Having gotten comfortable, he stuck the edge of a napkin into his shirt collar.

Zinaida, emerging from the kitchen, showed no sign of recognizing me and walked past as though I were a life-sized sculpture, not a human being. She had the same dour look on her face. She brought out a white porcelain soup tureen filled with thick, cream-colored liquid that exuded the incomparable aroma of porcini mushrooms.

Sergei was in, too. As we walked through the apartment, I caught sight of him through a door that had been left ajar. He was wearing his usual white undershirt and blue overalls, and was methodically buffing the parquet with a pig-bristle brush attached to his foot. He looked like a figure skater attempting a fancy jump and then changing his mind.

"Are you going to cooperate?" Korenev asked, drilling me with his tiny eyes. "I mean after your boss has given you a serious talking-to at my request?"

"I am, Matvei Nikanorovich," I said. "However, there has been almost no news."

"What do you mean, almost no news?" Korenev exclaimed, quickly becoming irritated. "Don't you start with me again, Lieutenant. I can't believe there have been no developments over the past three days."

"I'm working on it," I said. "I'm trying to make sure it has not been sold in the black market."

"Are you talking about my car again, Lieutenant? Forget my car. It's the murder I'm talking about. And don't tell me you don't know anything about it or are not authorized to talk to me. Your boss told me that you'll be keeping me informed. So? Has the case been solved?"

"Not yet," I replied.

"Why not? What about the neighbor? You've had him in custody since day one."

"He has not confessed to anything yet. Evidence against him is still just circumstantial."

The playwright had had his eye on the soup even as he bombarded me with questions. He swallowed hard and dug in. Unfortunately, the nasty pseudo-English maid had placed the tureen on the far end of the table, just out of his reach. He extended his short arms as far as they would go and just managed to touch it, but didn't hazard to pick it up. Standing next to the table, I pushed it over to him.

A wooden ladle, decorated with a red and black flower motif, literally stood upright in the creamy thickness of its aromatic content.

"I could've told you that from the start," he declared as he ladled himself three brimming scoops. "Of course he wasn't going to admit to a vile crime like this, no one would. Trust me, as a writer, I can penetrate the criminal mind by the force of my imagination. You should confront him with some incontrovertible piece of evidence, push him to the wall and then he'll confess."

People love to give advice to detectives. Detection is like soccer. Everyone knows how to coach a soccer team.

"Would you like a shot of vodka?"

The playwright had realized that I wasn't paying attention to his musings and changed the subject. Indeed, I was concentrating on the rustle Sergei was making as he polished the floors somewhere in the depths of the playwright's apartment. The sound was getting closer.

I wanted to have another talk with him, but I thought maybe I should wait until I heard from Nastya. I grinned as I thought of Rubashkin, the king of stolen ZIMs.

"So you do want a shot, after all," the playwright exclaimed, mistaking my grin for assent and grabbing the crystal decanter off the table.

I shook my head. "No, none for me, please."

This time the vodka was tinged with purple, having been steeped in tiny wild blueberries.

"Are you sure? One shot? It's very good."

"I can't," I said. "I'm on duty."

"Well, you're making a huge mistake. It happens to be the elixir of life, the dew of the soul, so to speak. It can cure you of a variety of ailments, physical as well as mental, if you take it in moderation, as I do."

He poured a shot for himself.

"Know what they call it in Sweden? Aquavit. Which means living water in Swedish. A high-ranking party official told me that. He served as our ambassador to Sweden for five years. You should have heard some of his stories about the Swedes. Especially their women. Apparently they have no shame. They've got bathhouses like ours, except they're all in there naked together, taking the steam. Personally, I'm not surprised. The West is decadent."

He winked at me, drank and poured himself another shot. A few berries escaped the narrow silver neck of the decanter into his shot glass.

"There we go," he said, smacking his lips and exhaling. "You know what the French say? Appetite comes with eating. What do they know, the frog-eating wimps? Appetite comes with drinking."

Whether or not it was indeed the vodka that had stimulated it, the playwright's appetite was prodigious. He garnished his soup with finely chopped dill and green scallions and began to eat.

I swallowed hard, turning away. The silence in the room was interrupted only by Korenev's methodical slurping and the sound of Sergei's floor brush in the next room.

"The soup came out exceptionally well today," Korenev declared contentedly and shouted to the kitchen door: "I'm ready for the main course, Zinaida, my dear."

A few minutes later, the scowling Zinaida brought out a silver serving dish. Korenev and I were refracted on its polished cover into ugly dwarves with balloon-like heads and tiny bodies.

Zinaida placed the serving dish on the table and lifted its cover, revealing a hunk of boiled beef clinging to a juicy marrow bone that looked like the barrel of a cannon pointing directly at Korenev. Two boiled potatoes and a fresh tomato resembled oversize yellow and red cannonballs at the base of the cannon. The sides of the cannonballs glistened with amber-yellow sunflower oil and were speckled with tiny pieces of green scallions.

"It's a simple country dish," Korenev observed, despite the fact that a tomato and green scallions were unheard-of delicacies in the dead of winter. "No matter how high you fly, you must never forget your roots. What am I, come to think of it? A famous playwright, a laureate, a literary official enjoying access to the highest levels of government in our country? Yes, it's all undeniably true. But underneath it all I remain a humble peasant, a country bumpkin, salt of the earth. I never for a moment lose sight of where I come from. You shouldn't either."

While cutting the beef and mashing the potatoes into a mixture of beef juice and oil, he told me about his life in a village and what tasty, honest dishes his mother used to make for him when he was a boy.

"There is nothing better than a wholesome country meal. And I've tasted it all: the rotten eggs Chinamen eat, the frog legs the French love, the noodles with ketchup at the best restaurant in Rome, where our Italian comrades took us during their party congress, all of it."

Feeling the emptiness in the pit of my stomach, I resolved to stop in at the smoke-filled dive at the corner of Sretenka and the Boulevard Ring, where they serve deep-fried Uzbek *bureks*. I liked the place but I rarely got to go there for lunch, given Lenny's keen interest in the pretty waitress at the Petrovka restaurant. At the *burek* place, on the other hand, two Central Asian men alternated behind the counter and the only female on staff, a middle-aged cashier, was a careworn hag, embittered by the constant struggle with clients who were forever trying to smuggle alcohol to the grimy oilskin-topped tables.

The telephone began to ring in the next room and continued ringing for a long time.

Korenev looked up from his plate and shouted:

"Couldn't one of you pick it up? Zinaida? Sergei? Tell them I can't come to the phone and I'll call them back, whoever it is. Unless it's someone important."

After a few more rings, Zinaida finally came out of the kitchen and, wiping her hands on her uniform apron, answered the phone with an irritated "What?" She listened and then, without another word either into the phone or to us, came into the dining room. The long cord trailed behind her.

"Who is it?"

Annoyed, Korenev began to wipe his mouth and hands on his napkin.

"I told you I didn't want to be disturbed," he told Zinaida.

"It's for him."

She shoved the receiver into my hand, giving me a look that suggested that by getting a call I had acquired a bitter personal enemy.

"For me?" I asked idiotically. "I'm not expecting any calls here. Hello?"

There was static on the line. I couldn't make out anything and shouted into the thicket of crackling noises. "Lieutenant Matyushkin speaking. Who's this?"

A hoarse, constrained voice come into my ear. I didn't recognize it at first and only gradually, as it went on, did I realize it was Lenny.

"Bad news, Pavel," he croaked at the other end. "Very bad news."

"What happened?"

I picked up the telephone and carried it to the window, as far as the cord would reach. Outside, kids big and small were spinning around the skating oval like spots of bright colors in a kaleidoscope. Tykes barely big enough to walk held on to the rink's wooden fence or to their parents; figure skaters in pink skirts glided through the middle effortlessly, like elves; and teenagers swooped in and out of the crowd, showing off their hockey skills. On the sanded paths of the park, mothers in fur coats pushed strollers, and a team of cross-country skiers in identical red outfits raced along the far wall. The rays of the bright wintry sun shone into my eyes through Korenev's curtainless windows.

"What happened?" Korenev asked anxiously in the background. "Who is it?"

"Another murder," Lenny said. "The same as before. Another kid."

Lenny's voice was struggling through the noise on the line. Two women were heard discussing something amusing, interrupting each other and laughing. Sergei was in the next room now, on the other side of the wall, polishing the parquetry with furious energy. I jerked my head toward the double French doors.

"Ask him to stop for a moment," I said to Korenev. "I've got a bad connection."

The rustling ceased and I was able to hear Lenny a little better.

"A boy this time. Also strangled. A communal apartment, neighbors out, a kid staying at home all by himself. His mom found him. I'll wait for you here."

Lenny dictated the address and hung up.

"I have to go," I said, taking the phone back to the table.

"Was it another murder?" Korenev asked.

He had taken a surreptitious bite of his boiled meat and had to speak with his mouth full, looking guilty and trying to swallow his food quickly.

I nodded.

"Who is it this time?"

"Another kid," I replied. "A schoolboy."

"Another kid?" Korenev exclaimed, pulling his napkin off. "It's outrageous. We obviously have got a gang of murderers operating in the city. We've gotta catch them."

"We're doing our best," I said.

"I'm going with you. I'll be ready in a moment."

He leapt out of his armchair and headed for the living room.

"I don't think you can come with me," I said firmly. "Only police and medical personnel are allowed at the crime scene. And, to be honest, there is nothing for you to do there."

"What do you mean nothing for me to do there? You've failed to do your job and I'm sure you can use a fresh pair of eyes. Very likely you're missing some important clue that a new person might notice."

"I'm sure you're right," I said, struggling to keep my temper. "But all the same you can't come with me."

"Fine," Korenev agreed suddenly. "I'm sorry, detective. It's such a terrible crime, my indignation got the better of me. But you must keep me informed about every detail of this investigation. I insist: every detail. And I don't want you to spend another minute on my car, do you hear? Not until you've found the murderer."

By the time I got to the apartment, the Forensics and Crime Scene people were still hard at work, but Gordeyev and Tumakov were gone. The body of the victim, fourth-grade student Dima Sadykov, had been taken away – I had seen the ambulance depart, waddling on the uneven asphalt of the courtyard like an awkward pachyderm, without the usual lights blazing and sirens blasting.

The boy's parents and nineteen year-old sister sat on unpainted wooden stools in the communal kitchen. The mother was weeping silently, the father sat next to her, staring at this huge hands. Half moons of dirt fringed his chipped fingernails.

The boy's sister gave us a reproachful look.

There was no more for me to do there than there would have been for the playwright Korenev. Lenny and I left almost as soon as I arrived. Lenny was contrite and quiet all the way back to headquarters. Even his driving improved. He obeyed the speed limit and braked for vehicles merging from side streets. I talked about Korenev, complained about him trying to stick his nose into our investigation and avoided any mention of Grushnikov.

I didn't think Lenny was paying attention to what I was saying. He fixed his brooding stare on the road, the surface of which had started to freeze again after our all-too-short thaw. But as we got closer to Petrovka he muttered under his breath:

"Like an old woman."

I took it as a reference to the nosy playwright.

There was a long line for the elevator on the ground floor. After a few minutes Lenny gave up and we took the stairs. Arriving out of breath, we discovered that an emergency meeting of the entire department had been called, and that we were late.

"Where the devil have you been?" the Boss growled once Marina had hustled us into his office and we tiptoed in, trying not to attract attention.

The situation was easy to assess. The Boss's accent was heavy and a civilian jacket hung like a potato sack around his square shoulders.

Our entire department had been gathered around the conference table. It was covered with green baize and placed at a right angle to Budyonny's desk. The Boss's desk stood on an elevated platform, so that he hovered over meetings, dwarfing other participants.

"We've gotta check the alibi of everyone who was in any way linked to Tanya Drozdova's murder," he said, repeating what he had been saying as we entered and found two vacant seats in the back. "Matyushkin, you've been talking to the doctor. Your job is to find out what he and Tanya's other neighbors did this afternoon. Including the girl's mother, just in case. But none of that psychiatry nonsense, please."

"Yes, sir," I replied.

"Connections between the two victims will be our next line of inquiry. Both kids seem to have known their killer. We'll look for adults who could have known them both – relatives, family friends, neighbors, teachers, summer camp counselors, doctors, librarians, athletic coaches, anyone."

He added two more detectives, Gromovsky and Mikhailov, to our team and went on with distributing assignments to others. The Boss was taking control of the investigation from Gordeyev, who was seated next to him looking sick to his stomach.

It was clear, too, that I was now considered a full member of the team. I would have felt better to be rid of the playwright and his shifty driver, had it not been at the price of another kid being killed.

"What about Grushnikov?" Lenny asked suddenly.

Budyonny stared at him.

"What about him?" he asked. "We're holding the wrong man. He'll have to be let go."

"Then it doesn't matter that he had sexual relations with an eleven-year-old?" Lenny persisted.

Lenny spoke reluctantly. He didn't like to contradict the Boss, and the fact that the eyes of the entire department were fixed on him made him uncomfortable. But he felt he had to speak out.

"Well," Budyonny said. "Your own partner Lieutenant Matyushkin doesn't think Grushnikov is guilty. Perhaps you should have a chat with Dr. Lazius. You might change your mind, too."

Lenny gave me a venomous look, as though I had betrayed our partnership and friendship and was personally responsible for the gym teacher's imminent release.

"But I don't want to hear any more crap about psychiatry," the Boss added. "I want Grushnikov detained for a few more days, until we check everyone's alibi, and then let go."

"That's just great." Lenny grimaced as though in physical pain. "We'll send him back to molest his students and go on hikes with third graders. Kids who've got no one to protect them from a sexual pervert. Just great. Well, he's not a murderer, just a rapist and a child molester. Perhaps we should give him some kind of a medal."

"Of course Urumov doesn't want to see Grushnikov go free," Tumakov unexpectedly broke in. "Because if the gym teacher is not guilty, Urumov will have to go on his hands and knees to his boss at the boarding school."

Budyonny had no idea what Valera was talking about.

"Whose boss?" he asked, drilling Tumakov with hooded eyes. "Why on hands and knees? What are you talking about?"

"The principal of the boarding school," Tumakov explained. "Urumov has been questioning her teachers and students behind her back and against her explicit orders. She's certain to lodge a complaint."

"Let her go to hell," Lenny said. "All the more so if Grushnikov goes free."

"Brilliant," Tumakov said sarcastically. "She's already told me she's going to write a formal letter to the City Party Organization. She's well-connected and can cause us a lot of trouble."

Ordinarily, Budyonny feared nothing more than words like "well-connected," "formal letter" and "City Party Organization." But this time it was different for the Boss, too.

"Who cares?" he shouted. "Is this the time to worry about such nonsense? And by the way, Tumakov, I have a special assignment for you."

Tumakov snapped to attention.

"You and me will be checking out all known sex offenders. We'll dig up all sexual crime cases involving children from the past ten years or more – rapists, child molesters, pedophiles and other perverts all around the country. We'll make sure we know where they were when those two kids were murdered."

Next to me Lenny gasped. He would've loved nothing more than to get that assignment. Since attacking Grushnikov, he had been itching to do more violence to a child molester. Budyonny knew Lenny well and it was the main reason why he had chosen Tumakov for the job.

"And unless we find something concrete on Grushnikov, we'll have to let him go," Budyonny concluded, shifting his gaze to Lenny. "And now, comrades, you've got your work cut out for you. Get on with it."

TWELVE

The following morning, winter returned with a vengeance, and nature emptied onto the city all the biting cold and bone-chilling wind it was capable of, as if trying to counterbalance our short-lived breath of spring.

Dr. Lazius's clinic was officially called The State Mental Health Research Institute for Workers and Peasants. Situated just inside the northwestern boundary of the city, its five-story glass-and-concrete cube loomed among hundred-year-old pines like the first colossal building block of some future pyramid, dropped there from an alien space ship. The impression was confirmed by the fact that it wasn't built with square walls, but, thanks to some newfangled modernist whimsy, had an angular twist.

Budyonny had turned down my request for a driver, claiming they were busy doing various errands. The suburban train spewed me out onto a deserted, ice-encrusted platform two stops from the Riga Railway Station. Giving me a short, derisive whistle, it pulled away and soon dissolved into the white mist, in the direction of snow-bound suburban dachas. The ancient bus idling by the padlocked station house, waiting for arriving passengers, generated barely enough warmth to keep the thoroughly swaddled driver from freezing to death behind the wheel. I was happy when the short, gut-wrenching ride at last came to an end. I exited by the side of the road, at the head of a footpath running through a pine forest.

The two-kilometer walk uphill warmed me up and had the added benefit of clearing my head. The air was crisp and the melted and refrozen crust on the snow glistened with the reflected sunshine. A service road ran parallel to the path, its paved surface plowed and sanded. As I walked, I heard two or three trucks pass by, their engines laboring and their gray sides flickering between the purple tree trunks.

The interior of the cube was restrained and functional, with antiseptic white walls and hallways that were silent, uncluttered and empty. The elevator shuttled silently between floors, opening and closing its automatic doors with a soothing pneumatic sound.

Checking the alibis for Lazius and his wife was a formality that took no more than five minutes. The doctor's schedule was set and events on it were repeated day after day without many variations. He saw patients, lectured, reviewed his students' work and wrote articles in his study. His secretary kept a log in which the hours of the day were divided into six ten-minute periods, and each was filled with notes written in the doctor's neat, economical hand.

Other employees, including Nadezhda Lazius, were also required to log their activities, albeit not in such minute detail. It was Dr. Lazius's clinic, and his Teutonic thoroughness and attention to detail were evident in the way it was run.

Having finished with my task, I knocked on the door of the doctor's office. His secretary, squirreled away behind a tiny desk in the anteroom, was awe-struck.

"Do you have an appointment?" she exclaimed in a theatrical show of horror. "The doctor doesn't like to be disturbed!"

But I felt it would be impolite to come to the clinic without seeing Lazius, or at least announcing my presence. He was reading an article in a foreign journal, resting an elbow on a hard-bound copy of an English-German dictionary. He frowned when he saw me, resenting the interruption.

"I didn't expect to see you again, Lieutenant."

He gave me a look that told me he had not forgotten my indiscretion last time we met.

"I had to check your whereabouts yesterday afternoon," I explained.

"Why is that?" he asked.

"We have our reasons," I replied.

"I have already told your colleagues that I'm the easiest person in Moscow to track. All my appointments are entered in my agenda well ahead of time, and my movements during the day are all accounted for, as I keep one appointment after the other. Everything is recorded and documented."

I nodded.

"Yes, I saw your appointment book and your schedule."

"Then you know that I'm a very busy man. I have been blessed with many things: I have the best job in the world, I enjoy international renown and respect of my colleagues and students, I have a beautiful young wife whom I adore and who loves me back, I'm raising two healthy, smart, athletic boys, I own a car and have a comfortable apartment. I'm in peak mental and physical condition. But when it comes to time, I'm a pauper."

He sighed.

"You know, Lieutenant, people who have no money are forced to live on a strict budget. I similarly have to be absolutely without pity in budgeting my time."

He stopped short, as though struck by a sudden thought:

"Wait a minute. If you're checking my alibi, there must have been another murder?"

"I can't talk about it," I said.

Behind their gold-framed lenses, the doctor's eyes lost their spark and for a second it was as though he was looking inward, his face suddenly expressionless, dull and aged. But then he shook his head and a moment later he was his usual self once more.

"Well, for the sake of argument, Lieutenant, let's assume there has been another murder. It goes to show how wrong I was when I ventured onto unfamiliar ground, discussing Grushnikov as though he was Tanya Drozdova's murderer. You must be quite relieved that I turned down your rash offer to testify at his trial. Which is not even going to happen now. I assume there's nothing left for us to discuss, since even the police ought to acknowledge that he has a strong alibi for the second murder."

It was time to change the subject.

"Dr. Lazius, I must apologize to you for what happened last time," I said.

The doctor frowned. "I'm not sure I know what you're talking about," he said, but the way he said it I knew he understood the reference only too well.

"You were absolutely right, Doctor. I had been misled by gossip and it was a mistake on my part to have taken it at face value without thoroughly checking it first."

"Oh, that," he said, dismissing my explanations with an airy wave of his hand. "I haven't given it a second thought. I ignore hearsay as a matter of principle. But, since we're on the subject of suicide, I hear you've been expressing concern about Irina Drozdova."

"Yes, and I would like to ask your professional opinion about her," I said, wondering how he knew that, since I hadn't shared my concerns with anybody but Irina and Lenny.

"I hope she isn't on your list of suspects, God forbid?"

"Of course not. She's been under a severe strain and she doesn't seem to have anyone she can be with."

Lazius took a long time to reply, which I now realized was his trademark. He leaned back in his soft office chair and raised his eyes to the ceiling. Unlike his cramped workspace at home, here he had a large office that was almost cubical in shape and contained no furniture except for a large desk and two chairs. Like the building, the desk was ultra-modernist in design, consisting of two bent and twisted aluminum tubes supporting a slab of thick green glass. There were no bookshelves and no books, and the walls, pristine in their whiteness, were hung with three almost abstract lithographs: three splotches of primary colors that only with considerable difficulty could be identified as female nudes. But the real artwork in the office was the window, or rather an entire wall offering a breathtaking top-floor view: a dark-green ocean of gently undulating pine trees, its waves cresting in white puffs of snow, a bend in the river locked beneath a black sheet of ice and the city on the opposite bank silhouetted by the sun, its smokestacks belching black and grey streams into the blue sky.

"It's a nice view," Dr. Lazius commented. "But I find it distracting. It sometimes keeps me from focusing on my work."

He pressed a button on his desk and a Venetian blind came rattling down from the ceiling. The ocean and city disappeared behind plastic slats.

"I'm not worried about Irina Drozdova in the least," the doctor said when the blind had stopped. "It's natural that she should be depressed. She's lived through a major shock. Grief needs time to settle down. Her recovery will be slow. But, in my opinion, she's moving along nicely. I have prescribed her some chloral hydrate to help her sleep. She shouldn't take it too often, and in minimal doses. It's a dangerous drug. Yes, it would have been better if she had a friend with whom she could talk, but in any case I'm sure she's going to be fine."

He paused.

"Drozdova has a strong psychological makeup. I mean the older one, the mother. The daughter was a very different matter."

"Do you mean Tanya Drozdova?" I asked.

Lazius nodded.

"The girl had a rare form of sexual obsession. In layman's terms, she had a premature interest in sex which was, of course, abnormal in a girl her age. She was attracted to much older boys at school. Naturally, she sensed that it wasn't acceptable. I don't believe she ever confided in any of her friends."

"I'm sorry, doctor," I said, opening my notebook. "How did you happen to come by this information?"

"I examined her."

I stared.

"Do you mean her mother asked you to examine her?"

Lazius hesitated briefly and shook his head.

"Not exactly," he said. "Actually, she didn't at all. It was her grandmother, not long before she died, who asked me for a professional opinion. She had noticed that something wasn't quite right with her granddaughter. She had seen her grow secretive and nervous, and she wanted me to get to the bottom of it."

"I thought sexual deviancy wasn't your specialty," I said.

"It was a special case. The grandmother wanted it to be done discreetly, because the girl's mother was refusing to acknowledge it. Mothers are often incapable of looking at their children objectively, and thus themselves become part of the problem. She and the grandmother had argued about it."

"So, Tanya's grandmother asked you to examine her and you agreed. Is that correct?"

"I was glad to oblige because, quite frankly, I found it to be an interesting case. I had observed strange behavioral patterns in the girl."

"Irina Drozdova knew nothing about it?"

"God forbid, Lieutenant."

"Why didn't you tell us this when Tanya was killed."

Lazius sighed.

"You know perfectly well why. I didn't want the mother to know that I had examined her daughter and that her own late mother had asked me to do so. It would have been cruel, given the circumstances."

"I understand why you wouldn't have wanted to make this information public," I insisted. "What I'm asking you is why you didn't tell it to the police?"

Lazius grinned.

"You would have had to check my story with her."

"Never mind what we would have done. You realize that this information is critical to the course of the investigation, don't you?"

"It is nothing of the sort, Lieutenant. Whether or not the girl had a precocious interest in sex, it's still a vile crime. It was committed by a maniac, not a normal person, even if we assume that the girl had flirted with her murderer. She was eleven years old, for God's sake. And now that there has been a second murder—"

He let the sentence hang.

He was right, but I wasn't about to give up.

"Forget the second murder." I said, raising my voice. "You concealed important information from the police. It's a serious offense."

"Please, lieutenant, are you going to charge me with obstruction of justice? I have just told you all this myself, without any prompting on your part. Before, you seemed to have a suspect in custody and I didn't think this information would matter. By the way, now that Grushnikov is no longer a suspect, do you have anybody else in mind? Assuming you're satisfied with our alibis. I mean my wife's and mine."

I shrugged. Lazius gave me an ironic smile.

"I assume we're about to see the triumphal return of Comrade Grushnikov to our apartment, fully exonerated and cleared of all charges. Splendid. We don't want to convict an innocent man and we're going to welcome him with open arms. But to get back to the original subject. I do not for a moment believe that Irina Drozdova is capable of taking her own life. In such matters, at least, you can fully rely on my judgment. Suicides is something I know a lot about."

He rose from his desk, indicating that our meeting had come to an end.

Outside, the cold air – smelling of pine sap and snow – filled my lungs. But my meeting with Dr. Lazius had left a bitter taste in my mouth, and now the brilliant December day had lost its luster.

Walking back to the bus stop, I went over our conversation, reviewing every detail. So he had examined Tanya Drozdova, presumably at the request of her grandmother, who was no longer around to confirm or deny it. That would have certainly made him a suspect had we known about it from the start. The suspicion would have been strengthened if he had tried, as he did during our previous meeting, to help me build a case against Grushnikov. But after the second murder, Lazius felt it was safe to tell me about his examination of Tanya. Had he not done so, and had we found out about it from someone else, Lazius could have been charged with concealing information.

He was a clever man, Dr. Lazius.

I stopped at home to change out of the heavy felt boots and rubber galoshes I had worn for the trip to Dr. Lazius's clinic. I was in no hurry to get to 1st Kolobovsky, where I still had to check Baba Dasha's and Irina Drozdova's whereabouts on the previous afternoon, and so I decided to pay a brief visit to Korenev first. True, the Boss had put me back on the murder case, but I knew that if I didn't show up at the playwright's after leaving his apartment so abruptly the day before, he would be back on the phone with Budyonny, complaining about me.

Dealing with Korenev, and navigating between him and the Boss, was like taking an accelerated course in politics and diplomacy.

I took a shortcut past the playground at the far end of my courtyard, which was turned into a skating rink every November, once the temperature fell below freezing and our perpetually tipsy handyman, Uncle Mitya Borisov, doused it with a garden hose. Every November I promised myself to get my old hockey skates from the storage bin on my balcony and take a couple of spins before work. For one reason or another, there never was enough time.

A few kids were chasing the puck around the rink, but it wasn't the game that drew my attention. The small boy watching from the sidelines was Tosya's kid brother. He was even smaller than I had recalled, and standing on his tiptoes he could just keep his eyes above the fence boards. It was a cold day and there was also a wicked wind whipping around the corner of our apartment building. Still, the boy kept watching the game, mesmerized, sniffling now and again and wiping his nose with the back of his hand.

I stood next to him for a few minutes. He gave me a quick look, checking me out, and went back to watching the game. The players stopped playing and started to argue. There were little kids on one side and a few older ones on the other, and the argument divided them along age lines.

"What's the score?" I asked Tosya's brother.

"That's the thing, there is no score," he replied readily, as though he had been waiting for me to ask. "Those big lugs never pass. My friends were playing, and then the big guys came and said they wanted to play too, and now they just pass to each other and ignore them."

His face, red from the cold, turned even redder with indignation.

I nodded.

"I know you," I said. "I saw you talking to Tosya."

"Maybe," the kid replied. "Who's Tosya?"

"What's your name?" I asked.

"And what's yours?"

He was a cagey kid.

"Pavel Matyushkin," I said.

"Mine's Sevka."

"Are you Tosya's brother?"

"Are you?"

"Me? I don't think so."

The game resumed. Sevka put an end to our conversation abruptly and watched it intently. Just as he had said, the older kids kept passing the puck to each other, frustrating their opponents as well as Sevka. But then one of his friends finally managed to intercept a pass and began skating circles around the older teenagers. When two of them cornered him, he pushed the puck to a friend, who turned out to be an even better skater. Stopping on a dime and spraying snow into the faces of his pursuers, he found an opening between them, banked the puck off the back wall, passing it to himself through a thicket of legs, jumped over a stick the other one had thrown in his path and was back on open ice in a split second.

"Great play," Sevka yelled. "That's the way, Andrei!"

His clapping was muffled by the mittens, and his attempt to whistle fizzled out, but his enthusiasm knew no bounds.

Meanwhile, one of the bigger boys pushed the kid off the puck and regained possession. Another argument ensued, about whether or not it had been a legal check. Two figure skaters in pink skirts who had been practicing jumps near the back wall joined in. They had a different complaint, alleging that the hockey game took up the entire rink, leaving them only a small corner of the ice, where it was all broken up and uneven. The boys, big and small, now made a united front against the girls.

"You should stop them before they start fighting," little Sevka said to me.

"Why should I?" I asked.

"Aren't you a policeman?"

I winked at him.

"How did you know?"

"Everybody knows everything about everybody else around here," he replied. "Are you the kind of cop who rides motorcycles?"

"No," I said. "I'm a detective."

"Oh, I see. You've got a desk job," Sevka said, disappointed. "It's no fun. You don't even wear a uniform."

"Well," I said trying to salvage my crumbling reputation, "I've been thinking of buying a motorcycle."

Sevka was instantly interested.

"Which one? An Izh? You should get a Java. Javas are way better, even though they're made in Czechoslovakia."

"No," I said. "A Zundapp."

"Never heard of it," Sevka said, disappointed once more.

"It's a war-booty model," I said. "Made in Germany. Nazi Germany no less. And it comes with a side-car."

I knew that was going to impress him.

"A Nazi bike?" he exclaimed, now full of admiration. "With a sidecar? Now that's really cool. Are you really going to get it?"

"I really am, if I put together enough money to pay for it," I said. "See, there are some things even you don't know about me."

"That's true," he conceded. "Will you give me a ride when you get it? But not in the sidecar."

"I will," I said, thinking that I would also love to take his older sister along. "Certainly not in the sidecar. You'll ride in the back seat and we'll put your sister in the side car."

"My sister?" the boy said, frowning. "I haven't got one. You mean my mom?"

"Wait a minute," I said, my jaw dropping. "Your mom?"

Sevka nodded.

"Only she's embarrassed about me."

"Embarrassed of you?" I asked, shaking my head incredulously. I was still trying to process this new information. "Why should she be embarrassed about you?"

"I mean she loves me and all that," Sevka replied thoughtfully. "But she's embarrassed that she had me. I mean because she had me without a normal father."

Sevka cast an eye on the rink, where the kids were playing hockey again and the two figure skaters had resumed their practice jumps.

"If you want to ask her out and give her a ride in your sidecar," Sevka went on, "or if you're thinking of taking her to the movies, you should know that she'll never go with you. Not in a million years."

"Oh, yeah?" I said. "What makes you think I want to take her to the movies?"

"Because other guys have tried. But she turns them all down. 'Once burned, twice careful,' she says."

He sighed.

"And this way we've got nobody in the whole wide world, just me and her. No other relatives. That's because mom grew up in an orphanage. All she's got are her friends, the ones she grew up with. It's not enough, right?"

Oh, the orphanage, I said to myself. That's why she's so good with her fists. If you learn anything growing up at the orphanage, it is how to take care of yourself, and that goes for boys and girls equally. I had had plenty of dealings with kids from orphanages in my line of work. Few stick to the straight and narrow once they get out into the real world, and plenty of them come into contact with Criminal Investigations.

"She has just one friend at work," Sevka went on. He turned out to be a lot more talkative than he had seemed at first. "Mom is a bookkeeper at the Tryokhgorka Textile Plant. A senior bookkeeper, actually."

I raised my eyebrows to show how impressed I was.

"A senior bookkeeper, no less?" I said admiringly. "That's nothing to sneeze at."

THIRTEEN

The concierge in the playwright's building had become used to me and waved me through without asking any questions. But coming in ahead of me, a thickset, grey-haired man wearing a full-length wool overcoat over a pair of pajama bottoms, for whom I had politely held the door, suddenly turned around and said, "Who's this comrade, Dusya? I don't recall seeing him."

"It's alright, Comrade Major General," the concierge replied deferentially. "I know him. He's going to apartment No. 64."

They were talking about me as though I wasn't there.

"You must always ask, Dusya," the man declared. "When I go visit my old squadron at the Bykovo airfield, all the sentries know me, because I used to be the base commander there. Nevertheless, I always insist they ask to see my papers. If they don't, I report them to their superiors and there's hell to pay."

"You've been retired how many years now?" the concierge asked, giggling. She didn't seem to take his lecture to heart.

"It's irrelevant, my dear Dusya. Rules are rules. Besides, I'm pretty angry with that Korenev fellow."

The retired general turned around and glared at me.

"What was it this time?" the concierge asked.

"They kept me up all night," the old man replied while still glaring at me. "They made so much noise I didn't sleep a wink, even though I'm deaf in one ear. German antiaircraft guns, you know."

"Oh, my," said Dusya. "What were they up to?"

"Fighting, what else?"

I had been waiting for the elevator. It had finally come down, but all of a sudden I was in no hurry to get in.

"Who's there to fight with? That driver of his got his own place. He was a fresh one, to be sure. Now it's just Zinaida, his old domestic, who's living there with him. Though I'll give it to you, she's a tough cookie."

"Well, I have no idea who the woman was. All I know is that her language would've made the Siberian gunner on my old Pe-8 blush like a schoolgirl."

Scandalized, Dusya threw her arms up and then covered her mouth with the palm of her hand, a gesture that meant to express both outrage and disbelief.

"Oh my," she exclaimed. "What on earth were they fighting about?"

Her curiosity aroused, she was settling in for a long bout of gossip. But the general took an energetic stride toward the elevator and, turning his head, said over his shoulder, "Some car or something."

He and I rode the elevator in silence. He got off one floor below the playwright's.

There was a lot to think about in that exchange, and if I were ever called upon to investigate the disappearance of the playwright's ZIM again, I would certainly give it plenty of thought. Be that as it may, now I was on my way to see Korenev strictly as a social visit, nothing more.

Little did I know what I was in for.

One day when I was a teenager, my class went on a school trip along the Moscow-Volga River canal.

We gathered at dawn at the Northern River Terminal, two dozen boys in blue shorts and white shirts and the same number of girls in blue skirts and white blouses, all with blood-red Young Pioneer scarves tied around our scrawny necks. We lined up in front of the gleaming *Josef Stalin* paddleboat while our teachers took the head count and instructed us for the fifteenth time on the rules of conduct on board. The early morning, the fresh air, and the excitement of the boat ride made us all giddy. For us, growing up in postwar poverty, the trip was the highlight of the year. Despite the teachers' warnings and threats of punishment, we ran around, played catch, and jostled each other on all three decks and the stairs.

Later, when the sun rose above the red and yellow crowns of trees lining the eastern shore, and the boat was held up at a lock, slowly churning its enormous wheels and puffing soot into the October sky, the girls sang and the boys, tired out by the running, sat around admiring the bronze caravels crowning the ornate lock towers. By lunchtime we were all starving.

We had been told to pack our own picnic lunches, but I couldn't bring myself to ask Mother to make me a sandwich. As it was, getting from one payday to the next without borrowing a thirty from neighbors was a constant struggle, and there was never any extra food lying around the house.

In our neighborhood, where, after the war, we were given a room in a makeshift clapboard tenement, many families were in the same situation. They had lost fathers and older brothers and came back after being evacuated to the East and South along with their factories and offices to find their old apartments either bombed out or requisitioned by the state. They lived just like us, hand to mouth. For the picnic, their kids had only a hard-boiled egg, a pear or a potato. But some, like me, brought nothing at all.

Yet our neighborhood was no longer uniformly poor or working class. Soon after the war, luxury apartment buildings began to go up on vacant lots on the other side of the train tracks. We called them Generals' Houses, because they had spacious apartments with high ceilings and luxurious entranceways watched over by stone-faced doormen. You couldn't just walk into one of them to warm up in winter and smoke a cigarette on their marble staircases.

Kids from the Generals' Houses attended our school, shared desks with us and didn't seem very different – except their mothers could afford to make proper white bread sandwiches for their picnic, spread with real butter and topped with sausage and cheese. They were our friends and would have gladly shared their food with us, except we would never ask. Our motto in those days was Poor but Proud.

Our homeroom teacher Anna Ilyinishna understood these dynamics better than anyone, since she grew up in our neighborhood and still lived there. She had used her own money to buy some inexpensive sausage and cheese and a couple of loaves of black bread.

It was the height of Indian Summer, and, after a cool, frosty morning, the day grew warm and the sun began to bake. We settled in on the top deck. The boys debated the displacement of various barges we encountered along the way and the throughput of the steel frame bridge carrying the Dmitrov Highway from one bank of the canal to the other. The girls admired the sun-drenched foliage of the woods, which stood so close to the shores of the narrow canal, it seemed like the *Stalin's* paddles would clip the longer branches of the trees.

The deck was crowded. Anna Ilyinishna was slicing bread and sausage to make sandwiches. She pretended to give them out as seconds, but of course her main customers were those of us who had come empty-handed.

The sausage went quickly, but there was still some cheese left over.

"Could you go down to the lower deck," Anna Ilyinishna asked Sveta Polovtseva, a straight A student who had been helping her make sandwiches. "There should be another loaf in my bag down there."

I had a crush on Sveta Polovtseva. She lived in the newest and best of the Generals' Houses and her dad was a real general, the hero commander of a tank division that took Berlin. Sveta's mother was dead and she lived with her father and a stepmother, with whom the general had two small boys, Sveta's half-brothers. Sveta's stepmother was so young, she could pass for her older sister. They were both radiant, fragrant and beautiful.

My crush on Sveta was purely theoretical. I attended classes in the evening and didn't even run into her at school on most days. But I had high hopes for the class trip and had spent the morning gathering up the courage to talk to her. I was also hoping we would have a shipwreck or run into a real-life spy, so that I could demonstrate my strength and courage by saving her from danger.

When, ten minutes later, Anna Ilyinishna noticed that Sveta had not come back up, I promptly volunteered to go down to look for her.

The glassed-in aft-cabin on the lower deck was empty. I glanced into the fore-cabin where we had piled up our knapsacks on the floor and wooden benches and where Anna Ilyinishna's knitted bag hung from a hook on the wall. The loaf of bread was gone, but Sveta was nowhere to be seen.

Bewildered, I started up again and then heard a throaty call coming from somewhere in the direction of the stern. I stopped and listened. The call was repeated once and then again a few seconds later. It was a strange sound, plaintive, aggressive and demanding all at the same time.

The engine rumbled steadily on and the ship swayed up and down on the calm waters of the canal as it glided forward.

I walked behind the cabin and stopped. It took me a few minutes to figure out what was happening. Sveta stood by the banister, between two red and white lifesavers with the words *Josef Stalin* emblazoned along their circumferences in gold letters. A small seagull was making concentric, swiftly tightening circles around her head. The bird assaulted Sveta now from the left, now from the right, pecking at her and uttering the harsh call I had heard on the stairs. Sveta kept her hands in front of her, shielding her face from the bird's razor-sharp beak. Her forearms were bleeding and tears ran down her cheeks. Every few seconds she would break off a piece of bread and toss it to her attacker. Catching it on the fly, the bird would swallow it greedily and be back assaulting her, pecking at her arms again and again, until it got a fresh portion.

I shooed the seagull away and dragged Sveta into the cabin, slamming the door behind us.

Even though I had come like a knight in shining armor to rescue her, nothing came of my crush on her. And not only because we inhabited different worlds, she being a general's daughter and me a poor kid from the wrong side of the tracks. That incident with the seagull made both of us embarrassed of each other, as if we had taken part in some shameful act. After that, whenever we ran into each other at school or in the street, she would turn away and pretend she didn't know me.

The distant memory flashed through my mind when the playwright placed me on the couch in his office, pushed back his armchair, cutting off my path of retreat, and began to interrogate me about the murders. Leaning forward, he hovered over me and flew virtual circles around my head, lobbing razor-sharp questions at me from every side. I defended myself as best I could, periodically tossing him a piece of information. It went down the bottomless maw of his curiosity, giving me a second of respite as he pondered it and filed it away inside his head. But it was never enough to keep him busy for long, and he was back at it almost immediately. Questions followed one another in quick succession, probing now this, now that angle of the investigation.

His armchair was large and heavy; it had a gilded frame, and its seat and back were upholstered in stamped pink and aquamarine leather.

He was as greedy and insatiable as the seagull. There was nothing about my work he didn't want to know – but when I, in my desperation, tried to turn the conversation to the loss of his ZIM, he would wag his finger and tell me to get back to the murders.

"Who's the murdered boy? Who are his parents? What do they do? What did his body look like? Who's in charge of the investigation? What are the names and ranks of other team members? What is Captain Gordeyev like? What is his theory about the murders? Do you agree with it? Do others? What does your boss think about it? How long has Urumov been on the force? Has there ever been a serial killer in the Soviet Union? How many school friends did Tanya Drozdova have? Who questioned them? Lieutenant Tumakov? How old is he? I just want to know how old he is, it's a simple question, Lieutenant. Is he married? Does he have any kids?

He would make the occasional mark in his notebook but that was more for show, since he never needed to consult his notes before asking another question. He absorbed information like a sponge and, when he suddenly changed the direction of his questioning, keeping me off balance exactly the way the seagull had by changing direction while attacking Sveta, returning to the subject he had dropped a few minutes before, he simply retrieved all the relevant details from his steel-trap memory.

In addition to the desk, the sofa and the armchair, his study contained a smaller end table supporting a black Underwood typewriter and numerous bookshelves, including one holding all forty-eight volumes of the Great Soviet Encyclopedia, along with its annual supplements. The vast surface of the playwright's desk was clear except for a stack of typewriter paper and a dozen carefully sharpened pencils, each with a pink eraser.

"What about Lieutenant Tumakov? Does he have a theory? I like his last name, Tumakov. It has a ring to it. What do you mean you don't know whether Lieutenant Tumakov has a theory. Don't you share your theories with each other? What if one of you is on the right track and others, instead of helping him, keep going off on tangents?"

"That is not how it works," I said. "Criminal Investigations is a government agency, not a detective agency run by Sherlock Holmes. We have a line of inquiry and everyone works on some aspect of it, based on his assignment from a senior officer."

Korenev kept on probing. When he wasn't asking about the investigation, he wanted to know everything about the personal and professional lives of my colleagues, and then we were back to discussing whether or not Grushnikov was still a suspect and, if not, who was.

"No suspects yet? What you need is a list of potentials. When you put one together, let me know who's on it. Also, what theories

Lieutenant Tumakov has about the case. I'm very interested in the progress of your investigation. I expect you here with a regular report."

"As far as your car—" I started to say, but Korenev grimaced as though he was suddenly afflicted with a toothache.

"I don't want to hear another word about my car," he declared. "Not until the killer is caught and brought to justice."

"That's what I was about to say," I said. "My boss wants me to assure you that the moment we catch the bastard, there will be a full team of detectives working on your case."

"We'll talk about it when the time comes, Lieutenant. Don't worry about it for now. Concentrate on the murders. I'm pretty sure the car will turn up one way or another."

Sergei was waiting for me by the front door. He seemed to always be on duty. His absence on the day the ZIM went missing was starting to seem like an aberration.

"Did you find that guy?" he asked in a conspiratorial whisper.

"Which guy?"

"You know. The one who wanted me to help him steal the car."

I was genuinely perplexed. So much had happened since our conversation by the metro station that his story about a mysterious guy from the Caucasus had completely slipped my mind.

I looked him in the eye. He was staring back at me insolently. It was a fabricated story and both he and I knew it, yet he still had the balls to ask me about it.

"Don't take me for a fool, Sergei," I said.

I changed back into my winter boots and put on my coat. He waited until I opened the front door before saying:

"Well, it's up to you. You'll find him when you decide you want to find the car."

I said nothing and went out, closing the door behind me.

I was used to being kept waiting outside the apartment on 1st Kolobovsky, and that was why I didn't rush to pull out the keys that I still carried on the bottom of my briefcase.

The light bulb had not yet been replaced, and I rang doorbells at random, still unable to read the names of the tenants next to them in the dim light on the landing.

As before, I was eventually rewarded for my patience. The door was opened for me after about ten minutes and I was greeted by Baba Dasha. Her gray hair was tangled and her eyes puffy with sleep.

"You woke me up," she said reproachfully, her mouth stretching in a massive yawn. "It's Thursday, my day off."

"Do you sleep during the day on your days off?" I asked.

"I've been working the night shift for thirty years, young man. I can only sleep in daytime."

"Were you here sleeping yesterday afternoon?"

"Yesterday was Wednesday. I slept till six and went to work."

"Was there anyone else at home?" I asked.

She eyed me suspiciously.

"Only the Drozdova woman. She's the only one left here. Not counting the doctor and his bunch."

"So, Irina Drozdova can confirm that you were in the apartment until six o'clock? Was she here the entire afternoon?"

"How would I know? I was asleep."

"Was she in when you woke up?"

"Why do you need to know?"

"It's my job to ask questions," I said sternly. "Yours is to answer them. Was she in or wasn't she?"

Baba Dasha shrugged.

"She got two weeks off from work. Bereavement leave they call it. So she's always at home during the day. Except in the evenings, when she goes out."

I was glad to hear that. Nice that she goes out to see people. At least she isn't sitting around an empty apartment chain-smoking and brooding. Dr. Lazius's assurances notwithstanding, I was still very worried about her.

"Where does she go?" I asked.

"How would I know? She doesn't report to me. All I know is she comes back all drenched and dries her clothes by the radiator in the hallway. They're hanging there when I come home in the morning."

"Is she at home now?"

Baba Dasha gave me a look as though she thought I was slow.

"How would I know? I was asleep when you came. What time is it, anyway?"

It was eight thirty. I knocked on Irina Drozdova's door, from which the seals had been removed two days before.

"By the way," I said. "Why did you tell me Dr. Lazius's first wife committed suicide? He says she died of a heart attack. He's quite certain about it."

Baba Dasha turned pale. She was suddenly very scared.

"Hush," she said, pressing a finger to her lips. "You never know who's listening around here."

I waited for another minute at Irina Drozdova's door and gave up.

"I'd like to know more about Dr. Lazius," I said.

"I don't know anything," she said quickly.

"How did you know about his wife's suicide then?" I asked. "Do you realize that you gave false evidence to a police officer? You could get into a pack of trouble."

"I never told you anything, young man. Not me, no sir."

I shook my head reproachfully and took out an official-looking notebook.

"Well, Comrade," I said. "Now, you're telling me an outright lie, and this is getting serious. I may have to take you in."

We were still standing in the hallway, not far from the front door and the armchair in which Irina Drozdova had sat chain-smoking on my previous visits. Even though it was no longer filled with cigarette smoke, the air was stuffy and oppressive, and the lighting was dim and bluish.

Baba Dasha hesitated, then took two quick steps toward me, getting so close I could smell her bad breath, the stale odor of sleep mixed with rotting teeth and yesterday's boiled cabbage.

"Sure he'd tell you she didn't kill herself," she said softly in my ear. "You shouldn't have mentioned it to him."

"Why not? Presumably he had nothing to do with her suicide."

"Oh, yeah? Then how come he married his good-looking assistant two months after his first wife died? Do you think she didn't know what was going on behind her back? She took those pills for sure, poor thing."

"How do you know that?"

"Everyone knows that. It's the truth, and you can't hide the truth from people."

It still sounded like unsubstantiated gossip.

"I don't believe it," I said. "There were other doctors involved. There was a coroner, and he could surely tell the difference between an overdose of sleeping pills and a heart attack."

Baba Dasha shook her head.

"They're all in cahoots. The coroner wrote whatever death certificate Dr. Lazius wanted him to write."

There were footsteps on the landing, and the jingling of the keys being hastily taken out.

Baba Dasha's nerves were on edge. She jumped and her face fell. Pulling her head in, she scurried back into her room, slammed the door and threw the bolt just as the front door was pushed open.

Irina Drozdova, whitened by the snow clinging to the front of her overcoat, stepped onto the doormat and began brushing herself off. The snow had started to melt, dripping on the floor around her.

"Good evening, Irina Borisovna."

She squinted at me near-sightedly and nodded in recognition.

"It's you again." she said softly. "What do you need now?"

It was clear she hadn't been visiting any friends. Her face was paler and more drawn than it had been a few days ago, and the circles under her eyes had become darker. Checking her alibi at the time of Dima

Sadykov's murder, which was the reason I was there, seemed like a preposterous idea.

"I wanted to tell you something," I said, following her down the hall. "May I come in?"

She shrugged, pulling off her wet overcoat.

"I wanted to tell you that Comrade Grushnikov is going to be released. It seems we arrested the wrong man."

No one had authorized me to tell her that, but I didn't want Grushnikov's release to come as a surprise.

She nodded, staring straight ahead. She had placed Tanya's photograph on the dining table. I caught sight of it and it again struck me unpleasantly how much she looked like my little sister. Suddenly, I felt anger swelling in my chest. Unlike Urumov's, mine couldn't be released in angry screams and bitter words. It had to stay bottled inside, making me almost physically ill.

"I swear to you, Irina Borisovna," I said more solemnly than I had intended. "I swear to you we'll find whoever is responsible for your daughter's death. I give you my word."

"It makes no difference to me who killed Tanya," Drozdova said, sitting down in a chair, the one in which Tanya had been found. "If it wasn't Grushnikov, so much the better."

"The reason we no longer think it was Grushnikov is because another child was murdered yesterday afternoon."

She lifted her head.

"Another little girl?" she asked.

"A boy this time. In similar circumstances."

"That's very sad," she said.

Going home after a long, frustrating day, I stood on the back landing of the tram car with my eyes closed, leaning my throbbing, aching head against the cold window. The tram car waddled slowly uphill and I swayed in time with its motion. The streetlights were transformed into blurry blue stains gliding slowly across the transparent layer of frost on the windowpanes.

Next to me, two women were having a conversation.

"It's all those man-made seas," said the older of the two. "They keep damming rivers and building power plants all around the city. And those seas make the climate warm. Soon we're going to have palm trees here, like Sochi. And men from the Caucasus, with big moustaches, wearing wide round hats on their heads."

They discussed the weather and then complained about the price of butter, which had recently gone up. The younger one then told a long story about her sister-in-law in Tula, who had to come to Moscow once a month to buy staples. I stopped listening and nodded off.

And then, suddenly, I was wide awake.

"—and then he chops them up with an ax."

I had missed most of the previous conversation and had just managed to catch a snippet of the last sentence.

"You mean the kids?" the older one asked.

"Yes, the little kids. All day I've been hearing people talk about it. Just now, for example, at my cousin's. A woman he works with told him the maniac killed a little girl in her apartment building. A first-grader. He chopped her up and they had to work hard all afternoon just to wash the blood off the landing."

Her companion was having none of it.

"It's nothing but silly rumors, my dear" she said. "I've heard more such stories in my time than I'd care to remember. It's always the same thing, mind you: a maniac, a psychopath or a serial killer – or else a spy poisoning the drinking water. If a third of those tales were true, Moscow would have been depopulated by now."

FOURTEEN

I honestly couldn't satisfy the playwright's curiosity on the subject of Grushnikov. Was the gym teacher still a suspect or not? I couldn't really tell, and the answer depended on whom you asked. Lenny paced the hallway from the door of our office to the smoking room, scowling at everyone who crossed his path. And despite Lenny's objections, Grushnikov was released two days later. The seals on his door were removed and he returned to his room on 1st Kolobovsky.

Tanya's and Dima's bodies were cleared for burial and released to their families. Their funerals were held on the same day. Dima being a Tatar, his parents, even though they weren't strictly speaking Muslims – we're officially an atheist country – objected to his being kept at the Forensics morgue for so long. Irina didn't complain about anything. She was numb, indifferent. There had been enough time for Tanya's father to travel to Moscow if he had wanted, but he stayed in Volgograd. Tanya's funeral was spare, almost austere. Her casket was taken to Vagankovo Cemetery and interred alongside that of her grandmother. The family had a private plot, a fenced off enclosure set slightly apart from the overflowing anarchy of nearby graves, those with Orthodox crosses and names chiseled in gilded letters into the black meat of their granite headstones. Only a few of Irina's colleagues from the *Literary Gazette*, an old college friend, Tanya's music teacher, and Baba Dasha came to say goodbye.

There were numerous fresh tracks in the snow around the plot, snaking behind the cast-iron fence. That explained where Irina Drozdova had been spending her evenings. I watched her bluish face and sunken cheeks and tried to imagine what she felt, looking at that thick cluster of family headstones and crosses. She was now the last of her long line. There would be no one else.

Grushnikov did not attend the funeral.

The services for Dima couldn't have been more different. The funeral was a well-attended, emotional, even noisy affair. There were cousins from Astrakhan and Moscow, members of the extended family and their friends, almost all Tatars. There was a Tatar mullah, even though he held back and tried to blend in with the crowd at the sight of Criminal Investigation cops circulating in the crowd. Dima's mother and grandmother wept loudly. Dima's sister must have been extremely popular at her Textile Design and Technology College. It seemed like the entire student body had come to give her moral support.

So different were their funerals as to make a mockery of our search for connections between the two murdered kids. The only link was us. We were watching the mourners, secretly studying their faces and casting occasional glances up and down the wintry pathways. The killer might be lurking somewhere behind snow-covered tombstones. Psychopaths are often drawn to the funerals of their victims.

Lenny had been assigned to the Sadykov family. He was angry at the world because of the slow pace of the investigation, but not as angry as the Sadykovs. Dima's parents were angry at their neighbors, who didn't stay at home the day of the murder, at their daughter, who lingered at school chatting with her boyfriend instead of going straight home, at the instructor of the airplane modeling workshop at the local House of Young Pioneers, who had had the flu and cancelled his class that afternoon, and even at the pediatric dentist at the local clinic, who had pulled the last of Dima's baby teeth the previous Saturday. Their daughter was angry at her parents for raising Dima as a trusting, naive kid who was always open with strangers. All three were angry at us for not catching Tanya Drozdova's killer before he could strike again. They took their anger out on Lenny who patiently, steadily, deliberately filled the pages of his notebook with his illegible chicken scratchings. He was possessed of indomitable energy. In just two days he interviewed teachers, schoolmates, street sweepers on Dima's block, and cashiers at the store where the boy had frequently stopped on his way home from school to buy a sweet roll.

It seemed inconceivable that two kids of nearly the same age, living in the same city, separated by less than five kilometers, could have had no common acquaintances and no connection whatsoever. Yet none could be found.

To keep Lenny's – and my own – mind off the subject of the murders, I shared my thoughts on the Korenev case. But first I had to remind him about the facts. Uncharacteristically, Lenny had no recollection of the case I had been investigating on Budyonny's orders. His mind was completely absorbed by the murders, and I could hardly blame him for that.

"It's a clear-cut case," Lenny declared. "The driver took the car for a ride, either to impress a girlfriend or to make a few rubles picking up fares."

Lenny had been filling out a stack of index cards, cataloging those who might be connected to Dima Sadykov and affixing a colored sticker based on how much additional work that person required. Having given his expert opinion on the theft of the ZIM, he forgot all about it again and went back to his task.

"That's what I thought originally, and that's probably what happened. Still, there are some strange aspects to this case. Why would Korenev, after calling in Criminal Investigations, frustrate my inquiry every step of the way? And what about that fight they had the other night? Why would he be discussing his car with his cleaning woman, of all people?"

Lenny reluctantly lifted his face from his index cards again. In only a few seconds he had become completely absorbed in his work once again.

"Wasn't it she who had discovered the car missing?" he asked.

"The playwright claims she knows nothing about anything."

"He's lying, most likely," Lenny opined. "You should bring her in and have a chat with her."

Lenny couldn't work up any interest in the ZIM case, that much was clear. But I persisted.

"I can't," I said. "I told you it's a delicate investigation. Budyonny doesn't want me to cross the playwright. I'll have to work carefully around him."

"Well, it's his car, after all," Lenny shrugged. "If the owner doesn't want you to put the heat on his driver and you don't want to question the cleaning woman behind his back, so be it."

"That's the problem. In the meantime, the driver might go ahead and sell the damn car. I don't think Budyonny would like it if I never found the ZIM. Nor would the playwright. He'd whine about it even though he says he wants me to focus on catching the killer."

"He's absolutely right. You should focus on catching the killer. I think you're wasting your time on this case."

"True enough," I conceded. "Still, it will have to be looked into at some point, and I don't understand it. Where is the car now? Why doesn't Sergei simply confess to Korenev? What is he afraid of? It doesn't add up. Psychologically, it's all wrong."

Lenny sneered.

"Psychologically, you say? Dr. Lazius seems to have infected you with his psychology mumbo-jumbo. Speaking of which, I noticed in your report that the doctor examined Tanya Drozdova and decided she was some kind of a nymphomaniac, and that is why you don't think it was Grushnikov who raped her."

I was surprised that Lenny had read my report – I had submitted it to Budyonny and Gordeyev only the night before – and I was even more surprised that he had drawn such perverse conclusions.

"That's not what I wrote," I said, blushing and, for no particular reason, feeling defensive under Lenny's relentless stare. "There is no evidence one way or the other. I have no opinion whether or not Grushnikov had sex with Tanya – and neither should you."

"That's where you're wrong, buddy," Lenny retorted sharply. "And so is Dr. Lazius. I can tell he's guilty just by talking to him."

The call came later that afternoon. After our sharp exchange, we had fallen silent, each doing his own work and stepping out for a quick cigarette separately and at different times. But once we got the call, our differences were immediately forgotten. We left the office together, driving to Basmannaya Street in the neighborhood of Three Stations Square in Lenny's Moskvich.

Up four flights of stairs to the apartment we found a middle-aged sergeant from the local precinct and two recent police recruits, fresh from the countryside. The sergeant stuck his head into the hallway when he heard us come in, nodded in acknowledgement and disappeared once again behind the bedroom door. The two boys in stiff police uniforms were leaning hard against the wall. Mumbling and repeating themselves, they took several minutes to explain that they had been told by the sergeant to wait there for the ambulance. Both kept their eyes glued on our faces and studiously avoided looking toward the kitchen.

Dismissing them with a wave of his hand, Lenny stepped into the kitchen. I followed close behind. There, stretched on the white linoleum of the kitchen floor, lay the body of nine year-old Vova Silin. Lenny lifted the checkered oilskin covering the body, pressed two fingers to the side of the neck and shook his head. When he turned toward me, his face was twisted with impotent rage. It was all he could do not to howl or punch the walls.

"You talk to these two," he said, jerking his head in the direction of the two cops as if they were suspects. "I'll go take a look around and question the neighbors. In case someone has seen anything."

It is always a good idea to question witnesses promptly, but it wasn't the reason Urumov wanted to get out. He needed to be doing something, anything, to get outside, to get moving, to fill his lungs with fresh winter air.

I envied him, but someone had to stay in the apartment and get on with the investigation. Soon enough, I got the two peasant oafs in uniform to start making sense. Having heard their confused tale and, after inspecting the three-room apartment, the following picture began to emerge:

Vova Silin lived with his parents and a grandfather. The grandfather had taken the kid to school in the morning and headed to the recreation room in the building's management office, where he played dominos, read the sports page, and discussed hockey and soccer with other retirees in the building. It was a kind of club. That day Vova was set to be dismissed early, but, since the school was just around the corner, he was allowed to walk home on his own. The grandfather returned around lunchtime and found the boy's body in the kitchen. Either old age or shock made him disoriented. Instead of calling an ambulance or the police, he rang the bell of a next door neighbor, who then called the cops. The rookie policemen had been on patrol down the block and were unlucky enough to cross paths with the sergeant, who commandeered them to the crime scene.

"We also had Karpenko with us," they added earnestly as if it was important or relevant. "Comrade Sergeant sent him back to the precinct with a report."

"Where's the grandfather?" I asked.

"He's in the bedroom with Comrade Sergeant and the neighbor. The old man is crazy with grief."

The doorbell rang.

"That must be the ambulance," one of the rookies said hopefully.

I opened the door, hoping to see Lenny, and found myself face to face with Budyonny.

Giving me no opportunity to speak, the Boss pushed his way through the door and into the apartment. He headed straight for the kitchen and, seeing the body under the oilcloth, nodded grimly. His reaction was very different from Lenny's, but under his calm exterior he was boiling with the same all-consuming rage, waiting for the slightest opportunity to give it vent.

"Who else is in here?" he asked, drilling me with hooded eyes that had the disconcerting tendency to glow like orange, oxygen-fueled embers when he was angry.

"Senior Lieutenant Urumov, sir. He's canvassing other apartments looking for possible witnesses."

"Is that all? Where's Gordeyev? Where's Tumakov? What happened to Gromovsky and Mikhailov? Did they fall off the face of the earth?"

His voice gained strength as he ran through the list of his subordinates. While he thundered, the unlocked front door was pulled open and our medical expert, Sasha Grigoriev, stepped in. Over his shoulder loomed the tall frame of crime scene photographer Dima Savitsky. Two young women from Grigoriev's department, whose names I didn't know, came in behind him, wearing lab coats and caps. One was carrying a large metal case. More forensics people crowded the landing behind them. Budyonny must have driven over with them, but had rushed up to the apartment, leaving the others to unload their equipment.

We were making a lot of noise. The bedroom door opened again and a gray-haired woman came out. A pair of horn-rimmed glasses hung on her narrow nose. She had one of those faces that was difficult to imagine without glasses.

She shut the door behind her carefully.

"What's going on here?" she asked.

By then there were at least a dozen of us milling around in the hallway.

"Moscow Criminal Investigations," Budyonny introduced himself. "Lieutenant Colonel Martirosyan. I'm in charge of the investigation."

His voice softened when he spoke to her. "Who are you? I mean, what is your relationship to—"

He stopped short without completing his sentence and gestured guiltily toward the kitchen.

"I'm a neighbor. I share a landing with the Silins. Pyotr Sergeyich, Vova's grandfather, is in the bedroom. He can't answer any questions right now. He's in a state of shock."

Budyonny nodded.

"I understand," he said. "Go back in. I'll join you in a minute."

The moment she went in, Budyonny turned on Grigoriev. His voice hardened.

"What the hell are you waiting for? Don't you know where to start? I suggest you take a look in the kitchen. The rest of you, too. Do I have to stand over you as if you were a bunch of toddlers?"

Gregoriev's team knew perfectly well what to do. They also knew the Boss's temper and instantly melted out of sight, fanning out in the apartment. If Budyonny had hoped to vent his fury at them, it proved impossible. He looked around for a new victim and his eyes lit up as they fell on the two hapless rookies, still standing stiffly by the door.

"Who the hell are you?" he hissed, letting his anger swell and gather force. "What are you doing here? Who asked you to stand here and get in everyone's way?"

The boys looked at each other and said nothing.

"They were brought here by the local sergeant," I said, butting in, knowing that if Budyonny were to go off, the two might be taken away by the very ambulance they had been told to wait for.

Swatting at me as though I were a fly, the Boss shouted at the cowering cops, "Out of here you two. Go down and keep watch by the front door. Make sure there's no crowd gathering by the building and no tongue-wagging. No tongue-wagging, d'you here? That means you, too."

They hesitated and Budyonny roared into their faces:

"Did you hear me?"

Hearing him was not the problem. They surely heard him, but I doubt they understood a word he said. The angrier the Boss got, the thicker his accent became. At that point, he might as well have been speaking in his native Armenian.

At last, it dawned upon them that this huge, hairy man with a red face and fulminating eyes wanted them out of the apartment – something they had been wishing for dearly for the past hour. Budyonny watched them retreat and slammed the door behind them.

"Let's go, Matyushkin," he said.

We knocked at the bedroom door and entered.

The sergeant sat on a narrow, twin bed next to an old man dressed in a suit and tie. The cop was tall, broad-shouldered and soft and spongy all over. Prominent on his pockmarked southern Russian face was a thick salt-and-pepper handlebar moustache and a bulbous nose. The old man was small, slender, bald and neatly put together. They were a study in contrasts, and yet, there was a similarity between them, perhaps a kind of solidarity or mutual understanding that two older males shared. The sergeant held the old man by the hand. The old man sat motionless, staring straight ahead and blinking frequently, as though he was about to cry.

Seeing a lieutenant colonel, the sergeant let go of the old man's hand, jumped up and stood at attention.

"At ease," the Boss commanded in a tired voice. His rage had evaporated.

He turned to the old man.

"I'm very sorry about your grandson, sir," he said. "Tell me how you found the body."

The old man didn't seem to hear. The room was tidy, full of good furniture and china in glass cases. Pots with dwarf cacti and small aloe vera plants ranged on the window sill like toy soldiers. The room felt a little feminine, and a handsome middle-aged woman in a large photograph regarded it with approval from the opposite wall.

"Pyotr Sergeyich," the sergeant said softly. "Comrade Colonel is asking you a question."

The old man didn't react. He was staring at the photograph. His lips, thin and colorless, kept moving without making a sound.

"Don't worry about it," said Budyonny. "We'll talk later. Stay with him, Sergeant."

The old man spoke suddenly, addressing no one in particular.

"How will I break the news to Lera?"

"It's his late wife," the neighbor explained in a whisper. "She's been gone for five years."

We went out of the bedroom, leaving the old man alone with the cop. In the hallway, the neighbor told us what she knew.

The old man had rung her bell around one in the afternoon. She knew something was wrong the moment she saw him standing on the landing, looking lost. He seemed to be trying in vain to gather his thoughts.

"My grandson is playing a strange game with me," he said absently, rubbing his temples. "He fell asleep on the kitchen floor and refuses to wake up. I keep shaking him by the shoulder, but he pretends to ignore me."

Still wearing an apron and clutching a potholder, she followed him into his apartment, where she found the boy's body. She was a retired pediatrician and proved an excellent witness. She didn't move or touch anything in the apartment. Having ascertained that Vova was not breathing – the body had started to go cold – she covered it with a piece of oilskin and took the old man back to her apartment to wait for the cops and the ambulance.

She had been at home all morning, but had noticed nothing suspicious or out of the ordinary. At noon, when Vova was supposed to come home from school, she was in her kitchen, making soup.

"We haven't called his parents yet," she added and suddenly broke into tears.

"Please," Budyonny said stiffly, taking a step toward her and placing a beefy paw on her shoulder. "Let's pull ourselves together, Comrade."

Half an hour later, Grigoriev filled out the rest of the picture. The lock on the front door had not been picked, and the door had not been forced. The boy was strangled from behind, like Dima Sadykov. But he may not have been a passive victim like the other two. Grigoriev thought he may have tried to run. They found a teapot and its lid on the kitchen floor. The cover had slid under the stove and gotten chipped. That could have happened when the boy or the killer swept the pot off the table as they ran past.

The boy was still wearing his school uniform and his briefcase lay on the floor not far from the front door.

"That's all for now," Grigoriev concluded. "I'll let you know if there's anything else."

"What do you think, Matyushkin?" Budyonny asked.

He was almost calm now.

"It looks like the first two victims knew their murderer and didn't have any reason to fear him," I began. I was flattered to be asked for my opinion. "That's why they didn't try to run away. This one, Vova, may have been scared of him. This suggests a stranger."

Budyonny nodded.

"What else?"

My other suggestions were not particularly original. If the killer rang the doorbell, the boy could have opened the door without asking, assuming it was his grandfather. But the killer could have also followed the boy from school and pushed him in once he had unlocked the door.

"This is what we'll need to focus on," Budyonny said. "Maybe a classmate or a teacher saw the boy either leave with someone or strike up a conversation on his way home."

"We need to find out whether the boy was tidy," I said.

"What for?"

"We need to know whether he usually changed out of his uniform or continued wearing it at home. He had plenty of clothes, they weren't poor like Tanya Drozdova. In families like this, parents usually insist that kids change their clothes after school. Plus, his briefcase is right here. It may have been his habit to throw it down by the door when he came in, but he could have also dropped it if he were pushed in."

"Good," said Budyonny.

"We should also check what time the grandfather left to go home."

Budyonny shook his head dubiously: "You don't suspect the old man, do you?"

I shrugged.

"Well, maybe," Budyonny said.

The ambulance finally arrived, more than an hour late. Budyonny came out onto the landing to send them away. By the time he finished bawling them out, Urumov had returned from his rounds.

"Nothing," he said in answer to Budyonny's unspoken question.

His rage, unlike Budyonny's, had not diminished.

"I want to check Grushnikov's whereabouts this afternoon," he said, gnashing his teeth like a cartoon villain.

Lenny was followed by other members of our team. We gathered in the old man's bedroom, after the sergeant had taken him back to the neighbor's apartment.

Everyone looked shocked, angry, and at a loss for words, apprehensively eyeing the Boss's immobile figure by the window. We remained standing, not wishing to disturb anything in the room. At last, Budyonny came back to life with a violent shake of his head, as though chasing away gloomy thoughts. It took him five minutes to distribute assignments. It was all routine police work, nothing fancy: canvas the neighborhood and talk to teachers and kids at school.

"Make sure you don't spread panic," he concluded. "Gather information, but do it cautiously."

"I'll take the boy's parents," he added with a sigh.

When everyone started to file out, I stayed behind and waited for the room to empty.

"What's your problem, Matyushkin?" Budyonny asked me sharply. "You've got your assignment."

"Comrade Colonel," I said slowly. "I need a word with you."

Startled by such a solemn beginning, Budyonny stared at me and waited.

"We've obviously got a maniac on the loose. This is the third murder in less than two weeks. He goes from house to house strangling kids."

"I know that, Matyushkin. What are you trying to say?"

"I have an idea, Comrade Colonel," I said slowly. "You have mentioned panic. Well, I think it's too late. The panic has already started."

I recounted what I had heard on the tram the previous night.

"So," the Boss said grimly. "What do you propose we do about it?"

FIFTEEN

This time, Korenev greeted me with open arms and started to prattle the moment I walked in, oblivious to my somber mood and sour face. But considering the kind of favor I was going to ask him, I had no choice but to sit and listen to him for as long as it took.

"I'm so glad you came," he repeated every few seconds as he led me to the dining room.

"I want to tell you a secret, detective. I'm writing a new play. No, not the one for the Army Theater. This one is about you. Yes, about Criminal Investigations. About the work of Soviet detectives. Maybe this should be the title, *The Detectives*. It has a ring to it, no? Sit down, Lieutenant, I'll tell you the plot. I'm having so much fun, I'm already done with the first act. Let's have some tea."

Korenev sat me down at the table and called out to Zinaida to brew us some tea.

"I want to hear your honest opinion, Pavel. Because you know the material first hand. You're not like some fruity theater critic who has never done a day of police work in his life. You'll recognize my characters right away. What's the most important thing in Soviet theater? Socialist realism, of course. As Maxim Gorky used to say, we draw our characters from life. I changed all the names, naturally, but otherwise they're all real people."

He jumped up, ran out and returned with a stack of paper covered with a meticulous, economical handwriting. At the same time, Zinaida brought in a metal tray containing teacups and silver bowls brimming with cookies, preserves and honey. She set it unceremoniously on the table and marched back out. Korenev poured me some black tea essence, diluting it with hot water from an electric samovar.

"Take some honey, preserves, chocolates. Me? No, I don't want any tea just now. I'm itching to start reading."

The play's main characters were three detectives: Senior Lieutenant Trofimov, Lieutenant Uvarov and Sub-Lieutenant Malyshev. Childhood buddies growing up in the same neighborhood, thick as thieves so to speak. After completing their military service, all three went to work for Moscow Criminal Investigations. In other words, the three musketeers: one for all and all for one. Except not all of them were good guys.

"Who does Sub-Lieutenant Malyshev remind you of?" Korenev asked, winking at me archly. "Anyone you know, Senior Lieutenant Matyushkin?"

As he went on reading, it transpired that Malyshev, in fact, was the villain of the piece. The first act closed with the announcement that the first kid had been murdered, followed by an emergency meeting with the detectives' boss, Police Major Martynuk. Thus, Lieutenant Colonel Budyonny had been simultaneously demoted in rank and given a Ukrainian last name.

"How do you like it so far?" Korenev asked when he finished reading. "Mind you, it's only the first act."

"It's very good," I forced myself to declare, summoning the assistance of the inner hypocrite who, I believe, lives in the deep recesses of every person's soul and comes out on exactly such occasions.

"Does it seem realistic?" he probed. "Don't worry about sparing my feelings. I want to hear what you really think."

"Extremely realistic," said my inner hypocrite, this time with a little more conviction. "I recognized all the characters right away."

All creative people are vain, at least the ones I have ever come across. Korenev blushed with pride and looked quite pleased with himself.

"That's great. It's just the beginning, of course. The main part is still to come. This is what's going to happen. Trofimov is the highest ranking officer of the three friends. But he's a careerist who plays by the rules and tries to be on the boss' good side. Uvarov, on the other hand, has a real passion for police work. All he wants to do is catch criminals and put them behind bars. He doesn't give a damn about bureaucratic rules, as long as he gets results. As kids are murdered one after another, tensions rise between him and Trofimov. Malyshev, who pretends to be a friend of both, is really an angry, vindictive type. He feels slighted because he has not been promoted. He knows that Uvarov is right, and that as long as Trofimov goes by the book they will never catch the killer. But when his two friends finally have it out, he opportunistically sides with Trofimov. I don't want to give away any more of the plot, but at first Malyshev's plan succeeds. Uvarov is fired, then Trofimov fails and Malyshev, using Uvarov's original plan, which Uvarov shared with him, lays a trap for the killer and becomes a hero. He gets his promotion, a medal, and marries the beautiful Zoya – did I mention that there's a love interest? No? Well, there always has to be one. Since their school days in the old neighborhood, all three of them have been in love with the same girl. Until Malyshev's apparent success in catching the killer, she gives preference to none of them, but then she, too, is swept away by the wave of fake hero-worship."

"Interesting," I said, thinking that the real life Uvarov – meaning Lenny Urumov, of course – would have had no difficulty seducing any pretty girl in the neighborhood, even if he were kicked off the police force.

"In the end, of course, it all comes out and Uvarov finally gets the recognition he deserves," the playwright concluded. "The scales fall from Zoya's eyes, and she realizes she's always loved Uvarov. But it's too late, she made her choice and is now stuck with a coward, a liar and a hypocrite."

Korenev paused, regarding me triumphantly.

"It's going to be really exciting," he concluded.

"I'm sure," my own inner hypocrite declared. "It sounds great."

Korenev rubbed his hands and was about to continue, but I used the pause to interpose.

"It's a great plot, Matvei Nikanorovich. But we're in real life now. In real life, there was another murder."

Korenev turned pale.

"What? Another one?"

I nodded.

"Yes. Another child has been killed. A third victim in less then two weeks."

"Why didn't you tell me right away? Here I am, babbling away about my play. What happened? Do you think it's the same guy?"

I told him everything we knew about Vova Silin's murder, summarizing what we had learned by questioning Vova's classmates, teachers and neighbors. The questioning had stretched late into the night and resumed in the morning, when I left to visit Korenev. Unlike our previous meetings, when I had been reluctant to talk about the case, I was now relating every detail we knew.

Korenev shook his head.

"It makes me sick," he said. "I realize now how stupid it was, to want to write a play about these terrible crimes."

He looked deflated and defeated. He had taken the news very hard and his usual ebullience ebbed out of him.

"What if you never catch the killer?"

That was where I saw my opening.

"We will, Matvei Nikanorovich," I said. "But we need your help."

"You do?" he perked up at once. "I knew you needed my writer's intuition. What do you want me to do? I'm entirely at your service."

"We need you to write an article about the murders," I said, looking him steadily in the eye.

"I'm sorry. I don't understand. Write what kind of article?"

"There are wild rumors flying around. About a maniac who's chopping kids up with an ax, for example. I heard people talk about it.

No one knows the true facts. And at the same time they still leave their kids at home alone and the kids still keep opening doors to strangers. We need to tell them the truth and tell them how to protect their children."

"But that is not possible," he said, his voice changing again, becoming cold and official, as though we were at a party meeting. "Our newspapers never publish stories about crime, natural disasters or major accidents that occur in this country. It has been the long-standing policy of the party and the government. We're not in America, after all, where they sensationalize tragedies and take pictures of traffic fatalities in order to thrill readers. Our people need positive news."

"I know that," I said. "That's why we need you to write it."

"Enough said, Lieutenant. It's a decision that has been made at the highest level."

"That's why we're asking you," I insisted. "You're the only one who can do it."

Korenev stared at me, his eyes narrowing. Hardening, too.

"You mean you want me to go to *him*?" he asked slowly.

Him meaning Nikita Sergeyevich Khrushchev, First Secretary of the Communist Party of the Soviet Union, Chairman of the Council of Ministers of the Soviet Union and President of the Supreme Soviet – the country's most powerful man. He was the only one who could authorize the publication of this sort of article.

I said nothing, only waited.

"It's ridiculous," Korenev sneered. "You've lost your mind."

Frankly, this was exactly the sort of response I had expected. And it was exactly what the Boss had said when I first brought up the idea in Vova Silin's apartment.

"You're a goddamn dreamer, Matyushkin," the Boss declared as soon as I started talking. "He's not his own worst enemy. He didn't rise up so high, to be the secretary of the Communist Party organization of the Writers' Union, by sticking his neck out like some kind of goddamn Don Quixote. Do you see him putting his nice life and privileges on the line and risking getting his plays banned? I don't."

The Boss shook his head violently.

"No, no way, Matyushkin. And you'll get us in trouble, too. It's not our job to come up with all kinds of crazy ideas. Our job is to investigate crimes and make arrests. Do me a favor, forget the whole thing."

He sighed and added quickly, "I forbid you to raise this issue with Comrade Korenev. That's an order."

"Yes, sir," I replied, clicking my heels.

I turned and headed for the door. Vova's grandmother looked down upon us reproachfully from the wall. From the kitchen came the clang of dishes, where Grigoriev's people were going on with their work.

"Wait a second," Budyonny said as I turned the doorknob.

He stood by the old man's narrow bed, shaking his head. There was deep silence in the room and I became aware of an alarm clock ticking loudly on the night table.

"You win, Matyushkin, damn you," the Boss said softly. "Go ahead, ask him. Let Korenev be the one to tell you to go to hell with your nutty ideas. At least my conscience will be clear."

I could have kissed him on both of his stubble-covered cheeks, but I merely saluted again and went out.

And now the scene was repeating itself. I was waiting, wondering whether Korenev would in fact tell me to go to hell. There was silence in his dining room, too, also broken by the banging of dishes behind the kitchen door.

The silence lasted for a long time. Korenev stared out the curtainless window, shaking his head now and again.

Suddenly, he turned to me and began to scream. "I forbid you to bring it up. I don't want to know anything about your investigation and I don't want to hear about any more murders. You've got to put an end to it. You're police detectives. If you can't do it, then perhaps we need to shake up your agency and bring in competent officers in your place, damn you."

Had the Boss been there, he probably would have fired me on the spot and then died of a stroke.

I kept silent, my eyes still fixed on Korenev. The outburst exhausted him and when he spoke again, it was still our murder investigation he wanted to know about.

"What are your plans now?"

"We haven't got any," I said. "We have hit a brick wall. The killer is on the loose and is obviously determined to go on killing."

"But you've got to do something about it!" Korenev cried out. "This can't continue like this."

"It won't," I said, nodding in agreement. "If he keeps killing, he's bound to make a mistake sooner or later and get caught. Unless of course he has the good sense to stop, in which case we may never catch him."

"Do you mean he could escape justice?"

"Yes, that could happen. So far he has not left behind any evidence or been spotted by any witnesses. He may be just as lucky next time. And the time after that. But what if he is someone who only has infrequent bouts of insanity? This one will pass, he'll stop killing, and return to his normal life. Until something else sets him off, maybe two years down the road."

"It should not be allowed to happen."

"I agree. We were hoping you'd write an article describing the circumstances of the murders and naming the three victims. A witness may come forward. An associate, a colleague from work, a neighbor, a relative, a doctor. No one lives in a vacuum. I'm sure there is someone somewhere who has noticed something."

"Nonsense," Korenev declared, but with less conviction. "Besides, there will be a panic."

"There already is a panic, Matvei Nikanorovich. And every new murder will add more phantasmagorical details to the rumor mill."

"You're probably right," he admitted.

"And there is something else you must keep in mind. It's the most important thing. Once people read about the murders, they will take precautions. Think of it: a life could be saved. A child's life."

That was my best argument and I had saved it for last.

"Do you really think so?" Korenev asked.

He was thinking it over, pondering, calculating. A thin line of perspiration appeared on his upper lip. His tiny brown eyes lost their sparkle and grew misty, opaque.

"It will never get published," he said at last. His voice had regained its firmness. "No paper would dare publish a thing like that."

"I know," I said.

"No," he said. "No way. I can never go to *him* with such a request. No one can, not even his own daughter. You're mad, Lieutenant."

At that point I knew that begging, cajoling or arguing would be of no use. As with Budyonny, what I needed to do was to plant a seed. His conscience would have to do the job for me, if it were to be done at all.

"Do you want a shot of vodka, detective?" Korenev asked.

This time I didn't turn him down. We drank to the memory of the three murdered kids, without clinking glasses, as tradition requires, and then he raised a toast to Criminal Investigations and the murderer's speedy capture. Then, as my tongue started to slip its moorings, I toasted the success of his play. This time we clinked our shot glasses and Korenev grew despondent.

The door to the dining room opened and Sergei stuck his head in.

"I'm done for the day, Boss," he announced. "May I go?"

He was addressing the playwright but looking at me. There had been none of the usual rustling of his floor-polishing brush, and I wasn't even aware that he had been in the apartment all this time.

"Yes of course," Korenev replied.

He waited for the front door to click shut before observing: "He's a nice young man, Sergei. Very reliable."

Korenev's vodka was excellent, but drinking it with him was work, and hard work at that. Downing one shot of the frosty blueberry-infused fire after another, I had to make sure I wasn't going to lose control. I had to let Korenev talk – whatever he wanted to talk about. I knew that sooner or later he'd come around to the topic that hung unspoken between us, even as we were getting loaded.

"Kids" he declared. "I love kids. They are the flowers in the garden of our lives. Do you have any kids, detective?"

I shook my head.

"Not yet? Well, then you can't put your soul into this investigation. If I were your boss, I'd put together a team of fathers. And not just fathers, but fathers of young kids."

I thought of Urumov and how he had dumped his soul into the investigation, and how his colleagues had to work hard to keep him from maiming suspects. And I thought of my sister Natashka, too.

"Are you married?" Korenev asked.

"Not yet," I replied.

Thinking of Natashka made me think of Tosya and her kid brother who had turned out to be her son. I sighed, and so did the playwright, but surely he was thinking different thoughts. The vodka was making us both melancholy.

"I was married twice," he announced. "Both times before the war. I was married to Adelaida Feoktistova, the actress. You know who she is, I'm sure. Every guy in the entire country wanted to go to bed with her and many did, even while we were married. It didn't last long, under the circumstances. Never marry movie stars, detective."

We finished a decanter and Korenev left the room, returning after a short while with an unopened bottle of Stolichnaya. It was nowhere near Korenev's own stock, but by then it no longer mattered to either of us.

"My first wife's name was Anisya Nikulina," the playwright continued. "Boy, how I loved that woman. She was a real beauty. But I wasn't good enough for her. You see, a beauty like hers is an asset. If you marry some obscure guy named Matvei Korenev, you are wasting your most valuable asset. So she dumped me for another man. A very powerful man. As powerful as they come. The head of the NKVD section for the entire Rostov region. He stole her from me, and I did nothing to try to win her back. I was even scared to punch him in the face for sleeping with my wife while we were still married. I was petrified of him, if you want to know the truth."

Korenev grabbed his bald head between his hands and began swaying from side to side, distressed by the bad memory.

"They used to throw wild parties. Champagne and caviar and lots of guests. They lived in a mansion requisitioned from Alperin, a Jewish grain merchant. They invited me over once, and I didn't dare not show up. It was more like a summons. But the real reason they wanted me there was to mock me. They made fun of me and humiliated me in all sorts of ways, and their guests laughed at me. They put me at the head of the table, making believe I was the master of the house. I had no choice but to fall in with their nasty game and pretend to laugh at all their jokes at my expense. I never told this to anyone, Pavel. Can I call you Pavel? You can call me Matvei. Skip the patronymic. My heart was breaking with grief, but I had to go on playing the buffoon."

He began to cry, shedding copious drunken tears, and then added ominously, "But what goes around comes around."

He took out a handkerchief, wiped his eyes and blew his nose.

"I'm a coward, detective," he resumed in a few minutes. "I'm afraid to go to Nikita Sergeyevich. I have always been afraid of everything. But you know what? I don't want to be afraid any more. First thing tomorrow morning, I'm going to go to Comrade Khrushchev. I mean, I'll write the article first thing, and then go straight to him. Maybe in the early afternoon. I'll call his secretary and make an appointment. Nikita Sergeyevich will understand. He's a father too. He can be gentle and understanding when it comes to children."

"Do you have kids?" I asked.

"I do and I don't," he said. "It's a long story. But I feel sorry for all those parents who lost their little ones. That's why I'm going to write that article. I give you my word, detective. My word of honor. I, Matvei Korenev. That's gotta count for something, right?"

It was the dead of night when we finally parted. He walked me to the door, insisting on hugging me around the shoulders along the way, so that we barely squeezed into his foyer. But at least we supported each other and swayed a little less violently from side to side.

I also nearly walked out still wearing the playwright's felt slippers, which made him laugh uncontrollably for at least five minutes.

"Forget about my car," he announced. "I forbid you to look for it. The Lord giveth and the Lord taketh away, even though there is no god, as we know, and everything around us is nothing but science and when you die you stay dead. There's no god, just man. And you've gotta have courage to be called a man. The courageous rule the world, the timid perish. You've gotta have balls."

Once out on the landing, I had to lean against the wall to catch my breath.

"Who gives a damn about that car," I asked myself out loud.

Really.

"If he doesn't care about it, why the hell should I? My hands are too full with a goddamn serial killer to worry about some stupid ZIM."

My words, slurred and hoarse and too loud for the time of night, echoed up and down the stairwell.

SIXTEEN

I wondered whether Korenev, when he woke up the next day with a bad hangover, would remember the solemn oath he had given to me that he would go to see Khrushchev first thing the next morning – or at least in the early afternoon. There was always a danger that, even if he recalled something vaguely, he would change his mind upon sober reflection.

So it was a nice surprise when, two days later, Budyonny called me into his office and made me sit while he read aloud an article that appeared in that morning's edition of *Izvestia* and was reprinted, word for word, by *Trud* and *Soviet Russia*. Later in the day it would also be carried by the local rag, *Evening Moscow* – a paper especially popular with the city's grandmothers. The article had no byline and was short, terse and to the point. It warned citizens of a psychopathic killer preying on schoolkids. No names and no gory details. As Comrade Korenev had said, we were not in America and there was no need to sensationalize crime. It concluded by calling upon residents to be alert and vigilant, never to leave small children alone and unsupervised and to warn them to never under any circumstances open doors to strangers.

Budyonny read the article in all the papers in turn, nodding gravely whenever he came to the phone number of our office, printed in boldface at the bottom of each article and accompanied by an appeal to report anything that might be pertinent to this case.

"You've got to make sure you thank Comrade Korenev properly. From now on, consider him a member of our team."

That was the sum total of the commendations I received from the Boss. My colleagues had less reason to praise my good work. The calls began early, pretty much the moment the morning papers hit the newsstands. Muscovites were reporting their friends and neighbors, suspicious characters loitering around their buildings and bosses at work suspected of a fondness for their younger female employees. The initial trickle of calls would inevitably turn into an avalanche once *Evening Moscow* had been delivered to mailboxes around the city in the late afternoon.

As I was getting ready to go out to see the playwright, I became a reluctant witness to a conversation between Lenny and an exceptionally tall woman who had dispensed with the bother of a mere phone call and had presented herself at Petrovka in person to denounce her ex-husband.

Lenny offered her a chair, which meant that my desk had to be pushed all the way back and I was pinned against the wall. The woman was holding a copy of *Soviet Russia* on her lap and speaking in a deep operatic bass.

"My ex-husband is your man, Lieutenant," she declared. "We've been divorced for two years. Not that he wanted to marry me in the first place. Even when I got pregnant with Vasya, he kept saying he just wanted us to be friends. Then he figured he could move into my parents' apartment. He's an out-of-towner and that's how he got a Moscow residence permit. And then he had the nerve—"

"Please, comrade," Lenny said, rudely interrupting her monologue. "This is Moscow Criminal Investigations. We're investigating a serious crime. I don't have time to listen to the story of your marriage."

"And I'm here to help you catch the killer," the woman asserted. "It's about this article."

She shook her copy of *Soviet Russia* at Lenny.

"Then stick to the relevant facts, please. Is the story of your marriage relevant?"

"Of course it is. Don't worry, I'll get to the facts shortly. The fact is that my former husband is the maniac going around and killing all those kids. What he did to his own son is both criminal and insane."

"Just tell me what you base your suspicions on," Lenny said, tapping his desk with a pencil in a show of impatience.

"With the greatest of pleasure, Lieutenant. We have an eight-year-old son, Vasya. Naturally, he lives with me. My ex-husband lives with another woman who is at least ten years older than he is."

Lenny sighed.

"Is this relevant too?" he asked.

"You bet it is. Vasya has lived with me ever since we got divorced. Once my ex-husband went to live with that harpy, I stopped letting him see the boy. Because I don't want my son to be emotionally traumatized."

Lenny kept tapping his pencil and the tattoo was growing more and more urgent. He was getting angry.

"I told my boy not to take his phone calls, never to open the door to him, never to see him anywhere. And still his father continued to harass him. Coming to school to try to pick him up after classes, trying to talk to him. But Vasya is a well-behaved boy, he would never disobey his mother. And you know what that monster did?"

"I can't imagine," Lenny hissed through clenched teeth.

The woman missed the venom positively dripping in Lenny's voice.

"He came to our door when Vasya was at home alone. He rang the bell and when Vasya asked who it was – which I had told him to do every time somebody rings the bell – the bastard pretended to be a MosGaz repairman coming to read the meter. Well, naturally Vasya opened the door, because like all little boys he adores various workmen, repairmen, firemen and other proletarians. His father then kidnapped him for an entire afternoon, plying him with sweets and taking him to see a grown-up movie that was completely inappropriate for a child his age. Imagine how I felt when I got back and Vasya was gone. I thought

I'd lose my mind from worry. Thank God I knew nothing about the killings."

"So, this is why you think your former husband is a serial killer?" Lenny asked her politely. Too politely for my taste. "The story you've just told me?"

"Is it not enough? What else do you need?"

"Did he ever try to get into *other* people's apartment by playing the same trick?" Lenny asked, still outwardly calm. "Do you know if he ever played a similar trick on some other child, not his own son, a stranger?"

"How would I know? I don't go around spying on him. But it wouldn't surprise me if he did."

"Why is that?" Lenny asked.

"Because only a man with a pathological personality disorder could play such a trick on his son. Believe me, he's capable of murdering Vasya, his own flesh and blood, just to get back at me. It's a miracle that nothing happened to the boy while he was with him. And then the devilish cunning of the man. You must absolutely detain him and check his alibi."

She turned and looked at me, as though to seek my support.

It was not her fault that she had happened upon Urumov. It was her bad luck, and she paid dearly for it. Lenny had been in a foul mood for days and he poured his accumulated anger, frustration, bitterness and scorn upon the poor woman. He turned crimson, stomped his feet and bellowed at her to get out. Lenny is a gentleman and to my knowledge had never laid a finger on a woman. But if she hadn't hastened to get out, I fear he might have been capable of physically throwing her down the stairs.

"Many thanks for getting this damn article published, Matyushkin," he said when he returned, after making sure she'd exited the building. He was still fuming.

His anger, while genuine, didn't prevent him from recounting the story in the smoking room five minutes later, to the full complement of Budyonny's detectives. Lenny had a talent for stand-up and, even though there was nothing funny about the fact that our entire department was now doomed to spend tedious hours listening to similar nonsense, everyone, including the Boss, laughed hard as he mimicked the tall woman's deep voice.

My retelling of it to Korenev was a pale shadow of Lenny's display, but the playwright giggled and grabbed a pen and paper to write it down.

"But I'm sure we'll soon be getting real leads," he said.

I said that I very much hoped so.

Korenev was in the best of moods. He accepted my thanks with a gracious bow, which managed to convey both modest self-effacement and acknowledgement that he had made a valuable contribution to our investigation.

He then paid me the highest compliment by inviting me to share his midday meal. Zinaida, wearing her usual fake English maid's costume and displaying our genuine Soviet lack of good graces, shoved a soup plate in front of me and filled it from a tureen. The soup that day happened to be a particularly thick, sour *shchi*, made with sauerkraut, pearl barley, sour pickles and beef kidneys.

Korenev once again offered me a shot of vodka, which I had to decline, since I was still feeling queasy from the other night.

The playwright downed two shots in quick succession and that was a cue to Zinaida to take away the empty tureen and bring out a dish of baked salmon, which came with sides of roasted vegetables and steamed cabbage with caraway seeds.

"I told you all sorts of nonsense the other night," Korenev said softly once Zinaida was out of the room. "About my first wife and so on."

"I don't remember," I shrugged. "I had too much to drink."

I found myself being drilled by those tiny eyes of his, and I held his stare with as innocent an air as I could muster.

"We both did," he said at last. "In any case, whatever I might have babbled, it was the vodka talking."

The dessert was the usual glutinous cranberry drink. By the time it was served, his face had acquired a uniform pink tinge. There was a mischievous bad boy gleam in his eyes.

"Well, Lieutenant, now you've got no excuse to conceal anything from me. Your boss, who called me just before you came, said that from now on I might as well be one of you, and that it is your job to fill me in thoroughly."

He then went on to question me again, but this time he went about his task with all the deliberate thoroughness of a master of the situation.

"I thought at first I'd have to make lots of changes in the plot of *The Detectives*," he said after wheedling from me lots of personal details about the murdered kids and guys on the investigative team. "To be honest, I nearly junked the whole idea and replaced the serial killer with a car thief because I didn't think the play would clear the censors. But it's a new situation now. Now when the play comes up before the censorship board, and some idiot member starts objecting to the child killings, I know exactly what I am going to say. They're quick to get on their ideological high horse, you know. That's why they've been made censors. I'll have some fun with them first, before telling them who it was who cleared my article for publication. I'll have a good laugh at their expense."

He rubbed his hands together, anticipating how much fun he would have putting the censors in their place.

"The composers came to see me the other day," he said, changing the subject. "A whole official delegation of them. Now they come hat in hand, literally begging me to sell my garage to them. It makes you wonder, Lieutenant, how they found out it's been standing empty these past weeks. It's a theory, no?"

I didn't reply and Korenev guffawed, winking at me.

"Don't be too serious, Sherlock," he said, poking me painfully in the ribs. "I'm just pulling your leg. But you've got to admit it's a funny idea for me to be selling my garage to them. What would I do with their money? Do you know how much I've got in my bank account at the State Savings Bank?"

I shrugged.

"Come on, venture a guess, detective," Korenev insisted.

"I don't know," I said, trying to think of a really large sum. "A thousand rubles?"

Korenev found it very amusing. He laughed for a good long time, even making a show of pulling out a handkerchief and drying his eyes.

"You're a card, detective. I haven't had a good laugh like this for a long time. You're no Nat Pinkerton, that's for sure. Don't take offense. I'm saying this as a friend."

He grew serious.

"Almost a million," he declared. "Minus two or three thousand."

I was impressed in spite of myself. A million rubles was a sum straight out of a radio broadcast about American fat cats – suspender kings, hamburger monopolists and oil magnates. And there I was, saving for a year the three hundred rubles I needed to buy a twenty-year-old war booty Zundapp.

"Yes, my friend. And every single kopek of it, all one million of them, legally earned. You want to know how it all adds up? Elementary, Watson. Whenever a play is produced anywhere in the country, I get royalties. There is a drama theater in every city, plus every republic has a Russian theater and a national one, too. Add to this Eastern Europe, China in the old days, and now Cuba, even though they're only now getting round to translating my plays into their language, which in case you didn't know is called Spanish, and not Cuban as you might think. I may not be as popular as I was while the Big Man, Josef Vissarionovich, was alive, and there are plenty of new authors coming up, which I don't mind, but I still get royalties. No longer a flood, but certainly more than a trickle. So why on earth do I need the composers' money? What am I going to do with it? Burn it in the stove to heat my dacha?"

He went on for a while, explaining to me that some composers were also rolling in money, especially the ones who wrote popular patriotic and love songs that were played on the radio over and over again. I was getting bored.

Fortunately, the phone began to ring and Korenev abruptly stopped talking. It had an unusual ring, shrill and urgent, coming at uneven intervals, as though somebody at the other end was pressing the ringer by hand.

"Oh, my, that's my special line," the playwright said quickly.

He jumped out of his chair, nearly upsetting the half-finished glass of cranberry drink, and ran out, sliding and balancing on the freshly polished parquet floor and pulling off his napkin as he ran. As he turned the corner, he wiped his suddenly glistening forehead.

The ringing stopped when Korenev reached his study and his voice came to me through the open French doors. It was a very different Korenev answering the phone, not the man who had been sitting at the table with me a moment ago. His voice had become high-pitched, differential and strangely upbeat, as though the middle-aged playwright had been replaced with an enthusiastic young pioneer.

"Yes, of course, Nikita Sergeyevich. Naturally, Nikita Sergeyich. No question, Nikita Sergeyich."

He kept repeating endless variations of this phrase in his new, syrupy voice, with the same relentless false cheer.

"Naturally, Comrade First Secretary. I understand completely. I agree wholeheartedly. Thank you very kindly indeed. Naturally, Nikita Ser—"

Then I heard nothing more, as Korenev had shut the door.

I got up from the table and walked to the window. In the fading light of a short December day, the Composers' Union building rose behind its concrete fence and, as far as I could make out, no work was being done on its carcass.

The weather was worsening, the low black clouds were foretelling a snowstorm, but at the skating rink there was still a clockwise merry-go-round of tiny skaters, oblivious to the imminent change in the weather. It seemed unimaginable that one of those laughing, heavily swaddled kids could be strangled – the way Tanya Drozdova, Dima Sadykov and Vova Silin had been. I hoped every nanny and grandmother watching their kids from the sidelines had read *Evening Moscow* or *Trud* or *Soviet*

Russia. To me, looking down from the height of Korenev's sixth floor, they seemed on high alert, and if that was true, it was worth wasting time on cranks and idiots like this morning's vengeful ex-wife, and worth listening to Korenev's endless prattle – every minute of it.

I was deep in thought and I didn't hear the playwright return. Suddenly, he was a changed man. Gone was the vivacious, rotund bon-vivant, the self-assured famous playwright enjoying the luxuries of his position. A short, overweight man with sloping shoulders and a sagging belly made his way back into the dining room with a shuffling, halting gait. He face was suddenly old and pale, the bags under his eyes drooping onto his flabby, wrinkled cheeks. He repeatedly wiped his face with the napkin that had also somehow wilted during the past few minutes, its starched crispness sodden with sweat.

"You've got me into hot water, Lieutenant," he muttered, lowering himself into his chair. His voice had changed yet again. It was now hoarse, colorless, deadly tired. "If you don't catch the killer, and catch him soon, I'm finished."

He sighed and added, "And so are you, my friend. And so are you."

SEVENTEEN

I left the playwright slumped over his dining table, a vacant expression on his suddenly aged face, staring at his own portrait on the wall. He waved a hand, dismissing me. A glass of his favorite cranberry drink sat untouched on the table in front of him.

I quietly let myself out of the apartment. As I walked along the long hallway past the multitude of rooms of Korenev's house museum, I couldn't resist peeking in, hoping to spot Sergei. He was either out or had chosen to avoid me.

Just as the front door was closing behind me, I heard a noise in the apartment. Stepping back quickly, I slammed the door, making believe I had gone out, but staying quietly in the foyer. Almost immediately I heard Zinaida's voice. What took me by surprise was not her nasty tone – that I had gotten used to – and not even that she would be laying into her boss, but her vulgar prison language.

"Serves you right, asshole. Who the fuck asked you to stick your stupid neck out?"

I stood there with my face against the closed front door, listening. She went on for some time, occasionally pausing to draw breath, which was when Korenev's soft, guilty voice attempted to reason with her.

I had heard enough. I realized now what I had found so jarring about Zinaida, ever since I first lay my eyes on her. I had assumed all along it had been the disparity between her position and her proprietary bearing, as though she had been the true mistress of the house. In fact, it had been the incongruity of a proper English uniform worn by someone who had spent time in a Soviet jail. The uniform had kept me from recognizing Zinaida for what she was: an older version of my pickpocket friend Nastya.

I opened the door softly and slipped out. As I did, I happened to glance behind me, and in the narrowing crack between the closing door and the doorjamb I caught the sight of Sergei's motionless figure, observing me from the hallway.

It had grown dark outside and the snow was falling thickly amid the headlights of rush-hour traffic. Korenev's building loomed against the black sky, its intricate turrets and plaster statues swaddled between the low-hanging clouds. The lighted windows of its upper stories were like yellow and blue squares suspended in air and generously speckled with swirling snowflakes. The snow had only now started to stick to the wet pavement, parked cars, and the wool overcoats of pedestrians hurrying home to get warm and dry.

I headed toward the metro station. I had set myself another task for the evening and I felt I had to carry it out, despite the gathering snowstorm.

To get to Vagankovo Cemetery, I had to take the metro to Red Presnya station and then change for the No. 35 trolleybus, which dumped me off under a dim streetlight a block from the front gate. It was a few minutes after seven. The snow continued to come down hard and, unusually for such a snowy night, it was also getting bitterly cold.

The vast cemetery was shaped like a triangle, bordered on one side by the train tracks of the Belarus line, and on the other two by busy thoroughfares. The residential street that leads to the main entrance is crowded with apartment buildings on one side, with the cemetery's crumbling brick wall running along the other. The sidewalk on the cemetery side of the street was usually deserted, even in daytime and in good weather, as many people are superstitious, feeling an unwarranted dread at the sight of densely packed plots interspersed with rusty crosses and full-grown tree trunks.

I was the only passenger who exited the bus at Vagankovo; there were also no other visitors on its snow-covered paths. Yet with the help of the light from a nearby streetlamp I could just make out Irina Drozdova's lonely figure in the distance. She stood with her back to me, oblivious to the snow that was slowly frosting her winter coat and black shawl.

I stopped a good distance away and waited. Soon, my own coat was heavily dusted and my toes had stared to go numb. The entire time she stood motionless. I waited another ten minutes and headed back to the main gate.

An elderly guard called out to me, wishing me a good evening.

"You still have a visitor back there," I told him. "Don't lock her in."

"I know," he replied. "She's been coming here almost every evening."

I took out my cigarettes.

"She started coming here a couple of weeks ago," he continued, casting a covetous eye on my pack. "At first I couldn't figure out why, all of a sudden. And then they had the funeral. Turns out her daughter was murdered. Those mothers. Once they start coming, they just can't stop."

I offered him a cigarette. He took it cautiously, examining the filter – I had recently switched to filtered Laikas. We lit up, shielding the flame of a thin wooden match with our hands. In its flickering light I could see his hands – black from soil that had long since become as one with his skin and arthritic knuckles.

Protecting a frail matchlight and sharing a smoke creates a bond between men.

"It's coming down hard," the guard observed, exhaling.

We smoked for a while in silence.

"Is she a friend of yours?" he asked. "I mean the woman visitor."

"You could say that," I replied.

"I don't like it," he said. "Your friend coming here like this. Sooner or later those mothers go mad. I'd keep her out of here."

He spat on the ground, took a last draw on his cigarette and tossed it into a snowdrift. The wind howled in the branches, making the snowflakes dance in intricate swirls between the graves.

"I've seen a bunch of them over the years," he said. "First she starts coming here all the time and then, all of a sudden, she just stops. And then there is no one to care for her child's grave. It gets overgrown with grass and the railing starts to fall apart. I would try keeping it up for a while but it's no use. If she's not coming back, why bother? It'll all crumble some day, this whole place," he concluded philosophically.

I offered him another Laika. Just as we lit up, Drozdova appeared silently, without warning, emerging from the chaos of dancing snowflakes like a ghost and startling both of us. She drifted past, looking through us with unseeing eyes.

I caught up with her beyond the gate and gently touched her elbow.

"I'd like to accompany you home," I said. "I don't think it's a good idea for you to be coming here every night."

She turned, recognized me and smiled bitterly.

"I'm going home anyway," she said, adding, "I don't seem to be able to get away from you."

I took Irina Drozdova back to 1st Kolobovsky. The trolley car, taking us across town all the way to Trubnaya Square, moved slowly, wobbling through the snowdrifts and sliding on patches of black ice in the road. I made attempts to engage her in a conversation, but with no success. She did not want to talk and responded to my effort with disjointed, monosyllabic answers, keeping her eyes fixed on the tropical fronds that the frost had traced on the inside of the trolley's window panes. I gave up and we rode the rest of the way in silence.

I walked her to her room, said good night, and then, obeying some strange impulse, gave a soft knock to Grushnikov's door on my way out.

I knew he was home – I had seen the light glowing around the edges of the wool blanket over his window as we came in.

"Who's there?" he asked, a note of apprehension in his voice.

"Criminal Investigations," I replied.

"One moment, please."

He turned the key in the lock, undid the bolt and jingled the chain. The precaution of keeping himself so securely locked seemed excessive, I thought. He was sweating and breathing hard.

"I've been exercising," he apologized.

His obsession with staying fit was in a stark contrast with the unhealthy and disorderly appearance of his room, which was, if anything, even messier than when he was in jail. The transience of his existence was even more apparent now, heightened by the remains of another sordid, hastily assembled meal on his table. A heavy, locker room odor hung in the air, mixed with the smell of alcohol, though no bottle was visible.

"I just wanted to see how you're getting on," I said, already regretting that I had stopped by and desperate to get away.

"Is that all?" he asked.

"Yes, that's all."

"Does this mean that I am a suspect again?"

"I don't think so."

"There won't be any questioning then?" he asked.

I shook my head.

"Good," he said. "In that case let me ask you a question, as long as you are here."

His voice rose and turned shrill.

"Why can't you leave me alone? You did your best to entrap me, but you couldn't find any evidence. Nothing. You know I'm innocent."

"You've been released. You're free."

"Free? You call it free? You destroyed my life. My neighbors shun me, little kids at school are afraid of me, and older ones laugh in my face and say nasty things behind my back, because teenagers are cruel. I used to be their favorite teacher. I used to coach their volleyball team, a dozen strong, athletic girls playing a great sport. We used to win prizes in city tournaments. Now they've all quit. That's the kind of freedom you created for me."

He was shouting now.

"I'm being ostracized. You trail me whenever I go out, you spy on me. Even now you're lurking outside my window."

He ran to the window and tore the blanket off, sending the clothespins flying. The window was encrusted with frozen condensation and all you could see were splotches of yellow lights from across the courtyard.

"Calm down and don't talk nonsense," I said. "No one's watching you."

"You search through my things. You steal my clothes."

He was getting incoherent and slurring his words. I had trouble following him.

"I don't think so," I said, trying to sound calm and hoping that my tone of voice would calm him down. "I admit that we made a mistake and I'm sorry for that. When the real killer is caught, I'm sure your arrest and the suspicion that fell upon you will be instantly forgotten."

"Sure. Who are you kidding? Besides, you haven't caught anyone yet. You may *never* catch the real killer, if you go about it the same way you did with me. You keep wasting your time trailing and harassing me. Meanwhile, Tanya was in Dr. Lazius' office unaccompanied – she'd started going there a long time ago, even before I moved in here. That you don't care about, do you? I bet you didn't even know."

"Actually, Dr. Lazius told me that himself."

That shut him up.

"He did?" he asked, suddenly deflated.

There was a knock on the door. Grushnikov gave me a quick, suspicious look. Fear suddenly crept into his eyes. Pulling his head into his shoulders, he went to the door. I followed a step or two behind. Peering over his shoulder, I thought at first that the hallway was empty and only after a few seconds did I make out Irina Drozdova's pale face in the darkness.

"Could you please keep your voices down?" she asked. "I've got a terrible headache and I'm trying to go sleep."

As I left the apartment I ran into Nadezhda, the doctor's wife.

"Dr. Lazius isn't here," she said in a colorless voice. "Did you want to talk to him?"

I had no need to see Lazius. All I could talk to him about, after the Boss forbade me from discussing the course of the investigation with him, was Irina Drozdova, but I already knew his opinion of her, which with all due respect I didn't share. He might be right, that she was not a type to hang herself or take an overdose of sleeping pills – I didn't know much about such things – but I was sure that in her condition she could easily starve to death, or lose her mind.

But standing there in the hallway of their communal apartment, I was unpleasantly struck by Nadezhda Lazius's appearance. She was no longer the cheerful, happy young woman I had seen on previous occasions. Over the past week or two she seemed to have lost weight. Her face was sallow and drawn, the tips of her nose and chin had become sharper and more prominent. Even her hair, blonde and lustrous the last time I saw her, had become lifeless. I thought she might have had a bout of flu or something.

"Where is your husband?" I asked.

"He's out with his boys," she replied, her voice strained.

The four of them had seemed inseparable. There was something not quite right about Dr. Lazius and his sons being out while Nadezhda was staying in.

"Are they going to be long?" I asked.

"I don't know. They're at the theater. Or the conservatory. I don't know. But you can leave a message. I'll be sure to pass it on to my husband."

I had become used to leaving the apartment in 1st Kolobovsky with a heavy heart. Irina's state of mind worried me and I was sad and angry about Tanya, the eleven-year-old who looked so much like my little sister. But now I felt an almost superficial dread. After going to see Grushnikov and running into Nadezhda, it was as though the smell of mold and decomposition had penetrated my nostrils, overpowering even the frosty air outside, which should have smelled delightfully of freshly fallen snow. Perhaps the old hag Baba Dasha was right after all: there was something rotten in that apartment.

As I turned into the long archway connecting their courtyard with the street, I turned around quickly and just managed to spot a dark figure in the doorway of the house opposite before it drew deeper into the shadows.

Lenny was nothing if not persistent, I thought, shaking my head.

At the entrance to my own courtyard, I ran into Tosya on the approaching side street. The snowstorm had abated, but the temperature had plunged lower still and it was just as cold as the first time we met. Tosya was once again cocooned in her winter clothes from head to toe, which is how I knew it was her walking down the deserted street. She spotted me, too, and promptly turned away, trying to sneak away. I picked up the pace and for a while we were walking side by side, saying nothing to each other.

I stopped before we reached her door.

"I want to ask you something," I said.

She stopped, too, and waited for me to continue.

"Did you read the article in today's papers?"

Lots of things had happened since that morning, and it was hard to believe that Budyonny had read the three identical articles out loud, one after the other, only twelve hours before.

"What article?"

She eyed me warily from the tiny opening in the folds of her thick fluffy shawl, as though expecting to be tricked. That was how she'd looked at me the other time, too, while we were fighting over her frozen Hungarian chicken.

"The one about the serial killer."

She shrugged contemptuously.

"That's all everyone was talking about all day. All the girls at Tryokhgorka. I never take what the newspapers say seriously. It's a lot of nonsense, most likely."

"It isn't," I assured her gravely. "I'm working on the case. I can tell you it's all true. You have to be careful. You've got a little kid and he's probably at home alone now."

I bit my tongue.

Blushing is not only a change in coloring; it's a facial expression that you can't mistake for anything else. Even in the darkness of our courtyard I could see her blush. And get angry, too. But it was too late – and, in any case, I thought it was more important to warn her.

"I met your boy a few days ago," I said. "He's a great kid."

I could see she was pleased to hear that. Her eyes, almost in spite of herself, lit up with pride before she looked away, still embarrassed. But I needed to drive the point home.

"You've gotta take care of him," I said. "I've just been with the mother of the first victim. You wouldn't ignore what the papers said if you saw her. She's really in a bad way."

"Very well," she said, turning to go. "I'll be careful. And I'll tell Sevka not to open the door to strangers. Even though he already knows that."

And then, with her hand already on the handle of her front door, she turned to me and said.

"Thank you," she said.

That was progress – she actually thanked me for something. And all of a sudden, I had an inspiration.

"What are you and Sevka doing for New Year's?" I blurted out.

EIGHTEEN

New Year's was at Lenny's.

Lenny was constantly in a funk and our personal and professional relationship had seriously deteriorated. Grushnikov had become a fixation with him – if not as Tanya's killer, then as a rapist – and he was angry with me because I didn't share his suspicions. It grated on him and flew in the face of his code of honor that his partner did not back him up, right or wrong.

But New Year's was New Year's. Raisa was determined to have a celebration. Yet Lenny would only accommodate her so far. Raisa called me on December 30, the embarrassment evident in her tone, "I'd better warn you, Pavel. It's going to be just the two us and the girls. You know how difficult Lenny's become. We're not inviting anyone else."

Had I known that, I would never have invited Tosya. She had other plans, which she cancelled because I promised her a very good time at Lenny's. Every other year, their New Year's parties had been full of joy and fun, with a crowd of cheerful guests and plenty of great food – something Raisa was a master at finding in half-empty grocery stores.

"But I've already invited someone to come along," I objected. "You told me I should, for a change. Is it going to be a disaster?"

"Are you now? Are you really bringing a girl?" Raisa exclaimed, ignoring my question and waving aside my concerns. She was a curious sort and, like many women who have been married a long time, was eager to see all her friends paired up. Misery loves company, as they say. "So there is someone after all. I'm intrigued and look forward to meeting the poor wretch."

Snowstorms are common in Moscow in December. So no one was particularly surprised when on New Year's eve the sky suddenly darkened. Still, it had followed a couple of bright and sunny days, when the city seemed particularly festive. Even the ordinarily grim wintertime faces on the street were transformed – there were even cheerful Russians, smiling at strangers and forgetting to glower at fellow passengers on overcrowded trams. Everyone had hoped that the good weather and good cheer would last into the next year. Yet now, as heavy black clouds positioned themselves atop snow-covered rooftops and tram wires, the air grew thick and sour. The wind rose, and a savage winter blizzard began scattering snow across the ground.

Tosya and I arrived at the Urumovs' wet, frozen and covered with snow. I was clutching a bottle of Soviet Champagne I had been saving for three months, plus a kilo of tangerines that Tosya's friend at Yeliseyev's Grocery had set aside for her from their holiday shipment. We also had Sevka in tow, who was sleepy and cranky and certainly didn't want to be there.

In the end, Sevka ended up enjoying himself more than any of us. Raisa and Lenny had two daughters, Lilya and Little Raisa, both of them younger than he. They looked up to him and their eyes shone with admiration. They took turns showing him their drawings, dolls and other girly treasures. To them, he was Prince Charming, and even though ordinarily he would have disdained their attentions, he somehow seemed to feel he had to live up to their expectations. He even played house with them, despite warning Tosya en route that he would never in a million years play with any girls. While Raisa and Tosya weren't looking, the three of them stuffed their faces with sweets, then, giddy with all the sugar they had eaten, pranced around the New Year's tree with red cheeks and an unhealthy gleam in their eyes.

Raisa had inherited a few delicate pine cones, cucumbers, and other tree ornaments made of fragile multicolored glass, and she and the girls had made animals using matches, aluminum foil, egg shells and paste, painting them with bright colors from the girls' watercolor set. Raisa had a gift for things like that, and their tree was beautiful and festive.

Raisa even had New Year's gifts for the kids. Little Raisa got a rag doll and Lilya, the older of the two, received a book of fairy tales. Even Sevka, who hadn't expected anything, got a model MIG-21 fighter jet to assemble. The kids wandered off to examine their new treasures, while Tosya frowned at me because I hadn't warned her about the gifts, and she had come empty-handed.

Eventually, the girls got out a projector and a box of films, which they screened over a window curtain that Lenny had stretched out between special hooks. Sevka joined them without protest, despite being far too old to enjoy *Puss in Boots* and *The Adventures of Buratino the Wooden Puppet.*

Raisa was a remarkable woman and a great cook. She served roast duck with traditional Olivier salad, richly dressed with mayonnaise, along with other salads, beef aspic with horseradish, canned sprats, marinated mushrooms, roast squash and many more delicacies. Lenny and I drank Georgian cognac, and there was a bottle of sweet Moldavian port for Tosya and Raisa, while the kids made do with apple juice. A few minutes before midnight, when the old year was breathing its last, Lenny switched their old Yunost radiogram on and, after a while, once its tubes were fully warmed up, we heard the clock on Savior's Tower strike midnight. We toasted the arrival of 1962 and kissed. I kissed Raisa first and then Tosya. She smelled sweetly of gentle soap and, ever so faintly, of a vague but exciting promise.

Even Sevka was given a little champagne in a glass, which he didn't like but gulped down with a brave face before the hero-worshipping eyes of Lilya and Little Raisa. But by then it was all the three kids could do to keep their eyes open.

There was a lot of good food and plenty of alcohol, and I kept stealing long glances at Tosya from across the table, getting a sweet feeling in my chest every time she looked back at me and smiled.

But the evening was not a success. Raisa tried hard to maintain her good cheer and Tosya, after being a bit shy at first, hiding behind her usually prickly exterior, warmed up to her host. The problem was Lenny. He was gloomy and withdrawn the entire evening, scowling as he downed one shot of cognac after another. I quickly gave up trying to keep pace. He finished the bottle and his foul mood loomed over us like a dark storm cloud.

"Well, at least this shitty year is over now," he declared once the National Anthem had finished playing. For that, he got a sharp elbow in the ribs from Raisa. Fortunately, the kids, half-asleep, seemed to have heard nothing.

We too were yawning and fighting back sleep, and not having a very good time. But we sat around the table long into the morning, pecking at tangerines sections and pieces of chocolate candy, drinking cups of thick Turkish coffee and waiting for God knows what. Maybe it was the blizzard howling outside that kept us from leaving. The red and green lights on the tree blinked hypnotically, reflecting against the snow-spattered windowpanes.

We finally left around two in the morning. The kids had long since nodded off. The girls' folding beds were in the corner of the large room the Urumovs shared, behind a large armoire and set off by a heavy curtain. Sevka, after declaring that he was going to stay up all night, had fallen asleep on the couch.

Tosya tried to shake him awake.

"Let him sleep," I said. "I can carry him home."

"Leave him with us," Raisa protested. "Seriously. He and the girls got along so well, they can play some more in the morning. We'll need help finishing the leftovers, anyway. Come back to pick him up tomorrow afternoon."

Tosya didn't want to leave Sevka in an unfamiliar house with people she had met only a few hours before. But she also didn't want to wake him. Reluctantly, she agreed and when she bent over to give him a parting kiss, Raisa winked at me behind her back.

Lenny and I shook hands.

"I hope we make headway in the New Year," I said.

"A nice New Year's wish," Lenny said grimly. "But it's not gonna happen. We've been going the wrong way since the start. We've gotta return to Grushnikov. He rapes her and it can't be a coincidence that she ends up murdered. We need to put some heat on him. I mean real heat."

Lenny's foul mood had been a nagging irritant all night, and I couldn't bear it any longer.

"Come off it, Urumov," I said. "You've gotten an idea in your head and you can't see anything beyond Grushnikov. You should stop harassing him. What good does it do, watching his place all night and searching his room?"

Lenny flushed crimson with rage. I thought he was going to explode, but Raisa put her hand on his forearm and he regained control of himself. Raisa was likely the only person in the world who could make Lenny understand the simple truth that starting the year off with a fistfight with his best friend and partner was not a good idea.

"Mind your own business," he hissed. "Who told you I've been going through his stuff?"

"He did. I saw him the other night."

"He's lying. Had I searched his room, he wouldn't have noticed a thing."

He was right about that, I had to give it to him.

"Come on, boys," Raisa said. "You'll have plenty of time to sort things out in the New Year. Now is not the time."

The storm had not blown past the city entirely, but the snow had stopped, at least for the moment. The cold wind blew, shredding the clouds and chasing their remnants across the blackened sky. The stars shone upon the thick cover of fresh snow that accumulated to knee-height on the street corners. In front of Lenny's apartment, the vast Taganka Square echoed with the prehistoric roar of snow-removing machinery. A diligent street sweeper was hard at work despite the hour, scraping ice from the pavement, his shovel grating on the asphalt.

It was too early for the metro to re-open, and ground transportation had come to a standstill on the snow-covered streets. There were few other pedestrians, except for a drunken celebrant or two wading uncertainly through the snowdrifts and singing loudly.

We got ourselves to the deserted Clear Ponds Boulevard and stood next to the frozen pond. It had been converted to a skating rink and was ringed with garlands of colored lights. The lights were on, and the music was playing softly over the loudspeaker, barely audible over the crackling of static. In the raised audio booth at the edge of the rink two lovers were kissing. The stepladder that led to the door had been pitched into a snowdrift and lay half-concealed under a snow. They kissed, unaware that their exit route was gone.

We too kissed – both of us shaking a bit from the cold. Her lips were soft and sweet, naturally, as well as thanks to all the chocolate she had eaten in the course of the evening, and smelled of Raisa's strong black coffee and citrus.

We had been talking during the long walk from Taganka to the Boulevard. I told her about myself, even though my life hadn't been very eventful or interesting or filled with adventure: school, military service, police training and now Moscow Criminal Investigations. I told her about my dad, who was killed in the war, and my little sister, who went missing on the day Stalin was buried. It wasn't particularly exciting, but I told her about it anyway.

She spoke about herself, too. Her life also hadn't been very exciting or happy. There was the orphanage, bookkeeping courses, and the Tryokhgorka plant. And Sevka.

She was reluctant to talk about Sevka's father, and whatever she told me about him she did cautiously, worried how I would take it. What was I going to say? Things happen, especially to a young girl straight out of a school for orphans, who knows nothing of life and has no one to guide her in the world. It's easy for a man to take advantage of someone like that, and it was easy for her to fall for someone like Sevka's father: good-looking, experienced, well-off. Someone who showered her with gifts and attention. And someone who left her in the lurch the day she told him she was pregnant. Tosya was understanding and didn't blame him. What could he do? He had a wife and a ten-year-old kid at home.

"Life was simple at the orphanage," she said. "It was us against the world. We were family. You would never lie to your brothers and sisters or steal from them. We had no secrets from each other. It all changed. We changed. The real world is different and it changes you. Usually for the worse."

It was easy for me to talk to her. I told her about the murders and the investigation that was preying on our minds and that had put Lenny in such a foul mood. I also told her about Irina Drozdova and how worried I was about her.

"She has no one to talk to," I said. "That's the worst thing in her situation. She keeps visiting her daughter every evening at the cemetery."

"She's getting used to it," Tosya said. "To the cemetery, I mean."

She wasn't a world-renowned psychiatrist, like Dr. Lazius, but I felt that she had put her finger on it.

"New Year's is a difficult time to be alone," she said. "Perhaps you should have invited her to come with us."

I thought about Irina's gloom being combined with Lenny's and didn't think it would have been a good idea.

"I really couldn't," I said. "We're cops investigating her daughter's death, after all."

"Maybe I should go over to see her," Tosya said. "To keep her company."

"You can try," I said. "She doesn't seem to want any company and she's not a talkative type."

"Neither am I, ordinarily," Tosya said. "Tonight has been an exception. We can be silent together."

Perhaps because we had been talking about Irina, the rest of our walk had an air of sadness about it. Or maybe it was that it was New Year's. It has always been my favorite holiday, but, come to think of it, it is a sad occasion, marking the passage of time and the death of the old, rather than the start of something new, with all its bright hope and expectation. And also because, after we kissed by Clear Ponds, we both knew what was going to happen next, which was both exhilarating and, somehow, sad.

We kissed again by her front door. Then she walked me to my front door and we kissed there, before I walked her back to hers. We didn't want to part, and in the end we didn't.

"I'm sorry, it wasn't such an exciting New Year's," I whispered as we tiptoed into her apartment, careful not to wake her neighbors.

"It's not over yet," she replied softly as she started to undo the top button of my overcoat. "There is still plenty of time to make it right. We don't have to pick up Sevka until late afternoon."

NINETEEN

If I had entertained any hopes of some kind of a breakthrough in the murder case resulting from Korenev's article, they were dashed two days into the New Year.

Olga Ilyina lived with her parents on Chekhov Street, in the center of town and not far from Pushkin Square. Olga was older than the previous victims: thirteen and very responsible and independent for her age. She wasn't at home when her parents returned from work, but that wasn't unusual. School was out for the two-week New Year's break, and their daughter, who was very popular with her classmates, was often out visiting friends. She had even started going on dates – nothing serious yet, and no steady boyfriend, just an eight o'clock show at the newly opened Rossiya movie theater, and an ice cream on a park bench afterwards. Maybe a kiss or two.

When Olga hadn't turned up by ten thirty, which was her curfew during the holidays, her parents began to get worried. They called around to her friends. No one had seen her or talked to her on the phone since that morning. When it got to be after eleven o'clock, her father called the local precinct. The cops said that they didn't consider someone a missing person until they had been gone for twenty-four hours. She'd turn up, they assured him.

Gordeyev was in Budyonny's office, reporting the details of the case. We were all assembled around the conference table. The Boss interrupted him, booming from his elevated desk, "What the hell is their problem? All the precincts have been instructed to respond to any reports involving school children on a priority basis."

Gordeyev shrugged and continued.

Needless to say, the parents weren't waiting for twenty-four hours to pass. Olga's father roused his brother and they walked the streets all night, while her mother stayed at home in case the girl turned up. She didn't.

They started making calls again in the morning, and then, in the late afternoon, they discovered the body. It had been stuffed into a utility closet at the back of the kitchen, where they kept the vacuum cleaner, the ironing board and other household items. The mother then remembered that when she had come home the previous evening, a kitchen chair lay on the floor by the closet. The girl had not been considered missing, so she didn't think anything of it.

Gordeyev finished his report and we sat in a dejected silence. Everyone was consumed by their own unpleasant thoughts. Then Budyonny distributed assignments and we began to file out, still in silence, passing by Marina, who was weeping quietly at her desk.

My assignment was a tough one: to inform Korenev that a new murder had been committed. After his conversation with Comrade Khrushchev just before New Year's, he wasn't going to take it well. It was getting late and I decided to postpone the unpleasant task until first thing the next morning.

The phone rang in the hallway. It wasn't very late, about eleven thirty, but no one in my communal apartment wanted to get it. They had their reasons: calls that came at night – and most of the ones that came during the day, too – were usually for me. The neighbors would have complained, except all the calls were work related. And no private citizen in the Soviet Union was brave enough to tell the cops that they were bothering them with a work-related call.

The phone rang and rang, until finally I accepted the inevitable.

"My God, Matyushkin, you're quite a sleeper," Lenny bellowed as I picked up the receiver. "You've gotta get down to the office, buddy."

I had left him three hours ago, slumped in his chair, leaning on his elbows and hugging his head. Now all of a sudden he was energetic, sarcastic and upbeat – in short, his old self.

Lenny was wrong about my sleeping habits. I had not been sleeping at all. Rather, the other way around. After putting Sevka to bed, Tosya had come for a visit. I had told her about the murder and she held me in her arms as we lay on my bed, fully clothed and tormented by misery and disgust.

"There's gotta be a break in this case soon," I repeated over and over, mostly to convince myself. "It can't go on like this. There's gotta be a break."

After a while, I calmed down and sought out Tosya's lips. Her mouth was wet and salty from tears and it met mine eagerly in the dark. I started to undo the buttons on the back of her dress. The buttonholes were tight, her wool dress was new and prickly and I gave up halfway as Tosya caught my hand and guided it down, under the hemline.

That was when the phone began ringing.

"What's the matter," I blurted into the phone. I was speaking slowly, trying to breathe normally and rein in my madly pounding heart.

"You'll find out when you get here," he said, and then blurted out, as though unable to keep his joy bottled up any longer: "We know who it is. It's Valera Tumakov. I mean, you won't believe what he's dug up."

In his excitement, he wasn't making much sense, but I got the gist. And yes, it was typical of Valera. While we were all despairing and moping about, he was doing his job and playing by the rules, even if he had to pull witnesses out of bed.

By the time I squeezed into his and Gordeyev's office down the hall, it was packed to the gills. Some guys had never gone home and others, like me, had been called back. All the chairs and tables were taken, and four people had managed to squeeze onto the windowsill. The air was hot and, in violation of Budyonny's iconclad rules, dense with cigarette smoke. I found a spot by the door, craning my neck to see over a row of closely cropped heads.

Tumakov stood in the middle of the room, flanked by an old woman and a boy of about nine. The old woman was the picture of a Moscow pensioner – and a typical *Evening Moscow* reader, I noted with satisfaction. She was dressed in a long wool skirt, a well-worn wool cardigan buttoned crookedly (and missing a button), and a brown wool shawl.

When I came in, she and Tumakov were arguing.

"Why would I have gone to the cops?" she asked. "They're useless, if you want my opinion."

"You were supposed to report the incident," Valera insisted. "If I hadn't questioned you, we would have never found out."

"So what? He's gone. Where are you going to look for him?"

"It's our job to find him, Comrade. And now, thanks to you, we have plenty to go on. Your information is extremely valuable."

"Enough already, Valera," Lenny shouted from the front row seat he had secured. "Let her tell her story."

"That's right, Comrade," Tumakov said, addressing the old woman. "Tell us what happened."

"It's not much of a story, son, and I've already told you three times. He scared me half to death, and I'm still shaking. And with my heart condition! The doctors told me not to get excited. Easy thing to say, harder to do. This whole thing could've killed me. Thank God I was at home."

After that, she told us a very coherent tale, demonstrating the advantage of several repetitions. She and her grandson had been at home. The boy's parents – the woman's daughter and her son-in-law – were at work and the neighbors were out. The grandmother felt weak after making lunch. As she said, she had a heart condition. While taking a nap, she sent the boy out into the hallway to play, where he would not bother anyone, since the rest of the apartment was empty.

"Stepa is good boy," she said. "He went out and played quietly by himself, careful not to wake his grandma."

While the boy was playing in the hall, she nodded off and then, a few minutes later, the doorbell rang. Stepa had been told not to open the door to strangers, and the warning had been emphatically repeated in recent days since his grandmother read the article about the serial killer in *Evening Moscow*.

"He wasn't supposed to open the door at all when he was alone," the woman said, shooting daggers at Stepa, who seemed to have little fear of his grandmother and was excited to be the focus of attention for Criminal Investigations detectives.

"I wasn't alone," he declared. "I was with you, grandma. So what if you were asleep?"

Be that as it may, he hadn't opened the door without first asking who it was – as he had been instructed.

"MosGaz," came the reply from the other side. "Open up. I need to look at your gas meter."

Urumov turned around, found me at the edge of the crowd and shot me a meaningful look. I acknowledged it with a nod.

After some deliberation, Stepa decided to let the MosGaz man in. He was old enough to know that MosGaz supplied the gas for cooking. His father had shown him a large green box hanging beneath the kitchen ceiling, and Stepa was proud of his newfound knowledge.

"Your gas meter is malfunctioning," the man said, once the boy opened the door. "I need to see whether it can be fixed."

Before coming in, however, the man said, "Call an adult for me, will you?"

Stepa didn't want to wake his grandmother, so he replied, "There's nobody at home. But I know where the gas meter is."

The man seemed glad to hear this. He entered and patted the boy on the head, after closing the front door carefully behind him.

"You're a very good boy," he said. "So where is it?"

"In the kitchen," the boy replied.

"Let's go then, you little devil," the man said.

After patting Stepa on the head, the MosGaz man didn't remove his hand completely, but placed it on the boy's shoulder. He now nudged him down the hall and they started toward the kitchen.

Meanwhile, the doorbell had woken up the grandmother and she was lying in bed, listening to their conversation, still half-asleep. Something about the man's words or tone of voice put her on her guard – perhaps it was how he called her grandson a "little devil." She got up, put on her slippers and went out into the hallway.

"To tell you the truth, sonny," she said, still addressing Tumakov, "at first I was more worried about a gas leak. Gas leaks are dangerous. I didn't want the place to explode."

She followed Stepa and the man into the kitchen, where Stepa was proudly pointing to the meter. But the repairman had apparently lost interest in it. He placed his other hand on the boy's right shoulder and jerked him sharply toward him.

"Come over here, you little devil," he whispered, shifting his fingers to his throat.

"At first I didn't even realize what he was doing," the grandmother said. "I just asked him, like he was a real repairman: 'What's wrong with our gas meter, young man?' But when he heard me, he jumped three feet in the air, as if I had pricked his ass with a knitting pin. And then he started dashing about the kitchen like a trapped rat. First to the window, then to the gas stove, then to the sink, all in a panic. I thought he might grab a kitchen knife and do away with both of us. But he was more scared than I was. He just pushed me out of the way and was gone."

She sighed and grabbed her chest.

"I still get palpitations whenever I think what could have happened had I come out five minutes later," she said. "There was no way I could catch him, though, not with my heart condition. He slammed the door in my face and by the time I got to the landing he was down the stairs and out of the building."

"You should have called the police," Tumakov said, returning to the subject of their earlier altercation. "You understand that you could have lost your grandchild."

"But he's here, isn't he?" Lenny said, jumping from his seat. "What's the point of wasting any more time? We know who he is. Let's go."

"Wait," said Valera. "We need to wait for the Boss and then he'll need to hear her story first. He'll decide what we need to do."

"What, me telling the whole thing again?" the grandmother protested. "It's late as it is, and it's long past Stepa's bedtime."

"I'm not sleepy in the least," the indomitable Stepa declared.

Most of us moved to the smoking room to wait for Budyonny.

"It all fits," I said. "That's why Tanya and Dima opened the door to their killer without any hesitation, and why Vova Silin's body was found in the kitchen."

"Remember the chair in Olga's kitchen?" Lenny added. "She must have brought it in for him, so that he could reach the meter."

His face, which had been beaming for the past hour, darkened suddenly.

"Damn it, I laughed off that hag's MosGaz story about her husband," he said. "I could kick myself."

"Come on," I said. "We all thought it was strange."

But he kept shaking his head and cursing under his breath.

Immediately after getting Tumakov's report, Gordeyev sent Gromovsky to canvass the old woman's apartment building to see if anyone else had been visited by the MosGaz man that afternoon. Sasha Grigoriev's people went along to check out the old woman's apartment. The intruder hadn't been wearing gloves, or at least the grandson didn't think so, and might have left fingerprints.

Lenny pulled out his report on the old complaint about the MosGaz prank and found the man's address. Gordeyev immediately dispatched a couple of guys to watch his apartment.

It took Budyonny a few minutes to hear the old woman's story, which she repeated without a word of complaint: she was petrified by the Boss and his ferocious moustache. After that, he sent her and her grandson home in our office Pobeda car and he called everyone else in.

It was the middle of the night and the windows of the communal apartments along Petrovsky Boulevard had gone dark. A bright, orange diagonal light reflected in them above a line of bluish streetlamps: it was our office windows blazing against the night sky.

"First things first," the Boss declared. "What do we know about this fellow?"

"The old woman's eyesight is not very sharp," Gordeyev replied. "She says he's an ordinary guy, young, a little above average height. The grandson by and large confirms her description. Lieutenant Gromovsky has since learned that the same suspect tried to get into a third floor apartment, also representing himself as a gas company employee. An old man lives there. He opened the door without asking because he's half deaf."

"How did he know someone was at the door if he couldn't hear the doorbell?" Budyonny asked.

Gromovsky chuckled.

"He's an amateur inventor, a tinkerer. He's installed a light over his door that goes on and off whenever the bell rings."

"Fine," the Boss said. "How did he know it was a MosGaz repairman? Does he have a gizmo to tell him who's on the other side of the door, too?"

We were all in a far better mood now than we had been a few hours before, and the Boss's sarcastic remark was greeted with loud guffaws around the conference table.

"He asked the guy to speak louder once he opened the door. The man saw him and then said he had made a mistake, it was the wrong apartment. The old man confirmed he was pretty ordinary looking, nothing that would stick in the memory."

"I hope his eyesight is better than his hearing," the Boss said with the same note of levity, and then grew serious. "What about the ex-husband of the woman who complained about the MosGaz prank? Anybody seen him and can describe what he looks like?"

He yellow eyes circled the table. There was no reply.

"Who checked out the wife's story?" he inquired ominously, squinting at every face around the table in turn.

Again, no one replied. We were all trying to shrink into our chairs, hunching our shoulders and looking as guilty as a bunch of first-graders in the principal's office.

"It's my fault," Lenny said at last, his face red and sweaty and his words barely audible.

"Excellent," Budyonny said, his voice dripping with sarcasm. "Congratulations, Senior Lieutenant Urumov. You interviewed the wife and you decided that checking out her story would be a waste of your valuable time. You were probably busy with some far more important case. I understand. I take it you have no idea how to get in touch with her, either."

"We do, Comrade Lieutenant Colonel," Gordeyev intervened promptly, trying to put an end to Lenny's public humiliation. "We have her ex-husband's address, too. I have people watching his apartment."

"Good," Budyonny said. "It was the right thing to do, Captain. He'll be lying low now. He had a near-miss, but then he went into a building next door and found Olga Ilyina."

"I wonder about that, Comrade Lieutenant Colonel," Gordeyev said. "If he strangled Olga after he had had his near-miss, he would be taking a huge risk. The old woman didn't call the police, but he didn't have any way of knowing that."

"So you think he'd already killed Olga?" Budyonny asked. "And was getting the taste for it, so to speak, looking for a second victim."

Gordeyev nodded: "That's what it looks like to me."

"That woman seemed crazy," Lenny muttered, still smarting from Budyonny's criticism. "They'd been divorced for a long time. She couldn't have had any idea he killed those kids. She was just looking for revenge."

"Look, Lieutenant," the Boss said. "You were supposed to follow up on *every* lead. You made a judgment call and you blew it. Now you just have to live with it and be a professional."

Urumov turned an even deeper shade of purple and started to examine a broken thumbnail with a look of utmost concentration.

"And I don't buy your line of reasoning, either," the Boss went on. "She didn't want her son to see his father, right? You should've been asking yourself why. Maybe she sensed that there was something wrong with the guy. Some deep-seated problem, maybe something of a sexual nature? A normal person doesn't become a serial killer. And who knows a man better than the woman who shared his bed for several years?"

Suddenly, as though remembering something, the Boss turned to me. "This is the kind of hard-nosed, practical thinking you should be doing, you and Urumov. Instead, you're asking advice from some feeble psychiatrist."

"Yes, sir, Comrade Lieutenant Colonel," I said.

Urumov and I had been designated scapegoats for the screw-up, but everyone in the room felt guilty in equal measure. No one had taken the MosGaz story seriously, and everyone had laughed when Lenny did his impersonation of the angry wife. Including the Boss, for that matter.

"Very well, then," Budyonny summarized. "What's past is past. It was everyone's fault, really. Mine, too. Now, let's see how we're going to take the bastard. What do we know about him? Name, place of residence, place of work?"

Gordeyev glanced into a folder that he had already labeled "MosGaz" in large block letters. He pulled out a typewritten sheet and began reading in a colorless voice.

"Oganesov, Grigory Mikhailovich. Residing at Krivokolenny Lane 14, apartment 45. Age 30 years. A degree in chemical engineering from the Mendeleyev Chemistry Institute. Employed at the Liberty Soap and Cosmetics Enterprise. Family status: divorced, one son. No party affiliation, no prior convictions, etc."

"Good," said Budyonny.

Gordeyev paused for a breath and was about to continue when I interrupted.

"It's not him," I said softly.

Gordeyev put down his sheet and stared at me. Budyonny also turned heavily in my direction. An uneasy silence fell over the room, with two dozen pairs of eyes now trained on my face. I was silent, gathering my thoughts. I had to think it through before saying anything more.

Oganesov was the guy I had been haggling with over a war-booty Zundapp, the dark-gray hunk of rusty German steel supplemented by a clunky sidecar.

I had been given his name by the regulars at the flea market, a group of biking enthusiasts who gathered every Sunday on a muddy elevation near the back wall. They could give you all sorts of advice about every known model of motorcycle, domestic or foreign, and could either sell you any spare part you needed or tell you where to find it. You could bring your poor disabled hog to them, pushing it through the milling crowd of buyers and sellers of everything from an ancient radio set to a magazine from a PPSh automatic rifle excavated from a World War II battlefield, and they would immediately diagnose the problem and explain how to fix it. They told me last fall that an engineer at the Liberty Enterprise had been thinking of selling a Zundapp, if he could get the right price.

Even though I knew nothing about the guy, not even his name, finding him proved easy. The first management type wearing a jacket and tie coming out of the Liberty plant gave me all the information I needed.

"That's gotta be Oganesov," he said. "You'll find him at the House of Culture, rehearsing."

Oganesov was a member of an amateur folk ensemble. They were on stage, him playing the accordion and two others furiously strumming the balalaikas. A barrel-chested giant of a man in a white turtleneck was belting out the popular song: "My trunk is full of wondrous treasures," and the effort was making his magnificent salt-and-pepper pompadour bounce up and down in time to the music.

Oganesov was a dark, nervous type of less than medium height. He exuded a strong, effeminate smell of either cologne or perfumed hand soap. The smell was as strong as it was repulsive, and it assaulted me as much as the stench of underarm odor that it did nothing to cover. I was momentarily taken aback by this assault on my olfactory senses before realizing that handling fragrances was what it meant to be a chemical engineer at Liberty.

It turned out that Oganesov and I were practically neighbors. Over the fall I visited him several times. I knew he'd been divorced and that he rented a room in a communal apartment. I even met his landlady, a heavy-set, dark-haired woman. She would come into his room without knocking and linger, listening to our haggling over the price of the bike and inserting a word or two every few minutes. This suggested that their relationship was somewhat more intimate than is customary for a tenant and a landlady, and she took great pains to demonstrate this to me. Oganesov, on the contrary, turned quiet in her presence and seemed a bit embarrassed.

"It's not him," I repeated at last, surprising even myself by the certainty in my voice.

"Why not?" Budyonny asked sternly.

When I first said it, I had not thought the idea through. Now, however, I was absolutely certain. Oganesov could not have been the killer – or at least not the person who had tried to strangle little Stepa.

"Oh, no, not again," Lenny groaned. "You're a hard man to please, Lieutenant Matyushkin. First you say that Grushnikov is the wrong man and now this guy doesn't fit your exacting standards. Yes, why not?"

"Grushnikov, you may recall, turned out to be innocent and has been released," I said.

I sounded pedantic, a little like Tumakov.

"We still have no suspects in Tanya Drozdóva's murder and as long as we don't, Grushnikov is not innocent. Not in my book. Just think of the so-called 'friendship' he said he had with her—"

"The pissing match stops right now," Budyonny said. "Otherwise both of you go back to kindergarten."

Then he turned to me: "What makes you so sure it's not him, Lieutenant?"

Urumov clammed up and stared at me stone-faced.

"I know, because I know him. And if it were him, the witnesses would have described him differently," I said. "We've got three witnesses – the grandmother, the little boy and the downstairs neighbor – and none described a man who looks like Oganesov."

"Which is what?"

"Oganesov is small, dark and fussy."

I stumbled before adding, "He's Armenian."

Budyonny, whose real name is Ashot Martirosyan, is also Armenian. But it had no bearing on the matter, of course.

We waited while Budyonny gave my information some thought.

"Very well," he said. "If it is not him, the witnesses will tell us soon enough. And he'll have some kind of an alibi. But we can't ignore the coincidence, either. Right now, we're going to act as though he's our man and bring him in, I'll get an arrest warrant and we'll be able to search his place. Gordeyev, you'll be in charge of the operation."

"Are we moving in right away, Comrade Colonel?"

Budyonny nodded.

"Immediately. Take Matyushkin with you, since they know each other. Tumakov and Mikhailov will be your backup, along with whoever you've got there watching the place."

Urumov convulsed as though in pain. He felt that the Boss was punishing him by keeping him off the arresting team. Budyonny noticed his frustration and appeared to be enjoying it.

"Your job is the ex-wife, Lieutenant," he told Lenny coldly.

"But that's only in the morning," Lenny pleaded.

Budyonny ignored him.

"Get moving," he said to Gordeyev.

TWENTY

Krivokolenny Lane was dark and cold. Breaking up into pairs and walking fifty feet apart, the four of us approached Oganesov's apartment building from the boulevard. We had left our departmental jeep and its driver around the corner, engine idling, lights off.

A dark figure emerged from the shadows, shivering in the wind.

"Dzhanbekov?" Gordeyev asked curtly, in a tense whisper. "Everything under control?"

"Yes, sir, Comrade Captain," Junior Lieutenant Dzhanbekov replied, also in a whisper. His face was swaddled in a checkered scarf, and a thick fur hat sat low over his eyes. "The subject is in."

"Let's get out of the light then," Gordeyev commanded.

We stepped into the shadow of a vacant two-story house across the street. Behind us loomed the Menshikov Tower of the Archangel Gabriel Church, its pinecone-shaped dome lit and gleaming golden in the black sky.

Gordeyev turned to me, "Where are his windows? On the façade?"

I nodded.

The building was dark but for a pair of windows on the top floor, under the protruding gutter that was trimmed with a row of icicles. The ice formations sparkled yellow and blue from the light of a New Year's tree in the room as it filtered out through the drawn curtains.

"Are those his windows?" Gordeyev whispered.

"No, Sir. His are the two dark ones on the third floor," said Dzhanbekov.

"We're going in," Gordeyev said curtly. "Matyushkin and I are going first. Tumakov and Mikhailov will be the backup and will go in after if everything goes smoothly. Dzhanbekov, you go to the back. Send one of your guys up the back staircase."

Dzhanbekov nodded, indicating that he knew the drill. Gordeyev took out a stopwatch.

"Five minutes," he said.

Exactly three hundred ticks later, Gordeyev pressed the doorbell of apartment number 45 on the third floor. He let the bell ring for a long time, sending its shrill, peremptory sound through the early morning silence of the stairwell, with its hissing radiators and creaking elevator cabin at rest on the ground floor. The sound ricocheted off the walls inside the apartment and echoed down the corridors. Gordeyev let go of the button, waited a few seconds and rang the bell again, even longer this time.

"What do you want?" came a voice from the other side.

"Him?" Gordeyev inquired with his eyes.

I nodded.

I knew that the Oganesov I had met, skinny and shy as he was, could not be a danger to two burly police detectives, even if he was a pathological killer. Nevertheless, I shifted my hand closer to my coat pocket, feeling it sag reassuringly under the weight of my service Makarov. Out of the corner of my eye I saw Gordeyev do the same. He was tense, his square jaw set and his eyes narrowed to slits. As though on cue, we both breathed in and held our breath.

"Who's there?" Oganesov asked, coming close to the door but not undoing the locks. There were three of them on the door, to judge by the number of keyholes. He was coming awake and fear was creeping into his voice. Visitors ringing the bell insistently at two o'clock in the morning were rarely the bearers of good tidings.

"Lieutenant Matyushkin," I said. "Open up."

"One moment," Oganesov said, sounding surprised but also relieved at the same time.

The locks clicked and the door opened a crack, to reveal Oganesov wearing a pajama top and a pair of blue boxers. There was a look of utmost surprise on his face.

"Why are you here at this hour?" he asked petulantly. "Do you know what time it is?"

He suddenly spotted the silent figure of Gordeyev next to me and stopped short.

His spindly legs protruded from the oversized boxers; they were knock-kneed and covered with thick black hair. The hair on his head was also black, thick and matted. On his feet he had high-heeled women's slippers that were several sizes too small for him. The familiar mixture of perfume and sweat drifted through the crack and fanned out onto the landing.

"Are you Comrade Oganesov?" Gordeyev asked, his voice steely.

It was the kind of official police voice every Soviet citizen feared instinctively, even if he had never received a knock on his front door in the dead of night.

Oganesov's landlady appeared in the hallway behind him. She was in a slovenly housedress thrown over a nightgown. In the harsh light of the bare light bulb hanging from the ceiling, her face looked bloated, pasty and old.

"What's going on here?" she asked. "Do you have visitors, Grisha?"

Another door clicked open somewhere in the darkness of the communal apartment, as the neighbors had started to wake up and grow curious.

"Go back to your room," Gordeyev ordered Oganesov's landlady and then shouted into the hallway. "You too, everybody. Stay in your rooms. Shut the goddamn doors. This has nothing whatsoever to do with any of you."

Oganesov's landlady retreated hastily and the unseen door was promptly shut.

Oganesov gave me a bitter look.

"I understand what's going on here," he said. "You're going to arrest me for trying to sell you my Zundapp. I expect I'm going to be charged with illegal commerce or speculation."

"Let's go get your stuff," Gordeyev barked. "Take only the essentials. You're being detained."

"I didn't want to sell it," Oganesov continued as he led the way to his room. He was walking awkwardly, dragging his feet with his toes turned inward, to keep the small slippers from falling off his feet. "I had a feeling it was going to end badly."

The bed in Oganesov's room was made up. He had not slept in it. He sat on the edge of it and continued in the same plaintive voice:

"But I didn't expect it from you. After all, you came to *me* with an offer to buy it in the first place. Are there no crimes left in the city that you need to go inventing them? Plenty of real speculators and black marketeers around, you know."

"Take only the essentials," Gordeyev repeated. "Hurry up."

The doorbell rang again. Gromovsky and Mikhailov had come to make sure everything was under control. I went out to let them in and all three of us, wearing thick winter overcoats with bulges under the arms, trooped into Oganesov's room. The room immediately felt overcrowded and stuffy, as though all the air had been sucked out of it.

"Is this your landlady's door?" Gordeyev asked Oganesov and, opening it without knocking, said into it. "Your rooms are going to be searched. You're to assist the operatives and not touch anything or try to hide any of your belongings. Is that clear?"

A deep-throated groan came in reply.

Budyonny was waiting for us in his office. The rest of the guys were also there; no one had gone home. As we led Oganesov down the hallway, they all poured out of their offices and stood along the walls, silently observing him. Lenny waited by the door of Budyonny's office.

Oganesov kept looking around, blinded by the bright lights after the darkness in the back of our departmental jeep. He had no idea who all those people were, and why they were ogling him as if he were some kind of a movie star or soccer player.

Once we had brought him in, I turned to leave, but the Boss called me back.

"You stay here, Matyushkin. We may need your help."

A tense silence hung in his office while Budyonny studied the suspect. Without all the people in there, the Boss's office had grown back to its normally impressive size. Outside, the night was black, and there were many long hours before dawn. Strings of electric lights crisscrossed the empty streets below, and the red stars on top of the towers of the Kremlin glowed solemnly in the distance.

The size of the office and Budyonny's bulk made Oganesov seem even shorter and skinnier than he really was, standing handcuffed in the middle of the floor.

Gordeyev and I flanked the door like an honor guard.

"Speak, man," Budyonny said at last. "Tell me everything."

He voice was soft, compassionate, paternal. I'd even say tender. In any case, it was not the voice he had ever used when addressing any of us.

"What am I supposed to tell you?" Oganesov asked angrily. "I'm sure you know everything already. Just keep in mind that it was he who asked me to do it in the first place."

He jerked his head in my direction.

"Do what?" Budyonny asked, turning to me.

"Don't play the fool," Oganesov exclaimed bitterly. "Sell my Zundapp, of course."

"Your Zundapp? What the hell is that?"

I felt it was time for me to step in.

"It's a motorcycle, Comrade Colonel," I explained. "A German wartime model. This was how we met last year. He thinks he has been arrested for illegal private commerce."

"No, my friend," Budyonny said softly. "Your motorcycle has nothing to do with it. What I want to hear from you is MosGaz."

Oganesov frowned. "MosGaz?"

It was his turn to be puzzled.

"Yes, my friend, MosGaz. About the clever way you thought up to get little kids to open apartment doors for you. By telling them you're a MosGaz meter reader or repairman, I'm not sure which."

"Oh," Oganesov said. "I know what you're talking about. You mean the little trick I played on my son? Did she file a complaint against me? Is this why you come to my house in the middle of the night and drag me away?"

Budyonny kept silent, letting Oganesov go on, which he did, at length.

"I had every right to see my son. He's mine, too, not just hers. I have my rights as a parent. I don't mind that he lives with her, especially since my own living arrangements – well, anyway, they're complicated, but that's beside the point. She doesn't let me see him at all, which is not fair. If there is anyone you should arrest it's her, because she has to let a boy see his dad. But I don't go about denouncing her to the police."

"Why do you think she doesn't let him see you?" Budyonny asked. "Did you ever strike him or hurt him in any way?"

"Of course not," Oganesov said.

"Did you ever try to strangle him?"

Oganesov stared at him.

"Why would I do that? I love him. And he loves me. She just wants to get back at me because I divorced her. But I want to see my boy, I want to have a normal relationship with him."

"What is a normal relationship, in your opinion?" Budyonny asked.

"Normal is when a father and a son are allowed to see each other regularly," Oganesov replied.

"So your ex-wife has been getting between you and your son," Budyonny said. "Does it make you mad?"

"Of course it does."

"Do you think she's wrong to keep your boy away from you?"

"What do you think? Every boy should have a father to grow up with."

"Did it ever occur to you to get back at her by hurting the boy?"

"That's the stupidest thing I've ever heard," Oganesov cried out in exasperation. "Are you insane?"

He looked around Budyonny's office as though he had indeed found himself in an insane asylum. Their conversation was taking a strange turn and he seemed genuinely perplexed.

"Of course you wouldn't want to hurt him," Budyonny said soothingly, sounding as though he was now taking Oganesov's side. "I'm a father, too. I'm raising two boys. They're older than yours, but in any case, I think you have every right to get into your son's apartment the way you did, by employing a little subterfuge."

Oganesov nodded, happy that the big man behind the desk was starting to see his point.

"Why did you arrest me then?" he asked.

"Because it wasn't the only time you used this subterfuge," Gordeyev croaked behind his back. "Because you gained access to other people's apartments by the same means."

When Gordeyev spoke, Oganesov turned to face him swiftly and combatively.

"Who said I did?" he said quickly. "Why would I want to get into other people's apartments?"

"You tell me why," Gordeyev said.

He took a step toward Oganesov, his body language suddenly threatening.

"I never did that, I swear ," Oganesov cried out, taking a hasty step backward and tangling in his own feet. "I only wanted to see my son."

"How many times did you do it?" Gordeyev asked.

"Do what?

"Tell people you were a MosGaz employee to get into their apartments."

"Why, just once. To get own son to open the door. He was happy to see me, by the way."

"Just once including that time involving your son, or one other time as well?" Budyonny asked, his tone especially friendly and encouraging when contrasted with Gordeyev's thuggish barking. The two of them had the routine down, even though the Boss playing the good cop was not the best casting decision.

"Just that once," Oganesov insisted.

"What about yesterday afternoon?" Gordeyev asked, pushing closer, so that his tall, bulky frame loomed over the undersized prisoner. "Where were you at around two o'clock yesterday afternoon?"

"What do you mean where? At work, of course."

"Can anyone confirm this?"

Oganesov grew a little more confident, regaining his footing as he got on more familiar ground. At least questions about his job were concrete and practical and no longer left him baffled.

"Any number of people," he said. "Half the workforce at Liberty, and all of my chemical engineering department. I started the day in the repair shop, then I went down to the factory floor to talk to the shift manager, because one of his production lines had to be shut down for maintenance. Then I had lunch in the staff cafeteria, and that was about one or one thirty. Dozens of people saw me there."

"Excellent," Budyonny said, smiling. "We'll be certain to check on your whereabouts. What did you do after lunch?"

Oganesov stopped suddenly.

"I went straight to the lab," he said. "I stayed there until three thirty, which was when we had a staff meeting. I guess I was at the lab all by myself."

"All by yourself, eh?" said Budyonny.

"But, presumably, there were dozens of people who can confirm that," Gordeyev asked wickedly.

"Well, not really," Oganesov replied, getting defensive once more. "I was working on a problem and I was alone. I mean there were other engineers and lab technicians who saw me go in and come out, but there was no one there with me."

"Interesting," Gordeyev said. "How long were you in there?"

"I told you, between about one thirty and three thirty. Two hours more or less."

"Is there any way to get in and out of the lab without anyone seeing you?" Budyonny asked.

"Well," Oganesov admitted. "There's a window."

"So, you were at the lab and nowhere near the intersection of Chekhov Street and Boulevard Ring?" Budyonny asked.

Oganesov went quiet. Then, after a brief silence, he shook his head.

"It's ridiculous. Do you see me climbing out the window – a third-floor window, mind you – and going out into the street in my lab coat and mask? I'd have to go through security at the gate, too."

"And yet, Vyatka Street, where Liberty is located, is only a ten-minute bus ride from the intersection of Chekhov and the Garden Ring," Gordeyev observed thoughtfully.

"So what? I wasn't there. Anyway, why do I need to account for my whereabouts at two in the afternoon?"

"That's all for now," Budyonny cut him off, ignoring his question. "We'll continue in the morning. Get him sent to Butyrka, Gordeyev."

"What? To a cell?" Oganesov cried out in horror. "What did I do? I'm innocent."

Gordeyev got behind him and, steering him like a German shepherd herding sheep, pushed him out as he was protesting and waving his handcuffed arms about.

The moment the door closed behind them, the Boss shook off the last vestiges of his avuncular manner and gave me a venomous look.

"Well," he said bitterly. "That's what we got from your newspaper article."

"That's not the only thing, Comrade Colonel," I objected. "People are being more careful. That boy, Stepa, is probably alive today because his grandmother read Comrade Korenev's article."

"I'm not so sure about that. People are still leaving their kids alone and the kids still open the doors to strangers. And are getting themselves killed, don't forget. But enough about that. How're you getting on with finding the playwright's vehicle?"

I was taken aback by his question because, to be honest, the playwright's vehicle could not have been farther from my thoughts the past few days.

"I've got a good idea what happened and who is responsible," I said. "And I'm pretty sure I can recover it. But Comrade Korenev has told me not to spend any more time on it and to concentrate on catching the child killer. He's worried that if we don't have some results soon, he might get in trouble with Comrade Khrushchev. We could, too. I heard him talking on the phone to Nikita Sergeyevich and Nikita Sergeyevich wants results."

Budyonny was an exceptionally brave cop, but he had a fear of his own bosses that bordered on the pathological. And of course there was no boss in the country bigger than Nikita Sergeyevich.

"Well, no one wants results more than I do," he exclaimed, wringing his hands. "But we've already dropped every other case and got everybody working on this. Including you. I've got people pressing me to lend them operatives. Our colleagues from Leningrad call me literally every day, but where do they think I'm gonna get reinforcements for them? I don't manufacture them. It's as if they don't read the papers and don't know what we're up against in Moscow."

He sighed.

"I want you to talk to the suspect in the morning. Get him to list everyone whom he spoke to about that clever MosGaz ploy of his. And when exactly he came up with it, how long that was before the first murder. Urumov will do the same with the ex-wife. The others should go through the list of MosGaz employees, current and past. Coincidences happen, you know."

What this meant was that we were back to square one. We had no credible suspect and Budyonny knew it. Later that morning, the old woman and her grandchild would be summoned to headquarters to identify Oganesov, and I was sure that they would not pick Oganesov out as their MosGaz man. Our investigation was once again spinning its wheels and we were thrashing about in search of leads.

It was not my fault, but Budyonny was mad at me. I was the messenger who had told him that Oganesov was not our man. Someone had to be a scapegoat.

TWENTY-ONE

Tosya had fallen asleep in my bed waiting for me. It was still dark outside my windows, but then again, there's not much daylight in Moscow in December. I got under the covers quietly, trying not to wake her, and closed my eyes for what seemed like a minute.

The alarm clock, after ticking all night on the night table, went off at six-thirty. Tosya shifted, shut off the annoying buzzing, and slipped out of bed. I strained my eyes in the darkness, watching her move around the room as she gathered up her clothes. I reached across her pillow and flicked on the bedside lamp.

She squinted at me and smiled as she sat down on the edge of the bed. I watched the muscles of her back flow and tighten as she pulled on her wool stockings. Suddenly, she became conscious of me staring at her and turned around quickly, shielding her eyes from the light. She frowned and she pulled a blanket over her bare chest.

"What are you looking at? You've got no shame, Matyushkin."

I raised myself on an elbow, threw both arms around her and tried to pull her toward me.

"Leave me alone," she grumbled. "I'm trying to get ready for work. Tell me what happened last night. Did you arrest the guy?"

I turned away.

"We did," I said. "But I think we got the wrong guy again."

"I'm sorry," she said.

She got dressed in silence for a bit. There was only the soft rustle of her clothes and the sound of her breathing.

"I need to talk to you," she said.

"What about?" I asked.

I extended my hand and tried to caress her.

"Stop it."

She was suddenly angry.

"I'm serious. I want to tell you something about Irina."

I sat up in bed. Right after New Year's, Tosya had taken Irina's phone number and said she was going to call her. In the turmoil of the various unpleasant events that followed, I had completely forgotten about it, and now felt guilty for not even asking her how it went.

"Yes, how is it going?" I asked.

"She's warming up to me," Tosya replied. "Gradually."

"That's good."

"Yes, but as I get to know her, I worry about it even more."

"Dr. Lazius doesn't think there is anything to worry about."

"Fine. But what I'm trying to tell you is that she's suicidal."

"And I'm trying to tell you that Dr. Lazius doesn't think so. And he should know. Suicides are his specialty."

"Perhaps she's not going to actually hang herself. She won't need to. She's fading away. All she had in life was her mother and her daughter, and now they're both under the dirt at Vagankovo. She wants to be with them, that's the problem."

Tosya had pulled her dress over her head and slithered into it, turning her back toward me once more.

"Do my buttons, Matyushkin. But no funny business, I'm warning you."

"She's fading away," she repeated. "Maybe the doctor, instead of opining about her condition, should do something about it. Since he lives next door."

The non-identification of Oganesov by our witnesses went just as I had expected.

"Are you trying to tell me you think this is the guy?" the grandmother cried out in disbelief, looking from Oganesov's mugshot to Gordeyev and back at the mugshot. "Are you pulling my leg, young man? I'm not blind and I have not yet lost my mind."

She had failed to pick Oganesov's picture out of a stack of ten that had been placed in front of her, and was outraged when Gordeyev suggested that Oganesov had been the man.

Stepa also ignored Oganesov's mug shot and picked someone else's, a man who couldn't have looked more different from the chemical engineer. Nevertheless, when shown Oganesov's picture all by itself, he insisted to Gordeyev that he was the man. His testimony, however, was dismissed as frivolous.

To make matters even more confusing, a sketch drawn by a forensic artist under the grandmother's direction looked nothing like Oganesov but, as Lenny was quick to point out, strongly resembled Grushnikov. Even I had to admit that he was right.

"I'll be sure to check his alibi," he declared ominously.

Oganesov's alibi, meanwhile, stood up. In the morning, he recalled that a technician had walked into his lab some time around quarter after two, and apologized for interrupting him before exiting again.

That was when I was at Butyrka prison having a chat with him.

I got there before reveille, rousing a guard who had been slumbering peacefully at his desk, his head resting on his forearm. He got the other guards up as well, and they went to fetch the prisoner, cursing under their breath. Soon I heard them playing out their underslept anger on poor Oganesov, yelling at him and pushing him roughly down the long prison corridor.

Oganesov was even more disheveled than he had been when we got him out of bed in the middle of the night. His swollen, bloodshot eyes told me that he had gotten less sleep than I had.

Yes, he had seen an article in the paper and had heard people talk about the killings at work and at his landlady's communal apartment.

He had been concerned about his son, of course. However, not being on speaking terms with his ex-wife, he could do nothing about it. No, it had never occurred to him that his MosGaz trick and the murders could have been connected in any way.

"Are they?" he asked, dumbfounded. His surprise seemed so genuine that I almost believed him. But with Lenny accusing me of being soft on our suspects, I worked hard not to let my own feelings interfere with the interrogation.

But when asked whom he had told about his MosGaz prank he showed no hesitation, "Nobody."

"Are you sure?"

"One hundred percent. But I'm sure Valeria did. I mean my former wife."

He went on to explain that he didn't want people to know that his ex-wife wouldn't allow him to see his own son.

"Not even your landlady knew?"

"She least of all," he said, averting his eyes. "She never wanted me to see my boy."

Lenny protested and even slammed a fist on his desk in impotent rage, but in the end Oganesov, too, had to be let go. We sat in our office in silence, Lenny staring out the window and drumming his fingers on his desktop.

Lenny had his hands full. Unlike Oganesov, his ex-wife had told the MosGaz story to everyone who'd listen, from her colleagues at work to fellow-passengers on the tram. The Boss insisted that Lenny check every lead – every person she could recall with certainty, and Lenny had a tall stack of index cards on his desk onto which he had started to transfer the names he had gotten from her so far, color-coding them based on the degree of urgency with which they had to be checked. But now he sat there paralyzed, unable to move.

In the afternoon, the Boss's secretary Marina came into our office. She gave a charming smile to Lenny, who frowned and turned toward the window, and announced to me coldly that Budyonny wanted to see me in his office. Then she pushed past me and began patting Lenny on the shoulder.

"What's the matter with you, darling," she cooed into his ear, oblivious to the fact that I had not yet left. "Those murders have upset me terribly and yet you've been paying me no attention."

Lenny shot daggers at her and I decided not to stick around to hear his reply.

With Marina busy in our office, the reception area was empty. I knocked on the Boss's soundproof door and pushed it open. He was on the phone, but he signaled for me to come in, indicating that he was almost finished.

"There is no way I can spare a single person," he was saying into the receiver. "We have our hands full, too. Worse than full. What?"

He listened. Apparently, he didn't like what he was hearing at the other end, because he interrupted brusquely.

"I'm sorry, Colonel, do you read the papers? Which papers? *Soviet Russia*, for instance? Sure, I know you're in Leningrad, but it's still Russia, last time I looked at the map. Well, then you know what we're dealing with. Don't you think this should take priority over a bank robbery? I'm aware that a young woman was killed and an officer was wounded, but it's over. It's a question of catching the bastards and putting them on trial, whereas here in Moscow we're in a developing situation. Every day I wake up dreading that I'm going to hear about another murder. It's you who should be giving me assistance, not the other way around. Please, that's enough. I'm not going to listen to you any longer."

However, he listened some more and then said, "Yes, I understand that the district party secretary is on your case. I would be too, if I were him. I'm not even going to tell you who's looking over my shoulder."

With that, Budyonny replaced the receiver with a bang and uttered a profanity.

"Those goddamn Leningraders. Now they want the fingerprints that they sent to our lab to get priority treatment. It's like they think our people have been twiddling their thumbs, waiting for our Leningrad colleagues to give them some work to do."

Having blown off steam, the Boss turned to me.

"Sit down," he said.

I sat in a chair and got ready to listen. Budyonny was hovering over me from behind his high desk, and there was the long expanse of the conference table between us.

"I want you to go see Comrade Korenev again," he said.

"I was planning to this afternoon, sir, to keep him informed about our latest developments."

"Good," he said. "But it's not that, Matyushkin. You should ask him to write another article. We need to tell the people about this MosGaz guy."

A week ago, it had taken all my powers of persuasion to get Budyonny to let me approach the playwright about the first article. Now we had switched roles. He thought we needed another article, about MosGaz, and this time I was sure it wasn't going to fly with Korenev.

"But it did us a lot of good, that article," the Boss exclaimed, countering my objections after I had recounted to him again what I heard of Korenev's conversation with Khrushchev. "People are more cautious. You said it yourself, the grandmother read the article and she was watching out for her grandson. The article probably saved his life. And we got a lead because of it. What? It was a dud? Well, yes, it was, but we now know how the killer gets into people's apartments. And it's our duty to get this information to the public."

Budyonny's accent was much stronger. He was getting more and more emotional. He was also using my own arguments against me. I felt flattered, but not convinced.

"Since it's not Oganesov," I said, "the real killer probably thinks that his cover has been blown. He won't use it again. Especially if the story gets into the papers."

I thought it was a pretty good argument, but Budyonny was suddenly tired of my objections. As it was, he found himself in an unusual position of having to argue with a subordinate.

"You may be right, Lieutenant," he said, wearily wiping his large hand across his face. "But I'm telling you to go to Korenev and ask him to write an article about MosGaz. Consider it an order."

Which of course it was. And it had to be carried out, regardless of what I thought of the chances that my mission would be successful or what kind of reception I was going to get at Korenev's.

I had not been to see Korenev since just before New Year's, and so much had happened over the past several days that I felt a little guilty not keeping him abreast of all the developments.

"Happy New Year, detective," Korenev said in greeting, hugging me at the front door. "Come in, bring me up to date. I hope you've got good news for me."

"Not too good," I said. "But there has been progress. Thanks to your article."

I looked at him closely. Contrary to my expectations, his face didn't spread in a gratified smile and he didn't immediately bombard me with questions.

"You haven't come to see me for a couple of days," he said, "but I don't mind. My play about you guys, *The Detectives*, has been spinning its wheels. But I've been working on my commission. The deadline is not far off."

Korenev had always been overactive, but this time he seemed a little slow and dejected. He skipped from one subject to the next more quickly than usual, and didn't seem particularly interested in our investigation.

"Let's have lunch, detective," he said. " I hear Zinaida setting the table."

He linked his arm through mine and took me to the dining room.

"No Sergei today?" I asked along the way, listening to the silence in the apartment. "Or at least he's not polishing the parquet?"

"He's done with the floors. He's taking a break and watching TV. I honestly have no idea what he'll be doing in the spring if the car doesn't turn up."

"Oh, I'm sure it will," I said.

I had skipped supper the night before and passed an almost sleepless night. I suddenly realized I was starving. Korenev, on the contrary, ate with uncharacteristic restraint. He pushed the creamy potato and leek soup around in his bowl and then, after his customary internal struggle, lifted the stopper from the vodka decanter.

"I need something to spur my appetite," he explained apologetically, pouring himself a shot. "I assume you're not going to keep me company."

I mumbled something unintelligible, since I had just shoved a heaping spoonful of hot soup into my mouth. The last thing I needed at the moment was something to spur my appetite, which seemed to be doing just fine, especially since Zinaida's cooking was truly superb.

He drank and poured himself another shot.

"Now tell me the news," he said.

I described the failed attack the day before and reminded him about the MosGaz story I had told him previously. Then on to Oganesov's arrest. Korenev listened, shaking his head now and again, but he was no longer giving me his usual third degree.

"I hope that Gordeyev and you kept an eye on him at all times," he observed when I was describing Oganesov's arrest. "And on his so-called landlady. Because they could've easily destroyed important evidence if you were not looking. They're most likely in cahoots, the two of them. I would detain her, too, if I were you. What are you going to do now?"

"We've already released him," I said

"What? Released him? But he's your prime suspect!"

"It's not him," I said. "He's got an alibi."

"What about accomplices? If his landlady was part of the gang, then they must have had others."

"We'll continue to work on all possible leads," I said. "We're also checking who else his wife could have told the MosGaz story to."

"That's good," Korenev said approvingly. "This should give me plenty of material to go back and finish my play. Otherwise I seem to have hit an impasse. Besides, I can't sleep. I've lost my appetite."

He reached for the decanter, pulled back momentarily and then shook his head decisively, pouring himself a third shot.

I waited for him to toss it back before mustering my courage.

"Matvei Nikanorovich," I said. "We need your help again."

"In what way?" he asked, becoming apprehensive.

The jailbird English maid Zinaida came in to take away our soup plates. I observed her closely as she plopped down a large serving platter piled with fluffy chunks of filet of cod in peppery sauce and a tall volcano of mashed potatoes with a yellow lake of melted butter in its crater. I waited for her to leave.

But when she did, and before I could reply, the playwright beat me to the punch.

"If it's another article you want, forget about it," he declared categorically. "Don't even ask."

"It's not a new article," I said. "It's an addition to the first one. We need to add new information, that the killer gets kids to open their door by impersonating a MosGaz employee. All we need is a few lines."

"I said no," said Korenev, suddenly cold and formal. "As you can imagine, I can't write it without Nikita Sergeyevich's approval and Nikita Sergeyevich wasn't too happy with the first article. Even though he gave it the green light."

"He obviously saw how important it was," I pleaded. "The boy, Stepa, was saved because of your article. Because of Nikita Sergeyevich's wise decision. You should have seen him. He's such a great little kid. I'm sure if you give Comrade Khrushchev the whole picture, especially using your talent for description—"

Korenev put out his palm bidding me to stop.

"Nikita Sergeyevich doesn't have time for this. He's been quite busy with the affairs of state. American imperialists are plotting all sorts of nastiness against the freedom-loving Cuban people. They sent pigs to invade the island, but Cuban soldiers slaughtered them as they came ashore. I'm not going to bother him at a time like this. It would risk irritating him."

I knew I wasn't going to make him change his mind, but I was carrying out Budyonny's orders and I had to persevere.

"Matvei Nikanorovich, it's not a nice thing to do," I said, shaking my head reproachfully. "You can't be concerned only with your own career. You're a Soviet writer, a member of the Writers' Union and that imposes on you the responsibility to care about people. Think of it for a moment: little kids' lives are at stake."

"Kids," grumbled the playwright shifting his eyes and looking at the wall. "Don't talk to me about kids. Small kids – small problems, big kids – a whole lot of very big problems. You never know, detective. It might be better if children die while they're little. They may be happier that way."

It was a strange thing to say, but I ignored it and continued to shower him with various communist party slogans. I felt they would be more effective.

"Children are the future of our society, Matvei Nikanorovich," I declared, as though I was speaking at some party congress. "It's for their sake that we're building the just and fair communist system in which everyone will be happy. We can't allow them—"

The playwright, who must have heard things like that more than once during his career, was unmoved.

"I told you I'm not going to go to *him* with this kind of request," he said at last, cutting off my sloganeering in mid-sentence. "It's not just my career that I'm concerned about. I'm probably the only member of the Writers' Union Nikita Sergeyevich respects. And rightly so. He is very unhappy with our writers and artists. He's given us a lot of freedom and some of our number have abused it shamelessly, embracing new-fangled forms and styles that the insidious West sends our way. There are some artists who don't understand that Americans have invented all that abstract art with the sole purpose of undermining our socialist culture."

Korenev had not touched the food on his plate and I too had started to lose my appetite. I wasn't looking forward to reporting my failure to Budyonny.

"Besides," Korenev added, "I've already done one article. That should be more than enough for you to catch the killer. If you know what you're doing, of course."

It was clear that he wasn't going to change his mind.

"Very well," I said. "I can't force you to do anything you don't want to. I've got to go now."

I pushed away my cup of cranberry drink and went out. Korenev stayed seated at the table, looking guilty and, somehow, doomed.

On the way out, I caught a glimpse of Sergei. He gave me a look that was full of apprehension and hastened to retreat toward the dining room, to the protection of his boss.

As to my Boss, he made only the briefest of appearances at the office over the next two days. He had had to report on the progress of our investigation to the top brass in the Ministry of Internal Affairs – or, rather, on the lack thereof, and the talking to they gave him upset him tremendously. He became physically ill. When he returned on the morning of the third day and I went to report to him on my conversation with the playwright, fully expecting him to vent his anger and frustration on me, I found him in an unexpectedly jovial mood. Before I could utter a single word, he pre-empted me.

"I don't know, Matyushkin, whether it's you who did it or whether Comrade Korenev acted on his own conscience, but it's a great job," he said, rushing toward me from behind his desk and giving me a fatherly squeeze on the forearm. "Congratulations."

"What happened, Comrade Colonel?" I asked, puzzled.

"As if you don't know," said Budyonny, winking and breaking into an almost tender smile. "An article about the MosGaz man, to let people know whom to fear and to report to the cops if he ever comes knocking."

It wasn't much, just three short lines buried at the bottom of the last page of the previous night's edition of *Evening Moscow*, next to the TV schedule and just above a couple of obituaries, enclosed inside their black frames. But it was better than nothing. A lot better, because our audience, the grandmothers, read the paper cover to cover and had an eagle eye for tidbits like this.

"Comrade Korenev has done his job," Budyonny added. "Now we simply must catch the bastard. Don't forget to thank him. We're forever in his debt."

TWENTY-TWO

As I had promised Tosya, I stopped by the apartment in 1st Kolobovsky to talk to Lazius. Irina Drozdova was out – I had a pretty good idea where she was – and so was Dr. Lazius.

The door was answered after a considerable delay by his wife Nadezhda, and once again I was struck by her bedraggled, unhealthy appearance.

"Could I leave a message for your husband," I asked, when she informed me that he wasn't in.

She nodded.

"Actually, there's no message," I said after a moment's hesitation. "Could you just tell him that I stopped by and that I wanted to ask him a question?"

She had an absent look on her face and I wasn't at all sure that she took anything in.

"Good bye," she said before closing her door.

I went away shaking my head.

Baba Dasha lay in wait for me in the hallway. Somehow I wasn't surprised to see her.

"Another day off, Baba Dasha?"

"Did you see her?" she asked me in her usual mock conspiratorial whisper.

"See whom?" I asked.

"The doctor's wife, who else? You were just talking to her. What did you think of her?"

"Nothing," I shrugged, keeping my opinions to myself.

"Oh, come on," she suddenly began talking faster, as though overcome by a great sense of urgency. "You couldn't help noticing it. She looks dreadful."

"I don't know." I said, shrugging again. "Why?"

"She's going nuts, that's why. It's the apartment. I've always said it's a cursed place."

She made a sign of the cross.

"All she talks about is how we've been damned. How these murders, the ones that started with our poor Tanya, are a punishment for our transgressions. That they'll never stop. How you'll never find out who's doing it, and it's useless to even try."

"What does her husband say about it?" I asked.

"Are you kidding? She'd never mention a thing like this in front of him. She's too scared of him. Her fear is even stronger than her craziness."

Outside, I took a deep breath, filling my lungs with fresh air. It was still very cold, a biting early January frost, and there were over two months of hard winter stretching before us. But, all the same, there was a hint of spring, too, and a winter thaw was on its way.

Nastya was waiting for me at the end of the long archway leading out of the courtyard, across 1st Kolobovsky Lane. She stood with her back to me in her bright-red overcoat and black high-heeled boots, smoking a cigarette. That's how she liked to appear, in unexpected places like a crowded metro car or a line at the grocery store. Her ability to turn up without warning gave me an unpleasant sensation that she was spying on me, but so stealthily that I was never aware that she was.

"Listen, I've got something for you," she began rapidly, also speaking in a hoarse whisper, like Baba Dasha. "Happy?"

"You bet I'm happy," I said. "You're a clever girl."

"Me, clever?" she sneered, but she was pleased nonetheless. She liked being praised. "Not as clever as you are, not by a long shot."

"And why am I so clever? Usually you tell me I became a cop because I was too dumb to do anything else."

"That's true, actually," she laughed. "But not in this case. I always knew you'd figure the creep out sooner or later."

"What creep?" I asked.

"Don't go stupid on me all of a sudden, copper," she said. "The good-looking professor. Weren't you in his apartment just now? And it's not the first time I've seen you go in and out. And don't tell me you're dating the charming cleaning woman from the People's Court, because I'll be jealous."

She guffawed at her own joke.

"What was I supposed to figure out about him?" I asked cautiously.

She was talking about Dr. Lazius and I knew it was bound to be interesting. What I couldn't even begin to imagine was exactly how interesting.

"Not about him, actually," she said. "About his first wife. Aren't you investigating her death?"

"No, I'm not."

Nastya bit her tongue. She was no police informant. That had always been an unspoken rule with us. She never told me anything that could land her pals in jail, and I never asked. She and I were friends, but she never for a moment forgot that we were also on different sides of the barricades. I had always wondered, however, whether that rule extended beyond the criminal fraternity and covered people like Dr. Lazius.

She herself was trying to figure it out and in the end she had an answer: it didn't.

"If you are not investigating her death, copper, you should be," she said at the end of a long pause. "Because he murdered his first wife. In cold blood."

We had a corner table at a café on Gorky Street. It was Nastya's choice, and she had insisted we go there by cab. She wasn't about to trudge through the rapidly softening snow wearing her nice boots, she said. As a rule, she preferred to have men drive her around in private cars, preferably foreign models, but considering my ridiculously low wages at Criminal Investigations and the fact that I wasn't clever enough to be on the take, she was willing to settle for a cab. And, come to think of it, she'd pay for it out of her own pocket.

There was a mischievous spark in her green eyes. She enjoyed poking fun at me.

She was sucking on a straw, rapidly getting to the bottom of her third Northern Lights – a potent concoction of brandy and sparkling wine, shaken, not stirred – while also finishing a serving of ice cream. I ordered several cups of black coffee for myself as I waited for her to tell me what she knew about Dr. Lazius.

I didn't begrudge the money I was spending, which added up to at least twenty rubles, excluding the taxi fare but including a ten-ruble note I had to slip to the maitre d' to be let in ahead of the line and placed in a quiet section of the cafe where we could talk. The place was full of stylish young men in tight trousers and clingy synthetic sweaters, each with at least one platinum blonde on his arm and some with as many as three. They were all pretty far away from us, however, huddling around a semi-circular stage near the bar.

Nastya was getting drunk.

"Not a bad dive, is it? What do you think? A nice place to bring your main squeeze?"

I didn't reply, ignoring her heavy-handed hints and frank stares. She took another sip of her Northern Lights and lit a cigarette.

"Fine," she said, with a tipsy wave of a hand. "If you don't want to be romantic, let's talk business. About the seedy underside of life. About Dr. Lazius, if you prefer. Let me think. It must have been around the time you and I first met. Before I was sent down the first time. I was working the trams back then. Hard work for no money, but if you want to learn, you've gotta start at the bottom and work your way up.

I wasn't born with a silver spoon in my mouth and had to work hard to get where I am. The problem with picking pockets is that no one in this city has any real dough on them unless it's payday. Even then, how much does a working stiff make? Eighty a month? A hundred? By the time they get on the tram to go home they've already spent at least five rubles on vodka. Then again, stealing from a drunk is a sin."

"I get it," I said, not wishing to discuss her professional activities. Nastya's tales were always entertaining, if you liked the criminal genre, but she took a long time to get to the point. "How does this connect to Dr. Lazius?"

"Just you wait. I'm gonna get to it and it's gonna be as juicy as the most expensive steak at the Prague Restaurant. So, there I am one day, on a tram, looking for someone with a social status above the usual Baba Manya. It's chock full of people, and not one person worth bothering with. Unless of course you go for fifteen-kopek coins kids get for their school lunches."

She giggled drunkenly.

"So, there I am, riding that tram all sad and lonely, and none of my fellow passengers has enough cash in his pockets for a girl to make a decent living, and then I look up and I start to rub my eyes and pinch myself. It was like I died and went to heaven. A middle-aged gentleman, clean-shaven, graying temples, a pair of gold-rimmed spectacles, jacket and tie, a pair of leather shoes so shiny it hurts your eyes to look at them. But wait, it gets even better. Plenty better. Next to him he's got a fat cow, not that ugly for her age, and expensively maintained: white skin, no wrinkles, gray hair, some kind of foreign perfume. And lots of baubles on her, like she's a New Year's tree: on her sweater, in her ears, on her neck, on her fingers, even on her wrists - in short, a pawnshop keeper's wet dream. And, trailing those two, a young beauty. An ice queen come to life."

"Don't tell me," I said.

"Precisely," she sneered. "The blonde Hitler. The professor's new love. If only I had her looks."

She sent me a flirtatious glance across the table. I shrugged and waited for her to go on.

"She was with them, but I didn't figure it out right away, because they were sharing a seat and she stood a little apart from them and didn't interfere while the two of them were busy fighting.

" 'You're in luck, my girl,' I say to myself. 'Now is your chance.'

"But then I saw that something strange was going on with those two. As they fought, I realized that what they were fighting about was the blonde. The woman kept pointing to her and calling her names like 'that piece of crap' or 'that whore.' Not very lady-like, and she wasn't the least bit embarrassed using that kind of language in public, as if there were no other passengers on the tram. Besides, the girl could hear her perfectly well. The old cow just didn't care.

"Then, right in the middle of a sentence she starts to nod off. Every now and again she'd shake her head, trying to stay awake, but to no avail.

" 'I think I need a cup of coffee,' she says, dreamy-like.

"And now he, her professor husband, suddenly goes tender and solicitous, even though not five minutes before he had been telling her to shut up and to go to hell. But now all is forgotten and he starts saying in a sort of hypnotic voice, and very softly: 'Take a nap, my darling. You're tired. You're very tired. Yes, go to sleep. What a good idea. Go to sleep. Go to sleep. I'll wake you up when we get to Kirov Gate.' "

"What happened to Nadezhda?" I asked. "I mean the younger woman."

"She just stood there stone-faced, like none of it had anything to do with her. By the time we got to Sretenka, the old cow was fast asleep, snoring softly. At Kirov Gate, all the old women and school kids got off, but the three of them stayed on and the professor made no attempt to wake up his wife. Then, when the car was nearly empty, he got up and went over to stand next to the blonde, whispering something in her ear. Something sweet and tender. But not as tender as he had been with the old cow. The blonde started to laugh and then glanced at the old cow who was by then slumped over in her seat and got very uneasy. After that she kept looking back at the woman and trying to get some kind of an answer from the professor, and the professor kept telling her not to worry about anything. Like, everything's under control."

"Where were you all that time?"

"When the professor and his wife were both sitting, I came up and stood just behind them with my back turned. Not that they were looking at other passengers. When he got up, I took his seat.

"By then most of the passengers were new, and if you hadn't seen them get on together, you'd have had no idea the professor and the old woman were in any way connected. To tell you the truth, at the time I didn't cotton on to what was happening and only reconstructed it afterwards. I was just busy with the job at hand, even though in the back of my mind I kind of thought they were acting strange. Not at all like normal people."

"Yes, it's a strange story," I said.

"Wait," she said. "It gets stranger. We get to Yauza Gate, at the end of the boulevard. I'm ready to get off, because I have taken off the old cow a nice gold bracelet that was pretty thin and weighed nothing at all, but looked real expensive. I knew I could have done a lot better, but I figured I shouldn't get too greedy and risk being caught by the old cow's husband or by her if she woke up at a wrong time. But as I get up to go I see that the other two, the professor and his blonde, are already off the tram and walking away."

Nastya was speaking softly and slurring her words. I had to lean close to her to hear, and I was listening intently when a thunderous noise made both of us jump. We looked at each other and laughed a little uneasily. Two young men were now at the edge of the stage, one holding a trumpet and the other an electric guitar. A third, an older man with a deeply lined face, was positioned behind them, manning a gleaming percussion set. All three wore dark suits, black turtlenecks, square black glasses and black hats. The two young men had pomaded hair that stood stiffly on end, while the head of the older one was completely bald, gleaming in the spotlight almost as brightly as his drums. The kids at the bar jumped up and rushed to the dance floor.

"Twist 'n' Shout," the drummer yelled at the top of his voice and added: "Yeah baby!"

And twisting was what the couples immediately began to do. As to the shouting, it was mostly done by the drummer, while the other two concentrated on their music – if that was what it was.

"Shall we dance?" Nastya asked archly, eyeing me.

"No chance," I replied sharply. "What happened next to Dr. Lazius's wife?"

Nastya moved her shoulders playfully in time to the music, trying my patience.

"I'd love another drink," she said. "My throat is parched from all the talking."

"You've had three cocktails already," I reminded her.

"Big deal," she said. "If Criminal Investigations is too cheap to stand me a drink, you should be a gentleman and pay for it out of your own pocket. What do you need the money for, anyway. You already bedded your lovely neighbor, so you won't need to take her to fancy cafés any longer."

I gave her a sharp look. So I was right. She had been spying on me.

To stop her talking nonsense I called the waiter over and asked for another cocktail and another cup of coffee for myself, even though all the caffeine was making me jumpy and irritable.

"Tell him to hurry up, will you?" Nastya added loudly, her words crowding each other. "Last time it took him an age to serve it."

"Go on," I said.

"There isn't much else to tell." She was losing interest in the story and hurried through the rest. "I changed my mind about getting off and sat back down. The tram went on, and I let her rest her head on my shoulder like we were together, a nice elderly grandma taking a little nap next to her loving granddaughter. Or, if you prefer, a rich old lady with a poor distant cousin. It was a perfect setup. Even you could've pulled the trinkets off of her."

"And then what?" I asked.

"Nothing. When I was done, I just pushed her off and she leaned the other way, against the window. She went on sleeping without waking up once. By then I knew it had to be the kind of nap you don't wake up from."

"So, you know what happened to her."

Nastya nodded.

"The professor became a widower overnight, and a free man. How damn convenient. The tram driver must have been in a hurry to take the car to the depot, so he didn't notice her. Or maybe she slipped down onto the seat after I got up. They didn't find her until the next morning. But I wonder whether it would have made any difference if they had. The professor didn't look like an amateur."

"How do you know about the tram depot and the rest?" I asked.

"It's not so hard to find out. You know about it too."

She giggled. The four Northern Lights were making themselves felt.

"I didn't tell you the weirdest thing yet," she said. "When I opened her purse to get her wallet, there was a suicide note. Now, based on what I told you, does it look like a suicide?"

"Not really," I admitted.

"The professor must have snuck it in when she started to nod off. In her purse, she also had her documents with her address on them, so I figured out who they were. I even went to her funeral. And why not? Come to think of it, I was the last person to see her alive. Besides, I had a lot to be grateful to her for, as you can imagine. Those trinkets weren't cheap. And a fancy funeral it was, let me tell you, with lots of flowers and wreaths, especially from her disconsolate husband. He was weeping like a baby over her casket. It was very touching to see, and it goes to show that the cynics are dead wrong when they say that there is no true love left in this world. Two adorable little tykes, too. Such a tragedy. And the Snow White blonde standing in the crowd, looking like death warmed over. She was taking it very hard. But I suppose she rallied. Two months later they were married. That was when it all started to make sense to me. A fat old wife versus a young, long-legged one. Even I could see the difference."

"I suppose you tried to blackmail the doctor," I said.

"Where would you get that outrageous idea?" she exclaimed and then burst out laughing. "Well, the thought *did* cross my mind once or twice. But I knew I had no chance. He's not stupid, that professor. He'd just call my bluff and turn me in to the cops. It would've been my word against his and no one would ever believe me. Besides, I had taken her wallet and all those trinkets. He thought her stuff had been stolen at the depot and made a stink about it. I wasn't going to come forward to tell him it was me."

She grinned and then suddenly grew sad.

"We are like vultures, me and his new wife. I snatched up the dead woman's trinkets and she took her husband."

It was well past midnight when Nastya and I parted. She had become unpleasant and quarrelsome. She kept asking me to dance and leaning across the table, trying kiss me. She also started picking fights with the kids on the dance floor. The waiters were giving us dirty looks, especially since the line by the door was snaking down the block, its tail hidden from view somewhere around the corner. But they didn't dare say anything to us and I doubt they were afraid of me. Waiters in such cafes have a practiced eye and they surely figured Nastya out. The last thing they wanted was to pick a fight with someone from her social circle. You could easily end up beaten up or stabbed on a dark street on your way home from a late shift.

"You owe me big time," she kept saying. "I went out on the limb for you."

I couldn't understand what she meant until I had put her into a taxi and she mentioned Rubashkin.

"Yeah, I forgot to tell you," she said. "You were right, after all, copper. I've gotta give it to you. Someone did try to offer a ZIM to Rubashkin."

She slammed the door and, as the Volga cab was about to pull away from the curb, rolled down the window.

"Except Rubashkin sent him packing," she said.

"What, no customers for a hot ZIM?" I asked.

"That too," she said. "But mainly because of the kind of ZIM it was. Too dangerous. Rubashkin may be greedy, but he's no fool."

TWENTY-THREE

Despite the late hour, I headed back to headquarters, walking through the dark, deserted streets of the city. Nastya had given me a lot of information and I needed to look at my notes and think things over in the peace and quiet of an empty office. Besides, with all the coffee gurgling in my stomach, I knew I wasn't going to fall asleep any time soon, despite getting only a few minutes of sleep the night before.

But the office was far from empty. In our narrow TU-104 the lights were blazing and Lenny Urumov was giving me a wolfish grin from behind his desk. Our overheated office smelled of burnt dust and sweat.

"Good evening, Matyushkin," he greeted me. "I see you, too, have decided to lucubrate."

"To do what?"

I had actually come to distrust Lenny's good moods. Lately, there was a kind of strain in his good cheer, whenever he chose to affect it, and his smile was as crooked as a seven-ruble note. I'd much rather have him scowl at me instead.

His desk had been cleared and dusted, almost like Dr. Lazius's workstation at his clinic, and now contained only a notebook and a sharpened pencil.

"I was going to review my notes," I said.

"Sure," Lenny said. "Go ahead."

He grinned at me again and started to hum a tune. He had no ear for music, and aside from the fact that it was some kind of an upbeat march, it was hard to figure out what it was.

"Are you going to stick around for a while?" he asked.

"Yes, I thought—" I started to reply.

There was a knock on the door. Lenny, who had clearly been expecting it, sat up abruptly and yelled, "Don't be shy, baby. Come right in."

I was surprised to see a girl from Forensics still working at this late hour. Her name was Svetlana and, like all the young girls in our department, she was on friendly terms with Urumov. She was holding a thin manila folder and a large paper bag.

"What's the verdict?" Urumov asked eagerly.

"It's a match, Lenny," she said.

There was a long hissing sound as Lenny exhaled through his mouth. He jumped up, ran over and encased Svetlana in a bear hug. Then he tried to twirl her in a waltz, but failed because there was so little room in our office. He hit his hip on the edge of his desk and cursed. But the pain, which must have been sharp, did nothing to dampen his high spirits.

"I told you so," he yelled, violating the night silence. "We've got him. I knew it all along. Thank you, Svetlana, thank you my angel."

She handed him the bag and the folder and left the room. Lenny, his eyes flashing madly, turned to face me.

"Aren't you curious to know what this is, Matyushkin?" he asked, shaking the paper bag in my face.

"Should I be?"

His ebullience was breaking my concentration and I had started to think about going home.

"Absolutely," Lenny said. "You of all people."

"Well, if you insist, let me ask you a question: What is it?"

He shook the bag again.

"This ordinary looking paper bag contains one pair of warm-up pants belonging to Comrade Grushnikov, taken from his room two days ago, while said Comrade Grushnikov was at work."

He put down the bag and raised the manila folder.

"And this ordinary looking manila folder contains the results of a chemical test on said warm-up pants, particularly on the dried black stains on the bottom of the said warm-up pants. It may come as a surprise to you, but the chemical test has determined that the stains are identical to the ink found at the scene where Comrade Grushnikov murdered his neighbor Tanya Drozdova."

I sat up, batting my eyes.

"Surely you remember the inkwell that fell and spilled all over the floor," Lenny said. "I knew there had to be a pair of pants somewhere with spots matching that ink. And here it is."

"So, it's Grushnikov after all," I said, still perplexed.

"I suppose it is, yes. Now who looks like a total idiot, Matyushkin? The ones who arrested Grushnikov on the day of the murder, or their one colleague who insisted throughout that he be let go?"

I still couldn't find any words. There was nothing to say. I was shocked, humiliated. It wasn't Lenny or Budyonny or any of the guys I was thinking of at that moment, and not my own career at Criminal Investigations that would not survive this blow. Rather, I was thinking of the other kids who had been murdered after Grushnikov had been released, and of Irina Drozdova who was living side by side with her daughter's murderer.

"But what about Dima Sadykov? He couldn't have been killed by Grushnikov. He was in custody at the time."

I had to ask him the question, even though I knew it would sound petty in the midst of Lenny's great triumph.

"Let's look at it one murder at a time," Lenny said. "We've just solved the first murder and we'll get to the second one in due course."

He opened the folder and began to read the typewritten report.

"That's right," he said. "Just as I expected. Exact match. Same chemical makeup, same color."

He went on reading.

"Oh shit," he exclaimed suddenly, squinting at something in the file. He cursed and tossed the folder onto his recently cleared desk.

"Look at this bastard," he said through clenched teeth. "Listen to what they found in the pockets. A pair of girl's underpants. I bet you anything they are Tanya's."

I glanced at the folder.

"I'm going to bring him in," Lenny said. "Right now."

"Does the Boss know?" I asked.

"He does," Lenny said. "He said if the test comes back as a match, I was to put Grushnikov under surveillance and wait until he got an arrest warrant."

"I want to talk to the Boss," I said.

I had now made up my mind, too.

"He's gone. And he won't be here tomorrow, either. He's on his way to the Crimea."

"Where?"

I couldn't believe my ears. Budyonny going to the Black Sea in the middle of this investigation? It didn't make any sense.

"Is that some kind of sick joke?"

Lenny grinned at me. He could afford to be jovial now, even while he was seething with anger at Grushnikov – and at me, too.

"Relax, Matyushkin. He's not taking a vacation. The Minister of Internal Affairs is. The top brass have summoned Budyonny to the Council of Ministers' dacha in Crimea. At least now he'll have something to report and they may go gently on him."

"When is he coming back?" I asked.

"I don't know. The day after tomorrow maybe. It depends on when he gets to see the Minister. The Minister is taking the sun."

Lenny paused and jerked his head decisively:

"I'm not going to wait for him to come back," he said. "If I take the bastard in, the Boss will be able to tell the Minister we've arrested the killer. I'm going right now. On my own responsibility. You can come along if you want."

"I do, actually," I said.

He unlocked the top drawer of his desk and pulled out his service Makarov.

"I think you should take yours, too," he said.

I didn't think it was going to be necessary, but I didn't want to argue with Lenny. I unlocked my desk, pulled out my own Makarov, checked the magazine and slipped it into my coat pocket.

"I need to tell you something," I told Lenny when we got into his car.

He squeezed the steering wheel to the breaking point. The drive was short, only two or three twisty blocks down narrow lanes that were completely deserted.

"Not now," he replied.

"I need to tell you something about this report," I said.

"I know what you're going to say," Lenny said savagely. "But I'm no longer interested."

I still had the key to the apartment that Lenny had given me after Tanya's murder. I held it at the ready when we passed through the long archway where I had met Nastya only a few hours before, and used it to unlock the front door on the dark landing. I was first into the dark, silent corridor. Urumov was behind me, stepping on my heels and flipping the switch in the hallway. He tried to push past me, but I stepped up, reaching Grushnikov's door first.

"Turn off the light," I said over my shoulder. "Keep quiet."

I felt Lenny's breath on the nape of my neck and sensed his tense restraint. I knew he had not been prepared for this turn of events, of me seemingly assuming command of his operation. And now he was starting to suspect some mischief on my part. I just hoped he wouldn't go off before I could talk to Grushnikov.

I knocked softly on the gym teacher's door and waited, and after a while knocked again.

"What are you waiting for?" Urumov urged me loudly. "You've got his key. Just open the goddamn door."

"Be quiet," I said.

There were footsteps in the room but at the sound of Lenny's voice they abruptly stopped.

"Damn it, Lenny," I said, elbowing him in the ribs. "You're gonna make a mess of it."

The door opened silently. Grushnikov stood in the doorway wearing a pair of long johns and a very wrinkled dress shirt. He had been asleep, and a fold from a pillowcase was imprinted on his unshaven cheek, looking like an ugly reddish scar.

A panicked expression appeared in his eyes when he saw us, and he made an involuntary motion as though he was going to make a run for it. Then, he took hold of himself.

"Let me guess why you're here," he said. "You took my pants from my wardrobe and now you have come to arrest me again. I suppose now you've got some uncontrovertible proof that I'm guilty, since you were the ones who planted them here in the first place."

"Shut up for a minute and listen," I said quickly, playing up the rudeness for Lenny's benefit, in the hope of keeping him quiet for a few seconds longer. "Were those pants actually yours?"

He started to say something but I interrupted him, "Yes or no?"

"Yes," Grushnikov replied. "These are my old warm-ups."

"When did you last wear them?"

I had been blocking the doorway with my body, keeping Lenny from entering the room. He didn't like it, but there was nothing he could do for the moment. He kept trying to nudge me aside, gently at first and then with growing persistence, and now he had finally decided not to stand on ceremony and give me a shove in the back, making me stumble.

That finally created an opening for him to get through.

"You, stupid bastard," he bellowed. "I know all about you now."

"Get away from me," Grushnikov shouted, taking a step back and putting up his fists.

Grushnikov had large fists, heavy and knobbly. But Lenny didn't so much as glance at them. He grabbed Grushnikov by his shirt collar and pulled him down violently. Several buttons flew off and the fabric tore. Grushnikov, who was half a head taller than Lenny, was bent forward and their faces met at the same level. Lenny threw a left hook that caught the gym teacher over his left ear. Grushnikov's head jerked to one side, but Lenny had a firm grip on his shirt. The result was the loss of the remaining buttons. Lenny raised his fist to strike again, but I caught it in mid-air.

Furious, Lenny turned on me.

"What's the matter with you? Back to your old tricks?"

"Wait a minute," I said.

But there was no stopping him. While I had a hold of his left forearm, he used his right to push Grushnikov off, and then added a vicious kick in the groin. The teacher reeled backwards, falling heavily onto his unmade camp bed. The flimsy structure collapsed under his weight, sending a half-liter bottle of "Moskovskaya" rolling on the floor and filling the room with the dingy stench of stale vodka.

"He's playing the fool again," Urumov yelled. "And you're protecting him. Back to where we started. You never learn, do you, Matyushkin?"

Lenny jerked himself free from my grasp and, hovering over the collapsed bed, slapped Grushnikov's face several times.

"That's enough, Lenny," I said. "Stop this shit and listen."

Lenny was furious and tightly wound, but he was not impervious to reason. There must have been something in my voice that made him stop. I pushed him out of the way and came close to the bed on which Grushnikov now lay spread-eagle, gasping.

"When did you last wear those warm-up pants?" I repeated.

"You're just playing the good cop while your idiot partner beats the crap out of me. I don't want to talk to either of you."

"I'll make you," Urumov said darkly, making a new attempt to push me out of the way.

"Stop it, I said," I said to him. "Let me speak to him for a moment."

"Think logically," I said, turning to Grushnikov again. "If we planted evidence tying you to Tanya Drozdova's murder, what would be the point of talking to you now? We would have arrested you and convicted you on the evidence we planted. Right?"

He thought it over.

"Because you want me to admit that I killed Tanya. That would make your job so much easier."

"I don't want you to admit anything," I said, becoming exasperated. "I don't think you killed anybody."

Next to me Lenny groaned, but this time he didn't try to attack Grushnikov. That was progress.

Grushnikov, who may have gone to bed drunk judging by his puffy face and red eyes, was now sober and appeared to be more sensible than Lenny.

"Why are we having this conversation then?" he asked.

"That's better," I said.

"What do you want from me?"

"I want you to think when you last wore those warm-up pants."

"That's what I'm trying to tell you," Grushnikov exclaimed. "I haven't worn them since last September. I got myself a nylon suit from Czechoslovakia and I've been wearing it ever since. I wouldn't have thought of those pants, except they keep disappearing and showing up again."

"Did you wear them on the night Natashka was killed?"

Grushnikov and Lenny stared at me.

"Natashka?" Grushnikov asked, suspicion promptly leaping back into his voice. "Who's Natashka?"

I shook my head. I must have been under an emotional strain and the name of my little sister had slipped from the tip of my tongue.

"I mean Tanya," I corrected myself. "Tanya Drozdova. What were you wearing when you found her body?"

"I hadn't had time to take my street clothes off. I was wearing the same pants I wore to go to the doctor. My good pants."

"Now, did you have any of Tanya's underwear in your possession?" I asked.

Grushnikov gave me a sidelong look. It was the kind of expression that could not be faked.

"Let's go, Lenny," I said, straightening up. "We're done here."

"No way," Lenny said firmly. "I'm not letting him off the hook again. Get up, you creep. You're going with me."

"You can take him along if you wish," I shrugged. "We're not going far."

We went out into the hallway. I turned the light on and knocked on the door leading to Dr. Lazius's part of the apartment. It was opened to us almost immediately, as though we had been expected. Contrary to his avowed early-to-bed habit, Dr. Lazius was up, wearing a pair of house pants, a striped shirt, a knitted vest and a tie. His gold-rimmed glasses reflected the yellow light bulb in the hallway and I could not read the expression in his eyes when he saw us.

We must have been a strange group. I was in front, Urumov and Grushnikov stood just behind me. Urumov's hand rested heavily on Grushnikov's shoulder. Grushnikov was still wearing a torn shirt with all the buttons ripped off. A pair of long johns clung tightly to his thick athletic thighs.

I had not warned them and everything had happened very quickly. Lenny and Grushnikov were both dumbfounded in equal measure, staring at the doctor. He, on the other hand, showed no surprise at our unannounced nocturnal call.

"I've been waiting for you," he said softly. "You have no idea how hard it is to wait."

A pale, drawn, strangely plain face framed by strands of lanky blond hair appeared in the doorway behind him. Nadezhda Lazius looked at me, then at Lenny and, finally, at Grushnikov.

"What's going on here?" she asked.

Dr. Lazius turned around swiftly, as though he had been stung, lashing out at her in a fit of unspeakable, dangerous rage.

"What the hell are you staring at?" he screamed, his voice rising to a shrill, hysterical falsetto. "Ah, what the hell! Go on, stare if you wish, damn you. Yes, they've come to arrest me. Yes, I killed her. And what are you going to do about it, you bitch?"

TWENTY-FOUR

I never expected a promotion or even praise for collaring Lazius, but the avalanche of abuse that was poured over me came as a surprise. Budyonny, informed about Lazius's arrest on the tarmac of the government airport at Bykovo, abruptly cancelled his flight to Crimea and was back in the office by morning.

He asked me to stay behind after Lenny and I had finished reporting to him and stared at me for a disconcertingly long time.

"What kind of circus do you think you're running here, Lieutenant?" he asked at last, his Armenian accent getting stronger by the minute. "Why are you playing tricks on me and the other guys? Do you think you're some kind of a magician, pulling rabbits out of a hat?"

I was trying to respond, but the Boss wouldn't let me.

"Hold your tongue, Lieutenant. You're not even part of this investigation. You've been privateering. You're not a stupid civilian but a uniformed officer of the Ministry of Internal Affairs. It's gotta stop if you want to continue working here."

"Yes, sir," I replied, clicking my heels.

Budyonny began pacing his office, circling the spot where I stood at attention, as motionless as Dzerzhinsky's statue.

"Sure," he said, his voice dripping with sarcasm. "I understand what you wanted to do. You wanted to be a hero and bag the killer all by yourself. I'll have you know, however, that because you kept us in the dark, you gave him time to kill again. And again. Kids died because of you. When did you first start to suspect him?"

"Comrade Lieutenant Colonel," I said, "I didn't begin to suspect him until the last minute. Until Senior Lieutenant Urumov told me that Tanya Drozdova's underpants were found in the pocket of Grushnikov's warmup pants. I just thought it was way over the top, that's all. And once I thought of Lazius, it all started to make sense."

"Be quiet, Matyushkin. I don't give a damn about your excuses. Think about what I have told you. Dismissed."

As it turned out, however, it was only the first shot across my bow. Many more salvos would soon follow.

On the first day after his arrest, Dr. Lazius was interrogated for 24 hours straight, day and night. It was done to keep him off balance. A couple of guys from the Special Interrogations unit of the Ministry of Internal Affairs, whose names and rank no one knew and who operated in complete secrecy, were calling the shots. Top brass from upstairs kept popping in and out of the interrogation. Lenny, Gordeyev and the rest of our guys were like poor relations barely allowed to be present at the feast. They were asked now and again about some minor detail of the murders, but otherwise they had been pushed to the wings. The floor was taken by others.

I was not part of the interrogation at all.

I hadn't been to see Korenev for a few days, and there was now plenty of news for me to report.

I also wanted to get Sergei out of earshot of his employer for a few moments. I was interested to hear his side of the story about his offer to the infamous Rubashkin, Moscow's premier broker of stolen vehicles. Despite the brouhaha surrounding Dr. Lazius's arrest, I hadn't forgotten what Nastya told me about a stolen ZIM being shopped around.

Korenev and I were now the best of buddies. His old effusive manner was on full display again; he started talking the moment he opened the door, not letting me get in a word edgewise.

"I've got a piece of great news, detective. Actually, two pieces of great news, but let's start with the first. You'll never guess what it is, Sherlock. Wanna bet?"

I opened my mouth but he interrupted me before I could say anything.

"Don't even try. I'll give you a hint. It's directly connected to your job responsibilities. I mean *real* job responsibilities. No? You give up?"

Korenev had walked me to his office and sat me in my usual seat, climbing into his massive armchair and blocking my exit. Then he executed a theatrical pause, shook his index finger at me for emphasis and was about to make an announcement, but at that moment I decided to steal his thunder.

"They found your car."

The playwright's mouth fell open. "How did you know?"

I shrugged.

"A lucky guess, I suppose. Where did they find it?"

"In the city of Klin," Korenev said, visibly disappointed. "One hundred kilometers from here. Some local cops called me after checking the license plate. Sergei was as happy as a kid. You managed to convince him that the car was as good as gone. Not me, though. I always knew it was going to turn up sooner or later. That's why I wanted you to concentrate on those child murders."

"I wonder who took it in the first place," I said.

"I don't know. I'm not a detective. It's your job to figure that out. I still think it was the work of the damn composers. But let bygones be bygones. I'm just happy to have it back."

"Was it in good condition?"

"Top notch. The first thing Sergei did was inspect it for any damage. The only thing, a little too much distance on the odometer, maybe fourteen hundred kilometers."

"Which makes it unlikely it was the work of the composers," I said.

Korenev gave it some thought. I was enjoying his obvious discomfort. The only thing I couldn't quite figure out was whether he knew that it was Sergei's doing and was lying to me intentionally, or genuinely looking for a plausible explanation.

"Who knows," he said at last. "They've got a composers' resort in Jurmala, on the Latvian coast. It's about seven hundred kilometers each way. So there. But, as I said, I no longer care who took it. There are more important things in this world. Like for example the fact that we finally have the real killer."

It was my turn to be surprised. Actually, I was surprised equally by his knowledge of the fact and by his use of the proprietary "we."

"How did I know, you may ask? Writer's intuition, of course. I always told you that you need someone like me on your team."

He giggled.

"Well, actually, to be completely honest, your boss called me first thing yesterday morning. And that's what my other piece of good news is about. I'm pretty much done with my play."

"Which play?" I asked. I was getting confused between the two plays he was working on.

"The one about you, *The Detectives*. All this time I've been struggling with the character of the killer, but now I finally got it. It's pure evil. And, what's important, not a Soviet citizen."

"What is he then?" I asked, still bewildered. "Dr. Lazius may be a Lithuanian, but he's a Soviet citizen as far as I know."

"Right. I merely took Dr. Lazius as my model. But I'm a writer, it's a work of fiction, after all. I changed his name and my killer is called Dr. Moriarty. Capitalist imperialist scum. Otherwise it's all exactly as it happened in real life. Dr. Moriarty befriends one of the detectives, sub-lieutenant Malyshev. Malyshev is ambitious and wants to solve the case single-handedly. But he's naive and Dr. Moriarty can twist him around his little finger. Malyshev gives him all sorts of information about the investigation, thinking that Dr. Moriarty would help him catch the killer. But Dr. Moriarty is devious."

In retrospect, I should've paid more attention to this insane new plot twist of Korenev's. Instead, I sat there only half-listening to his prattle, thinking about his ZIM.

"I hope we got the right man," I said at last.

Korenev stopped talking at once.

"What do you mean you *hope*?" he asked. "I thought it has been all sewn up."

"He's still being interrogated, as far as I know. He has admitted to Tanya Drozdova's murder, but that's all."

Korenev jumped up and began to pace his office. Walking past a pile of books in the corner, he brushed against it accidentally with his shoulder, sending several of them tumbling onto the floor. He ignored them, then, stepping on one, kicked it angrily under his desk. At one point, he reached for the special phone by the window, his private line to Khrushchev, picked up the receiver, hesitated and replaced it.

"He's got to be the right man," he said at last, stopping in front of me and wiping a constellation of tiny droplets from his forehead. "For your sake as well as mine. Because Nikita Sergeyevich has been informed about Dr. Lazius. And I was the one who told him."

This time, too, I had to find the door on my own. Any mention of Nikita Sergeyevich seemed to sap the playwright of all his strength, leaving him slouching in a chair. Just as I reached the front door, Sergei stepped into the foyer.

"Oh," I said cheerfully. "Just the man I wanted to see. I'm glad to know that the thief took my advice and brought the car back."

"It wasn't me," he replied with an insolent smirk. "I have no idea what you're talking about."

"Don't worry," I said. "I'll let you know who the thief is the moment I find out. I promise that you'll be the first to know."

"I don't think you will find out. He doesn't want you to work on this case any more. That's what he told your boss, too. My boss is more important than yours. He can give your boss orders."

"I do not intend to measure bosses with you, Sergei," I said. "In any case, it's out of Comrade Korenev's hands. It's a crime and crimes have to be investigated, no matter what."

"I don't think you know what you're in for. You're in a whole lot of trouble yourself, and you might be the one who's going to be investigated."

He still had that smirk splattered all over his face and I wanted to wipe it off with my fist.

"Look, it doesn't matter whether it's me or one of my colleagues," I said. "Whoever investigates the so-called theft of Comrade Korenev's ZIM will sooner or later find out that there was an attempt to sell it to professional car thieves – no doubt in hopes that the thieves would be blamed for stealing it in the first place."

That worked. Frankly, I hadn't expected my words to make quite the impression they did. Sergei literally turned green and then crimson and, like his boss, began to sweat copiously. He took a step back and leaned heavily against the doorjamb. For a second, I thought he was going to slide down. By then I had changed back into my boots and put on my winter coat. I went out and closed the door without giving him another look.

In less than an hour, I had managed to shock both Sergei and his boss without really trying.

With Korenev's ZIM now safely in his garage, and the Boss keeping me off the team interrogating Dr. Lazius, I didn't have much to do. I was sitting at the office putting my files into some kind of order when Lenny came in.

"How's it going?" I asked.

"Not so good," Lenny said tersely.

Despite the participation of Secret Interrogations specialists and valuable advice from our top brass, progress in Dr. Lazius's interrogation had been minimal. Lazius had had no trouble taking the responsibility for killing Tanya Drozdova. He was willing, even eager, to talk about the murder and to provide copious details: how he had been able to leave work unnoticed and get back to the apartment on the day of the murder, and how he had arranged for his alibi by putting it into the head of one of his patients that she had been with him all afternoon.

"Suicidal types are highly suggestible," he told his interrogators. "The only thing was to make sure she hadn't done away with herself before confirming my alibi."

"The scum likes to make macabre jokes," Lenny observed.

Lazius knew that no neighbors would be around when Tanya came home from school that day. He also admitted that he and Tanya had been "engaged in a relationship that was essentially sexual in nature," as he put it.

"Of course it was sexual," he declared. "You don't expect me to conduct learned conversations with her. She seduced me, plain and simple."

Recounting it to me, Lenny spat on the floor, saying furiously, "Ever heard anything like that? A ten-year old seducing a fifty-year-old goat? It simply boggles the mind."

Lazius was convinced he had to kill Tanya.

"She had power over me, over everything I have. She could have ruined everything: my clinic, my family and our athletic and cultural hobbies. Even my work, for God's sake. Do you realize that my research is of great international importance? I'm looking into the question of why man is the only mammal who deliberately takes his own life. This holds the key to an even more important question – why we kill each other. Not for food but for sport, for fun. No other animal can bring itself to kill its own species the way we do. And yet, that little girl could have destroyed all this in one stroke. Not to mention that blackmail is a criminal offence, even when committed by a minor."

Lenny's great talent as a mimic didn't desert him even when he was enraged. He imitated Dr. Lazius's clipped, pedantic, slightly peevish manner to perfection. It was as though the good doctor was in the office with us, trying to justify his despicable actions.

Lazius had also admitted trying to frame Grushnikov. He had gotten his hands on the gym teacher's warm-ups and sprinkled their bottoms with the ink that had been on Tanya Drozdova's table. He added a pair of Tanya Drozdova's undergarments and planted the evidence at the bottom of Grushnikov's closet.

"I did it before the second murder. Who knew that another murder would be committed and Grushnikov would be let go? No, I've got no scruples about it. To be honest, I was helping you guys. In my professional opinion, Grushnikov is a dangerous psychopath. Isolating him from society *before* he has committed any crimes is a good idea for all of us. You should think about doing that in any case."

"Did you ask him why he didn't remove the planted pants when we released the teacher?" I asked.

Lenny shrugged.

"It no longer mattered, I suppose," he replied.

However, when it came to the other murders, the investigators hit a brick wall. Lazius resolutely refused to admit that he had anything to do with them.

"Why would I kill a kid who has done me no harm and is no danger to me?" he kept repeating. "I didn't know any of them. I'm a normal person. I'm not a homicidal maniac. If you want to catch the real killer, you've got to look for a psychopath. Somebody like Grushnikov. I refuse to take responsibility for other people's crimes."

"Don't you think it's strange?" I said. "I mean his refusal to admit to any other murders even after he has confessed to Tanya's?"

Lenny waved his hand dismissively.

"I don't think so. There is logic in what he's doing. If he admits to only one murder, makes a full confession, shows sufficient remorse in court and so on, he might beat the death penalty. Especially since he's such an international luminary in his field, which he reminds us of at every turn. He's concocted pretty solid alibis for the other three killings, and he thinks he's sitting pretty. Sure, he'll have to spend fifteen years behind bars, but you can't blame him for choosing jail over the firing squad."

Lenny's theory made sense. It was confirmed earlier that day when the witnesses who had seen the fake MosGaz meter reader – the grandmother and her grandson Stepa – picked Dr. Lazius out of a lineup, especially when he was paraded in front of them without his gold-rimmed glasses. He was older than they had originally described him, but the grandmother's eyesight was not particularly sharp and to a boy Stepa's age anyone over thirty looked old.

The old downstairs neighbor didn't go along with their identification, but it didn't really matter. He was just too old.

The case against Lazius got a further boost when a search at his clinic turned up a blonde wig and a fake moustache - even though the doctor claimed those were props left over from amateur theatrics during his university days in Kaunas.

"All we have left to do is to crack his other alibis," Lenny told me. "Actually, we only need to crack one. Once we do, the rest will tumble like dominos, I'm sure."

That afternoon I was summoned to the Boss's office. Lately, such summonses had meant trouble, and this one was no exception.

"Do you remember I told you not to discuss our investigation with Dr. Lazius?" the Boss asked the moment I came in.

"I never did, sir," I responded.

"You've not answered my question, Matyushkin. Do you remember my order not to talk to Dr. Lazius about the investigation?"

"Yes, sir, I do."

"But you disobeyed it, didn't you?"

"All I did was to check his alibi, Comrade Lieutenant Colonel."

"Is that all?"

Budyonny was scrutinizing my face as though trying to catch me on a lie.

"Well, we did talk about a couple of other things," I said tentatively.

"Like what exactly?" he asked.

I tried to think what subjects we had discussed during the two or three conversations I had had with Lazius, and I turned up a pretty long list.

"The death of his first wife," I began. "Irina Drozdova's mental state and whether she was likely to commit suicide. The fact that he had examined Tanya Drozdova."

"Did he really?"

"I put it in a report I submitted to you and to Captain Gordeyev."

"Did you really? I'll have to go back and check whether that's true. What about Grushnikov?"

"We did have a discussion about Grushnikov's personality. That was while Grushnikov was still being held as a suspect. I thought Lazius could make a good expert witness."

"Exactly. Captain Gordeyev and I both remember that very well, much better than your report about him examining Tanya. I also remember that I told you then that Lazius was still on the list of suspects and that you were never to discuss any of the particulars of the case with him. Do you admit it?"

"I do," I said.

"But you ignored my order, Lieutenant, and you kept talking to him freely. He confirms this. I'm pretty sure that he twisted you around his little finger, Lieutenant. While stuffing your head with his psychiatric mumbo-jumbo, he wheedled crucial information out of you."

My head began to spin. Suddenly, I found myself in some parallel world. It was exactly like the plot of Korenev's play, except it was no longer fiction. It was reality. Or it seemed to be.

Meanwhile, Budyonny continued.

"It's clear to investigators that Lazius was able to use the information he gained from you to evade capture and to construct alibis for his subsequent murders. He convinced his patients, students and the staff at the clinic that he was at work at a time when he was returning to the city and committing his vile crimes. It is because of you that we have not been able to link him to any of them."

"Why was he killing all those other kids?" I asked.

"It's obvious, Matyushkin. Every new killing, committed apparently at random by some psychopath, was making it less and less likely that we would tie him to the murder of Tanya Drozdova. Think back, Lieutenant: maybe you could figure out what information you gave him during your conversations and how he could have used it to plot the other murders. Obviously it was from you that he got the MosGaz idea."

"It certainly was not," I exclaimed. "I never mentioned the MosGaz story to him."

Whatever I personally thought of it, it was a theory and it needed to be thought through. I went back over all of my conversations with Dr. Lazius, reviewing every detail carefully, exactly the way Budyonny asked me to. There were probably things I didn't remember exactly, but on the face of it, it made no sense.

"Where do you keep your service weapon," the Boss asked suddenly, breaking a long silence. "Go get it and leave it with me. As of this moment, Lieutenant, you're suspended from all active investigations. You're not to talk to anyone in this department and they have all been instructed not to share with you any information pertaining to their work."

He paused and added, "As things now stand, you've been dismissed for insubordination. It may get much worse for you. Lazius will be charged with all four murders and unless he admits his guilt, you'll be tried alongside him as an accomplice. I believe you were duped by him. Had I thought otherwise, Lieutenant, you'd be sharing his cell at the Butyrka."

TWENTY-FIVE

A day or two later I ran into Nadezhda Lazius at Gastronom No. 40. It's the nearest large food store to my house, but a long walk from 1st Kolobovsky Lane. Nadezhda had a large bag full of groceries and I offered to help her with it. She greeted me warmly, but I wasn't sure she knew who I was.

We came out onto the vastness of Vorovsky Square, which was used as a parking lot by the official Volga sedans belonging to the nearby Committee on State Security. The drivers huddled in a cloud of blue cigarette smoke, a dense clump of leather jackets and fur hats at the foot of the awkwardly squatting statue of Ambassador Vorovsky, the Soviet diplomat gunned down by a White terrorist back in the 1920s.

We headed down Sretenka, me carrying Nadezhda's groceries as well as my own knit bag containing a bottle of kefir, a half-loaf of black bread, and a small package of butter, and Nadezhda walking next to me in silence. She still wore expensive clothes, but seemed to have stopped taking care of them; one elaborate button on her elegant winter coat was hanging by a thread and her silver fox hat needed brushing. So did her blond curls, which hung lifelessly around her ears.

I waited until we were nearly at the Boulevard Ring before asking, "Correct me if I'm wrong, Nadezhda. When you married Dr. Lazius, he was a widower?"

She stopped and started as though she had forgotten all about me.

"I mean, he had been married before?" I said.

"Yes, of course," she said, shaking her head. "His wife was dead by the time we were married."

That was a strange way of putting it, but I wasn't going to spend time on that.

"Did you know him when his first wife died?" I asked.

She nodded and I was going to prod her with another question when she suddenly spoke. "What you've got to understand about Dr. Lazius is that he doesn't believe that our life is real. Or rather that the world around us is real. He has said it many times. He's convinced that each person's world is of his own making. That it is created for each one of us individually."

It was a lot of nonsense, but I decided to humor her in the hope that, while talking, she'd let slip something important about Dr. Lazius. After all, my life and freedom now depended on whether or not it could be proven that he was guilty of the other three killings.

"Does he mean the world was created by God?" I asked. "I always thought he had a scientific bent and more that of an atheist."

"No, not by God," she said. "Even though God enters into it somehow. I don't really understand about God. What he says is that it is a world created by each person according to the way that person is. He says that life is like a dream – something that each person conjures up in his head, something that only he can see. As far as other people are concerned, their dreams don't exist. But characters in a dream do have their own personalities. They act independently of the dreamer, who doesn't control what happens in a dream and can't change it."

"Maybe," I shrugged.

I had a feeling she was not really talking to me, but responding to her own thoughts. She wasn't looking where she was walking, either, having bumped into a couple of passersby along the way.

"Look where you're going, you cow," a pensioner with a walking stick screamed after she nearly knocked him down.

We were passing by the main church of the Sretensky Monastery, which had been converted to a restoration lab. Fluorescent lights struggled against the early dusk of a Moscow January afternoon. The building had narrow windows cut through thick, whitewashed walls and covered with cast-iron bars. Behind its rusted green domes loomed the red brick building of a school. Vacation had ended, and school was once more in session. Some schoolboys were having a snowball fight in the schoolyard next to the church.

"You can't change your dream, but you can end it," Nadezhda said. "It's the same with life. That's why Dr. Lazius was so interested in suicide."

I let her babble on. I walked next to her, trying to steer her out of the paths of other pedestrians, making sure she wouldn't get run over when we crossed side streets.

Suddenly, she stopped and turned to me.

"Come to think of it, he is right, that queer husband of mine," she said. "When we're born, we think that we come into a pre-existing world. But we don't have any proof of that. As far as you are concerned, this show starts the moment you open your eyes as a newborn baby. And it comes to an end when you close your eyes for good."

"If the world doesn't exist and is invented by me, why can't I go back and change something in the past?"

"Because there are rules. That's where God comes in. The film can only go forward, not backwards, and it can't stand still. And it has to have a beginning and an end."

Two kids ran into the street, one holding a snowball and pursuing the other. They used us as props in their game, running circles around us and shielding themselves behind our bodies. They were laughing and cursing each other at the same time, using grown-up obscenities.

"You can't influence things directly, but you always shape them subconsciously," she resumed when the kids were gone. "Things happen to you, and they happen a certain way, because of the way you are. Ignorant people call it premonition. But if you spend time learning about yourself, you'll understand exactly why your life shapes up in a certain way. Because it comes from within you. And you can learn to steer it."

"What about other people," I asked, getting drawn against my will into a stupid conversation with a crazy person. "You have said it yourself: there are dreams and there are real people living in the real world who can't see your dream. How can I be nothing but a character in your dream?"

"And yet you are."

"Or maybe it's *you* who is nothing but a character in my dream?"

"That's possible, too. But it doesn't matter. Because as far as I'm concerned, you'll end forever the moment I do."

I looked at her. She was completely logical and totally sane. Or did she seem so completely logical and totally sane because I had lost my mind?

Insanity is contagious.

That night, I lay awake for a long time, tossing and turning and listening to Tosya's quiet breathing next to me. When I finally managed to nod off, I had a vivid, insane dream.

I dreamt that I was very little. I was eight or nine years old and living in a very nice apartment.

I dreamt it was early in the morning and I was in my own bed, half asleep. I was lying warm and comfortable under the covers. My mother had gone out to buy bread. She had kissed me on my forehead, patted me on the head and said, "Sleep, Natasha, my little girl."

She didn't look like my real mother. Rather, she looked a little like Irina Drozdova, except she was young and beautiful. I could smell the menthol tooth powder on her breath. Her hands were soft and they smelled nice, too, of sweet flowery soap. She had called me Natasha and she thought I was a girl, and it didn't surprise me in my dream. I didn't necessarily like being a girl in my dream, and being called Natasha, but I couldn't change it.

"You can't change your dream," someone had said recently. "But you can end it."

But it was a nice dream, and I didn't want to end it.

I was wrapped in a blanket and I was still sleepy, because it was early in the morning and it was a Sunday, and I didn't have to get up to go to school. I may have fallen asleep again after my mother had gone out, and if I had I didn't know how long I slept.

The doorbell woke me up.

I dreamt that I got up, found my slippers under my bed and went out into the hallway. It was a long way to the front door because our apartment was so vast, and it had many rooms on either side of the hallway. It didn't surprise me, either, that I knew my way around and I knew where to find light switches to turn the lights on as I walked. I also knew which door led to which room. This one was Mom and Dad's bedroom, that one, across the hallway, was Dad's study. I knew I was not allowed to go into Dad's study, even if I found the door unlocked – which never happened, anyway – and even when he was out of town on a business trip. Especially when he was out of town on a business trip. He was out of town now, at a place called Chita, which sounded cold and remote, and which Mom and I had looked up on the globe the night before.

Another long hallway, twisting to the right.

Walking along, I realized that it was No. 42B in 1st Kolobovsky Lane, except it was configured differently. It was light and airy and didn't have the partition that separated the Lazius's rooms from the rest of the apartment.

I knew I was not allowed to open the door to strangers. Always, in all circumstances, even if I expected somebody like Grandpa or Grandma, I was to ask first and never open the door until I knew for sure who it was. Or better yet, not open it at all if no grown-ups were there with me.

"Who's there?" I asked in my dream, coming close to the door.

"MosGaz," came a muffled reply.

I was very little in my dream but I knew that word. I didn't know what it meant but I had heard it before. It was short, only two syllables long, and full of ominous sibilant sounds, like the language of snakes. It was an evil word, too. A long time ago, I had seen Grandma turn on a stove and let a foul-smelling, suffocating substance fill the air around us. It penetrated my chest, enveloping everything inside in a kind of transparent polyethylene film and laying heavily at the bottom of my lungs. Grandma then struck a match and pulled me away from the stove, and the foul-smelling substance hissing out of the burner exploded. But then, instantly, it arranged itself into a harmless blue halo. Grandma had done it several times and if she was too slow to pull back her hand, there would be a burnt smell, like when our cook Nyura got a fresh chicken at the market and had to singe its feathers over an open flame.

But MosGaz was also a name. Somebody had told me that a man called MosGaz went from house to house murdering little kids.

"MosGaz," the voice on the other side of the door repeated, and again, over and over, several times, like a snake crawling in the grass: "MosGaz. MosGaz. MosGaz."

I knew I must never open the door to MosGaz. I was afraid of what Dad would say when he came back from Chita if I opened the door, and I was afraid of MosGaz on the other side, and of the door itself, too. I knew I should get away from it but the voice reaching me was hypnotic. It enveloped me in a kind of polyethylene film, like the smell of raw gas coming from a burner. It sapped my will to move.

No longer feeling my legs, which had become soft as cotton, I went up close to the door and leaned against it, next to where the door met the jamb. I felt a gentle draft blow through the crack and onto my cheek. It blew through my long hair, and there was a sweet smell reaching me from the landing, something like vanilla or strawberry, or maybe even perfumed soap. It was mixed with the familiar smell of our staircase, the smell of yesterday's borshch and boiled cabbage and something going bad, too. I could smell MosGaz and it was scary and irresistible at the same time.

On the inside, our front door was painted dark red, the color of dried blood. It was smooth, warm and pleasant to the touch, like Mom's cheek.

"No one is at home," I whispered into the crack. "No one. Just me."

"I know," MosGaz replied through the door. "That's why I'm here. Open the door."

"No," I said trying to sound strong and resolute. "I won't."

"Open up" came a soft, tender, cajoling voice smelling of strawberry soap. "Open up. I'm MosGaz. I've come to play with you."

His words troubled me and thrilled me at the same time. When I was very small, I used to climb into bed with Mom and Dad on Sunday mornings. Dad would tell me a scary story about three little piglets and a big bad wolf. The story scared me every time and I climbed under the blanket and listened to my heart beat rapidly. But I also knew that Dad was near and he would never let anything bad happen to me.

That same sweet, thrilling danger emanated from beyond the door, from mysterious MosGaz. The danger lurked in his words, smooth as sea pebbles. The door was thick, it was made of hard, durable wood and it was secured by two locks and there has a chain hanging on the side, ready to be used. There was nothing for me to fear. I could hook the chain and it would make me even more secure. There we go. Nothing bad could happen to me inside my vast, silent apartment. I felt almost as safe on my side of the door as I used to feel in my parent's bed, their thick wool blanket thrown over my head, and safety and darkness surrounding me, full of the astringent, cloying and strangely exciting smell of Mom and Dad sleeping. I was like one of those piglets from Dad's fairy tale. I could stand there forever and keep taunting MosGaz and thrill to his softly whispered words that came to me with the cool, sweet-smelling draft from the landing.

"I'll never open the door to you," I whispered into the crack. "I'm all alone here."

"Open up. I'm MosGaz."

I returned to my room but I couldn't stay away from the front door. I was on pins and needles, drawn back to it, to MosGaz. I had to know what was happening there.

MosGaz rang the doorbell again and I went back, putting one cottonwool foot in front of the other. I was moving as though in a dream. I was in a dream.

The door was still locked. MosGaz was still on the other side, still on the landing, breathing into the crack. His breath smelled of menthol tooth powder.

"Are you still there?" I asked.

"I'm not going anywhere. I'll be here until you open the door. I'm MosGaz."

There was no harm in opening just one lock. Just as an experiment. Cautiously, barely moving my fingers, I turned the dial on the top lock. It was brand-new and black, installed by Dad on Grandma's special request in order to keep MosGaz out, and it gleamed in the electric light of the hallway.

"Good girl," said the voice. "Now try the other one."

I tried to say No, but I couldn't make myself do it. My mouth was dry and I wet my lips with my tongue.

"There is also a chain," I said.

"Take it off," said MosGaz. "Open up. I'm MosGaz."

My voice was failing me. I just shook my head, even though I knew that MosGaz couldn't see me through the door. I removed the chain. It jingled as it fell and again MosGaz commended me.

"Good girl."

There was silence for a while. My throat was constricted, and MosGaz was waiting on the other side, saying nothing and breathing softly into the crack in the door.

"What is your name," he whispered.

"Natasha," I whispered back.

"What? I couldn't hear you. Say it louder."

"Natasha," I repeated.

On the other side, MosGaz rapped gently on the door – rap-a-tap, rap-a-tap, rap-rap.

"Natasha," he whispered softly. "Natashenka."

My Mom often called me Natashenka. Maybe it was her, and she was only pretending to be MosGaz as a joke. She wants to scare me and then laugh at me and my fears.

"Of course it's Mom," I said to myself. "It's her menthol tooth powder that I smell through the door. And her nice-smelling toilet soap."

If I opened the second lock now, she would come in and we would have a good laugh together. It would be a relief. But I had to get there first. I had to open the second lock.

"You got away from me once already, Natashenka," MosGaz said through the door. "You climbed on top of all those people and you ran off – a skip and a jump – stepping on their heads, on their fur hats, on their knitted wool caps, on their fedoras. They stayed below and died, but you escaped. You're a bad girl."

I was scared now. I was trembling and pressing my weight against the door, which was being pushed from the outside more and more insistently.

"I'm MosGaz, Natashenka. Open the door. I'm getting angry."

He kept knocking and an indescribable horror took hold of me. I hated myself for being so scared, but I couldn't help it. Slowly, I turned the second lock until it clicked. The door opened very slowly.

The landing was blinding, with the winter sunlight streaming in from the stairwell window. The window was dirty, streaked with rain and droplets of melting snow, and in the shafts of sunlight particles of dust danced like snowflakes.

There was no Mom on the landing. There was MosGaz. I knew him instantly. His shape was huge against the sunlit window, huge and dark. He smelled of Russian Forest aftershave, the one Dad always used when he got ready to go to work in the morning.

MosGaz took a step toward me.

"Don't try to run away. You've got nowhere to run."

TWENTY-SIX

"My, you can be a heavy sleeper sometimes, Matyushkin," Tosya said, shaking me by the shoulder.

She was fully dressed and had her heavy winter coat on, ready to leave. It was late and the winter darkness beyond the curtain had started to thin out. I shook my head, trying to rid myself of the remains of the nightmare.

"I was wondering whether you could stay with Sevka today? If you don't have to be at the office."

I had not been going to the office at all. Even if Budyonny's threat to put me on trial as Lazius's accomplice still seemed a little phantasmagorical, I was as good as fired and had plenty of time on my hands.

The situation had a silver lining: I was spending a lot more time with Tosya. I would get supper ready by the time she came home from the Tryokhgorka, the three of us would have it in her room and then she and I would go to the movies while Sevka stayed home doing his homework. Tosya loved the movies. If she liked a film, she could see it over and over again, until she practically knew it by heart.

And now I could do her a good turn. Sevka had come down with the flu at the start of the week and Tosya had to take a couple of days off to care for him. Now she really needed to go back to work: her boss kept calling her at home with various bookkeeping questions. Sevka was convalescing, his fever had abated, but Tosya still wanted someone to stay with him. She was an orphan and had grown up in an institution where such niceties were unheard of, which was why she was so protective of Sevka.

"Sure," I said. "I'll go over to your place when I get up. He'll probably be sleeping until noon."

My room was usually cold in the early hours of the day. The radiator, exuding waves of heat all night, struggled to counteract the cold draft from the window that became especially frigid right before sunrise. Once Tosya left, I wrapped myself more tightly in the blanket with the intention of going back to sleep. But the thought of the nightmare, brutal, fantastical, and yet strangely vivid and realistic, kept me awake.

Sevka and I had not yet become good friends, which is always difficult when a third person breaks in on the mother-and-child intimacy. He was jealous of me, and also embarrassed because he soon figured out that she spent most nights at my place – even though he was a deep sleeper and Tosya made sure to leave only after he had fallen asleep. Only in the last few days, thanks to our suppers together, during which we talked a lot and laughed even more, had the two of us started to break the ice. Which was another positive result of my otherwise dismal situation at work.

On the few previous occasions when we have been left together, Sevka and I always play chess. I would gladly do something else, for example, play Naval Combat or draw funny faces, or discuss soccer and hockey, but Sevka insists on chess. I'm not a good player, and Sevka is worse. We play game after game until we're blue in the face and black and white checks dance before our eyes.

This time, we played for a couple of hours, and around two o'clock in the afternoon the phone began to ring. Sevka, still wearing his pajamas because of the flu, ran out to the hallway to answer it. Their neighbors were out, so there was no one else in their large communal apartment.

In his haste, Sevka had neglected to put on his slippers. If Tosya had caught him stomping around barefoot on the cold and dirty floor just as he was getting over the flu, she would've have given hell to both of us – especially me for not paying proper attention.

Sevka picked up the receiver and instead of a "Hello" automatically said "Check."

He had been so involved in the game, he had nothing but checks and checkmates and queenside castlings on the brain. His own error made him hysterical with laughter. He laughed so hard, he couldn't bring himself to say another word. He did try to get serious and to stop laughing, but the effort made him laugh all the harder. In the end he gave up, dropped the receiver, grabbed his stomach and collapsed on the floor. Nothing could be heard after that except for grunts, gurgles and giggles.

"Hello?" I heard a voice repeat insistently on the other end. "Who's this? Hello?"

I ran to grab the receiver from the floor, stumbling over Sevka who was now rolling on the floor gasping for air, but I was too late. Whoever it was had given up and decided not to call back. He had probably figured he had a wrong number and had reached the insane asylum by mistake.

Sevka and I went back to chess, with Sevka recalling the incident every few minutes and collapsing on the foldout couch in a fresh paroxysm of laughter. After a while, I thought he was starting to overplay it.

I took our games seriously and made no concessions to Sevka's youth and inexperience. As a result, even though my knowledge of the game was limited to two weeks at the Young Pioneer's Palace in the Urals town of Nizhny Tagil, where my Mom and I had been evacuated during the war, I won most of the time. Sevka kept careful score in his notebook and celebrated every one of his infrequent victories with so much hooting and cheering, you'd think he had just become world champion.

Our games were long and almost never resulted in draws. Sevka hated to lose, but he hated to surrender even more. Even when his situation was desperate and his eventual loss was a foregone conclusion, he always insisted on playing to the bitter end.

"It's not fair," he declared. "There has to be at least some hope left. Besides, there is always a chance you will miss something and I'll get your queen."

I was the same way when I was his age. It takes time and maturity to realize that there are no miracles in this world and that sooner or later you have to lose, and you might as well get used to it. That's what growing up really means. But everyone has to grow up by himself, make his own mistakes, and learn his own lessons.

Sevka wouldn't let me concede a lost game either, and never forgave me any of my mistakes or misses. But whenever he made a wrong move, I usually allowed him to take it back. That happened fairly often: he pursued my king with such abandon that he often forgot to defend his.

We paused briefly to warm up some chicken broth, which was supposed to be extremely good for Sevka and his flu. The two of us also shared a frying pan's worth of fried potatoes and meatballs, which Tosya had cooked the night before and which we ate straight out of the pan, dipping into it by turns with our forks. Sevka hated chicken broth and got it down only after I told him we were not going to resume playing until he had finished the last drop. I didn't want to get in trouble with Tosya.

I was taking the dishes to the kitchen when the doorbell rang. It was around three in the afternoon and we did not expect any visitors.

"Who do you think it is?" Sevka asked me, his voice catching.

"I have no idea," I said. "But we'll soon find out."

"It's too early for Mom. Besides, she has keys and never rings the bell, even when she knows I'm at home."

I put down the dishes on the floor in the hallway and went to answer the door. Then, something made me change my mind. I stayed back and sent Sevka instead.

"You go," I said to him softly. "But don't open it without asking."

We walked down the hall together, keeping quiet. As we approached the front door, I hung back, taking my position a little to the side.

"Who's there?" Sevka asked.

There was no answer, no sound at all. Sevka took another step forward and glanced at me.

"Should I open it?" he whispered.

I shook my head.

"Who's there?" he asked again.

This time, there was an answer. A high-pitched voice said softly from beyond the door, "Is your father at home?"

Since Sevka's father didn't live with them, it had to be a stranger. I shook my head vigorously in answer to Sevka's mute question. He understood.

"No, sir," he replied. "Nobody is here except me."

Sevka was a good liar. He sounded remarkably plausible.

"I'm a MosGaz repairman," came a muffled reply. "I need to check your stove. It's an emergency. Open the door."

My heart skipped a beat and then began to pound so loudly, I thought its heavy thudding against my ribcage would carry all the way to the landing.

Sevka gave me a worried look. If anyone in the city had been told never to open the door to a guy from MosGaz it was he. I was clenching my teeth together so hard my jaw began to ache. The front door was old, rickety, cobbled together from dry pine boards. There were sizeable cracks at the door jambs.

Sevka was waiting for my instructions. Battling the flu over the past three days had left him thinner and paler. His eyes were large, black and full of fear. I heard heavy breathing nearby and it took me a moment to realize that it was my own.

As our eyes locked, I nodded after another moment of hesitation.

"Open the door," the high-pitched voice repeated.

Sevka is a brave kid. Sure he was scared out of his wits – I was too. Being brave doesn't mean being fearless; courage is the will to overcome your fear.

Sevka battled his fear and won. He took two small steps toward the door, exhaled and undid the lock. Then, as a man came in, he jumped backwards, raised his arms to protect himself and shouted, his voice breaking, "What do you want?"

From where I stood at the side of the door, I couldn't see the man's face, but I wasn't going to waste time taking a better look. I stepped up behind him and, reaching out with my left hand, grabbed his left ear, which stuck out from under his fur hat. That took him completely by surprise. As I twisted him toward me, he stumbled and nearly lost his balance. While he tried to steady himself, I had plenty of time to aim a heavy right and he magnified the damage by involuntarily leaning into my punch. He was thrown against the wall and spun around. As his shocked, pain-twisted face flew by a couple of inches from mine, I recognized chemical engineer and Zundapp owner Oganesov even as my nostrils caught a whiff of flowery toilet soap. I felt rage and disgust rise up simultaneously from the pit of my stomach.

Oganesov hit the ground heavily next to Sevka, slid along the dusty parquet and knocked down the console table that held the telephone. The instrument fell with a loud thud, its rotary dial flying off and its cord twisting around Oganesov's snow-covered winter boot.

I took a step toward him and, giving vent to the rage that was now choking me, kicked him on the buttocks. Oganesov howled in pain. Still lying on his stomach, he brought his knees up to his chin and placed his hands over his head. I wound up for another blow.

"Stop it, Pavel, please," Oganesov screamed.

I kicked him again, but this time with less enthusiasm. My rage was starting to ebb.

"Stop it," Oganesov pleaded. "Let me explain."

The owner of the Zundapp was damn lucky. I had merely bruised his jaw and bloodied his nose. Had it been Lenny instead of me, he could have been dead by now, or at best badly injured.

I stopped kicking him and waited. But I remained alert, expecting him to pull some dirty trick – which I admit I would have welcomed, since it would have given me an excuse to give him a very satisfying beating.

"Wait," Oganesov said. "Let me catch my breath."

He was smearing everything with blood and I handed him my handkerchief. He examined it skeptically before pushing it under his nose. He sat with his head thrown back until the bleeding stopped. Then he raised himself on his elbow and sat down, checking the left side of his face, which had turned red and was starting to swell.

Sevka and I watched him in silence.

"You may have broken my jaw," he said. "And my nose. I can only breathe through my mouth."

"Are you ready to talk?" I asked, ignoring his complaints.

"I just wanted to see how careful you were," Oganesov said. "I knew that your son had a cold and was staying home from school. I had a talk with your wife last night, she told me she was going to go to work and leave the boy alone. I phoned you earlier because I wanted to tell you that I had another customer for my bike. The boy sounded strange on the phone. I came by to see whether you were at home, but then, as I stood on the landing, I thought I might check whether you had warned your boy to be careful. It happens all the time, you know. Doctors tell people that smoking is a very bad habit, but most doctors I know smoke. I was just about to give your son a big talking to for opening the door."

"So, you're worried about him," I said sarcastically. "How nice of you."

"Of course I was," Oganesov replied heatedly. "I'm a father, too. And I feel responsible, in a way, because of my silly MosGaz trick. There was an article in the newspaper about MosGaz, but I fear no one took it seriously. I thought that even if your own son—"

"I'm not his son," Sevka said, frowning. "He's my mother's boyfriend. He doesn't even live here."

"Is that true?" Oganesov asked, looking at me.

"What business is it of yours?" I asked.

"I was absolutely sure you lived here," Oganesov said. "Because I thought this kid is yours and that his mother was your wife."

"Wait a second," I said. "How do you even know so much about me?"

"I saw you at the movies with a woman the other day," he said. "I was sitting in the back row, because my landlady is hypermetropic. And then, after the movie, we turned out to be walking in the same direction and I was curious to see where you lived. Because you'd told me that we were neighbors."

"Why did you want to know?" I asked.

"Because I thought you were the only person who was nice to me when I was detained," he said. "That's why I would rather that you bought my Zundapp. I have another offer, for more money, but I want you to have it."

I shrugged.

"You've gotta buy it, Uncle Pavel," Sevka blurted out. He had recovered his spirits and I half expected him to ask me to continue our chess match. "You said it has a sidecar. Is that true?"

"It does," said Oganesov.

"You see? You could take me and Mom fishing."

"I'm not going to buy it," I said, pouring cold water on Sevka's enthusiasm. "It no longer matters, anyway. Get up," I added, turning to Oganesov.

The man got to his feet, still holding my handkerchief to his nose, and started to brush the dust off his coat. He touched his bruised jaw again.

"Let's go," I said.

"Where?" he asked in surprise.

"Where do you think? I'm going to take you to my colleagues who are investigating the MosGaz murders. I'm sure they'll find your behavior highly unusual and would want to know more about it. I wouldn't be surprised if you ended up back in jail."

"But why? I told you why I did it."

He kept protesting, explaining yet again why he had come looking for me and why he had wanted to test Sevka's vigilance, and that the idea had only come to him right there, on the landing—

I cut him short.

"I'm sure you'll be able to explain everything," I said. "Let my colleagues try and make sense of it. This goddamn case is way over my head."

TWENTY-SEVEN

Ever since I had the nightmare, a nasty premonition haunted me. It lingered like a bitter aftertaste.

Two days after Oganesov's arrest, Lenny called me at home early in the morning and told me to meet him at the Kirov Metro station in fifteen minutes.

"I want to show you something," he said tersely, which had lately been his usual manner when he spoke to me.

"I'm sure you realize that I no longer can take part in any investigations," I said. "By the order of the Boss."

"The Boss told me to get you," Lenny said. "He wants you to see it."

Lenny had come on foot, not in his beat-up Moskvich, which he drove everywhere since acquiring it the previous year. He was waiting for me by the Griboyedov monument at the head of Clear Ponds Boulevard, across from the squat Constructivist box of the Kirov metro station. Next to him, two grandmothers with strollers stood gossiping, ignoring their screaming babies.

Lenny greeted me with a reserved nod, without offering a handshake. He wore his full police uniform, a blue overcoat with shiny buttons and senior lieutenant's epaulets.

"Let's go."

Without waiting for me, he started down the central path of the boulevard. I caught up with him and we walked briskly. The thaw, after gathering momentum for some time, had finally arrived in earnest. It felt like early spring; the day was eerily warm for mid-January. The trees dripped melting snow and the path running between the two rows of park benches was spotted with puddles. Lenny made no effort to avoid them, almost deliberately splashing gelid water on the bottoms of his uniform pants.

We reached the Kharitonevsky Lane exit from the boulevard and turned right, crossing the tram tracks and taking Telegraph Lane into the maze of side streets off the Boulevard Ring.

This was where Oganesov had lived before his arrest, sharing his landlady's bed. I assumed that was where we were headed, but when we reached Potapovsky Lane, Lenny turned left, away from Oganesov's building.

"There has been another murder," he said, breaking the silence.

"Another child?" I asked.

That would mean, of course, that neither Lazius nor Oganesov had anything to do with it.

"Another murder, yes," Lenny said. "But not another child. You'll see."

We walked a couple of hundred feet down Potapovsky Lane, stopping by an abandoned building with a garbage-strewn vacant lot next to it. I knew the place. It was where Nastya, fresh from her time in the juvenile facility, had tried to seduce me. Except back then it was in the middle of the night and in summer, and the place was overgrown with burdocks. And now it was a sickly, sloshy, unbearably bright and strangely warm winter day.

Sasha Grigoriev's forensic staffers were scattered around the lot, the bottoms of their lab coats protruding from beneath their winter coats. There was mud and melting snow everywhere: on their winter boots, on the hems of their lab coats, and on the sides of their departmental jeep, parked on the edge of the vacant lot.

Suddenly, I knew what I was going to see, and the bright sunshine went black before my eyes.

There were deep puddles all over, and patches of ground, sodden and orange, strewn with broken bricks and household trash. Grigoriev spotted us and broke away from a group of his people surrounding him. He greeted me warmly and offered me a handshake. He was probably the only guy from Petrovka who would still shake my hand. I was grateful to him, even though I knew it was his image as a free spirit and a nonconformist that he was mostly concerned with.

Together we walked to the far wall, where a uniformed cop stood at ease, smoking. At his feet lay something bright red and black that was soggy with melted snow and smeared with clay.

I slowed down, falling behind the other two, then came almost to a halt. But I kept going, slowly putting one foot in front of the other. I knew that in the end I would have to make myself get over there and look.

Nastya lay on her back, her arms thrown wide. She could have been staring at the sky overhead, which was filled with jackdaws taking off from nearby Menshikov Tower and circling the rooftops. Except she had no face and only a bloody mess for a head. It was one massive mash of red, sinew and bone chips mixed in with long strands of red hair. There was a clump of mud and pieces of broken bricks where her mouth had been.

Sasha Grigoriev bent down and undid the buttons of her red coat, revealing the marble-white skin. She was naked under her coat. I turned away at first and then made myself look at her small breasts and the blue smears of tattoos snaking around her ribcage.

"So many nice pictures," Sasha commented with a smirk. "A portable Tretyakov Gallery of prison art. You go to bed with this beauty and you get a short course in art history."

The patrolman guffawed.

"You're disgusting," Lenny said, spitting on the ground.

"I don't care what you think," Grigoriev replied. "What I think is that it's a great day for lambs when wolves start killing one another."

"She's a woman," Lenny said. "A young girl. She might even have been beautiful."

"As far as I'm concerned, thugs don't have age, gender or nationality. They're scum."

"See that mud in her mouth?" Lenny said. "This means she talked. Maybe you should ask Matyushkin what she talked to him about."

I was staring at Nastya's mangled head, unable to take my eyes off it.

"Come on, we've gotta go," Lenny said.

I turned around and almost stumbled. My head was spinning. I took a step to the wall and threw up. I kept retching violently for several minutes, even after there was nothing left in my stomach, staring at my vomit as it seeped into the mixture of snow and mud.

"Let's go," Lenny urged.

"This is what getting fired from Criminal Investigations does to you," Grigoriev observed. "Even the most hardened cops get tender-hearted as young ladies."

I shook my head slowly. Tears had risen to my eyes, but it was from vomiting, not grief. I knew for certain who was responsible for Nastya's death. And I was going to have my revenge.

Lenny called me again on Sunday morning, telling me to come and see him at his office. That is, my old office. It wasn't an official summons or an order, but I knew it was an invitation that I had better not ignore.

Tosya and Sevka were getting ready to go out. Irina Drozdova was going to take them to the Pushkin Museum. Irina had taken Sevka's education in hand and was starting his instruction by showing him Impressionist paintings.

I had winked at Sevka when I heard that and said something about the danger that Sevka, being of an impressionable age, would be terribly affected by those Impressionists. Sevka laughed while Tosya give me a sidelong glance, squashing further attempts to be funny.

The words "Sevka's education" were music to Tosya's ears and even though she wasn't sure those Impressionists were going to be useful, she was happy he was going to learn about them. She also wanted to come along. She had never been to the Pushkin – or, for that matter, to any museum except for the Lenin Museum on Red Square, which she had visited with her class from the orphanage. But when she mentioned the Lenin Museum, Irina made a face and dismissed it definitively with a shake of her head.

I had assumed Lenny was going to talk to me about Oganesov and Nastya, and I was not wide of the mark. But I was in for a lot more than I expected.

Lenny left me waiting by the security desk downstairs for a quarter of an hour. My former colleagues went in and out of the building, averting their eyes when they saw me sitting patiently in the lobby. Knowing Lenny's obsessive punctuality, I had no doubt that he was marinating me there on purpose, driving home the point that I was no longer part of Moscow Criminal Investigations. The one consolation I felt when he finally came down and took me to our old office was that my desk had not been given over to someone else. It had merely been cleared of all the files and pushed against the wall, to free up more space for Lenny.

"I've gotta tell you something right away," he said, offering me my old chair. "Budyonny wants to charge you in connection with the murders."

"I know," I said. "He'd told me that last time."

It was still a preposterous idea and I couldn't bring myself to take it as seriously as the situation demanded.

"Yes, but it's a lot worse now," he said. "He's building up a version of events in which you figure as a link between Lazius and Oganesov. He doesn't have everything in place yet, and not all the pieces fit into the big picture, but he's working on it."

I honestly couldn't believe my ears. It surely had to be some kind of a joke.

"Yes," I said, laughing. "The one piece that surely doesn't yet fit the big picture is that I was the one who arrested them both."

Lenny didn't share my hilarity. He frowned at me and said, "That's where you are wrong, buddy. It's what makes it even more damning in Korenev's eyes."

"In whose eyes?"

I thought I had misheard him or else he had misspoken.

"That's right. Korenev. He's been brought in to work on the team and he's dead set against you. While Budyonny thought initially that you were Lazius's dupe, Korenev is actually peddling a different version. Which has you as the mastermind of the whole thing. He believes that you wanted to be the hero who solved the case and arrested the murderers. And that was why you turned the other two in. And how you knew from the start that Grushnikov was innocent. He spun that whole tale for the Boss, and now he's going away for a while, letting it sink in."

"Oh, is he?" I said.

"He is, in the car which, according to him, you had done nothing to recover. Only by a miracle it was found by some local cops in the city of Klin. Is that true?"

"I suppose so," I said.

"And now your informant turns up dead," Lenny went on. "It may be a crazy idea of Korenev's, but you must admit, Pavel, it kinda fits in. Things don't look good for you."

"Fine, we know now what Korenev thinks," I said. "And the Boss?"

"As I said, Korenev is working on him and the Boss is starting to lean in this direction too. You can't blame him, can you?"

I thought it over.

"I suppose I can't," I said. "And what about you, Lenny. What do you think?"

Lenny made a show of pondering my question over. He even pulled out a cigarette, twisted it between his thumb and forefinger and stuck it back in its pack.

"I don't know what to think, frankly," he said. "Maybe if you tell me what actually happened, and what was your real connection to Lazius and Oganesov—"

He left the sentence trailing.

It was an old trick and I was surprised and embarrassed for him for trying it on me. I was about to make a snide remark about their ham-fistedness when the phone on my old desk began to ring.

Lenny and I exchanged glances.

"Should I pick it up?" I asked.

Lenny shook his head.

"I'll get it," he said coldly.

He picked up the receiver and listened.

"Sure," he said into the phone. "He's here. I'll put him on."

"It's your girlfriend," he added softly, passing me the receiver and covering the microphone. "She seems hysterical."

"What the matter?" I asked Tosya. "Where are you?"

By my calculations, they should have been at the Pushkin a long time ago.

"You've gotta come over here, Pavel. Oh my God."

"Come over where? Aren't you at the museum?"

"What museum? Come over right away. Please, Pavel."

Lenny was eyeing me closely, straining to hear what Tosya was saying on the other end.

"I can't," I said. "I'm being questioned. Where are you? What happened?"

"You've gotta come, Matyushkin," she insisted. "We're at Irina's. Something is very, very wrong."

"Is it Irina?" I asked, my heart sinking.

Lenny got up and came over to stand next to me. He too suddenly looked worried.

"No, she's alright. But you should come here anyway."

"What happened, for God's sake?"

Tosya was starting to calm down and began to sound a little more coherent.

"It's the doctor's wife. Irina says she sent the boys away to stay with a relative last night. I mean the doctor's sons. And she has not come out of her room this morning. It's not like her at all. We tried knocking on her door, but there is no answer. One second."

There was noise in the receiver and a man's voice came on. It was very emotional and pinched and it was with difficulty that I recognized Grushnikov.

"You need to get over here right away, Lieutenant," he said urgently. "We've got to break down her door."

"Could she have gone away?" I asked him.

"Lieutenant, are you listening to me or not? I swear I'll break it down myself if you don't come."

He rang off.

"Did you hear that?" I asked Urumov.

He nodded.

"Let's take your car," I said, taking a step toward the door.

Lenny didn't move.

"I don't think you can come," he said. "The Boss—"

Now I finally got furious.

"Oh, who cares what you think, Lieutenant. Or what your boss and the playwright Korenev think, either. You can either come with me or stay here, I don't give a damn which."

"You can't go there," Lenny insisted.

"I'd like to see you stop me."

I walked out and headed for the elevator. By the time it reached our floor, Lenny was standing next to me.

"Let's take your car," I said.

"It's faster on foot," Lenny replied.

"No," I said. "We may need it afterwards."

If Nadezhda Lazius was alright, maybe Lenny could drive Irina, Tosya and Sevka to the Pushkin, I thought. But I feared there wasn't much chance of that.

The snow was melting everywhere beneath the rays of an unseasonably warm sun. Pigeons, their blue-purple plumage faded and discolored by the long winter, pecked greedily at something on the roadway, waddling under the wheels of oncoming cars. Rivulets and little streams had formed in the gutters, and gangs of kids walked on the sidewalk, racing matchsticks in the currents, past mounds of blackened ice.

Lenny put his hatchback into first, propelling it forward, skidding madly and leaving tracks of burnt rubber on the wet asphalt. We made an illegal U-turn against the traffic on Petrovka and rammed like a torpedo through a softened pile of snow into a side street. We splashed through puddles and screeched through turns, reaching the familiar archway in 1st Kolobovsky in fifteen seconds flat.

Every time I had been in the apartment before, there had only been one or two tenants at home. Now the hallway was crowded with people. Grushnikov, Baba Dasha, Irina Drozdova and Tosya stood by the front door waiting for us, their faces pale and worried. Sevka hung back, trying to make himself as inconspicuous as he could, so as not to be sent away from all the excitement.

His efforts were doomed. The first thing I did was tell Tosya to take him into Irina's room, disregarding his loud protestations. Lenny added his official voice, declaring that tenants and their guests should also clear the hallway. Now Grushnikov started to protest, but not vehemently, as he was still scared of Urumov.

Left alone in front of the Lazius' door, Lenny and I knocked on it repeatedly and waited. There was no answer.

"Nadezhda, please respond if you're there," I shouted into the keyhole. "This is Moscow Criminal Investigations. Otherwise we'll have to break down your door."

Lenny moved back, taking a running start.

"Come on, Lenny," I said. "I still have a set of keys."

The last time I had seen the Lazius's room was during the doctor's arrest. There had been two witnesses with us, a local street sweeper and an upstairs neighbor, both roused from bed and batting their eyes in the narrow hallway. We had turned the place upside down, not really knowing what we were looking for, just hoping that something would turn up. When we were done with it, the doctor's pedantically neat rooms looked worse than Grushnikov's, with items of clothing pulled from their drawers and old books in foreign languages and scattered on the rug.

When I unlocked the door this time, I was surprised to see that, except for the boys' rooms, everything was pretty much as we had left it. Nothing had been tidied up or put away; chaos still reigned in the master bedroom and in Dr. Lazius's study.

It was the door of the study that Lenny fixed his eyes on. Nadezhda's stiffened body was suspended from the ceiling, a length of rope knotted to a brass hook protruding from the stucco decoration. A long time ago, the hook must have supported a massive chandelier, which probably weighed more than Nadezhda. Her robe was skimpy and colorful, its splotches of red, yellow and green silk making her look like some kind of oversized, horrifying Polynesian lantern. Her feet, with chipped red polish on the toenails, swayed waist-high above the floor. She must have climbed onto her husband's desk, secured the rope and jumped off.

I stepped up and felt for a pulse. But I knew it was no use, and touching her wrist confirmed it. It was cold and hard and didn't feel like human flesh at all. She had been dead for several hours.

I walked to the window and stared outside, trying to gather my thoughts.

"What the hell," I heard Lenny's angry voice behind my back. "Get the hell out of here. You're not allowed in. We're treating it as a crime scene. I said get out."

Grushnikov had burst in and was hugging Nadezhda's body, trying to lift it in his massive, hairless arms. He was weeping, his shoulders twitching spasmodically.

"Get out of here," Lenny repeated, coming over to him and putting his hand on his shoulder.

"Let him be," I said.

Lenny let go of the gym teacher and turned to me.

"Why do you think she did it?" he asked.

"It's my fault," Grushnikov replied, and then added through tears. "And yours, too."

"Why ours?" Lenny asked.

"It wouldn't have happened if you hadn't arrested me," Grushnikov replied.

"What does your arrest have to do with it?" Lenny asked.

Grushnikov stared at him. His eyes were red and swollen and tears were still rolling down his cheeks.

"Don't you understand? She did it because she thought I had killed Tanya."

I now understood what he meant, but it was taking Lenny a bit longer.

"She thought that Grushnikov killed Tanya and so she killed Dima Sadykov to get him off the hook," I said.

"Is that true?" Lenny asked, staring at Grushnikov, who nodded and burst into tears again.

"She did it for me," he wailed. "But how could I accept it? I simply couldn't."

TWENTY-EIGHT

We were getting into Lenny's car when Gordeyev and Tumakov arrived at the scene. They eyed us suspiciously: after all, as far as they knew, I had been suspended and was facing a possible arrest.

Forensics were already in the apartment, crowding its hallways for the second time in less than two months. Tosya had taken Sevka home. Irina and Baba Dasha had seated Grushnikov in the kitchen and were trying to get him to calm down with a mug of tea and a stiff drink.

Lenny drove me home.

"And so it goes," he said bitterly. "We're going to keep solving these murders one at a time. Two down, two more to go."

I didn't reply. He waited for me to get out, but I remained seated in the passenger seat. I had an idea and it was pecking at my brain, giving me a bad headache.

"Listen, Lenny," I said slowly, still thinking my idea over. "I need to go down to Baba Yaga's basement for a few minutes. Do you think you could get me in without telling Budyonny?"

Lenny hesitated. He said nothing and patted his coat pockets looking for his cigarettes. He took one from the pack and lit it, still staring out the windshield. The cabin of his tiny Moskvich filled with foul-smelling blue smoke.

"I think it can be arranged," he said at last and threw the half-finished cigarette out the window. He took off from the curb with his trademark flourish.

Once back on Petrovka, Lenny went down to the basement with me and stuck around while the white-haired Baba Yaga got me what I was looking for. Whatever else might be said about her, she is an invaluable resource to any detective's work.

It took me no more than a few minutes to leaf through the thin file.

What I learned was this: On a busy morning in early December, three men and a woman wearing masks and long canvas coats drove up in a beat-up Volga to the Nevsky Prospect branch of the State Savings Bank. It was the main branch in the very center of the city, on its main avenue. They left the car at the curb, walked in, locked the doors and announced a stickup. One of the men was armed with a handgun and when the branch manager showed hesitation in opening his bank vault, he shot out a light overhead, signaling that they meant business and making the manager move a lot faster.

Meanwhile, the cops arrived at the scene, blocking the robber's getaway path.

The bank building was old, built in the late nineteenth century. Its two long hallways met at a right angle in the back, and offices with barred windows gave out onto the garbage-strewn remains of a winter garden. The garden, which was more like an airshaft running through the middle of the building, had no obvious connection to the outside. Except that there was a window, boarded up years ago, which connected it to one of the buildings in the back. The robbers had apparently staked out the place and prepared an emergency exit. They had loosened the bars on one of the windows at the bank and removed the nails from the piece of half-rotten plywood covering the back window. That was how they escaped.

But not before the cops tried to break down the front door, which turned out to be difficult since it was solid steel with stained glass sections that were protected by thick bars. As the robbers were getting ready to leave, one of the cops shot into the bank, hitting a 23-year-old clerk in the thigh. The robbers shot back, hitting a cop. Then they picked up the loot – nearly three quarters of a million rubles – and vanished.

There was no trace of them anywhere. The beat-up Volga turned out to have been stolen from a garage in neighboring Vyborg the night before, the tags taken from a car parked in a residential district of Leningrad. The clerk bled to death before the police forced the door, but the wounded cop survived. No leads, no further information.

"Let's go," I said to Lenny when I was done in the Cellar.

The only question Lenny asked me was: "Where?"

I didn't reply.

"When is Korenev leaving on his trip?" I asked him instead.

"He may have already left. Or is leaving pretty soon."

"Then we've gotta hurry," I said. "You know where he lives? No? Near Sokol metro station."

We were off. As he drove, I tried to explain my theory and he tried to listen, but since I was being thrown from side to side by his driving technique and bumping my head against the car's hard top every time we encountered a pothole, I found it impossible to keep my thoughts straight, much less come up with a coherent narrative. Nor was Lenny in a position to grasp all of the intricacies of a rather complex tale. He raced up Leningradsky Prospect, passing trolley cars within a hair's breadth of their shiny blue sides and, hand on the horn, crossing intersections against the light. Pedestrians scattered before us like hens on a village street.

"Anyway, this is how Nadezhda Lazius got involved in it," I would start, only to choke on my words and grab the strap over the door. I had to shout just to be heard over the straining of the Moskvich's midget engine, which Lenny was gunning past the upper limit of its powers.

Finally, Lenny put an end to my attempts to talk by screaming into my ear, "Later. You'll tell me later. When we get there."

To be honest, I was starting to doubt we ever would – at least not in one piece.

The worst thing about the situation was that our fiery death on Leningradsky would allow the killer to get off the hook.

We skirted a traffic jam near the Dinamo Stadium, nearly overturning as Lenny jumped the curb and veered on and off the sidewalk, barely avoiding at least two head-on collisions, leaving more rubber on the road and trailing shrill traffic cop whistles and invectives from other motorists.

Lenny was thoroughly enjoying himself.

"Where now?" he shouted as we reached Korenev's courtyard.

"Stop right here."

The moment he hit the brakes I was out of the Moskvich and running toward the front door of the playwright's ornate apartment building. I couldn't account for my sense of urgency, but I was convinced that I had to run like hell. Otherwise I'd be too late.

"Wait here," I shouted over my shoulder. "Don't go anywhere."

Pushing past the concierge, who was dozing peacefully in her glass booth, I ran upstairs, taking three steps at a time.

I pressed the doorbell and kicked the door. When it was finally answered, Zinaida surveyed me with her evil green eyes through the narrow crack permitted by the safety chain.

"At home?" I asked, still out of breath.

"Comrade Korenev is busy," she announced coldly. "He's working."

"Is he at home?"

"I have just told you that he's busy," she repeated, attempting to shut the door in my face.

Suddenly, I knew why I was in such a hurry. What was driving me was a blinding, bitter fury. It had first assailed me in the vacant lot where Nastya's body lay disfigured in a puddle of blood and melting snow. It ebbed after I threw up, and since then I had managed to keep it under control. But now I felt it flooding over me like a roiling ocean wave.

It must have been reflected in my face, because Zinaida's black pupils widened in fear.

It was the worst kind of rage: rage against myself.

I squeezed my foot against the doorjamb, keeping the door from being shut.

"I'm an officer of Moscow Criminal Investigations," I said softly. "Open the fucking door."

She was still pushing on the door, her fear making her redouble her efforts. If she could only place the heavy door between her and me, she would feel much safer, but as matters now stood, my face was uncomfortably close to hers. I leaned on the door, pressing it with the entire weight of my body and squeezed my fingers through the opening. I scraped the back of my hand on the doorjamb and it started to bleed, but I didn't feel the pain. I snatched her English maid's dress by its stiff collar, my blood smearing its starched lace, and, jerking her toward me, slammed her face against the sharp edge of the door. Her shriek of pain echoed up and down the stairwell.

"What's going on up there?" the concierge shouted from the lobby.

"Get the fucking chain off," I growled and, because she showed some hesitation, I hit her a couple of more times. Now her blood was streaming onto the front of her dress from a cut on her cheek, mixing with mine.

"I can't open the door without closing it first, you idiot" she wheezed, gasping for air as I twisted her collar in my hand..

"Go ahead," I said, releasing her. "But if you don't open it right away, I'll shoot you dead through the door. You won't have time to run. I'll count to three, very fast."

My Makarov had been taken from me, but she had no way of knowing that, and I didn't think she'd risk calling my bluff.

I was right. Once the door was reopened, I quickly stepped inside, sending her flying against the mirror in the foyer.

"Where is he?"

I took hold of her collar again, more securely this time, keeping her down.

"Did he go away?"

She rolled up her eyes, pretending to pass out. I released my grip and took a step toward the hallway, trying to figure out in what part of the apartment to look for the playwright. That is if he was still there.

Swift as a wild cat, she was on her hands and knees, lunging for my ankle. She has a mouth full of metal teeth and she tried to bite me. It took me almost a minute of intense struggle to get her to let go of me, but her desperate attack confirmed that Korenev had not left.

His was a huge apartment. I went from room to room, throwing open doors that led into various chambers, bathrooms and utility closets. There were plenty of places for a man to hide behind massive armoires and bookshelves, and even to escape by moving from one connecting room to the other.

"Where are you, damn it?" I roared, upsetting a small étageré with playbills, pictures and dry bouquets. The glass shattered thunderously, sending shards across the shiny parquetry.

Pushing at yet another random door, I suddenly found myself in the master bedroom. It was vast, like all the other rooms in the apartment, and luxuriously furnished. The crystal chandelier on the ceiling had been switched on, because the windows, alone in the playwright's place, were hung with heavy satin curtains blocking the sunlight. The playwright sat on the edge of a king-size bed covered with a brocaded bedspread and scattered with tiny pillows. He wore a pair of beige trousers with brown suede patches on the knees and a jacket of the same fabric, with elbow patches. He was bending with difficulty over his sizeable paunch, tying his shoelaces. A leather travelling case stood next to him.

"What's the matter?" he bellowed, raising his eyes at me. His face was a deep shade of purple. "Who the hell let you in? Didn't they tell you I was busy?"

"Busy doing what?" I asked.

"It's none of your business. I'm going away. I'm lucky my car has turned up just in time. No thanks to you, Lieutenant."

I took a step toward him.

"Do you know why I'm here?" I asked.

"I have a pretty good idea. It's because I figured out who was behind those murders. You wanted to be the hero, didn't you? Well, I'm not afraid of you in the least. The fact that you're here just proves that I'm right."

While speaking, he rose to his feet. He was full of dignity and self-importance, striding toward me and pushing his chest out, like an overweight rooster spoiling for a fight. He might have even cut an impressive figure had he not been so comical, especially as he stood there in his ridiculous nineteenth-century travelling outfit.

But I was in no mood to be amused. I pushed him hard and he ended up on top of his bed, making a splash among his tiny pillows.

"You'll pay for that, Lieutenant," he croaked.

I bent over him and slapped his face.

"Where is Sergei?" I asked.

"What do you need with him? The car's been found and no one cares who took it in the first place."

"It's not about the car," I said. "Or not only about the car. It's about the murders."

The playwright sat up on the bed.

"Ah, the murders," he exclaimed. "That has nothing to do with Sergei. It's you who needs to explain what happened. You're the only connection between the doctor and the engineer. You got them to commit the murders so that you could turn them in and get all the praise. You can't fool me, and I've already told your boss as much. Even if you kill me now, it will be completely useless. The truth is out."

"The truth?"

"Yes, the truth. It's the only theory that makes sense."

"Unless there is another theory that makes more sense," I said. "Let me ask you one more time. Where is Sergei?"

"He'll be driving me to the Black Sea. I'll be spending a month at the Creativity House of the Writers' Union in Pitsunda."

"I see," I said. "Nice try. So, you're hoping that in a month's time I'm going to be arrested and tried quickly along with Lazius and Oganesov and the case will be solved, right?"

"It's up to your boss to decide when the case is solved. I'm not a detective. I'm a playwright, and I need peace and quiet to finish my play. Because the atmosphere here is too nerve-wracking. The doctors at the Kremlin clinic tell me I may develop a heart murmur from all the nerves."

"And what about Sergei?" I asked. "Is he in danger of developing a heart murmur too?"

"I'm in a hurry and you're holding me up," said the playwright.

"Never mind," I said. "By the time you get back I may already be sentenced to death and executed by the firing squad. Don't you think you can spare a minute or two for a chat with me?"

"Perhaps I can. What do you want to talk about?"

He sounded weary now.

"About the disappearance of your car," I said. "Wasn't that what I came here to investigate in the first place?"

"Look, just to save a little time, let's say Sergei is responsible for the theft of my car. It's my car and it's up to me whether to press charges or not. Suppose I let him use it for a week and forgot about it. I'm an old man, my memory is not what it used to be. By the time we're back from the Black Sea, it will all be ancient history."

"I don't think so," I asked. "I would bet you that the disappearance of your car will not be forgotten soon, except I may not be around to collect my winnings. And, since you're the one who gave the car to Sergei, you'll be charged as an accomplice."

"An accomplice to what?"

"Well, you don't think it matters what your car was used for? And why it had exactly one thousand four hundred extra kilometers on the odometer?"

That got him interested, which was a good sign. At least he wasn't covering up for Sergei any more. But I wasn't entirely sure yet.

"You see," I said, "even if Lazius, Oganesov and I are convicted of murdering four kids, there will remain the open case of a bank robbery in Leningrad, in which a clerk was killed and a policeman wounded. And even if that case is never solved, there is yet another murder case, involving a young woman who was a friend of mine and whose murder will need to be looked into as well. What are we going to do about them?"

"You seem to be talking in riddles," the playwright said, but he didn't sound as sure of himself. "Perhaps we should talk to Sergei."

"That's exactly what I intend to do. Where is he?"

"He should be here somewhere."

But he wasn't. We searched the apartment with Korenev calling Sergei's name repeatedly.

"Where is Sergei?" I asked Zinaida, who was still sitting on the floor, her back against the front door.

"Did he go out?" Korenev asked.

The English maid, her lace collar and black uniform splattered with blood, turned away and sat there silently, blocking the door.

"I think he did," I said.

The playwright nodded.

"Let us get by, Zinaida," he said.

The woman didn't move.

"Get out of my way," I said, stepping up to her. She ignored me. I bent down and grabbed both her ankles. She kicked at me furiously as I pulled her away, along with the doormat on which she sat. Thank God for Sergei's polished floors, I thought.

"Come, we have to hurry," I told the playwright.

"You're a goddamn bastard, Matvei," she screamed after us. "How can you do this to him?"

Korenev hesitated for a second, then waved his hand and followed me out the door.

"Hurry up," I shouted, my sense of urgency, which had been blunted by the sight of the unhurried playwright getting ready for the journey, returning in a flash.

Lenny had turned his Moskvich around and positioned it by the front door. The concierge was now on the sidewalk, haranguing him while he reclined behind the wheel, smoking a cigarette.

"Did you see Sergei, Comrade Korenev's driver?" I asked her.

"I'm going to call the cops on him," she announced, ignoring my question and pointing to Lenny.

"They're the police, Anna," the playwright said. "Did you see Sergei?"

"Sure I saw him," she replied. "He ran out of the building like somebody was after him. He's a crazy one, your Sergei."

She waved in the direction of the park.

"The garage," I said.

I told Korenev to get in the car and show Lenny the way.

"It's faster on foot," the playwright objected. "If you drive, you've got to take a detour all the way around. There's that Composers' building on the way."

"Take the goddamn detour," I yelled at him and added, turning to Lenny: "Don't let his driver get away. Use your gun if you have to."

"No!" Korenev cried out, turning pale. "No guns, please. I forbid it!"

Lenny's Moskvich was off. The playwright in the front seat was still remonstrating when he was thrown back by the sudden acceleration. The last thing I saw as they took the corner at full speed was his bald pate bouncing off the headrest like a football.

Sergei had at least a five-minute head start on me and I had no hope of catching up with him.

I don't know if it was faster on foot. I was wobbling on the sodden paths in the park, sliding and stumbling on the melting ice and thrusting my arms out, trying to keep my balance. Sergei's footprints were on the ground, pressed into the softened snow and quickly filling up with muddy water.

I squeezed through the breech in the wall and, repeatedly falling down and crawling on all fours, climbed the steep ascent along the construction fence. Straightening up at the top, I was just in time to see the ZIM back out of Korenev's garage. It was a good-looking car, resembling a shiny black cigar.

I was still at least two hundred feet away. Sergei, who had spotted me, knew I was too far to reach him. He rolled his window and waved at me derisively. He was in no hurry. The ZIM jerked a little and its fenders trembled as he shifted gears. The tailpipe coughed up a cloud of blue exhaust and the car began to gather speed. It was accelerating slowly, as though taunting me.

There was nothing I could do. I didn't have my gun. Breaking into a funny kind of trot, I promptly slipped and fell face down into the wet snow. Cursing, I scraped together a hard, prickly snowball and tossed it at the ZIM, which gave me a friendly wink as a ray of the setting sun caught its nickel-plated bumper. Majestically, like an ocean liner, it started to turn the corner.

That was when Urumov's pesky Moskvich, moving at what seemed to be the speed of sound, burst onto the scene. It nearly hit the ZIM head-on, only just swerving out of the way at the last moment, and went into a crazy screeching skid, burning the rubber on its locked wheels. It came up alongside the ZIM and then swung wide, sideswiping the gleaming black fender of the ZIM. The Moskvich bounced back like a tennis ball hitting a brick wall.

The impact shattered the window on Lenny's side. Lenny reached into his coat, the universally recognizable gesture of a man going for his gun in his shoulder holster, and Korenev fell heavily on top of him. He was choking Lenny and grabbing for his right hand. Struggling against the playwright, Lenny steered sharply to the left and smashed into the ZIM once more, this time making it pitch nose first into a pile of snow and blocking the driver-side door. Lenny too was now locked in the Moskvich, his door having been pinned against the side of the ZIM. On his right, Korenev was practically lying on top of him, pummelling him madly.

Lenny's Moskvich was not constructed to accommodate hand-to-hand combat in its narrow cabin. Everything happened in a flash, and all at once. Lenny's right hand jerked forward, as he tried to shake off Korenev, and the muzzle of his gun hit the windshield, shattering it. After a considerable struggle, Sergei finally managed to open his door and squeeze his body out of the ZIM. At first he turned back toward the garages, but remembered that I was still there, now on my feet once again, barring his way. Turning around, he passed the Moskvich with the two men still wrestling inside it, and was about to round the corner when Lenny, momentarily freeing his hand from the playwright's grip, got off a shot through the shattered windshield. Sergei pitched forward, grabbed his left shoulder and fell. Lenny then kicked at Korenev and at the same time hit him in the face with his gun. Both of them, locked in a ferocious embrace, tumbled out through the passenger door.

"Damn you!" yelled Korenev as he disentangled himself, scrambled to his feet, and ran toward Sergei. He and Lenny reached him at the same time. While Lenny put away his gun, Korenev bent over Sergei's prone body. He lay on his back and a puddle of blood was spreading rapidly around his left shoulder, saturating the snow and coloring it bright red.

I came up to them. Sergei moaned. Korenev took out a starched white handkerchief and began mopping up the blood.

Another shadow fell over our group. I looked up and saw Zinaida, still in her maid's uniform, not wearing an overcoat.

"You're not gonna stop the bleeding that way," she said.

She removed Sergei's jacket, tore his blood-soaked shirt on his shoulder in a single motion and tied Korenev's handkerchief around his arm a few inches above the wound.

"Lie still, Seryozha, don't move," she said. "He needs to be taken to the hospital. Or else he'll bleed to death."

"Yes," Korenev pleaded with Lenny. "Take him to the hospital."

Zinaida gave him a contemptuous look. "How could you do this to your own flesh and blood, Matvei?"

TWENTY-NINE

Two days later, Lenny and I had an appointment with the Boss. He looked exceptionally pleased.

"Are you finally ready to talk about it?" he asked me.

"Yes sir," I said. "I believe so."

Budyonny had wanted me to report right away, after we had taken Sergei to the Sklifosovsky Institute to get patched up, leaving him there under police guard. But I needed more time. I spent the next forty-eight hours interviewing Korenev and doing more – and more thorough – digging in Baba Yaga's dusty archives. Lenny was helping me by phoning Criminal Investigations in Leningrad, the result of which had been the arrest of two men and a woman in Kiev and the requisitioning of the playwright's battered ZIM, which now stood in the police garage behind Kursk Railway Station.

And now, finally, I was ready. But before I could begin, the Boss felt he needed to make a short speech.

"Well, Matyushkin," he declared from behind his towering desk, "I don't mind admitting that we were wrong about you. But forgive and forget. I'm not even going to think of your previous transgressions."

Budyonny accompanied that declaration with a hearty laugh. He almost never laughed for real, only when he needed to hide his embarrassment.

"And now let's hear the whole story from the beginning."

I opened a manila folder in front of me.

"We have three distinct stories here," I said. "Or rather three parts of the same story connected by misunderstandings, tragic mistakes and coincidences. Because of those misunderstandings, mistakes and coincidences, people who had nothing to do with the story got entangled in it. Some were innocent bystanders, like Oganesov and Grushnikov, both of whom were arrested by mistake, while others were guilty."

"We know it all by now," Lenny grumbled. Grushnikov was his nemesis. He still felt embarrassed and humiliated for pursuing the man so maniacally.

"In fact, Grushnikov's arrest was the biggest mistake of the case," I said, not sparing my partner's feelings. "It became a catalyst for the chain of events that followed. Had he not been arrested, those events would not have happened."

Lenny pulled his head into his shoulders and turned away.

"We already know everything about Tanya's murder," I continued. "Dr. Lazius first suggested to Tanya's grandmother that she needed to be examined by a professional psychiatrist, and while examining her in his office, he raped her. He continued to abuse her regularly for several months and then, fearing exposure, strangled her.

"Tanya's murder wasn't Dr. Lazius's first crime. Several years ago he killed his first wife, the mother of his boys, by administering an overdose of sleeping pills. He did it because he was in love with his beautiful assistant Nadezhda. With devilish cunning, he implicated her in the murder, blackmailing her into marrying him."

"She seemed pretty happy to me," Budyonny interjected.

"Actually, she was horribly scared of him and lived in mortal fear of exposure, because Lazius had convinced her that she was an accomplice. He held it over her as a threat. If she didn't love him, he would go to the police and confess, and they would both go to jail. It was nonsense, of course – he would never have done such a thing – but it worked. Besides, being pathologically jealous, possessive and controlling, he never let her out of his sight – all the while pretending that they just loved to spend all their time together. It's true that he organized sporting activities and trips to the theater, trying to make her life interesting, but it was also a way of never letting her out of his sight and limiting her contact with the outside world."

"She even worked at his clinic," Lenny observed.

"Nadezhda was isolated and deeply unhappy. Then, after Irina Drozdova's mother died, a new tenant moved in. Nadezhda soon fell madly in love with him."

"With Grushnikov?" Budyonny exclaimed in disbelief. "How could it have been possible? He's repulsive."

"There's no accounting for taste," I said. "And Grushnikov is not a bad man. The truth is that it didn't really matter to her what he looked like. When your life is a secret hell that you can't share with anyone, any warm human contact can sweep you off your feet. Grushnikov, a loner himself, fell in love with his beautiful neighbor and then much to his surprise discovered one day that the love that he had thought was completely hopeless was actually reciprocated. And ardently, passionately so. But, despite sharing the same apartment and seeing each other every day, they could barely consummate their relationship. Their trysts were rare and hasty, which only heightened her passion and fanned her love."

"They must have been hiding their relationship pretty well," Lenny observed. "Otherwise somebody would have noticed something. Especially a nosey gossip like Baba Dasha."

"Actually, Baba Dasha was aware that something was going on. She's more discrete than we give her credit for."

"What about her husband?" Budyonny asked. "I always thought that, for all their supposed knowledge of human nature, those psychiatrists are pretty damn blind about their own lives."

"He knew, too. Or at least he suspected it. At first, he made the same mistake everyone else did. He thought Grushnikov was too unattractive to interest his beautiful wife. Especially in comparison to him, the good-looking, rich and accomplished Dr. Lazius."

"But then he found out?" Lenny asked.

I nodded.

"He would regularly search Nadezhda's things as a way of controlling her, and that was how he found Grushnikov's key. When Grushnikov was arrested, he saw an opportunity to sink his wife's lover – while also deflecting suspicion from himself – which was not a minor consideration in his calculations. He used the key to plant evidence and then hinted to me that we should search Grushnikov's room again."

Lenny blushed.

"But we didn't find it," Budyonny observed.

"No, we didn't," I said. "But not because we weren't thorough enough. You see, Nadezhda had found the evidence first and removed it before we could find it."

"How did she do it? The room was sealed," Lenny exclaimed.

His embarrassment made him sound all the more indignant.

"That's the thing," I said. "It's an old apartment and there is a secret door connecting Grushnikov's room to the Lazius's. Tanya's grandmother grew up there and knew about it. She used it to get her granddaughter to Lazius in secret from Irina, for what she thought were psychiatric examinations. But that was also how Lazius got in, to plant that evidence. As to Nadezhda, she discovered the door on her own, yet she didn't know that her husband also knew about it. There are plenty of secret doors in that apartment."

Budyonny chuckled.

"So, Nadezhda also thought that Grushnikov murdered Tanya," he said, winking at Lenny. "You're not alone, Lenny."

"The problem was that Lazius, who also wanted Nadezhda to believe that Grushnikov was guilty, succeeded beyond his wildest dreams," I said. "She was crushed. She was losing the only man she ever loved. Worse, her beloved turned out to be a monster, a child murderer. But it was also too familiar: wasn't Lazius also a murderer, and she his accomplice? If she was living with a man she feared and despised because she was tied to him by the fear of exposure, wouldn't she commit another crime to save the man she loved? Indeed, if there were another murder, very similar to the first, Grushnikov would automatically be in the clear. And if she committed it, she would become *his* accomplice. She was already starting to lose her mind and it was an insane idea, but she carried out her plan rationally, with deadly efficiency. She arranged an alibi for herself at the clinic and then came to the city, where she strangled little Dima Sadykov. She chose him at random, but it all went very smoothly as far as she was concerned."

"And, of course, the second murder got Grushnikov released," Budyonny said.

"Indeed. Nadezhda was overjoyed. She welcomed him home, telling him proudly what she had done. But Grushnikov was no murderer, and the idea of killing a child horrified him. Imagine Nadezhda's shock when, far from being grateful and proud of her, he recoiled in horror instead. He was still in love with her, but he couldn't bring himself to be with her any more.

"Nadezhda was still convinced that Grushnikov had killed Tanya and was mad at him for denying it. Unlike us, she knew who committed the first murder and she also was in possession of what she thought was incontrovertible proof of his guilt. That was why she returned the warm-up pants to Grushnikov's closet. She thought that it would be a reminder to him what he had done, and also would make him realize that she knew it too. But those pants had no meaning to him whatsoever. He was merely surprised that the pants kept popping up and disappearing again – especially after Lenny stole them from his closet. He naturally concluded that we had planted them in order to frame him.

"Meanwhile, Nadezhda's life became a nightmare. Grushnikov refused to have anything to do with her. She was hounded by guilt. And, worse of all, the murders went on. A third child was killed, then another. She knew about them because after every new murder we checked the alibis of everyone in the apartment. Then there were those articles. She started to blame a supernatural force, that it was some kind of divine retribution at work. And then her husband was arrested for Tanya's murder. The scales fell from her eyes and she realized that she had taken a young life for nothing. And that with her husband under arrest she and Grushnikov could have been together, bonded by love and not by shared guilt. It drove her over the edge."

"That takes us through the first two murders," Budyonny said. "What about the next two?"

I took a sip of the tea that Marina had brought in. She had also filled a candy dish with chocolates, but I resisted the temptation, recalling the soapy aftertaste our departmental chocolate tended to leave in my mouth.

"Now another character, Sergei, enters the story," I said. "By the time Tanya Drozdova was murdered, Sergei had already been implicated in a serious crime."

It took me a long time to tell Sergei's tale. It was a long and complicated story, which went back many decades. After considerable prodding on my part, Korenev, red faced and contrite, had revealed it to me over the previous two days.

As he told it, while we were finishing his blueberry-infused vodka, he had been married twice. His second wife was Adelaida Feoktistova, the famous star of the Collective Farm Cossacks and other popular pre-war movies. Their marriage and breakup were universal knowledge. His first marriage was another matter.

His first wife's name was Zinaida Nikulina. She worked at a tractor factory, while young Matvei Korenev was starting out as a journalist, writing enthusiastic, ungrammatical articles for the factory's newspaper. After thirteen months of what Korenev thought was connubial bliss, Zinaida suddenly announced that she was leaving him for another man, with whom she had been having an affair. His wife's lover was none other than the formidable Karl Engelbaum, the head of the Rostov NKVD.

Korenev was devastated – all the more so since he didn't dare to confront Engelbaum, who could have packed him off to the GULAG in a heartbeat. After a few agonizing months, when he both feared arrest and was treated to the spectacle of his former wife driving around in confiscated motor cars and whooping it up in Rostov, Korenev left for

Krasnodar and took an accelerated course for young playwrights at the local literary college. Six months later, his first play was unexpectedly picked up by a Moscow theater.

Times were turbulent, the country was going through massive purges, and there was a shortage of ideologically correct works for the stage written by authors of an impeccable working class background. This was something Korenev had in abundance. Stalin saw the production of his play five times and loved it, and so Korenev's spectacular career was launched. The next season, the same play was staged in three dozen theaters across the Soviet Union, several new plays were commissioned from him, and he was showered with favors, titles and medals. He was given an apartment on Gorky Street, a stone's throw from the Kremlin. He married Feoktistova, a celebrity, and forgot all about the perfidious Zinaida and her scary Engelbaum.

He probably would never have thought of them again, had one evening in the mid-50s a woman not accosted him in a dark alley near his house. She thrust a soiled envelope into his reluctant hand. The woman wore a pair of soldier's boots and the grey *vatnik* jacket of a workman. Although not old, she had a sharp, weatherbeaten face and only a few yellowed teeth left in her mouth.

Korenev was not naive. He took the letter and stuck it deep into his pocket. He asked the woman no questions. Times were starting to be less dangerous, Khrushchev's Thaw had begun, and former enemies of the people were trickling back from Siberia and the Far North. Some were even allowed to return to the capital, restored in their old jobs and given their Party membership back. They had been, the official line went, unjustly repressed. Be that as it may, in such matters caution never hurt anyone – Korenev knew that from experience.

The letter, which he read in the privacy of his home, was from Zinaida. Her life with Engelbaum, having had such a brilliant start, quickly took a dramatic downturn. For a while, Engelbaum rose rapidly through the ranks of the State Security apparatus, having earned his wings during collectivization. In those days, he had been ferreting out rich German farmers settled along the Volga and sending them to Siberian exile. Being of German stock himself, he knew the community well and could identify class enemies with remarkable accuracy. In fact, when he was done, eight out of every ten German farmers found themselves deported.

Her superiors were impressed with his thoroughness in finding class enemies and his efficiency in eliminating them, and he was soon transferred to Kiev, where lots of arrests and executions were waiting to be carried out. Kiev was a large cosmopolitan city with plenty of restaurants, theaters and other entertainment. There was a brilliant social scene and gay parties given by the new Party and State Security elites. The future looked bright for Engelbaum and his young wife.

But then purges began inside the NKVD. Engelbaum's boss, Genrikh Yagoda, was himself arrested and shot, and soon it was Engelbaum's turn to disappear down the black hole he had dumped so many others into. A month later, in the middle of the night, Zinaida was taken and their little son Sergei, like other children of enemies of the people, ended up in an orphanage.

"When Sergei was born, I was married to Engelbaum," Zinaida wrote to Korenev. "When Karl was arrested, I took my maiden name and I changed his name, too. He is now Sergei Karlovich Nikulin. But the truth is that my Seryozha is your son."

Writing to her former husband from a labor camp, Zinaida used the respectable *Vy* form of address and the tone of her letter was as humble as befitted the widow of an enemy of the people asking a favor of a famous playwright, the Laureate of two Stalin Prizes for literature, and a Deputy of the Supreme Soviet.

"I have no idea where he is or how to find him," the letter continued. "I have had no news of him for over fifteen years and I don't even know whether he is still alive. But if he is, I assure you that you will see right away how much he looks like you, dear Matvei Nikanorovich."

After divorcing Feoktistova, Korenev remained single and lived alone. He had no kids of his own, but liked children very much and even now stayed friends with Feoktistova's son from a previous marriage, whose stepfather he had so briefly been. Stealthily at first, and then more and more openly, he started to gather information about Sergei Nikulin. He was greatly helped by his numerous connections in the higher echelons of State Security, which he had developed as Stalin's favorite playwright. Once he was able to locate the boy, he took a trip to meet him and reconnoiter the situation.

Sergei had turned eighteen by then. He was out of the orphanage, working at a ball-bearing plant and learning to be a milling machine operator. Korenev could find little resemblance to himself in the young man, and actually thought he looked remarkably like Karl Engelbaum, as far as he could remember the man from so many years before. But, then again, Zinaida was a tall, strapping beauty and Sergei might have inherited her physique. Whatever he thought of his parentage, Korenev liked the young man immediately and, once Sergei had completed his military service, he took him back to Moscow.

Korenev didn't reveal the secret of the boy's birth or, for that matter, that Korenev had once been married to Sergei's mother. He introduced himself as a childhood friend of his parents, whom Sergei remembered only vaguely.

"At first I wanted to send him to college," Korenev told me. "I wanted him to become an engineer. Or maybe a designer of airplanes, cars or tractors. But he didn't want to go to school. He hated studying and didn't have much aptitude for it. So he stayed with me, did some cleaning and other housework, but mostly he was my driver and took care of my car. He really loved automobiles. I should have sent him to a vocational school for car mechanics. But I got to like having him around and working for me, and he didn't mind it either. He's very reliable, diligent and honest. You can tell right away that he grew up in a German household."

And then, one night, someone rang Korenev's doorbell. He opened the door and there she was, his first wife, Zinaida Nikulina, even though twenty years of hard labor and internal exile in the harsh climate beyond the Arctic Circle had changed her beyond recognition.

Sergei happened to be out. Korenev invited her in and made tea. They sat around his kitchen table for hours, talking about their lives and discussing Sergei. When morning came, Korenev realized to his consternation that, even though nothing in that hard-bitten, battered woman remained of the love of his youth, he still loved and desired her.

Times had changed, and political prisoners had been mostly released from the camps. But Korenev felt that marrying – or, worse, re-marrying – the widow of an enemy of the people would be a rash move, even if Engelbaum's name had been cleared and charges against him had been recognized as false.

That night they decided that Zinaida would stay with Korenev as a cook and a maid, and the fact that she was Sergei's mother would not be revealed to the boy – if only because Korenev was not ready to admit that he was his father. And there they were, a family living as strangers under one roof.

"Too bad Dr. Lazius has been arrested," Lenny sneered. "He no doubt would've had an appropriate explanation."

"And how is Sergei connected to the murders?" Budyonny asked, ignoring Lenny's remark. "And to the Leningrad bank robbery?"

"I'm getting to it," I said.

This was the part that Lenny had researched, but he didn't mind if I continued telling the tale. It was more consistent that way, he said. In general, this case, and the role he played in it, had made my partner remarkably humble. It was pleasant, but I wondered how long it was going to last.

"Sergei grew up in the orphanage and, after leaving it, kept in touch with a group of his childhood friends. They had been through a lot together. Their parents had disappeared into the GULAG in the thirties and they had grown up branded as children of the enemies of the people. Even while still at the orphanage, some turned to crime. Sergei did not, but he felt loyal to his friends. When they asked to use his employer's ZIM in a robbery, he never hesitated.

"Their plan was simple. They arrived to the bank openly, driving a stolen Volga. It was never intended to be a getaway car. Instead, they got out through the back, using the maze of connecting Leningrad courtyards to come out a few blocks away. The entire district had by then been cordoned off by the police, but that was part of their plan. Under their canvas overcoats, the two men were wearing smart jackets and ties. They looked like party functionaries, arriving for a meeting with a female assistant. A black ZIM with a uniformed driver was waiting for them and it became their getaway car. No one thought of stopping an official party ZIM with important-looking officials in it and with Moscow license plates."

"Very clever," said Budyonny. "Was Sergei the driver?"

"No, his role was to provide the car and not to get involved. But that was when there was a glitch. Normally, no one checked on the ZIM while it was garaged for winter. But this time, completely by chance, Korenev discovered that the car wasn't there. Worse, before Sergei could do anything about it, the playwright had called in Criminal Investigations. Sergei realized right away that, if we started to look for the missing ZIM in earnest, or went to Leningrad to help with their investigation as our colleagues there had asked us to, we would sooner or later connect the two ZIMs.

"Sergei and his friends didn't know how to solve this problem. They could have destroyed the ZIM, but then we would continue looking for it. They could have sold it to a fence, and at one point Sergei tried to find a buyer in the Moscow underworld. In the end, bringing it back became the best of several bad options."

"However, there was another problem: getting the car to Moscow now required more time. Since the ZIM had been reported stolen, it was risky to drive it back openly from Leningrad. That was when Sergei came upon the idea of child murders."

"Quite a way to buy time," Lenny muttered.

"Well, he didn't want his friends to get caught," I said. "Especially since a bank clerk had died during the robbery and a cop was wounded. They would have been brought up on murder charges.

"He overheard me talking to Korenev about the first murder. I had said then that we would put more operatives on his case once we were finished with Tanya Drozdova's murder. When he heard that we had arrested Grushnikov, he got nervous, but then we let him go after the second murder, and I got too busy with the investigation to look for the ZIM. Sergei put all this information together and figured that, if he kept us busy, he could gain enough time to arrange for the return of the car. All the time I was keeping Korenev informed about the course of the investigation – and supplying him with more and more details – Sergei was listening in on our conversations. He knew exactly where we stood at any given moment. He also knew how the first two murders had been committed and had no trouble replicating them."

"And that's how he discovered the MosGaz ploy then?" Budyonny asked.

"Yes, but first Sergei murdered Vova Silin. He followed him home from school, struck up a conversation in the elevator, and knew that there weren't any adults waiting for the boy at home. He got out on the floor above Vova's, then descended the stairs as the boy unlocked his front door. The rest was pretty easy.

"Once Korenev had written the first article and we had a report about MosGaz from Oganesov's former wife, Sergei concluded that this was a clever way to gain access to apartments. He was successful the first time, and succeeded in killing Olga Ilyina, but when he tried it a second time he nearly got caught. Yet he nonetheless achieved his ultimate goal: we certainly were not thinking of the missing ZIM or paying any attention to the Leningrad robbery investigation. That gave his friends plenty of time to bring the ZIM most of the way back to Moscow and dump it in Klin."

"The rest is pretty straightforward," Budyonny said quickly. "I'm sure Comrade Korenev knew nothing about Sergei's involvement in the murders or the Leningrad robbery."

It's amazing how the bosses always cover for one another. Not to mention that it was Budyonny who had told me to keep Korenev in the loop – which then resulted in the murders of two children. He seemed to have completely forgotten about that.

"I wonder about that," I said bitterly, "Sergei confessed to Korenev that he had taken the car for a joy ride, wept and asked for forgiveness. And, once he was forgiven, they sat down and decided that Korenev should take him away for a few weeks, until the car case was forgotten. Meanwhile, in line with a theory developed by Comrade Korenev, Lazius, Oganesov and I would have been railroaded into a child killing gang, tried for the four murders and convicted. After that, it would have been truly safe for Sergei to return to Moscow."

"I don't know what gave you that idea," Budyonny said. He met my eyes and held my stare. "In any case, it has worked out for the best. If you thought – mistakenly, I'm sure – that we ever suspected you, you worked all the harder to get to the bottom of this case. And, as a result, we have all the criminals in custody – not just Sergei, but the Leningrad robbers, too."

"Not really," I said. "There's one more person who's still at large."

"Who's that?" Budyonny sat up, suddenly worried. "I hope you don't think that Comrade Korenev—"

I shook my head.

"I accidentally let it slip to Sergei that I knew about his attempt to sell the ZIM. That got somebody else killed."

"Yes, Lieutenant Urumov told me that she was your informer," Budyonny said.

Nastya was never my informer. She was a friend, but I couldn't say that.

"Yes, she was," I lied. "And a very valuable one at that."

"But she was also a pickpocket with a record as long as my arm. I don't really care who killed her or why. In fact, you should be thankful for not being reprimanded, Lieutenant. You were essentially protecting her from arrest."

He gave me a stern look.

"And," he added, "just to return to the subject of Comrade Korenev, he had absolutely nothing to do with any of this. Is that clear?"

He waited to see whether I would object, and when I didn't, he concluded benevolently, "Good job, Matyushkin. And you too, Urumov. Dismissed, both of you."

ABOUT THE AUTHOR

Alexei Bayer is a New York-based author, translator and, by economic necessity, an economist. He writes in English and in Russian, his native tongue, and translates into both languages.

His first novel, *Murder at the Dacha*, for which this novel is a prequel, was published in 2013.

Bayer's short stories have been published in *New England Review*, *Kenyon Review*, and *Chtenia*. His translations have appeared in *Chtenia* and *Words Without Borders*, as well as in such collections as *The Wall in My Head*, a book dedicated to the twentieht anniversary of the fall of the Berlin Wall, and *Life Stories*, a bilingual literary anthology to benefit hospice care in Russia.